DEFIANCE VALLEY: THE COMPLETE NORTHWOODS STORIES OF FREDERICK NEBEL, VOLUME 1

Frederick Nebel

FREDERICK NEBEL

DEFIANCE VALLEY: THE COMPLETE

NORTHWOODS

STORIES OF
FREDERICK NEBEL

INTRODUCTION BY
ROB PRESTON

BOSTON • 2015

© 2015 Altus Press • First Edition—2015

SERIES EDITOR
Rob Preston

DESIGNED BY
Matthew Moring

PUBLISHING HISTORY
"Trade Law" originally appeared in the July, 1925 issue of *North•West Stories*.
"The Firelight Patrol" originally appeared in the September, 1925 issue of *North•West Stories*.
"Stuart of the City Patrol" originally appeared in the December, 1925 issue of *North•West Stories*.
"Raw Courage" originally appeared in the December, 1925 issue of *Action Stories*.
"The White Peril" originally appeared in the January 1, 1926 issue of *North•West Stories*.
"Eskimo Sorcery on Baffin Island" originally appeared in the February 22, 1926 issue of *North•West Stories*.
"Defiance Valley" originally appeared in the March 8, 22, and April 8, 1926 issues of *North•West Stories*.
"The Freight of Honor" originally appeared in the March 22, 1926 issue of *North•West Stories*.
"The Black Fox Skin" originally appeared in the April 22, 1926 issue of *North•West Stories*.
"Trail Tales of the North: Law of the Trapline" originally appeared in the April 22, 1926 issue of *North•West Stories*.
"Trail Tales of the North: Patrol of Courage" originally appeared in the May 8, 1926 issue of *North•West Stories*.
"The Big Moon Lake Patrol" originally appeared in the June 22, 1926 issue of *North•West Stories*.
"Trail Tales of the North: Alone" originally appeared in the August 22, 1926 issue of *North•West Stories*.
"Trail Tales of the North: Cache Law" originally appeared in the September 22, 1926 issue of *North•West Stories*.
"East of Big Moon" originally appeared in the November 8, 1926 issue of *North•West Stories*.
"Tell It to the Mounted" originally appeared in the December 22, 1926 issue of *North•West Stories*.

THANKS TO
Rick Hall, Bruce Harris, John Locke, Bill Pronzini, & Jonathan Sweet

TABLE OF CONTENTS

INTRODUCTION BY
ROB PRESTON

THIS IS a book of Frederick Nebel firsts: his first published story, his first series character, his first long novelettes (in a career filled with many of this length), and the first volume of his collected Northwestern yarns.

He broke into the rough paper fiction writing field with "Trade Law" in the July 1925 issue of *North•West Stories*. Nebel wrote in the September 10, 1928, issue of *Short Stories:*

> At sixteen or so I went off on a spree into the Canadian Northwest. It was in the springtime. I came home late in the fall and fell back on the railroads to make a living. Then I wandered off into the South for a spell. Back-trailed and struck west, getting as far a Tejon, Colorado. Then east again and then north again, up through Ontario and on up through Manitoba. Back to Montreal with a ticket to New York and a quarter to squander on three meals. Another job to jack up the battered bankroll that never was. Threw up that and bought a Corona and wrote steadily, for four months, almost day and night, gathering the most sweetly worded rejections slips on record.

Time has erased all knowledge of who these rejection slips were received from, but certainly some of them were from Fiction House. The hard work paid off and his first sale would lead to just over a hundred story sales—long and short—to Fiction House over the next six years.

At the start of his writing days he was published as Lewis Nebel, but within a few months the yarns begin to appear under his full name. It isn't for a few years that he finally dropped his middle name, or in many cases just shortened it to an "L."

Included in this collec-
tion are his first fifteen sales
to *North•West Stories* and
one to *Action Stories*. The
handful of "Trail Tales of
the North" short short
stories all feature the same
themes with recurring
figures. Although purport-
ed to be true, these are
obviously fiction. Ramblin'
Dad or "Free-trade" Jim
narrate yarns from their

Frederick Nebel

past stressing a trait of survival or unwritten code of living
(sometimes stronger than law) in the Canadian backwoods.

Northwestern yarns were obviously a genre that Nebel held
an affinity for, as every one of these stories has strong plotting
and a rapid fire—though not frantic—pace along with excellent
dialogue that many fledgling writers struggle with. A signature
writing style that would come to the forefront with his well-
known series characters for the detective pulps was already here
at the beginning, just in a slightly rawer form. More impor-
tantly these tales were a vehicle to showcase rough, elemental,
action-oriented men. These sort of characters continued to
appear throughout his entire career writing for the pulps.

The first series character, R.C.M.P. Corporal Chet Tyson,
appears in his second published story "The Firelight Patrol"
(September 1925) and turned out to be an important one. Tyson
appeared in numerous stories over the next six years and would
even team up with Jack Cardigan in 1931: a familiar-sounding
name, as Nebel went on to recycle it for one of his longest-
running series characters in *Dime Detective* just a few months
later. Tyson even had the distinction of being referenced in
passing in at least one other yarn, helping set up the cohesive
framework that would be in effect throughout his Northwest
tales.

R.C.M.P. Pat Quinlin was the lead character in the first long serial novelette, "Defiance Valley," starting March 8, 1926. Quinlin is—of course—a character in similar mold as Tyson, yet Nebel was a skilled craftsman and did not make him a carbon copy. The following quote in a letter in the October 22nd, 1927, *North•West Stories* applied to Quinlin as well as any character to develop from his pen:

> When you start a man of his type on a big adventure, big things are bound to happen. Above all I tried to make him human, and gave him his faults and his virtues.

Can you hear the blizzard blowing in? Can you see the pulse of the northern lights? In your mind, put on your *capote*, strap on the snowshoes, get your mitts on. It is time to get on the trail and face the coming storm. There is an enemy to be faced, a girl to be saved, a vendetta to be settled. There is not a better place to do it than from the comfort of your easy chair reading this groundbreaking collection.

TRADE LAW

**NORTHWOODS—JIM
DIKE DISCOVERS
A QUEER BRAND,
MISSING PELTS, AND
A FAITHFUL INDIAN.**

YOUNG CREE brought the news to the lonely post on Lac la Marthe. He came staggering across the lake at the fag-end of a blizzard with a bullet in his lung and a glassy look in his eyes. Six dogs and an empty sledge trailed behind him.

Jim Dike, once of the Old Company, once of Revillons on the Bay, and now the best known free-trader north of Great Slave Lake, carried the young buck into the trade store and laid him down on a pile of skins.

"My best runner," he said thickly, and then swore under his breath.

Two trappers rubbed life into the wounded man's hands and feet while Dike gave him a shot of brandy and went about cleaning the wound. He was saying:

"Take your time, Billy, m'lad, but tell me why you're in such a mess. I see your sled's empty. It looks like dirty work, I'm thinking."

The Indian, half-frozen, more than half-dead, was struggling for words. "I mak camp Grandin Lake. Shot get me lung. Men come from timber. I lit me on head. I dead long tam. I wak, furs gone...."

He lapsed into unconsciousness.

"So that was it!" exclaimed Dike, rising. "It gets me, it does, the scum that's in the country nowadays. Billy, as good an Injun as ever a white man had working for him, shot and banged over the head and robbed. I not only lose a slice of money on them furs, but I lose Billy. Damn the bums!"

He turned on one of the Indians.

"Joe, Billy's in bad shape. Maybe the mission doctor at Fort Rae can help him. Take your dogs and use my cariole—not your toboggan."

The Indian shuffled out and rounded up his dogs. Bundling up the wounded Billy thoroughly, they carried him out and placed him in the cariole. Not half an hour elapsed since Billy's arrival and the mission of mercy upon which Joe started, bound east for Fort Rae and medical aid for his brother.

Directly after he departed, Dike went for his own dogs; nine big Mackenzie hounds that held several records for speed and endurance. Meanwhile Ajeri, his assistant at the post, was loading a six-foot toboggan with provisions and robes, aided by a number of breed trappers who had just driven in their pelts from the Land of the Great Bear, from Lac Ste. Croix and points between and beyond.

In the trade-room, Dike was struggling into a carribou-skin *capote*, muttering dire threats against a certain "damn darn cut-throat." Taking a thirty-foot whip from the counter, he slipped on gloves and mittens and strode out, his broad jaw set hard, a cool, hard glint in his eyes.

He said to Ajeri:

"I may be gone two or three days. Take good care of things. And, remember, go the limit on blackies, but no more."

The whip snaked out, ending in a sharp report. With a snarl King-O, the whale of a leader, leaped forward and broke his mates into a fast trot. Dike, running beside the sled, kept snapping the whip and urging them on. Once upon the frozen surface of the lake they had good going, and Dike laid a westerly course.

It was an hour past noon, and the sun, a bruised red globe, was riding low over the southeastern bulge of the earth. At three the lake began to broaden out, and a little later Dike swung northward. As he traveled the shores converged until at last he passed through a narrow passage that merged into a sheltered bay. Speeding across this, he struck a waterway, followed it due north and came out upon Grandin Lake when night was full upon him. Here he halted for a hasty meal of tea and cold bannocks.

He traveled by the moon and the ghostly flare of the Northern Lights, which played weirdly down upon the broad surface of the lake. The temperature plummeted. A stiff wind was working out of the northeast, blowing full in Dike's face. His breath, spuming out, fell back against his beard and froze.

His face was beginning to freeze. But frost-bite was an everyday occurrence in Jim Dike's life. Sometimes they called him "Honest Jim." He often made the remark that he was born in a blizzard, and he'd been frozen more times than he could remember. Big, sturdy and rounding forty years, he had a name among men who admired him for his honesty and his cool courage.

At midnight he made the northern rim of Grandin Lake and camped for the night. The first touches of dawn found him on the trail, toiling with his dogs through a rugged country. He gave a grunt of satisfaction when he left the timber behind and found good going on Lac Tache. Two hours later he veered toward the eastern shore and led his team up to a clearing in front of a wide, high cabin. He went to the door, pushed it open and stepped in.

The room was almost empty. A French-looking breed lounged against a trade-counter. A heavy-set man, built low and wide, with a nose that sprawled all over his bearded face, sat in a split-log chair with his feet perched on the edge of the stove. His small, close-set eyes darkened beneath bushy brows when he beheld Dike. He removed one foot from the stove.

"Howdy, Dike," he said.

"Howdy, Pogue."

Dike kicked a stool up beside the stove and sat down, stuffing his pipe. "Hear you've got a new batch of prime blackies?"

Pogue frowned.

"What about it?"

"Who brought 'em in?"

Pogue took his other foot down from the stove and leaned forward, shoving out his heavy jaw.

"What's that to you?"

"Billy, my Injun boy, was shot over on Grandin the other night and robbed of a sled-load of pelts."

Pogue spat out of the side of his mouth.

"You mean to say I took 'em!" he jerked out. "You can't prove it!"

"I didn't say you took 'em," Dike came back coolly, his eyes narrowing. "Thought maybe you'd know who did. You haven't got a good name north of Athabasca Landing, Pogue, so don't look so damned outraged. The Company kicked you out for shady deals, you know."

"Now cut that talk out, Dikey," Pogue lashed out. "You're as much as accusing me."

"I never said anything to accuse you. You accused yourself, almost."

Pogue had drawn his gun.

"I don't like the way you talk, anyway, chum. Just about turn and slide out. You ain't got nothing on me."

"If you're not guilty, Pogue, you're sure getting in a heat over nothing."

"Get out!" Pogue was boiling.

Dike calmly knocked the ashes from his pipe, drew his *capote* closer about him and without another word walked out. Outside, he turned his team about and swung down toward the lake. Looking back, he saw two evil faces pressed against the window; Pogue's and that of the French-breed who had been leaning against the counter.

BACK IN his own post on the following night, Dike and one of his runners, a Dog-Rib named Toochoo (Big Water), were convened in the little living-room behind the trade-store. Toochoo had been extending credit to the trappers in the country between Lac la Marthe and the Yellow-Knife, and Dike considered him a valuable man.

Dike was saying:

"I'm not forcing this run on you, Toochoo, you understand. But I need a good man for the country between here and McVicar Bay. I'm sure Billy got shot by accident. They want the pelts; that's all. If you take that run you'll know there's dirty work afoot and you can keep a look-out. If they threaten to shoot you, let 'em take the pelts. For my scheme, I want 'em to take the pelts. Now it's up to you. You can take that run or leave it."

"Take," nodded Toochoo.

"Good man. Now here's the scheme." Briefly speaking in whispers, Dike outlined his plan.

Toochoo, his dark eyes impassive, listened. When Dike had finished, he rose. He was a stalwart fellow, of noble stature. He had first seen the light of day on an island in Great Bear Lake; hence his name, Big Water.

"For the honor of the trade," he said solemnly, in good English.

"For the honor of the trade," repeated Dike, and they shook hands.

Next morning, when it was still dark, Dike walked with Toochoo and his dog-team down to the lake, giving him last-minute instructions. With a farewell shake, Toochoo cracked his whip and swung off behind his dogs.

"Good man," muttered Dike.

Several days later a trapper who ran his fur paths in the Lac Tache country, stopped in on his way toward the Mackenzie. He told Dike just what he thought about that neck of the woods, and swore he'd never go within a thousand miles of it again.

Someone had been raiding his traps for the past month, he explained with much blasphemy, and he'd be damned if he'd squat in a country where a man's traps weren't safe. Dike sympathized with him, sheltered him for the night, and saw him off next morning without airing his own suspicions.

On the tenth day after Toochoo's departure, he climbed to the look-out tower which he had built a-top his station and swept the lake with his glasses. Three times during the day he made the search, and on the third time, in early afternoon, he spotted far off to the west a dog-team and a man riding on the sled. He left the look-out and went down to the lake.

Toochoo, with a bloody bandage showing beneath his plaid toque, drew up and leaped from the sled. Except for his trail equipage, the sled was empty.

"What now, Toochoo?" asked Dike.

"Made camp south shore of Lac Ste. Therese. Fell asleep. Banged on head. Furs gone. Big snow. No trail." He was concise if anything.

"So they got you before you reached Lac Tache, eh?" Dike clamped his jaw grimly. Then:

"You did as I told you?"

Toochoo nodded.

"All right. Now I'm ripe for anything short of murder. Come, Toochoo."

Dike was grim as he stamped into his trade-room. He told Ajeri to load the toboggan and get out his dogs. He kicked off his slippers and put on several pairs of socks, duffels and moose-hide moccasins. He buckled his gun-belt outside his caribou-skin *capote*, practised sliding the gun out of its holster, and finally was satisfied that it was in the right position.

Toochoo came in from the other room, pulling his toque over a fresh bandage.

"Feel all right?" asked Dike concernedly.

"Good," Toochoo shot over his shoulder as he passed out.

When Dike went out a moment later Toochoo had his snowshoes on and was standing up by the lead dog. Stepping upon his own rackets, Dike gave a few instructions to Ajeri; then snapped his whip.

Dusk was falling even as they started. Before they were an hour on the trail a flurry of snow smote them, and then a strong wind blew across the lake and the snow whirled in great clouds. But the outfit did not falter. Toochoo, his elbows pressed close to his sides, trotted briskly in the lead, his head bent into the teeth of the storm.

King-O, mighty leader, the harshest taskmaster a string of dogs ever followed, tagged close behind the Indian. Dike, already covered with snow, ran tirelessly beside the toboggan, shouting encouragement to his dogs, cracking his whip over their heads from force of habit.

The storm grew in fury, howling across the lake in reckless abandon. The outfit swung in and hugged the shore line, but it never wavered. They made a camp in the middle of the night on a wooded island in Grandin Lake. Next day they fought in the chaos of the blizzard, made bleak Lac Tache and halted in the afternoon to make final plans.

"I'll go into the cabin alone," explained Dike. "You watch by the window. Most likely he'll have his gang in on a day like this. If I think I need you I'll take off my hat and scratch my head."

They went on. At a point on the shore a little below Pogue's cabin they left the dogs. Then they crept up to the cabin, Toochoo sidling over to the window which, though pretty well frosted, offered him a fair view of the interior. Dike pushed open the door and stepped in.

Pipe smoke hung thick under the rafters. Six men lounged about; rough, tough-looking fellows. Pogue was again ensconced in his chair, his feet planted against the stove. He lifted drowsy eyes when the door opened, then sat erect and glared at the man who was wiping the salt-rheum from his eyes.

"Evening, boys," called Dike, coming forward.

Grunts greeted him.

"I see you're back again," drawled Pogue harshly.

"So I am."

Their eyes met; Dike's cool, level ones, and Pogue's querulous ones. Pogue rose, his big hand sliding to his right hip.

"Well?" he blurted.

"As man to man, I'd like to look over your pelts, Pogue," said Dike simply.

Pogue's lips writhed in a sneer. "The hell you say!"

"Just so. Another of my boys was robbed. I want to make sure you haven't got 'em."

Pogue was on the verge of drawing his gun. Then, crossing his arms, he threw back his head and laughed, turning to the others.

"Ha, boys! Dikey thinks we've got his pelts. He's as much as accused me of stealing 'em! Let's show him some rough stuff."

He whirled on Dike with a roar.

But the trader from Lac la Marthe jumped back and swung out his revolver. He said—"Not a move out of any of you!"

Glowering, his huge face contorted with rage, Pogue stopped in mid-career. His followers, muttering, riveted their burning eyes on the man with the gun. Hands strained at knife-hilts and revolver butts.

"Raise 'em high," went on Dike. "I want to look over your pelts, Pogue."

He raised his hat and touched his head. The door opened. Silently, his rifle leveled, Toochoo slid in and over beside Dike.

"Into the store-room, Toochoo, and get those pelts."

"Wait," snarled Pogue. "How do I know he won't fake it? How does he know which is which?"

"He knows," said Dike.

Toochoo had passed behind the counter and into the store-room. The trade-room was deathly silent. The men, tense as drumheads, watched wolfishly for a chance to outwit Dike. The minutes passed. Finally Toochoo, frowning a little, came out. He shook his head.

"No find," he said.

Dike seemed perplexed. In the momentary movement of his eyes to Toochoo, a breed swept his hand toward his knife. Toochoo's gun cracked. The breed slumped. That broke the tension. Another breed snatched at his revolver and Dike, shooting low, smashed his hand. Pogue, bellowing, had his gun trained on Dike when Toochoo, hiding behind the counter blazed and sent it spinning from his hand. Knives came into play.

A greasy Indian made a panther-like leap for Dike, who ducked under, spun around and shot another breed in the act of drawing a bead on Toochoo. He emptied his gun and picked up a stool as he saw Pogue hurtling toward him with drawn knife. He missed Pogue and caught another fellow flush in the face. That put the third man out of commission. The other three were concentrating their efforts on Toochoo, who was hidden somewhere among the stores behind the counter.

Dike met Pogue and missed the wielded knife by a fraction of an inch. He hurled Pogue away and dove for another stool. Raising it, he crouched, while Pogue circled around him with drawn knife. A gun spat from behind the counter and an Indian hit the boards. The two others fired. Pogue, unable to hold back, leered bestially and hurtled for Dike.

The stool grazed Pogue's head, ripped open his left ear and thudded against his shoulder. He groaned, but he was a hard-case brawler, and he forced Dike to the floor, his one arm helpless, but his knife-arm still in fighting form. Madly he jabbed it down, blind with rage. The blade grazed Dike's bearded face and sank three inches in the hard pine floor.

Dike caught his thick throat and struggled to force him up, but Pogue had worked his knee in his stomach and was pressing down with all his strength, while his one good hand was working feverishly for the brutal nose-grip. The cabin was foul with oaths and powder smoke. The two remaining breeds were creeping toward the counter, emboldened by no recent challenge from Toochoo. Dike and Pogue were fighting to the death, locked in each other's grips, streaming blood.

Pogue had Dike's nose between his fingers and Dike had Pogue by the throat in an unbreakable vice. Finally, with a mighty effort, Dike managed to throw Pogue on his side and thus broke the terrible knee-to-stomach grip. He worked him to his back, still with the throat grip, and then lifted one hand long enough to smash him between the eyes. Grudgingly, Pogue's nose grip relaxed and Dike, grimacing with pain, tore his hand away altogether and again smashed him between the eyes. Grunting, Pogue slid into a coma.

Dripping blood, his nose already swelling monstrously, Dike lunged after the two who were stalking Toochoo. He leaped on the one fellow's back and cracked him on the ear with a short, chopping jab, tearing his gun from senseless hands. The other fellow lurched back and swung his rifle, butt to hip. A shot boomed from the other side of the room, and Toochoo mysteriously appeared from nowhere.

"He'd a got me that time," muttered Dike, wavering. "Where'd you come from? Thought you were back here."

He pointed to the counter.

Toochoo actually grinned.

"Got pelts," he said in Dike's ear. "Come."

Bewildered, Dike followed Toochoo behind the counter, then into the room where pelts were stored. The Indian scrambled up a rope that dangled from a rafter, looked down to see if Dike were still watching, and reached up into the shadows under the roof. He tugged at something which finally gave way and came tumbling down. Toochoo worked his way toward the front of the cabin on the rafters, then dropped down near the door, thus showing Dike how he had fooled the two Indians.

Dike, opening the moose-hide bundle, found almost half a hundred pelts; silvers, crosses, one black-fox, marten, otter, and a few fisher-cats. Turning one of them over, he saw on the rawhide the outline of a little circle, apparently imprinted with a heated instrument.

Toochoo, pulling his revolver from his belt, fitted the muzzle on the little circle.

"You branded 'em all right," said Dike, "but these bums must have caught wise—there's Pogue."

Pogue was sitting up, rubbing his head. Some of his henchmen were groaning, fighting back to consciousness.

Dike straightened up, throwing the batch of pelts over his shoulder and moving toward the door.

"Good-by, Pogue. I wouldn't mind sleeping indoors tonight, but it's cleaner outside."

Pogue blinked up stupidly. Then:

"Go t''ell."

"And Pogue. You're booked for hell, all right, but in the meantime you'd better go where you're not known so well. Come on, Toochoo."

THE FIRELIGHT PATROL

NORTHWOODS—THE LAND OF THE NORTH TAKES A MIGHTY GRIP OVER THE LIVES OF MIGHTY MEN.

CORPORAL CHET TYSON, of the Mounted, pulled out of Fort Resolution one morning in November. Dusk was still heavy upon the land, and a shrill little wind was working out of the northeast. Between the post and Great Slave Lake there is a portage of about ten miles, and McAleny, the temporary factor, evinced his respect and friendship for the hard young corporal by escorting him to the lake. They were trotting side by side behind the big McKenzie toboggan.

McAleny was saying:

"It gets me, Chet, why the divil ye're in sich haste. Sure it's starvin' I am f'r news from the outside, an' here ye come blowin' in at twelve las' night, eat me out o' house an' home, sleep, eat again an' thin away wit' ye. I'm thinkin' yere manners are bad, Chet Tyson. A glutton f'r speed ye be, damme!"

Tyson grinned broadly.

"Forget it, old chum. If I had the time I'd sit and chat with you for a week, but I've got a little job ahead of me. I'm bound for Lac Ste. Therese, and it's no tourist country, you can bet. I'll have a big story to tell when I get back. So calm yourself."

"But, sure, ye should tell a mon whyfor all the haste."

"No, Mac. I can't spirt it now. Wait'll I get back."

"Ah-h-h, go way wit' ye!—Well, I s'pose it's as ye say, an' I won't be pressin' the matter."

Tyson shook hands with McAleny.

"God be wit' ye, Chet," said the factor. "It's a dommed country up that way, a blasted death patrol, I tell ye."

"I've been through worse," Tyson chuckled.

He snapped his whip, and the team of nine wolf-dogs snaked out and began the mush due westward across the frozen lake. A good team, that, bred by Tyson himself, with the wolf strain strong in them.

Fighters all, and good workers, with a powerful leader that was the most exacting taskmaster that ever toiled in the traces—Jock, offspring of a wolf and a MacKenzie River hound; and Bunty, the wheeler, pure wolf, who once had toiled through a blizzard with a helpless leg and fought Tyson when the latter had tried to cut him out.

The outfit pegged away all day, for the going on the lake was good. Tyson saluted several fur brigades bound for Resolution, caught up with and passed a trapper legging it for Lac La Marthe. He passed the mouth of the Yellow-Knife, still kept going when the moon and the multi-colored Northern Lights made twilight of the night.

It was near midnight when he drove into Fort Rae. He slept at the Mission House, ate a hurried breakfast and was off when only a faint hint of dawn was in the east. He left the lake and toiled northward through pine and spruce and juniper. At noon he made Lake Fabre and at night Lac Ste. Croix.

Still northward on the next day, and then due west through a ragged, battered country, dotted with nameless little lakes and cut up by bumpy ridges. One dog went under, and Tyson wrapped him in furs and placed him on the sled. The other dogs were ripping their feet on the rough trail, and he paused long enough to bind their paws with pieces of moosehide.

He made a bleak camp that night in the vortex of a snow squall. Next day he continued in a still, gnawing cold that cracked his lips and painted dark patches on his bearded face. His breath, spouting out, congealed as it fell back and formed a thin mask of ice. But he kept up the breakneck speed, and

made a record run between Great Slave Lake and Lac Ste. Therese.

Dusk was closing in when he reached Ste. Therese. He slowed down and trotted up to a settlement of half-a-dozen log cabins at a leisurely pace. His dogs, dead tired, dropped to their bellies. Tyson strode up to the largest of the cabins and pushed open the door.

In the middle of the low, spacious room was a long cylindrical stove about which were clustered a dozen rough-looking men; some few whites, a breed or two, and several stolid Indians. At the rear was a counter, behind which were tiers of shelves stocked with trade goods.

Tyson stood with his back to the door and swept his keen eyes about as he drew off his mittens. His gaze riveted on a big bearded man who had just emerged from a door behind the counter. The man frowned darkly. Tyson threw open his furs and strode across the room, still holding the other's eyes.

"You the trader here?" he asked curtly.

"Yeah."

"What's your name?"

"Braddock."

"Tyson, patrol corporal. Anyone in from the outside recently?"

"No," insolently.

Tyson chuckled softly.

"Let's talk it over privately."

Braddock started to say something, then changed his mind and indicated the door behind him. The corporal went around the end of the counter and entered. Braddock, following, looked over his shoulder, caught the eye of a small, dark man who was apparently waiting for some cue, and winked.

Tyson sat down, sighed and stuffed his pipe thoughtfully. When it was going smoothly he leaned back and blew a cloud of smoke ceilingward.

"Come, Braddock, I'm looking for a chap called Halsey. Where is he?"

Braddock was poking aimlessly at the stove. He said, without looking up:

"Halsey? Never heard of him."

Tyson regarded the bowl of his pipe.

"That's a lie."

"Whadeya mean!" Braddock heaved his bulk erect and glowered darkly.

"Don't look so damned outraged. Listen!"

Tyson banged his fist on the table.

"I'm not up this way for my health. I've been detailed to get Halsey and bring him in. Do you know why he's wanted? I guess you do, old sport, only you won't tell. He's wanted for the killing of Billy Jim, a packer formerly in your employ! Know Billy Jim?"

Braddock moistened his thick lips.

"Never heard of him."

"That's another lie. Billy Jim knew you and you knew him. Halsey thought he'd killed him outright, but the buck crawled into camp and spun a pretty story before he passed out."

"He lied!"

"About what?"

Tyson's eyes twinkled.

"About— Say, what the hell are you driving at?"

Tyson laughed.

"Almost gave yourself away, didn't you?" He shot to his feet.

"Sit down!" he lashed out.

Sullen, muttering in his thick beard, Braddock flung himself into an armchair, his big hands grasping the sides savagely, his bleary eyes shooting about evasively.

"Now," said the corporal softly, "where is Halsey hiding?"

"I don't know, I tell yuh."

"Bah! I'll tell you why you don't know. If Halsey's taken in he'll tell a little story about you, a little worse than the one Billy Jim told. It's not going to take much to drive you out of the country, remember that. You were kicked out of the old company for a crooked deal over on the Doobaunt. Revillons wouldn't have a thing to do with you. Artillery Lake got too hot for you and you pushed farther north. To all appearances you were working on the level up here, until Billy Jim spilled the whole game.

"Now it comes out that you've been poaching right along, in cahoots with a bunch of cut-throats that get paid a bonus for each trap they rob and for each trapper they bang over the head. Billy Jim crossed you and threatened to expose you. He was making for Chippewyan when Halsey overtook him and shot him, most likely under your orders. Now where is Halsey?"

"That's a damned lie!"

"*That* remains to be proved."

Tyson put on his mittens and moved toward the door.

"I'll give you an hour to produce Halsey. When I come in here again I want to see him here."

With that he pulled open the door and passed out into the trade room. Talk amongst the loungers ceased immediately, they stared mutely at the floor, then venomously after the corporal as he passed by.

TYSON ERECTED his tent in full view of the trading post. He built a roaring fire, threw frozen fish to the dogs and cooked his supper. Then he changed his sweaty socks for dry ones and settled before the fire for a thoughtful smoke. He could see scowling faces watching him from the trade house window.

The night was Stygian; no moon, no stars. A sullen wind was droning in the timber and the temperature was plummeting. The dogs huddled about the fire, curling up. Tyson rose and paced back and forth. The wind picked up and sang shrilly across the lake. The trees began to rock and groan.

Tyson bent down near the fire to look at his watch. The hour was up. He piled more fuel on the fire, looked aloft into the black starless void and shook his head gravely.

"H'm. I've got an idea this is going to be a lively night," he murmured.

He shoved open the trade house door and kicked it shut with a moccasined heel. The white men and the breeds were playing poker. The Indians looked on dispassionately. No one looked up at Tyson. Pipe smoke hung heavy in the low room, and the booming noises of the night only emphasized the silence that prevailed. After a meditative pause, Tyson proceeded across the room to the door behind the counter. Suddenly he swung about and beheld twelve pairs of evil eyes regarding him. Immediately they shifted elsewhere.

Tyson booted open the door abruptly, his hand on his service pistol. Braddock stood behind the table, his hands clasped behind him. For a long moment the two men locked eyes. Tyson said, simply—

"Where's Halsey?"

Braddock jammed his hands into his pockets and studied the toe of his moccasin.

"He wouldn't come out."

"Where is he?"

"In one o' the cabins."

"Show me."

Braddock hesitated, rubbed his jaw, then took down a mack-

inaw from a peg on the wall and rolled out of the room. Tyson
followed. There was a stir in the trade room—rasping whispers.
One breed leered evilly. Tyson stared them down one after
another, his eyes flinty. A hard man, Tyson, and unafraid. Braddock led the way outside and pointed to a small, nondescript
shack not thirty yards away.

"He's in there."

"Armed, no doubt?"

"He'll fight."

"So I imagine. Well, I'll get him. You'd better make ready for
a trip south. He'll probably tell all he knows."

Braddock spat out of a corner of his mouth.

"Y' think so?"

"That's what I'm going to find out."

Tyson gave Braddock a long, unwavering look, then went
over to the little shack. He rapped soundly on the door.

"Halsey, come out, in the name of the law."

He listened. There was a movement within but no reply. He
knocked again, repeating the words. Again there was a movement, but no other sound. Tyson drew his service pistol.

"Halsey, if you don't come out I'll come in shooting."

He waited another moment. Receiving no response, he banged
open the door and hurled himself into the gloomy interior. The
wind slammed the door behind him. He crouched in a corner,
his gun ready. Somewhere in the murk he heard a stir. Vaguely
he could make out a table.

He moved a trifle, bumped into something that made him
whirl, but found it to be merely a small stove. He wormed his
way cautiously behind this, raised his pistol and fired through
the roof. The momentary flare revealed, not six feet away, a lynx
with bared fangs, just making to spring!

Tyson brought his gun down and blazed away. The lynx was
already in the air and hurtling toward him. It struck the stove
and leaped away nimbly. Simultaneously Tyson dove for the

door and made to throw it open. It resisted. Locked from the outside.

"The scum!"

He fell back against the door, drawing his knife. Blade in one hand, pistol in the other, he awaited the great cat's next move. Despite the cold, perspiration stood out on his face in great beads. Unable to wait any longer, he fired again. The lynx was at him like an arrow from a bow, a chilling sound grating in its throat.

Tyson jerked himself aside. The lynx snapped the fur from his shoulder and crashed against the door. Tyson twisted and struck with his knife, slicing away the animal's ear, then lurched across the cabin as the great claws clicked not an inch from his nose. That close call chilled the blood in his veins.

The cat was at him again. It caught the sleeve of his right arm at the elbow and tore fur, tunic and undergarments completely off, leaving his forearm bare and bleeding. Had the fur and clothing been less stout, he would have lost one good arm. But, if his arm was still intact, his gun was gone, and he found himself with only his knife.

He met the next charge with a terrific slash that gouged out one of the cat's eyes. With a blood-curdling scream the lynx followed up and tore away part of his collar, barely missing his throat. Tyson thrust upward and slashed open its belly. Again and again he slashed, and each time his knife came away dripping red. There was no getting away now.

The cat was lashing at him continuously, snarling, its fangs, snapping, its claws ripping away Tyson's furs and seeking his face. He had no chance to aim his blows. He just hacked away, laying open the cat's face, puncturing its sides, tearing open its belly.

And still the blood-crazed animal fanged his furs and drew his blood. He did not know that, finally, he pierced the animal's throat. For minutes afterward he kept jabbing home the blade, until finally the beast slipped to the floor and lay inert.

Tyson lunged across the room, fell over a table and dived to the floor. He sat up, fumbled for a match and lit it. He recovered his gun, reloaded the magazine and stumbled about in the gloom.

"Damn pups! Humph! Damn, pups! Hell's going to pop now."

He tugged at the door, calling damnation upon Braddock and his whole gang. But the door would not yield. Then he heard a noise in the rear of the cabin. He whirled, saw boards being ripped away from what he made out to be a window. Then a face appeared, and the next moment a man was struggling frantically through the aperture.

"Hey, you all right? Where the hell's that cat? I say, you all right?"

"I'm alive," clipped Tyson. "Who the devil are you?"

"Get ready. They're coming. Braddock's hell-bent now and he won't stop at nothing. Cripes, I thought I'd be picking you up in parts. The screams o' that cat were terrible."

"Say, stranger," persisted Tyson, "who are you?"

"I— There they are now. Lay low!"

The door rattled. Voices floated in.

"Say, Corporal Tyson, we want that man in there."

It was Braddock.

"Since when am I taking orders from you, Braddock?" shot back Tyson. "I want *you!*"

"Nemmine that cheap talk, corporal. I happen to be top-dog right now. You just try and get me. If you don't shove him out we'll rush the cabin and we'll shoot!"

"Who is the man you want?" asked Tyson.

"Bud Halsey."

"The same," supplemented the man beside Tyson.

"In that case," rejoined Tyson, "I can't oblige. Halsey belongs to the law. I warn you not to take him."

There was a loud guffaw. Then the door rattled, a lock was

snapped open, and then the door swung wide. Side by side, Tyson and Halsey crouched behind the table. Tyson said in his ear: "I'll take your gun. This is my affair."

"They'll murder you. God's sake."

"Your gun, Halsey. Quick!"

He snatched the revolver from the man's hand.

"Behind me, now."

Braddock was speaking:

"Last warning, corporal. We're after Halsey."

"Put a foot through that door at your risk. I'm waiting."

There was a long pause. Then, like a flash, a slim figure hurtled diagonally through the door. Tyson broke his neck with a fast shot and dropped a second fellow who was in the act of trying the same stunt. A volley broke loose from outside and bullets spattered in the cabin. Tyson tipped the heavy table and crouched behind it.

"God's sake, gimme a gun," urged Halsey.

"Get in the corner, out of range. I can handle—"

He met a combined rush with two guns vomiting fire and lead. Two figures slumped down in the doorway, groaned, then stiffened. Bedlam predominated. Cries of rage came from without; more bullets clattered in, hitting the stove, sinking dully into the heavy pine table that protected Tyson.

The corporal was not awed. He had been too near death in the struggle with the lynx to be startled by a mere gun-fight. He lay behind the table, pumping one gun while he loaded the other.

THE ATTACKERS did not rush in a body again. Random shots sang through the cabin, and Tyson kept making the doorway an unhealthful place for a man to be. Then, for a while, no guns spoke.

Tyson became uneasy. He sensed that some other plan was hatching among the attackers. He took advantage of the intermission to load his and Halsey's gun to capacity. So intent was he on the doorway that he did not see a slim form ooze through the rear window.

But Halsey did. He materialized out of the corner where he was crouching and with a little chuckle drove his fist into the Indian's face. The Indian went limp and lay draped in the window. At that moment a burning faggot was hurled through the doorway, then another and still another, so that soon the room was lighted and the attackers could find easy targets.

"Damn 'em!" snapped Tyson.

"Gimme a gun, corporal. Cripes, give me a chance to fight 'em."

"You squat behind me. I'm handling this."

Quickly Tyson began shooting at the burning faggots, while from outside a rain of bullets stormed him and kept chunking into the table. In time he shot out the faggots, until only smouldering coals lay on the floor.

"I'll show the scum," he muttered. "Let's see now. There are four either dead or wounded, and there's that chap hanging in the window. That means seven outside. H'm."

"If you'd only give me a gun," bewailed Halsey.

"Shut up. I'm thinking."

Tyson slipped back to the window and pulled in the unconscious Indian. Cautiously he peered out, saw no one. They were concentrating on the door, no doubt. Softly he called to Halsey.

"Follow me," he said.

He slid out through the window, and the cold stung his one bare arm. Quickly he drew it inside his coat. Halsey was beside him. The corporal handed him a pair of manacles.

"Put 'em on and keep near me. Understand?"

A little bewildered, Halsey snapped on the hand-cuffs.

"I wouldn't have a chance, corporal, if—"

"If they got you, eh? Don't worry. They won't get you."

The corporal spat sharply.

"Come on."

Silently they slipped into the bush behind the cabin and began to work around to a point that finally brought them in a direct line with the cabin entrance. Here they paused. They could make out vaguely dim shapes crouched on either side of the door.

"Seven," murmured Tyson. "All there."

Finally he could make out the figures advancing upon the cabin. One or two fired shots, and upon receiving no reply became bolder. Presently one edged up beside the door and then flung himself across the threshold. The others waited for a brief instant, then followed.

Tyson was on his feet in a flash. He sped over the hard crust, swerved to the left and finally brought up at one corner of the cabin. Here he crouched, with Halsey behind him.

"I say, if you'd give me a gun…. I'll hang, but let me get a shot at Braddock." He spoke in a whisper.

From within the cabin: "Dammit, they sneaked all right." It was Braddock's voice. "Here, make a light. Why the hell didn't one o' you watch the window?"

A lamp was lit. The table was righted.

Tyson, a gun in each hand, crept up to the door. Then he stepped in.

"Not a move!"

They were grouped around the table. Braddock was struck speechless. Curses grated from the others' lips. One fellow's finger was worming around his gun trigger.

Tyson went on, tersely:

"Drop the guns—all of you. Lively!"

The weapons were released reluctantly. They clattered to the floor one by one.

"Back up against the wall; no crowding."

At this moment Halsey slipped in and sullen mutterings arose from the captives. Tyson advanced and kicked the weapons into a heap. He turned to Halsey.

"Now you can help me by tying up this crowd. Take the key out of my pocket and unlock your 'cuffs." This done, Tyson proceeded, "Take that skin that's lying on the bunk, cut it into strips and truss 'em up."

When the thongs were ready, Tyson ordered the captives to come to the center of the room, one by one, and Halsey bound them. The last to be called was Braddock. He took his time about it. He rolled up to Halsey like a big bear and held out his hands.

Halsey said, "I'll swing, no doubt, but I guess you'll pass away some of your years in a jail. You're through running me, Braddock."

Braddock made no reply. But with a deft movement he snatched the knife from Halsey's belt, turned so that the latter's back was to Tyson, and drove the blade into Halsey's chest. Halsey slumped with gritted teeth.

"Damn you, Braddock, back up!" snarled Tyson.

Braddock, grinning hellishly, watched the wounded man writhing on the floor. Tyson threw him the manacles.

"Put em on, you bum!"

Braddock snapped them on and lined up with his henchmen, gloating with unholy glee over his act. It was purely the act of an outlaw who realized that he was pretty well at the end of his tether.

Tyson had lifted Halsey to a chair.

"I'M GONE, corporal," he said thickly.

"Yes, I killed Billy Jim. Braddock held a mighty hand over me. When Billy threatened to expose Braddock and then ran away Braddock made us draw cards to see who would track Billy and kill him before he could tell. I drew low. So I went. I found Billy and followed him for three days before I could get up enough nerve to shoot. But I did shoot. Then I came back.

"When you blew in looking for me Braddock wanted me to hide in the cabin here and murder you. I wouldn't do it. I told him to turn me over, but he was afraid I'd tell on him. So he locked me in the trade house and planted a lynx in here that one of the Indians had trapped the other day. He told me he'd do that if I didn't consent to kill you. But I wouldn't consent.

"Then I heard the cat screaming. I broke loose and busted in here, thinking I could help you out. I—I hope I've helped you, corporal. I—I got in with Braddock a year ago. I couldn't break—away. I—I...."

His voice gurgled in his throat. Suddenly he pitched to the floor, twisted, groaned, and then lay very still.

Tyson looked across at Braddock stonily.

"And that's that. You heard? Well, in the morning we start south. You'll swing, Braddock, and I'm going to see if I can be the one to pull the rope."

Then he sat down and stuffed his pipe with one hand.

"Yes, Mac," he said, half aloud, "I'll have quite a story to tell you."

STUART OF THE CITY PATROL

FAR NORTH—MELTING ICE, CRUMBLING TRAILS AND A NORTH GIRL'S LIFE IN THE BALANCE.

I **NSPECTOR CRAIG** said tersely: "Stuart, I'm taking a chance on you, despite the fact that you've just come up from the City Patrol. Jacko Braun's wanted for the killing of Alf Olsen between here and Hart Lake.

"We have no description. Indian found Olsen just before he cashed in, and the poor beggar had only time to whisper a name and say that Braun would hit north. Get out right away. Take— let's see—take Pete Smart. He's a good Indian and he knows the country. Lively, Stuart. Braun's got a start."

"Yes, sir."

Stuart saluted and went out briskly. An hour later he pulled out of Athabasca Landing on foot, for there was a nasty country ahead of him and a horse would be an impediment. He carried a light pack, as did Pete Smart, for they intended to live for the most part off the land.

Stuart was on his first assignment, and he was not a little thrilled. It was about time, anyhow, he told himself. He'd been getting tired of pounding the pavement of Main Street and Portage Avenue down in Winnipeg. He was six feet and a product of the Lake Temiskaming country, and he had a body that was tough and wiry, for the lumber camps around North Bay and Cochrane had claimed him before the Mounted.

He had a mild, level eye that could turn cold as ice, and his hand was always ready to shoot out in friendship and just as ready to shoot out doubled up. He had been a bit of a roughneck in his very early youth, but at twenty-seven he was calm and cool and went off the handle only on rare occasions.

It was light until nine that night, and at half past they made a camp on the shore of a little waterway. After two days they made Lac la Biche, stopped only for a meal, and struck out north for Hart Lake, where they stopped for another meal of caribou ribs in a Cree lodge. Here Stuart tried to find out something about Braun, but the fellow was evidently a stranger in that vicinity, and to all his questions the Indian said *"Namowyah"* which is Cree for "no."

Later Stuart said to Pete Smart: "Well, Pete, old chum, it's a case of finding a needle in a haystack. But we'll get him, eh?"

"Always," nodded Pete, for he had accompanied other Mounties into the wilds.

One of the Crees paddled them posthaste across Hart Lake next morning, and before nightfall they reached and were whisked across Big White Fish by another Cree. Two days later, after fast and mighty trail-pounding, they drew up on the southern tip of Big Jack Fish Lake just as the moon rose. Stuart's tunic was dirty and torn from much travel through dense bush, and his face was dark with a thick stubble of beard.

After supper he lit his pipe and went off for a stroll through the poplar and spruce. The moon had risen above the treetops, and the night was pale, with an easterly breeze rippling the lake and rustling in the branches. Pete had not informed him of any cabins being nearby, so he was naturally surprised and interested when he beheld, through the interlacing foliage, a square of yellow light.

He found a settlement of three split-log cabins, one large one flanked by two small, unlighted shacks. The door of the middle cabin was open, so he walked in. A girl had just emerged from another room. He saw immediately that she was pretty, but what struck him most was the flush in her face and the dampness of her eyes, which she was now attempting to dry hurriedly with her apron.

"Good evening," greeted Stuart casually. "Just saw the light and thought I'd drop in. Constable Stuart, Athabasca Landing."

The girl gave a little start, then laughed jerkily.

"Oh, yes, Mr. Stuart. Mine is O'Neil—Joan."

"Just so. This looks like it might be a trading post."

"Yes, it is. My brother Dave is a free trader, I'm up from Edmonton, vacationing. I like the woods."

At that moment a man shambled in from the other room. Stuart looked him over rapidly, saw that his smile was greatly overdone and forced, and told himself that he disliked the man for just that reason. And there were other reasons, too. The man was built high and wide, with a leonine neck and a big crooked nose. He had an under-slung jaw, and his eyes were big and bleary and seemed about to burst from their sockets. He rocked forward, his smile breaking into a toothless grin.

"Howdy, cons'able. O'Neil's the name. A good Irish name, and I've got a good Irish sister here. Hey, sis?—Joan's her name, cons'able."

Joan fidgeted with her fingers and kept wetting her lips, and Stuart thought he saw a hint of suppressed terror in her wide, dark eyes. However, he took O'Neil's big, calloused hand and wrung it briefly.

"I suppose you're on patrol, cons'able," O'Neil ventured.

"No, not exactly. Little job ahead of me. Chap named Braun

killed a Swede, and I'm after him. Happen to know anything about him?"

Joan started to say something, but O'Neil fixed her with a baleful eye and stroked his beard. Then:

"Braun, y' say, cons'able? Huh! Can't place the name. What's he look like?"

"That's it," laughed Stuart. "I don't know. I'd like to find out."

"Huh! That's too bad. Sorry I can't turn a hand to help you out. I hope you get the bum, though. That reminds me. There's been a breed hanging around here and I don't like his looks. If you got a camp near here you'd better look out. Might rob your outfit."

Stuart knitted his brows.

"Breed! H'm. Well, I've got an Indian with me, and he's over at the camp now. But I'll keep an eye peeled anyhow. Thanks."

O'Neil studied the toe of his moccasin thoughtfully.

"S'pose you won't be staying around this way long, hey?" he asked.

"No. I'll be off before the sun. Might have to chase this chap to the Barrens. But I'll get him, of course."

"That's the spirit. —Well, I'm sorry you ain't hanging around a little while; but the law's the law."

Stuart looked beyond O'Neil to the gloomy corner where Joan was now standing. Vaguely he could make out her white face; the wide eyes, the mouth half open. He started to say something, then changed his mind and moved toward the door, mildly perplexed. There was something strange about the atmosphere of the trade room; something strange about Joan; something strange about her brother. Or so Stuart thought. He paused meditatively in the doorway for a moment, then shrugged his shoulders, called good-by to Joan and O'Neil and strode swiftly back to his camp.

Pete was squatting before the fire and smoking a greasy old pipe. Without a word Stuart sprawled flat on his back, hands behind head, and wondered if there really was something strange about the trade house or if he was just a plain fool letting imagination get the best of him. He started to count the stars to change his trend of thought, but the job was too big, so he reverted to ruminating on Joan and O'Neil, but mostly on Joan.

He gave a start when somewhere in the murk a branch snapped. He sat up, threw a glance at Pete for confirmation, but Pete was sleeping. He listened for a moment, then gave it up and stuffed his pipe.

"Say, Pete," he called.

Pete's eyes blinked open.

"Say, Pete. Question. Do you know a trader up along the lake by the name of O'Neil?"

"Know," grunted Pete, nodding his head.

Stuart thought over this for a moment. Then:

"H'm. We'll stop in there tomorrow morning. We'll—"

Another branch cracked over in the gloom. Stuart shot to his feet, his hand on his service pistol. Came more sounds, as of a body passing through the underbrush. Stuart drew his gun and dived into the timber. He made a poor start by crashing into a twisted windfall, and it took him almost five minutes to disentangle himself. Then he continued at breakneck speed, beating his way through stubborn willows and dense spruce scrub. He topped a ridge, paused to listen for more noises, heard none, and swore roundly. He went on aimlessly, cautiously, trying to pierce the gloom. He stopped again, to listen.

Then something hard hurtled out of nowhere and caught him across the head. He pitched to the ground, groaning deep in his throat, and everything went black. A raucous chuckle floated from the willows. Then there was silence.

Stuart was struggling to his feet long before consciousness returned. Everything seemed to spin and dance, and he kept reeling and stumbling until he tripped over a rock and went headlong into the cool waters of the lake.

The cold shock in some measure restored his senses. He heaved to his feet and crawled back to the shore, dripping wet.

He leaned against a slim poplar and rubbed the big bump on his head. Then his head cleared suddenly. He got down to his knees and searched for his pistol, found it and straightened up, coldly grim.

"Now we'll see!" he clipped.

With that he beat his way back toward the camp in high heat. When he arrived he found Pete sprawled on the blankets. He called crisply to him, and when the Indian neither answered nor rose, he frowned darkly and bent over him. Pete's eyes stared up at the pale stars, and a red blotch was on his shirt near the heart. His body was already cold.

A hot wave went through Stuart's body. His eyes blazed up, and his neck muscles bulged out like knotted cords. With a little snarl he left the corpse and plunged into the timber at a reckless gait. It was the recklessness of the old lumber-camp days when he used to mix in a scrap at least once a day and take and give beatings with a broad grin. But he did not grin now, nor did he smile. His eyes were flinty, and his jaw was set hard.

He burst out upon the clearing before O'Neil's trading post and saw the trader standing in the doorway, rifle in hand.

"Say, cons'able!" O'Neil bellowed. "That breed I told you about's been around again. I'm going to pump him full of lead. Trying to make up to Joan and all that. Funny you didn't see him. Last saw him heading for your camp."

Stuart brought up, a little breathless. "A breed is he? Well, dammit, I was banged over the head and then I blew into camp to find my Indian stabbed—dead! Cripes, O'Neil, I'm out for blood! I'll let no man, breed or otherwise, bang me over the head and kill my Indian. I'll be damned if I will!"

O'Neil spat out the side of his mouth. "It's him as did the dirty work, I'll bet. Joan was scared to death. She's in bed now. Let's beat up the bush for the bum."

Side by side they started out, Stuart running swiftly and silently. O'Neil lumbering along like the big bear he was. When they reached the lake Stuart called a halt.

"Here," he said shortly. "You go north. I'll zigzag south. If you see him, shoot your gun and I'll come running."

Stuart bounded off without further explanation. He kept to the shore for awhile, then dived into the spruces. His choler had not diminished even slightly. His Indian guide having been so foully murdered, he would have to find his way north alone or engage another guide, which is not altogether easy. In any event there would be a delay, and Braun would be getting farther and farther beyond his reach.

"And this my first big job," muttered the constable. "Damn the luck!"

In the wake of his words came, through the silence of the forest, a woman's scream. He stopped dead in his tracks, his hand freezing on his pistol. Then he whirled and galloped madly toward O'Neil's post. He reached the clearing and went through the door in one magnificent leap, swinging his gun low for immediate action.

The spacious room was empty. Stuart, tensed for a clash, threw his eyes about quickly, then relaxed. He moved warily toward the door that led to the rear room. He could hear no sound, not the faintest stir. The oil lamp suspended from the ceiling threw a sickly yellow light into the dark corners. Stuart put his hand on the knob, pushed the door open to a crack, then suddenly booted it wide and jumped to one side.

There was no shot to greet him. He struck a match, and even by its feeble glow he could see that the room was empty. He went into it abruptly, lit a lamp and looked about hurriedly. There were signs of a struggle. A chair was overturned, another was tipped against the table. A home-made rag carpet was crumpled in a heap. He gave the carpet a casual kick, and magically it came to life; that is, there was a vicious snap, and the rug jumped up along with a powerful-double-spring fox trap. The steel jaws had missed Stuart's foot by a mere inch.

"The fiend!" he grated, then gripped his gun tighter.

He hurried back into the trade room. He wondered if O'Neil

were still hunting the breed. Surely he must have heard the shot. And what about Joan? No doubt it was she who had screamed, and perhaps she now was at the mercy of some half-breed blackguard. He cast another searching glance about, and this time he saw another door, to the left of the counter. He guessed it was a store room and started to move toward it.

Just then he heard the sound of running feet outside. The next instant Joan burst into the room, wild and disheveled, panting like a hard-pressed animal. She carried a rifle, and before Stuart knew what it was all about she had crossed the room like a panther and was crouching before the door he had been about to enter. He frowned perplexedly.

"Don't you try to get in here!" she cried. "Don't you dare. I can shoot straight; and I'm not afraid to, either. Get out!"

Stuart could have shot her if he had been so inclined. However, he smiled and slipped his pistol into its holster. He stroked his stubble of beard, regarding her half-humorously, half-quizzi-cally.

"I don't know what's in that room, Miss O'Neil," he said. "But if it concerns the law I'm afraid you'll have to step aside."

The girl crouched lower, her rifle unwavering. "But I won't. Don't you take one step. I'll shoot, and I don't care about your red coat. I mean it. Don't move!"

Stuart was unruffled. "I shall have to put it in the form of an order. Miss O'Neil, in the name of the law, step aside or I shall have to arrest you. Out of the way!"

His eyes were hard as agate now. He took a step forward, his eyes riveted on the girl's. Her finger wormed nervously around the trigger, and in her eyes Stuart saw horror mixed with a faint suggestion of admiration; but he saw no fear. He was almost positive that the girl would shoot, and he was trying to crumple her with his eyes, which had crumpled many a man. But the girl was still determined.

He was ready to chance his life, started to take another step and discountenance the girl by sheer nerve, when a commotion arose outside, and then O'Neil came rumbling into the trade room. His shirt was torn, his face was bloody, and there was murder in his eyes.

Joan's gun dropped. Stuart, a little awed, let his hand slide to his pistol; and then O'Neil, with amazing agility for a man of his bulk, hurled himself at Stuart. Stuart's gun came out in a flash, but O'Neil pinned it down with a mighty hand and twisted Stuart's wrist until the gun fell to the floor.

Stuart drove out with his one free fist and caught O'Neil between the eyes, but the latter was a whale of a man and hard as nails. He merely grunted, shook his head and caught Stuart about the middle. The constable hit the boards with a crunching thud and O'Neil came lunging down at him. Locked in grips of steel, they rolled all over the floor, with one and then the other on top.

Joan still crouched by the door, her wide eyes following the struggling men. Still locked, they heaved up to their feet. O'Neil broke and chopped a knotted hand against the constable's ear. Stuart reeled and groped for his opponent. He dodged another vicious blow whose force was so terrific that the momentum carried O'Neil off his feet. He slid on his face along the floor and reached out for the pistol that Stuart had dropped.

But the constable kicked it out of reach with a quick movement. Snarling, O'Neil caught his legs and toppled him over, but lost the grip and scrambled to his feet just as the constable cut loose with a pile-driving fist that landed flush on his mouth. Roaring, spitting blood and a fragment of a rotten tooth, O'Neil picked up a split-log stool, hurled it with maniacal force.

It struck Stuart a glancing blow above his already bruised ear. Joan screamed. O'Neil cackled with unholy glee as the constable tottered around in a circle and then slumped to the floor. He rocked over and drove a boot into Stuart's ribs, bent down and cuffed him against the ear, then kicked him again.

"Stop that!" lashed out the girl. "You coward!"

O'Neil looked up slowly, then scowled venomously when he saw Joan had a gun on him. He straightened up, glowering.

"Put that down, you brat!" he snarled.

Joan met his fierce gaze with cool deliberation.

"I'll shoot you if you don't get outside and then keep moving."

He snapped his fingers at her.

"D'you forget what I said? Want me to spill it, huh? Just wait!"

"Get out!" persisted Joan, taking a step forward.

Under the steady gun O'Neil wavered.

"I'll—I'll spill it, I tell you. You put that gun away. I won't hurt you—"

"No, you wouldn't," laughed Joan ironically. "Never mind. Get out; do you hear? *Out!*"

Grimacing, chagrined, baffled, O'Neil retreated toward the door, shoulders hunched like a grizzly's. He put one foot out when Stuart's choked voice said:

"Don't move—you!"

And his retrieved service pistol, which he had fallen upon, was trained on the trader.

Stuart staggered to his feet and leaned against the table. Joan, in perplexed indecision, didn't know whether to cover O'Neil or the constable.

Stuart was saying:

"Step inside. Here."

He threw the trader a pair of handcuffs. "Put 'em on and let me hear 'em click. Lively!"

His head was clearing.

The trader obeyed sullenly. Stuart turned to Joan.

"I thank you for assisting me. Now for the little room here."

"No!" cried the girl. "No!"

She flung herself before the door, rifle leveled.

"I am sorry, but I must investigate." Cool as ice, he advanced, until her rifle was pressed against his chest. Still holding her eyes with his own hard ones, he raised one hand, grasped the barrel and calmly shoved it aside. With that the girl crumpled like a deflated balloon and cried pitifully.

Stuart tried the door and found it to be locked. Unceremoniously he took the girl's rifle and battered it down. He heard a stir in the darkness of the room. He turned for a moment to see O'Neil making for the outside.

"Stop!" he lashed out. Then, "Come over here."

Black with rage, the trader shambled over.

Stuart said:

"Go in there and bring out whoever's in hiding. Don't look at me like a blasted fool! Move!"

He chuckled then.

"Go ahead. I can hear he's gagged. If I went in you'd skin out."

The trader went in finally and came out a moment later with a man bound and gagged. Stuart indicated a chair, and the stranger was placed there.

"Would you mind cutting him loose?" he said to the girl.

Joan took a knife and slashed away the bonds, then fell upon her knees beside the man. He was a middle-aged man, grayed about the temples, with a face that at other times might have been kindly; but now it was flushed with hot indignation. He pointed an accusing finger at O'Neil.

"You—you *dog!*"

He was off the chair in a mad leap, but the constable caught him and held him back.

"Just a minute," he said. "What's this all about?"

"About!" exploded the man. "Good God, this dirty rat came into my post here, slammed me on the head and I woke up, bound and gagged, in the store room. Can you imagine such a man around here with a girl like my good Joan?"

"And who are you?" asked Stuart.

"Me? Patrick O'Neil, free trader. And a good name, too. Ask anyone north o' La Biche. You're new up this way or you'd know."

"Why," began Stuart, "this man said he was O'Neil."

"*Him!*" roared the man. "The liar! I met him some years back over in the Candle Lake Country. And a fine cutthroat he is, too. Jacko Braun—that's him."

Stuart spun around, his fists clenched.

"Jacko Braun!"

Then he relaxed, saying:

"Jacko Braun, you are under arrest for the murder of Alf Olsen on August fifth."

"Ah, so that's it!" breathed the genuine O'Neil.

Joan was now in his arms.

"God, it's been awful, dad," she said, and it was meant for Stuart's ears, too. "When I came in this afternoon after that tramp I found Jacko Braun here. I asked for you, and he said you were all right. But I asked where. Then he explained that he had known you over in Saskatchewan some years ago, that he had seen you kill a man, and that the Mounties were still looking for the criminal.

"He said he asked you to protect him from the police, said he had committed a minor misdemeanor—stealing a horse to get a doctor for a sick friend. When you refused he threatened to tell the police what you had done, and still you refused. So, to save *you*, he said, he bound you and threw you into the store room. He attacked me, made indecent remarks and finally ran off with me, but he stumbled down a ravine and I managed to get back here."

"God!" whispered the father. "What a liar he was! He had seen you, Joan, and wanted you. I never killed any one in my life. He was safe from the police, because he's new over this way. He just wanted you, so he got me out of the way."

"Yes," said Joan. "And when he saw Mr. Stuart coming he made me say he was my brother, or he'd tell on you."

"Well, it's all settled," spoke up Stuart. "He killed my Indian, too. Must have heard him say he knew you, Mr. O'Neil, by sight. He stabbed him. Then he invented a story about a mysterious half-breed. He'll swing, all right."

LATER, ALTHOUGH it was well past midnight, Stuart and Joan stood in the doorway and watched the westering moon.

"You know," Stuart was saying, "things have been popping so fast that I haven't had a chance to say much to you. When I first saw you here— I dunno— I felt— That is, you crept— Well, what I meant to say is— I— That is, you—"

With a little laugh Joan slipped from the doorway and sped across the room, pausing with her hand on the rear door.

"You'd better wait until the morning. I'll have an answer then," she called.

And Stuart waited… and not in vain.

RAW COURAGE

THERE'S ONE CALL REAL MEN ANSWER TO THE WORLD OVER, AND IT ECHOED IN THIS MAN'S HEART.

WAYO, THE VOICE, led the team of six wolf-dogs up the slope through the small junipers. Jim Barnes, bigger than men usually come, even in the tall woods, rolled along beside the heavily laden toboggan on broad snowshoes, snapping a thirty-foot whip dexterously. When they reached the summit Wayo shambled to a stop and kicked a heap of soft snow from one of his rackets. Barnes rocked up beside him and squinted down into the spruce valley that sprawled before them.

"See a smoke down there, Wayo?" he observed casually.

The Indian nodded. "Wolf Valley. Ugh! Lodge of the Evil Spirit, *Nennahbosho!*"

"H'm. Don't say! Wonder what kind of an outfit's down there?"

Wayo was making ready to start westward along the ridge, away from the valley. He was saying, "Come. We mush. Make La Marthe dam' soon or dogs starve. *Wah-he-oh!* (It is far!)"

Barnes, still watching the faint wisp of smoke, called: "Hold on there, old chum! I've got an idea we'd better give a look-see. Can't tell where Harry might be holed up. Come on, now, Wayo. Swing the dogs around and we'll camp down there for the night. Maybe we can rustle up some dog grub, too."

Wayo grimaced. "Bad camp, Jim Barnes. Bad Injuns, bad white men. My brother come down from the Great Bear long tam 'go; tell me 'bout Wolf Valley. Trader rob him, shoot, chase him 'way no meat. Ugh! *Nennahbosho*—"

"Blast your old Nenny spirit! We're going down there. Now see here, Wayo. You're my brother, ain't you? I raised you, fed you, and taught you what little I know about the king's English, which ain't much. And now you're going back on me. Wayo, I'm ashamed—"

"Go!" clipped Wayo sheepishly.

Barnes grinned, cracked the whip and plunged down into the valley beside the sled. They struck the valley floor and then swung out upon a narrow waterway that twisted aimlessly through mainly spruce and pine. Soon they emerged upon a little lake, and on the eastern shore they could make out a group of squat cabins. Wayo mushed from the lake onto the spacious clearing and checked his dogs. Barnes handed him the whip and strode up to the largest of the cabins.

There was a boisterous crowd in the large trade-room. Barnes, closing the door behind him, stood for a moment and swept his keen eyes about the room while he drew off his moosehide mittens. Indians were there, dirty, grinning devils, loaded with rank rum; French voyageurs in their saucy tongues and multi-colored sashes and leggings—bold, hard fellows, always ready with a smile and no less ready with a knife; a few degenerate whites, dirty as the Indians and as drunk; and off to one side, two big, raw-boned blonds, unmistakably Swedes—silent, cautious men, both wearing white-fox *capotes*. They saw Barnes, and only in their eyes did the man from the trail see any hint of greeting. The others were too drunk to notice him, and those who were not completely gone leered or stared truculently at him.

With a tightening of his wide lips he sauntered through the crowd to the counter in the rear. Here he met a broad, heavy-set man, hard-jawed and hard-eyed, who leaned indolently upon the counter and regarded him hostilely. Barnes divined he was the trader.

"My name's Barnes," he offered crisply. "I'm with the Hudson's Bay over on the Du Rocher."

The man spat lazily. "Yeah? I'm Canavan— Mike Canavan, free trader. What c'n I do for you?"

Barnes leaned closer. "I'm looking for a man named Larry Thorpe. Maybe you've seen him or know where he's at."

"Thorpe… Thorpe… H'm. Nope, can't say I do offhand. What's up?" He shot Barnes a dark look.

Barnes hesitated. Then: "Well, it's a long story. Thorpe had an idea he killed a man down in Edmonton three years ago and he skipt out for the wilds. Turns out another chap did the killing. Confessed a year ago and cleared Thorpe. That's the whole thing in a nutshell.—Well, I won't bother you, then. You see, I'm his stepbrother."

Canavan shifted his chew and stared hard at the counter, making no further comment. Barnes, always brief and to the point, having finished his business, turned away. Drawing on his mittens, he wormed his way through the lurching trappers. One tipsy Frenchman, in festive mood, made a pass at Barnes from behind, catching him soundly across the back of the neck. With amazing agility for a man of his bulk Barnes spun around, caught the Frenchman by the throat and hurled him fully six feet cross the room.

It might have been good policy for him to have disregarded the blow on the neck, but the fellow had hit exceptionally hard and in a nasty place, and Barnes' fist was always as ready to knock a man down as it was to meet a friendly palm and shake. As quickly as he struck the Frenchman he sensed that something bigger was to follow, and he whirled clear of the crowd and stood by the door, a towering giant in the low room. Out of the corner of his eye he saw the two stolid Swedes edging toward him, but with their eyes on the other trappers, and his heart thrilled. He felt sure that these two were honest men, ready to see and stand by a square deal.

The astounded Frenchman was now tottering to his feet and his hand was fumbling in his sash. A knife flashed out, glinted in the yellow glow from the swinging oil-lamps, and hissed across the room. It clanged into the stout pine door. Barnes' eye narrowed and grew coldly grim. He raised his hand and lashed out, "Canavan, if you've got anything to say here, call that dirty pup off, or I'll wring his neck!"

Canavan spat and leaned back, apparently disinterested. The Frenchman had mysteriously possessed himself of another knife and was creeping wolfishly toward Barnes. Barnes eyed him coolly, his fists doubled, his great shoulders drooping. The Frenchman dived at him, whipped the knife upward for his stomach even as Barnes cut loose with his fist and caught him flush on the jaw. The knife merely pierced the caribou-hide *capote* before the Frenchman jack-knifed to the floor without so much as a grunt. Barnes breathed with relief and watched the others. He saw hatred, malice, blood-lust in every set of eyes, but he met the gazes coldly, fearlessly, for he had a name where men are measured by their courage.

He took a firm, resolute step forward. A breed's hand was sliding toward a knife. Then the window to the left of the door crashed in, a rifle was poked through and the breed went down screaming with his hands clutching at his chest. Without turning Barnes knew that Wayo had come to his aid. He laughed harshly.

"I have nothing with you—any of you," he said. "I don't like to get cracked across the back o' the neck and I don't like to have knives heaved at me. Throw away the weapons and I'll take you two at a time and spread you over the floor."

Canavan said, "Nemmine that talk, stranger. Just slide out and let it pass." To the others, "Lay off, boys."

Barnes said, hotly, "Why the hell didn't you talk like that before?"

"Nemmine. Better clear out. I mightn't be able to hold these boys."

Barnes backed away, pulled the door ajar. The two Swedes were regarding him with no little admiration. He gave them a brief, appreciative glance, swung the door wide and backed out. Then he turned to greet Wayo. He gave a little gasp. A girl was just pulling her gun from the window. In the faint light that streamed out he caught a brief glimpse of her white, wondering face. Then she whirled and in a flash disappeared in the gloom.

"What the hell!" he jerked out.

Then he looked about quickly, saw no one, and hurried over to his dogs. They were lying on their bellies, dozing. But Wayo was gone. Barnes was perplexed. He gave a low call, strained his ears for an answer. There was none. Night had come down rapidly, but the snow near the sled revealed signs of a struggle, and there were some dark stains that he guessed was new spilled blood. He cursed bitterly. He grabbed his rifle from the sled, started back for the cabin, then changed his mind.

He drove his team into a juniper grove and made camp. He divided the three remaining jack-fish among his six dogs, and ate his own frugal meal without his usual heartiness. He kept his gun near at hand, sat so that he saw all who entered or departed from the trade house. He counted three other cabins, small and nondescript. After his meal he gave a low call of three notes, such as is made by the big gray owl. It was a call that

Wayo had taught him, and when in distress the answer was to be the thin, quavering call of the wolf. But there was no answer.

Wayo had been right. This was the valley of *Nennahbosho*, the Evil Spirit. Canavan was a tough, unscrupulous cutthroat, Barnes told himself, and he had a pretty crowd of henchmen, too. Something was brewing in the trade house, no doubt, and before very long hell would start to pop. Barnes had expected to spend *Ooshemegoo Kessigow* (New Year's Day) at his post on the River du Rocher with Wayo and his own half-brother, Larry Thorpe, who, through a misunderstanding, was hiding in the wilds because he thought he had killed a man. But now his hopes were smashed to smithereens.

He tensed a trifle. He saw Canavan issue from the trade house and enter one of the other cabins. Half an hour later he came out with two Frenchmen, and they were all talking excitedly. Before entering the trade house Canavan paused, looked toward Barnes' camp and spoke in a low tone to his companion. Then they entered, chuckling devilishly.

Barnes again gave the call of the owl. A moment later a similar call floated from the direction of the cabins. Barnes smiled.

"Fooled him. He doesn't know the answer."

But, nevertheless, Barnes took his rifle and slunk away from the campfire. He slipped through the dense spruce scrub, gave the call again and again heard the same answer not far to his left. Toward the source of it he crept, gun-butt to hip, ready for immediate action. Then he stopped dead in his tracks. "Don't move!" said a feminine voice, low yet very clear. "I've got you covered."

"All right, miss. But what's the idea?"

"You must leave here before morning."

"And why?"

"Because you are after Larry Thorpe."

"Oh-ho, so he is here. Well, in that case, I'm sorry to disappoint you. I'll just hang around until I find him."

"No you won't. I have saved you once, but if you stay I must kill you. You will not take Larry Thorpe. I'll leave you now, but you must be many miles away by daylight."

"I say, where is he? And where's my Indian? Where—" His voice trailed off. Receding sounds in the gloom told him that the mystery woman had left him to decide. Then, vehemently, "I'll be damned if I'll leave! I'll find Larry and I'll find Wayo, or, by cripes, I'll raise holy hell!"

He crashed back to his camp in high heat. No sooner had he arrived than a stick was flung from a nearby bush. He crouched, his eyes shooting sparks.

A slow voice spoke from the gloom, "We are de fellas dat was ready to help you when de fight started in Canavan's."

Barnes remembered the two Swedes and said, "Yes."

"An' me an' my partner, Alf, ve're ready to help you again. Somet'ings up in dere—ain't it, Alf?—an' ve'll be on hand to lend a hand. Von't ve, Alf? An' ve t'ink, Alf an' me, dat you an' us oughta not be seen together. Ain't it, Alf? But ve'll keep out our eyes an' follow any move you start. Alf— hey?"

"Ole's right," came a deeper voice.

"Thanks, strangers," spoke up Barnes, warmly. "I won't forget it. Thanks."

They slipped away. Barnes' confidence was bolstered up by his new allies. He piled more wood on the fire, stuffed a wad of tobacco into his mouth and rolled off toward the trade house. Suddenly he changed his course and made for one of the cabins, putting his ear to the door.

"Wayo," he called in a hoarse whisper. Then, "Larry."

No reply. He went to the next cabin, repeating the two names, but received no answer. Then to the third cabin, set deep in the pines. Here he called, then tried the door. There was a faint stir within, the pad-pad of moccasined feet on boards, but no other sound.

"Open up!" he snapped out.

A tense voice grated, "Get the hell out of here or I'll shoot!"

Vaguely the voice struck a chord of memory in Barnes, and he tried to catalogue, swiftly, the voices he had heard in his forty years. But the task was too great and he was pressed for time.

His own voice was coarse with the menace he put into it, "Shoot and be damned! I've got a gun here, remember."

Even as he spoke the cabin boomed with a deafening report. He felt no hurt, and with a mad little oath he returned the fire. He sprang to one side as another bullet crashed out. Then the trade house door banged open and Canavan, leading his motley crew, swung out and blazed away with a big revolver. The shot kicked up the snow between Barnes' feet and he whirled to meet the new attack, leaping backward into the bush.

"Come! Follow me!" It was the girl's voice near his shoulder.

"I'll not move!" he gritted. "I'll show these birds some fast and mighty shooting!"

"They'll murder you! Come! Ten against one!"

In a flash Barnes realized the futility of his stand. He turned, found the girl close beside him and then followed her helter-skelter through the murk of the forest. She was fleet, and it was apparent that she knew every foot of the country, for she neither hesitated nor faltered once.

They were on the lake for a few yards, then she dived into the forest and Barnes crashed after her, wondering among other things what it was all about. She had saved him once, then she had threatened to kill him, and now she was trying to save him again.

The sounds of his pursuers broke into his thoughts. He concentrated his energy, mental and physical, upon the immediate issue. Looking over his shoulder, he saw a dim figure just passing over a little ridge. Without stopping he turned half around and fired. He heard a cry, saw the figure pitch to the snow.

"Don't stop to shoot," panted the girl.

"I won't."

They crossed a little creek, plunged into slim white poplars and struggled up a steep slope. The girl misjudged a matted windfall and with a little cry crashed between the branches. She tried to rise. Barnes jumped to help her up.

She said, "Go on! They'll get you!"

"And what about you?"

He picked her up in his arms and hastened on, but the added weight caused him to sink through the snow's crust. At each step he sank deeper and swore between clenched teeth. Then, finally, he set her down and said, "Try to get out of this neck of the woods. I'm going back to meet that crowd."

"But—"

"Never mind. Just keep going the best you can and I'll hold 'em off for a while."

With that he back trailed to the summit of the slope and threw himself down behind a thicket. The pursuers had crossed the little creek and were now creeping up toward the ridge. Barnes caught a fleeting glimpse of a shadowy form, fired and cursed when he saw he'd missed. His challenge was answered with much gusto by half a dozen rifles, and lead droned low over his head and in one instance plowed the snow in front of his face and went through the snow beneath him.

"Almost!" he observed with a grim little chuckle.

He could hear noises in the bush to left and right, and he guessed that they were surrounding him. He looked around, hoping that the girl in some way had placed herself beyond the death ring. Then he drew his knife and laid it near at hand, emptied his pockets of cartridges and placed them beside the knife. He hugged the frozen crust of the snow, so that the thicket formed a canopy above him and in some measure concealed him.

Shots barked, from all directions, some close, some wide. They were feeling him out, guessing at his position. For a brief moment he saw a head rise above a bush down the slope. He sent two fast shots at the easy target, saw the man jerk upward and then heard him crashing down toward the waterway. A storm of bullets sought him, whining, thudding into trees; one grazed his cheek, another tore off the peak of his *capote* hood, others sprayed the snow in his face and for an instant blinded him.

The gloom was alive with sounds, then; random shots, bodies crashing through the underbrush, a snarl, a hoarse command, a foul oath. Barnes got to one knee, grim as death, shooting at dim shadows that hurtled from all sides. One Indian took a pretty leap with upraised knife. Barnes, cramped for room, twisted his gun and smashed the fellow's brain in mid-career. The body, carried by its own momentum, sailed over his head and collided with a voyageur who was in the act of clubbing Barnes over the head. Both bodies crashed down upon him and pinned him to the snow. Another voyageur had, at that moment, flung a knife which, instead of hitting Barnes, went through the neck of the man who had tried to brain him. He hurled both bodies away and heaved to his feet, swinging his now empty rifle with terrible ferocity. The knife-thrower, unable to move swiftly enough, was caught within the radius of the wielded gun, screamed a split-second before he was hit and then spun to the snow with a broken neck.

Four men, clubbing their guns, sprang upon Barnes at once, and the big man from the River du Rocher started to run down the slope with them, in an effort to tear himself loose. One man was flung high and far, but the other three clung to him and tried to throw him over. He fought them with his mighty arms and his strong heart, while knives tore his stout hide *capote* to ribbons and drew his blood. And then Canavan, leading two others, came hurtling out of the gloom and Barnes, breaking through the snow, was crushed down.

A gun-butt caught him neatly across the head and he groaned deep in his throat and fought even when he could no longer see. He slumped down, and when the attackers drew off he tried to rise. A voyageur, cackling fiendishly, raised his knife, lunged at the helpless man with a mighty sweep. A gun spoke

from the gloom and the Frenchman, his brain shattered, pitched
headlong upon the snow, his mad cry clipped short. The others
flung back into the spruce scrub. The mysterious gun barked
again and an Indian snarled, dropped his rifle and dangled a
shattered hand in the air.

Canavan and his henchmen, unable to comprehend the new
attack, left Barnes and fled down the slope. More bullets spattered after them. Barnes, his vision clearing, tottered to his feet
and then, losing his balance, pitched down the incline. Two big,
heavily furred figures lunged out of the thickets, brought up
short and for a moment crouched, scanning the valley below.

"Down dere, Alf," muttered one.

"Aye, Ole. Koom on."

They rocked down after Barnes and caught him before he
was half-way down the slope. Ole took a pot-shot at Canavan's
gang and then dropped to his knee. Barnes, knocked to consciousness by the tumble, sat up and rubbed his head. Alf was
shoving a revolver into his hand.

"Thanks, boys. God, they damn near finished me that time!"

"Aye. Koom on," said Alf.

The three of them plunged down toward the waterway and
Canavan, snarling, led his followers into the timber. Nor did
he stop to lay an ambush. He struck out for his post in mad
haste, with his henchman passing him in wild, frantic leaps.
They made the clearing and stumbled toward the trade house.

"We'll show 'em!" snapped Canavan.

Then he stopped dead in his tracks. From the trade house
window a gun was leveled and spoke when one of the Indians
tried to bring his rifle into play. He sank, clawing at his stomach.

Barnes and the two big Swedes came galloping out of the
timber and blazed away lustily. Canavan, his face ashen with
fear and horror, dived for one of the cabins. The gun in the
window swerved around, vomited flame, and Canavan, his
mouth choked with blasphemy, went to his knees and doubled
up. The others, caught between two fires, and without a leader,
huddled together and mumbled incoherently.

Barnes brought up before them, his torn *capote* blowing crazily in the wind, his face bloody and his wide mouth set hard.

"Drop those guns!" he lashed out.

Reluctantly they obeyed, cowering under his cold, piercing eyes. Ole shambled forward and gathered up the weapons. Alf was stuffing his pipe. Barnes took a vicious bite at a plug of tobacco and said, "Back up, you roughnecks, into the trade house."

The door opened and Wayo, the Voice, grinning, ushered them in.

"Well, I'll be damned!" exclaimed Barnes.

Wayo offered, "Smashed on head by white woman. Put in cabin. Wake up. Ever' dam body gone."

"So!" Barnes' eyes narrowed. Then, "Now to find Larry." He turned to the Swedes, "Say, boys, just keep these bums in here till I come back. Come on, Wayo, old chum."

They strode out and stumbled upon Canavan. He was stiff and cold, staring with glazed eyes at the pale stars. Barnes went on toward the last cabin. As he neared it a slim form came running from the woods, fell against the door, then whirled about and crouched with leveled gun.

"She smash me," grunted Wayo. It was the girl again. She was saying, breathlessly, "Stay away. Don't come near this door. I'll shoot. I mean it. I'll kill you! Don't take another step."

Barnes frowned perplexedly. "I tell you I'm going to get in that cabin. I—"

"No, you're not! I'll shoot if you take another step!"

He saw she meant it. She was tense, like a cornered thing of the wild, and her rifle covered him unwaveringly. Annoyed, baffled, he flamed up suddenly. "I must get in there, I tell you. It's my duty. I've been all over the blasted territory to find Larry Thorpe, and I'm sure he's in there!"

"And it's my duty to see he's not taken out. And you can't take him. You can't! You can bring the whole police force up here, but I'll fight to save him."

"Police! Good God, I'm no policeman!"

The girl blanched. At that instant the door burst open and a man, his eyes wild, lurched out and flung himself into Barnes' arms.

"Good God, Jim; Canavan said the Mounties were after me! Said you were a Mounty in disguise!"

"There, there, Larry, chum. Canavan's dead and the rest of the outfit's sitting tight. But tell me how the devil you ever got mixed up with that dirty crowd?"

Larry, half-laughing, half-crying, had released Barnes and was now holding the girl close in his arms. Wayo chuckled. Barnes turned and boxed his ears, and the Indian stared at the snow very sheepishly.

Larry was saying, "I'll be able to get away now, Jim. I blew in here over a year ago when I thought a Mounty was trailing me. I'd heard about Wolf Valley and about Canavan sheltering outlaws. I told him my story and begged for protection. He gave it to me, but it was the worst thing I could have asked for. Had to do as he said, you know, because he held the whip hand. Tried to get away, but he wouldn't hear it. No man ever gets out of his camp alive. Afraid their tongues might wag and spoil his game—robbing trappers and all that. Some tried to steal away, but his Indian cut-throats trailed 'em and murdered them. Kate, here, and I have had an awful time. I was driven into her father's mission house in a valley ten miles west by a storm some time ago. She's stood by me, though." He turned to the weary, half-conscious girl. "Kate, I want you to meet my big brother. Jim, my wife."

Jim gasped, then grinned broadly and nudged Wayo.

Larry went on, "Now we'll have to go in hiding some place else."

Barnes nudged Wayo again. "You didn't give me chance to say, Larry, that you're a free man. Packy Davis killed that chap in Edmonton. Confessed on his death-bed over a year ago. I've had every man in the North watching out for you, and I've been up as far as Coppermine looking for you myself. Congratulations to both of you, and especially to Kate for saving me a number of times tonight."

"She thought you were a Mounty, too," choked Larry, "and she knew what would happen if they killed a redcoat."

Barnes left the two lovers and shambled thoughtfully back toward the trade house with the Indian. "Well, Wayo," he said, "I guess you were right about that Nenny spirit."

"Um. Dawn we start east, *Kisse-Manito* land."

"Yes, old chum, and I'll be glad to see my wife and kids again. It's been a big mush."

THE WHITE PERIL

**FAR NORTH—
STRAINING DOG
TEAMS AND A RACE
FOR LIFE OVER
DRIFTING SNOWS.**

ED STRYKER drew up before his spruce log trapping shack as the swift Labrador night was closing in. He unstrapped his oval-shaped rackets, pushed open the door and booted it shut behind him. Little icicles hung at the corners of his wide mouth, and frozen ridges of rheum were under his eyes. For it was November, and the long cold had come to stay.

"Hello there, Keepee, old scout," he called to a tall Indian who stood by the sheet-iron stove, mixing fresh bannocks.

Keepee, which is Cree for "make haste," said, without looking up, " 'Lo."

Stryker, a whale of a man, shrugged out of his deerskin *koolutik* and hung it on a peg near the stove. They were not Labrador men, these two; their native habitat was many miles westward, beyond Hudson Bay, way over in the Saskatchewan River country. But furs run mighty fast along the Koksoak, and the Barren Lands produce no finer black foxes. Stryker, an Old Company "freeman," had seen wealth in the Labrador while still with the Company, and when he resigned he had persuaded Keepee, an old friend, to join him and try their luck there.

He was saying: "Say, Keepee, there's a blackie snooping around that deadfall you made. Bet we'll nab him before the week's out. Three prime marten today and a beauty silver. Some running, eh?"

"Um."

Stryker bathed his face with snow while the Indian set out the supper. The cabin was small, barely clearing Stryker's head. It was patched with earth and moss, which subsequently had been treated with water, so that a layer of ice covered it and checked the bitter winds that were always howling down from Ungava Bay.

Stryker was just about to sit down to a steaming meal when the door whipped open and a fur-swathed man pitched to the floor, clawing at the boards. Keepee closed the door. Stryker bent down and turned the man over, and gave a little gasp when he saw the stranger was white. There are not many white men in the Labrador wilds.

"That brandy!" snapped Stryker, at the same time tearing open the man's furs.

Keepee brought a black bottle from the larder and put it to the man's lips. Stryker went outside and came back with an armful of snow, bathed the man's feet and hands and face. The nose was in critical condition, and he pressed it in his cold hand instead of using snow, for at a certain state of frost-bite snow will tear the skin.

The man began to mutter unintelligible things. He stirred; his hands writhed. His red-rimmed eyes opened, and in them was an appeal that beckoned Stryker to lean closer.

"Letter… pocket… Kuglictuk… go… life depends… name o' God…."

A rattle choked the words in his throat. His eyes glared for a moment, then became glazed and expressionless. A sigh fluttered from his blackened lips. Then he lay very still.

STRYKER ROSE, a little awed, then bowed his head for a brief moment. After which he bent down again and rummaged in the dead man's pockets. He found a little note-book, a sort of diary, bearing the name, "Harry P. Kavanagh." He scanned the entries made under various dates, from which he learned that a certain sloop had put out from Fort Churchill in hopes of making Whale River Post before the freeze-up.

Things had gone wrong. The sloop had been wrecked by floe ice. The writer claimed to be the only survivor. He didn't know the country. He was without food.

"I guess that about tells the story," muttered Stryker grimly. "Now he said something about a letter and a life and for me to go some place. Let's see. Oh, yes! Kuglictuk, he said. That's a river."

After further searching he found an envelope bearing one word—"Jack." He paused before breaking the seal, then finally tore it open and read:

> "Dear Jack:
> Everything is all right. The beast disappeared into the Barrens almost a year ago, and no one has seen him since. I am counting the days till I see you. Harry was always a good boy, and he volunteered to go and find you, and both our hearts are broken while you are away...."

There were two pages of maternal sentiment, written in fine script, and signed, "Mother."

Stryker folded them after two perusals and sat down to think. There were two roads open to him. He could disregard the letter, continue with his trap-lines and bury the late Harry P. Kavanagh when the spring thaw came. On the other hand, he could take his dog-team, mush to Fort Chimo and then start east for the white, barren tundra that lies between there and the Kuglictuk River. If he chose the latter he would face death and starvation, and after it all was over he would return to the Saskatchewan with empty pockets.

A man named Jack was apparently in hiding. It is bad for a white man to stay in the Labrador alone. And Ed Stryker was of the brotherhood of the wilds. So he said to Keepee:

"Old scout, I'm pulling out to-morrow. Got a little job. You go right ahead with the trapping and make yourself rich. I may get back to nab a few more furs and I may not. When you got all the furs you want leg it to Chimo and I'll meet you there when it's over. I'll have to take the team, but I'll leave most of the provisions with you and stock up at the Post. You can have my traps, too. I don't know what this letter's all about, but this chum who just died tried to tell me to carry on, and I'm obliging him."

Keepee, having finished his meal despite the newly dead, mumbled:

"Want me help? Me go dam' quick, betcha."

"No, Keepee. I know you're a good sort. But this is a whim of mine. I brought you over here and I want to see you get something out of it. Maybe I'll try next year; maybe, as I said, I'll get back in time to run the traps again. Anyhow, I'm going, for some chum's struck a streak of bad luck and I'm going to lend a hand."

Keepee understood his white companion, and he pressed the subject no further.

In the morning, when it was still dark, they drove the six wolf-dogs out of the lean-to in the rear and then brought out the twelve-foot *komatik*, a sturdy Eskimo sled which Stryker had purchased at Fort Chimo. Quickly it was loaded with grub, blankets and sealskin robes, and some blackies which Stryker intended to sell at the Post. Then they shook hands, the white man and the red, and their hearts were in their palms.

"Luck, Ed," murmured the Indian, then waved his hand skyward. "*Kisse-Manito* watch um."

"Thanks, Keepee. I'll see you later at Chimo."

"At Chimo. Good."

The thirty-five-foot walrus-hide whip snaked out and ended with a sharp report, and the big wolf-dogs lunged ahead, passed through a growth of stunted larch and tamarack and then struck the Koksoak River, heading north.

CHAPTER II

CHEVIK, THE KNIFE

THEY FOUND good going down the Koksoak. The dogs were in fine fettle, and Stryker reeled off fifty miles the first day. At dusk of the second, when a cold moon hung over the frozen world, Stryker trotted into Fort Chimo at the head of his outfit and went directly to the H.B.C. store.

Flemming, the acting factor, looked up from a copy of "Pilgrim's Progress" and said:

"Hello, Stryker. What brings you up here already? Thought you were holed up for the winter."

They shook.

"Strange things happen," laughed Stryker. "Chap blew into my shack and cashed in. Had a letter on him. Asked me to find somebody named Jack."

Briefly he related the whole affair, showed Flemming the letter and asked for a guide.

"A guide?" echoed the factor. "I wish I could, but every Indian and husky's off to the traps. Seems you've struck bad luck to begin with. Why not take a run over to Revillon's?"

"H'm. Might as well try. Thanks. See you again."

Monsieur De Loge, the agent at the Revillon Freres Post, was a genial man. He said after Stryker had given him details:

"Ah, *m'sieu*, I should lak to help you ver' much, but you will see by glancing about dat no one ees here. It ees a bad time, dis, to secure guides. De traps, you know. Meantime, howevaire, you will be my guest? De table is ready."

After a splendid meal with monsieur *le facteur* Stryker went out to a clump of scrub spruce and fed his dogs. He had suspected all along that a guide would be unavailable, and now that the fact was thrust upon him he was a little undecided just what to do. He knew very little about the Ungava, and for a stranger to get stranded in the white peril of snow and ice and low temperatures, is suicide.

He went back to the French post. A lone Eskimo had just arrived from the east, and on his *komatik* was a dog that had been unable to stand the toil of trail and trace. The Eskimo's dark face glistened with a layer of ice, and his sealskin *netsek* was caked with hoar frost.

De Loge greeted him.

"Ah, Chevik, a bad trail, *oui?*"

Chevik grunted and threw open his skins.

"Chevik, me frien'," proceeded De Loge. "M'sieu Stryker, here, desires a guide to de Kuglictuk. It ees a mission of great importance. *M'sieu* desires to find some one by de name of Jack, who is white."

Chevik's eyes narrowed. He shot a quick look at Stryker, then at De Loge. Then he stuffed his pipe and moved away toward the stove.

"Say, Chevik, what do you say about that?" called Stryker. "Good pay, Chevik."

Chevik, holding a match to his pipe, looked up and straight into Stryker's eyes. Stryker saw hatred in that gaze. The whole face, with its pulpy mouth, its slanting forehead and flat nose, emanated danger. With a faint sneer, Chevik continued to light his pipe, then drew his skins about him and went outside.

"Now what do you know about that!" exclaimed Stryker softly.

De Loge said:

"He would be a good guide, too. Speaks ver' good English, unlak de Eskimo. A great fighter, *m'sieu,* and marvelous wit' de knife. Hence his name, Chevik, which means de knife. Ah—he dislaks you, howevaire."

"That's putting it mild," laughed Stryker. "He *hates* me. Why, I don't know."

Flemming managed to find sleeping quarters for him that night in a cabin that was also shared by one of the assistants. He was worn out from the day's hard traveling, and he turned in early. But he lay awake a long time, figuring things out, and before he finally closed his eyes he had decided that, guide or no guide, he would leave next day for the Kuglictuk.

He awoke some minutes later to find a dark, fur-swathed form standing in the doorway. For a long moment the stranger did not move, but Stryker felt that a pair of eyes were regarding him, despite the thick gloom. Cautiously he slipped his hand toward the stool beside his bed, where lay his belt and revolver.

Then the stranger moved. Instinctively Stryker dodged to one side. A knife whizzed across the room, grazed his cheek and stuck in the wall behind his head. With that he dived for his revolver, but the door slammed shut and the stranger was gone. Gun in hand, Stryker jumped to the door, hurled it open and swung his gun low for immediate action. But only a sharp wind and the cold night sky greeted him, and farther away the yellow square of light that marked the H.B.C. store. He thought of dressing and going over to tell Flemming and his assistant, but changed his mind.

In the morning he said nothing about the attack. He went over to see the agent at Revillon's and discovered that Chevik had departed more than two hours before. Stryker was almost positive that it was Chevik who had thrown the knife, and he felt that he would cross Chevik's trail before long.

WHEN HE announced his intention of proceeding alone Flemming threw up his hands. De Loge, a bit of a humorist, wanted to know what kind of flowers should be put on the grave. But between them they mapped out a course and gave him hints on the country, for they were wise in the ways of the Labrador.

Daylight was almost complete when, his *komatik* loaded with a month's provisions, he pulled out of Fort Chimo. As he put the Koksoak farther and farther behind him the timber died away, until finally nothing but bare, ragged hills swept away toward the horizon and the frosty air hung like gauze all about him. It was the land of *Torngak,* the Death Spirit of the Eskimo; but Stryker was entering it unafraid.

That night he took some wood from his *komatik*, built a little fire, ate bannock, pork, and beans cooked in seal oil. He cut blocks of snow and raised a snow wall against the wind. He went to sleep huddled in his blankets and robes. Some time after midnight he was startled awake by a big form that was bending over him. With a sharp oath he tried to heave himself up; but a mittened hand smashed him between the eyes, and things spun around and then went black.

When he awoke he was sitting against his *komatik.* On the other side of the fire sat Chevik, the Knife, regarding him impassively, with a rifle resting across his knee.

"Don't move," grunted the Eskimo. Stryker was cramming tobacco into his pipe.

"What's the idea of the big grudge you've got against me, Chevik? I'd like to be your friend."

Chevik sneered. "Me your en'my. Me kill you—you don't go back Chimo."

"You will, eh? Well, let me tell you something, Chevik, I'm bound for the Kuglictuk. See? I'm turning back for no damned husky, either. The factor at Chimo knows I'm over this way, and De Loge saw that look you gave me. If I don't get back he'll tell the Mounties, and he'll tell 'em about you."

Chevik frowned darkly and nursed his pipe.

"Me kill," he muttered thickly. Stryker got up. Chevik rose also, his gun still leveled, his eyes beady. They locked gazes. Then Stryker, shrugging his shoulders, bent down by the fire, looking for a fagot with which to light his pipe—or so it seemed. He pulled out a flaming stick of tamarack, held it to his pipe, then with a rapid movement flipped it up so that it struck Chevik across the forehead.

Snarling, the Eskimo hurtled backward. At the same time his gun boomed and the shot buzzed over Stryker's head. But Stryker cleared the fire in a mighty leap and bore Chevik down upon the snow. The Eskimo lost his gun in the mix-up and met Stryker with his short, powerful arms. Still locked, they struggled to their feet, reeling, staggering about the fire, while the wolf-dogs looked on with eager eyes. For they understood.

In a break Chevik whipped out a short, broad knife, crouched, then dived at Stryker with animal-like ferocity. It was a downward thrust, and it carried all the Eskimo's weight behind it, so that when he missed he toppled over and buried the knife hilt-deep in the frozen snow. With a mad little laugh Stryker was upon him and lifted him up with such force that he ripped away the stout hide collar. His next blow caught Chevik on the Adam's apple and he jack-knifed to the snow and writhed, struggling for his breath.

When he tottered to his feet Stryker had a gun on him.

"Where's your outfit?" he snapped.

Chevik nodded toward the gloom sullenly.

"Lead me to it," said Stryker.

Chevik started off and half an hour later brought up before his campfire. Stryker bound him hand and foot, piled more wood on the fire, then said:

"It'll take you about five hours to work loose. The fire'll burn till then. After this don't go fooling around with strangers. Good night."

CHAPTER III

CHEVIK'S REVENGE

AT NOON of the following day Stryker crossed the Whale River a hundred miles south of Whale River Post, one of the loneliest stations in all the Ungava. Chevik had not yet put in an appearance, although this did not cause Stryker to relax his vigilance, which he maintained night and day for the next two days. After passing the Whale and then the Mukalik, he headed northeast and at last came to the headwaters of the Kuglictuk. Flemming and De Loge had given him good instructions, and he knew that without the map they had supplied he would never have reached the river.

Desolation was all about him; stark, naked hills, fading into the cold film that always hangs over the Labrador, with here and there a wind-blown tree, and the frozen waterway winding silently to the distant Ungava Bay.

"It's a hell of a country for a man to live," he said aloud. "I wonder what the devil drove that there Jack fellow up this way."

He made a fire and put up his Eskimo *tupik* (tent), banking it with blocks of ice. Later a high wind worked across the tundra and snow began to drive down, pattering on the *tupik* like buckshot. The dogs crouched down on the lee side of the shelter. The wind became a howling maelstrom, hurling the snow madly before it, so that in short time the fire was beaten out and Stryker huddled deep in his robes.

He drowsed despite the bedlam. He was sound asleep when a man cautiously pulled aside the flap of his tent and looked in, then, satisfied that Stryker was sleeping, bent down and cracked him over the head with the butt of his rifle.

Stryker jerked awake, still able to see.

"Chevik—damn you!" he burst out.

The Eskimo chuckled.

"Me come. Me kill. Not with knife. Not with gun. Me let *Torngek* kill. Take dogs, grub, gun. You starve, freeze."

"You dirty—"

His words were cut short by another blow on the head. He passed out completely. Chevik chuckled, then began to tear down the *tupik*. Then he piled it on the sled along with the robes, lined up the dogs and drove off into the white cloud of the blizzard.

When Stryker came to his face was covered with snow. His shelter was gone. Only one 4-point blanket remained with him, and the awful cold was gnawing into his bones. He struggled to his feet, drawing the blanket about him, cursing deep in his throat. Everything was gone, even his ax, with which he might have built a snow wall. No food, no rifle, no robes—nothing.

"God!" he whispered.

He kept up a brisk pace to prevent his blood from freezing. He kept it up when the storm died and the dim dawn broke bleak and gray and cold, with all around him swells of virgin snow—and nothing more.

He figured he was about fifty miles from the mouth of the Kuglictuk. If he followed it to the sea and then struck west he might by chance strike Whale River Post, which was almost another fifty miles away. But then his snow-shoes were gone! How can a man trek through the Labrador without them?

He cursed the Labrador and every Eskimo in it. And he cursed himself for having penetrated it. He had a little tobacco and a dozen matches. He made a fire and had for breakfast one pipeful of tobacco.

Sinking knee-deep in the fresh snow, he began to follow the river northward. Perhaps that mysterious Jack was holed up somewhere along it. Perhaps he would meet a friendly Indian or Eskimo.

Three hours later, as he topped a barren ridge, he saw far ahead several wisps of smoke rising. His heart missed several beats and he gave a glad little cry. He summoned every bit of strength he possessed, until he rounded a bend in the river and saw on the west bank a settlement of three shacks and several *tupiks*. He tottered up to the largest of the cabins, pushed open the door and rocked in.

SMOKE HUNG heavily in the low room. There was a sheet iron stove in the center, and sitting about this were three men. Two were French *voyageurs,* and the saucy clothes they wore suggested the country west of Hudson Bay. The third man was big and thick-chested, freshly shaven, with a hard jaw and a hard, cold eye.

"Hello," called Stryker. "I'm a stranger over this way. Had a team but some blasted husky banged me over the head and ran off with every thing I had."

The *voyageurs* looked at each other sharply. The big man spat deftly out of the side of his mouth and said:

"Don't say! This is no tourist country anyhow, stranger. What brings you up this way?"

"Do I look like a tourist?" shot back Stryker crisply.

"Well, I didn't mean it that way." He winked at one of his companions. Then: "Sit down. What's the news?" At that moment the door opened and a young woman entered clad in sealskins. Stryker eyed her for a long minute, marveled at the beauty of her dark eyes.

The big man interrupted. "My name's Delevan. What did you say about that husky?"

"Oh, yes," said Stryker, and gave his own name.

The woman passed to the rear of the room. Stryker went on:

"Well, as I said, the fellow robbed me. Didn't like me since he saw me at Fort Chimo. I'm over here looking for some one whose front name is Jack."

The girl gave a little cry. Delevan fixed her with a threatening look. She turned away, trembling, and disappeared behind a curtain which separated part of the cabin.

"Yes, Jack's the name," continued Stryker. "I was running a

trapline over on the Koksoak when a chap blew into my shack, gave me a letter, mentioned this river and then died. The name on the letter is Jack; that's all."

"Let's have it," said Delevan.

"I'm sorry, chum, but it's only for Jack."

Delevan glowered. "Oh, you don't say? All right, then. Well, there's no Jack around this camp, so you might as well move on. Who'd you say was the man died?"

"I didn't say, but it was a chap named Kavanagh."

"Kavanagh!" Delevan half rose from the chair, his eyes wide.

A choked sob issued from behind the curtain. Delevan snapped to his feet and went behind. Stryker could not hear what he said, but he noted the low, menacing tone of his voice. Then Delevan came out again, his face a little flushed.

"Stranger, there's a cabin next door you can share with Paul and Rex, here. Show him, Rex," he said to one of the Frenchmen.

A little perplexed at the way things were going, Stryker followed Rex to the little shack. It had but one room; and robes on the floor served for bunks.

"You expect to go on soon, *m'sieu?*" purred Rex, his dark eyes sparkling.

"As soon as I get a guide. I'd like to run up against that husky that swiped my outfit. Crack team that was. I'd break his greasy neck." Rex chuckled liquidly.

"Good luck to you, *m'sieu,*" he said, and sauntered out.

And Stryker did not fail to get the sinister note in his voice.

CHAPTER IV

THE TRAP

REX AND Paul came into the cabin later, and the latter made supper. Stryker, sitting beside the little stove, told himself that both of them bore the earmarks of the devil. Rex was always chuckling, and Paul, as though understanding its meaning, would wink back and then favor Stryker with a wide, ingratiating smile. And Stryker was charged with a desire to get up and knock the fellow for a row of stumps. He bided his time, however, for he felt that he was on a warm trail, that Delevan and his henchmen knew something about Jack, and that the girl would be prevented from telling what she knew.

He tried to stay awake that night. He lay on one side of the stove, while Rex and Paul lay on the other side, and he damned the luck that had left him without a gun. But try as he would, his eyes refused to stay open. He fell into sound slumber.

Later on he awoke with a start and tried to cry out, but found a dirty piece of hide across his mouth. Then a bag was pulled over his head and tied about his neck. Hoarse whispers floated to him. Rough hands picked him up; and then he felt the bitter cold against his body, and he knew he had been carried from the cabin.

Five minutes later his captors halted. More whispers… a brief, rasping argument… silence. He knew that something terrible was going to happen. He struggled frantically. And then he felt himself released. A moment later an icy shock went through his body and his blood seemed to congeal instantly.

He was in the cold waters of the Kuglictuk!

He struck out. His feet touched the river bottom, and he guessed the water was no more than eight feet deep. He sprang up in an attempt to grasp the edge of the hole through which he had been dropped. His head bumped against the ice. He tried again, and this time his frozen hands caught onto the rim of the hole, but his fast dying strength was not sufficient to haul his body clear. With a groan he started to sink again.

Then, magically, he felt himself being drawn up. His body was too numb to sense contact, but he knew that he was clear of the water, that some one was carrying him across the ice. Already his clothing was frozen stiff as a board.

He heard a door slam. He felt a new warmth. Then his clothes were being torn off. Brandy was thrown down his throat. Deft hands were massaging and slapping his purple flesh. He could see nothing. He was in a semi-stupor, and he could only hear; and by and by he began to feel.

Warm, soft Hudson Bay blankets were wrapped around him. He was lying on a pile of robes. His eyes opened, but he saw through a haze. The red stove looked like a big evil eye. Several short, squat figures hovered near him. Another shot of brandy was poured between his lips. Things cleared. He was in a cabin. A round, swarthy face was near his own.

"Better?" a voice inquired.

He squinted, and as his vision became perfect he gave a little start.

The man bending over him, administering to him, was Chevik, the Knife!

"You!" he choked.

The Eskimo raised a hand in warning. "No noise. You better soon."

An hour later Stryker sat up. His vitality was remarkable, and anyhow a bath in frozen water is not so bad as it often is supposed, provided expert attention is given immediately. He looked around for Chevik. The Eskimo was gone, but another squatted stolidly by the stove.

"Chevik?" asked Stryker.

The Eskimo made signs which Stryker took as indicating that Chevik had gone out and would return shortly. He found his pipe and found some tobacco on the table. Then he searched for the letter and the notebook which had been in an inner pocket. His clothes, hanging by the stove, were still wet, and both letter and book had been removed.

"Delevan's work!" he muttered bitterly.

The door whipped open. Chevik waddled in, regarded Stryker studiously for a moment, then went to the rear of the shack and came back with dry clothes.

"Put on," he said shortly.

"Say, did Delevan and his gang heave me in the river?" Stryker asked.

Chevik nodded.

Stryker proceeded:

"Tell me what it's all about, will you? First you try to kill me, then Delevan tries his luck, and then you come along and save me. Dammit, what makes me so blasted important anyhow? And where does the lady fit in?"

Chevik pointed to the fresh clothes.

"Put on—dam' quick." He went to the door and looked out, then closed it quietly.

"Dam' quick!" he repeated.

While he dressed, Chevik went out. Ten minutes later he reentered, only to pause in the doorway and jerk his thumb over his shoulder. Stryker followed him outside. His old dog-team was there, and he saw that his *komatik* had been replenished with provisions. Chevik handed him the walrus hide whip.

"Go north," he said. "Turn west mouth river, reach Whale River. Go!"

"What's the idea?"

"Go. Delevan kill."

"Who sent you?"

"White woman."

Stryker thought over this. "What is she here?"

"Delevan's wife."

Stryker spat sharply. "But that letter. Delevan stole a letter from me. I want it."

"Go!"

"Damned if I will! Who the hell does Delevan think he is? I'm going to get that letter. Where's my rifle?"

Chevik pointed to the *komatik*. Stryker snatched up the rifle. Chevik grasped his arm.

"White woman say go. Delevan kill."

Stryker tore the Eskimo's hand away.

"No, Chevik, old chum. I'm indebted to you for saving my life. But I'm looking for somebody, and I've got a hunch this is the end of the trail. I'm going over there to Delevan's cabin and talk cold turkey to that bum. Hands off, Chevik!"

CHAPTER V

THE MYSTERY WOMAN

CHEVIK'S CABIN was only a quarter of a mile from the one in which Stryker first had met Delevan. When he left the Eskimo he trotted briskly along on the hard surface of the snow, topped a rise and then swung down toward the river, where he could see the lighted cabins. He drew up before the large cabin and put his ear to the door. He heard a loud guffaw, then the unmistakable, fiendish chuckle of Rex. He held his rifle tightly, then banged open the door, entered and kicked it shut with his heel.

Delevan and his two henchmen were sitting at the table with a bottle of whiskey between them. Delevan was the first to look up. His face froze. Rex almost toppled over. Paul crushed the glass of whiskey which he was about to raise to his lips. The room was deathly still.

"Not a move!" snapped Stryker. Then: "You, Delevan, out with that letter and book you swiped. Quick! Don't look at me like a damned fool! Show some life!" His voice rang with command.

Delevan, his mouth twitching, fumbled in his shirt pocket and brought out the letter and then the notebook. The two Frenchmen had overcome their momentary paralysis and were now eying Stryker craftily. Tension was high in the low room.

Stryker said: "Get up, the three of you. Put your guns on the table and line up against the wall."

Delevan, now sullen with rage, obeyed reluctantly. Rex and Paul followed their chief's example. As they backed against the wall Rex's hand rested lightly on his right hip.

"You, Rex, take that knife out of your sash," lashed out Stryker. "Something tells me you're not going to live long. Out with it!"

With a sneer the Frenchman pulled a knife from his sash and threw it upon the table. As Stryker stepped forward to gather up the letter and book, the curtains in the rear parted and the mystery woman stepped out. There was a big revolver in her hand.

"Back!" she warned Stryker coolly.

With a nasty laugh Delevan, thinking he had the better of the break, lunged toward the table for his knife.

"You too—back. All of you," said the woman.

Delevan snarled, "You brat!"

Stryker said, "What the devil!"

"Back!" warned Delevan's wife.

Perplexed, angry, yet marveling at the girl's cool nerve, Stryker held his peace. She picked up the letter and the book, then smiled across at Stryker.

"You'd better keep your gun on these fellows," she told him.

"But those—they're mine, madam."

Without another word she disappeared behind the curtains. A moment later she came out dressed for the trail. For a brief instant Stryker was undecided whether to detain her or keep his gun on the three others. But that brief instant, the split-second's relaxation, gave Rex time to dive for the table, snatch up his revolver and drop behind it. The next moment his gun blazed. Simultaneously Delevan and Paul jumped for their weapons. Stryker's gun boomed twice wildly. The girl was tugging at his arm.

"Come! Out!" she screamed.

"I'll not let these dirty—"

"Fool! Come!"

SHE HALF-DRAGGED him through the door and began to run off toward Chevik's cabin, yelling for Stryker to follow her. He was taking her advice a little against his will, for he felt that he had more than one score to settle with Delevan and the two Frenchmen. And his blood was up. And he was ripe for anything short of murder.

"I wish you'd let me—" he started to say.

"Never mind. It's only started," panted the girl. "You'll get all the fight you want."

Delevan and his henchmen were already on the trail. Half a dozen huskies came tumbling out of the smaller shacks and took up the pursuit, and the frosty night was shattered with rifle fire and mad oaths.

Stryker and the girl reached the cabin and burst in. Chevik and the other Eskimo were sitting by the stove, half asleep. The door was bolted.

The girl said: "Chevik, Tuktoluk, quick! Big fight!"

The Eskimos grunted, yawned and picked up their rifles. The girl took a handful of shells from her pocket and placed them on the table. Stryker loaded his rifle to capacity. The grimy oil lamp was extinguished, and the heavy table was braced against the door.

The pursuers arrived, and Delevan's voice boomed:

"Open that damned door! Open, d'you hear?"

"Go 'way; you make me laugh," shot back Stryker.

"I do, eh? All right, you pup, you'll laugh the other way when I'm finished with you."

"That's cheap talk, Delevan. Let's see what you can do."

Delevan swore and fired, but the door was of stout spruce and merely absorbed the lead. Then the attackers hurled themselves against it *en masse,* and it shivered but gave no hint of breaking down.

"I want my wife!" bawled Delevan furiously.

"You don't say!" replied the girl. "Try and get me, then." She was cool as ice.

There was a lull. Then there were sounds on the low roof, the crunch of many feet, and after that came the ring of an ax. Stryker stood so close to the girl he could look into her eyes.

"They're going to chop through," he muttered.

"Yes," she said, and let her hand fall upon his arm.

He thrilled.

"But we'll win through," he grated out.

"Yes—we will," she said.

The ax was still pounding away. The roof was straining and snapping. Then the ax stopped, and several men began to jump up and down. The roof strained more and more until finally the middle of it caved in and a deluge of snow and men crashed to the floor. Chevik caught Paul neatly across the back of the neck with a wielded gun and reduced their number by one. But more dropped through and guns and knives were swung with murderous ferocity.

Stryker, having killed one of the attacking Eskimos, swung open the door and led the fight out into the open with the girl beside him. Chevik, his face bleeding, rolled out after them, and close on his heels came Tuktoluk, shooting back as he ran. Delevan's gang, falling over one another, burst out in hot pursuit, their guns flaming, with Delevan himself, a gun in each hand and red murder in his eyes, at the fore.

Stryker reached the settlement of three cabins and drew the girl down with him beside the nearest. Chevik and Tuktoluk rocked up behind him and threw themselves to the snow. The attackers came up over the ridge, and as they swung down toward the cabins Stryker bowled over one of them with two fast shots. Chevik wounded another but did not put him out of the fight.

The attackers drew up and dropped to the snow, taking potshots at the cabins. The Northern Lights grew brighter, flinging their ghostly banners across the white tundra. The attackers, realizing they were too much in the open, retreated and worked away toward the river, but Tuktoluk dropped one of them and the girl's shot made another stagger until a companion helped him along.

CHAPTER VI

TREACHERY

"**ABOUT SIX** left," observed Stryker.

The girl started to say something; but at that moment a gun was poked in the air, and from it fluttered a piece of white cloth.

Stryker yelled, "Come on up, only one, and have your say!"

It was Rex who came forward over the little ridge that concealed the others, holding the flag of truce before him.

"Well?" snapped Stryker.

"*M'sieu,*" began the man, "we have no desire to murder you. M'sieu Delevan says to let his wife go and call t'ings off. It ees bad policy, *m'sieu,* to steal another man's wife."

Stryker looked at the girl. "Did you hear that? I'm here to help you out. I'm not interfering; but Delevan tried to murder me, and it seems he's none too good to you. I'll fight this thing out as you say. If you go over to him or not, he's got to settle with me for other things."

He paused. He was not a man to mince words. That is why he asked: "Do you love him?"

She shuddered, "No. But I'd better—"

"That's all. You were going to say you'd better go over to save me." To Rex, "Tell Delevan to go to the devil."

The Frenchman did not move. He regarded Stryker with a strange twinkle in his eyes.

Then something happened. There was a rush from the rear. At the same time Rex swung his gun butt to hip. Stryker, sensing immediately that the others had crept around while Rex was offering a truce, swung his rifle in a short arc and broke the Frenchman's jaw.

He whirled around and found the girl in his arms. She whispered:

"There's one bullet in my gun. I'll keep it for myself."

Scarcely without knowing what he did he kissed her, then pushed her behind him and fired his gun point blank at an Eskimo that was just about to brain him. The husky went down with a scream. Chevik and Tuktoluk were at close quarters with four others, and Delevan was lunging wolfishly toward Stryker.

Stryker, his rifle empty, advanced to meet him. They both swung at the same time. The rifles crashed in mid-career, broke, and the two men grappled. Delevan broke away and came back with a mighty fist that grazed Stryker's jaw and turned him completely around. Following up, Delevan caught him behind the ear with a short but terrific jab that sent him head first to the snow. But Stryker was a hard man and quick for his size. He was up and at Delevan, and everything he had was behind his blows.

It was furious, the way they mixed it, and before many minutes both were spitting blood, and their hide mittens were soggy with it.

Tuktoluk went down with a smashed skull even as Chevik broke one opponent's neck. The other three piled on him and, fighting to the last, he went down. As one of the huskies raised his knife to stab him, the girl, with a little cry, swung her revolver about and fired with her last shot—the shot she was going to save for herself. The husky dropped across the groaning Chevik.

The other two rushed at the girl and overpowered her, then began to carry her off, each striving to tear her from the other. With a mad snarl one let her go, whipped up his knife and buried it in the other's back. Then, cackling, he picked her up and disappeared behind one of the cabins. A little later he mushed out behind a *komatik* and a four-dog team, and the girl was strapped to the *komatik*.

Stryker and Delevan, struggling to the death, did not see this. Now they were down on the snow, locked in each other's arms, kicking, biting, cursing, with one and then the other on top. They carried the fight over the little ridge and right down to the river. Then they were up again and out upon the frozen waterway, slugging, taking and giving, streaming blood.

"Delevan," ground out Stryker, "this is the last fight you'll ever do. I'm going to pound you to death."

Delevan spat out a tooth. "D'you think so? G'on, you pup; the wolves 'll get you before morning."

They closed and rocked farther out upon the river. They neared a hole cut in the ice which apparently had been used for fishing. Delevan had Stryker by the nose and was trying to twist it off, and with the intense pain the latter's knees buckled as he tried to tear away. Then they went down in a heap, with Stryker underneath. Frantically Delevan pulled a long, slim knife from inside his sealskin coat and raised it high above his head.

Chevik was tottering and reeling down toward the waterway. He saw Delevan draw his knife. Chevik, the cleverest Eskimo with a knife in all the Labrador, hesitated for a split second. Then he fingered his own knife gingerly, gauged the distance with a calculating eye and threw it. It sang eerily through the air, struck Delevan point first in the side of the neck. His throat rattled. He heaved to one side, lost his balance and plunged through the hole in the ice to the bitter waters of the Kuglictuk.

Panting, Stryker struggled up and lunged toward the shore. He fell upon Chevik, grasped his hand and pressed it till the Eskimo winced.

"Thanks, Chevik! God—thanks, old chum!" Then, "Where's the white woman?"

"Gone. I see go. Man take."

The two badly mutilated men stumbled to Chevik's cabin, lashed out the dogs and followed the trail made by the abductor.

CHAPTER VII

THE LAST OF THE PACK

THE DAWN broke gray and leaden above the winter-locked Labrador. Stryker was running up beside his lead-dog. Chevik was trotting behind the *komatik* and cracking the whip. Men and dogs were covered with hoar frost.

Rounding a bend in the river, Stryker raised his hand, and Chevik called the dogs to a halt. Up ahead, on the west bank, was the smoke of a camp-fire, and Stryker could make out two figures beside it.

"It's them," he said.

He rummaged in his equipage and found a revolver, then continued at breakneck speed. Immediately there was a stir in the camp. One of the figures bundled the other upon the *komatik*, swung out the dogs and began to drive madly northward.

But Stryker had a powerful team, and in short time he was within pistol shot of the kidnapper. He fired. Missed. The other, without stopping, turned and returned fire. The shot went wild. Stryker stopped, took careful aim and shot again. This time the man stumbled, tried to grasp the gee-bar of his *komatik*, missed and sprawled headlong on the snow.

He was dead when Stryker drew up. A hundred feet farther on the team had stopped. He found the girl trying to struggle from her thongs. When she saw him she stopped struggling and lapsed into a coma.

Chevik made a fire. Strong tea revived the girl, and when she came to she found herself in Stryker's arms. And she did not seem to care.

"Thank God you came," she said with a shudder. "That beast of an Eskimo...."

"Yes, I understand," nodded Stryker. "I may as well tell you now that the whole gang is cleaned out, including your husband.

He was about to stick a knife in me when Chevik, here, pitched his own knife and hit the bull's eye. Delevan is now at the bottom of the river. This husky back here was the last of the pack."

"Good Chevik," she murmured. Then: "And my husband dead? It might sound cruel, but I'm glad. And—and thanks for bringing that letter. Poor Harry, he had to die."

Stryker, looked puzzled. "Letter? Harry?"

"Yes. You see, I am Jack. Funny name for a girl, isn't it?"

Stryker was stunned. "You—Jack?"

"Yes. Harry Kavanagh was my brother. It's hard to say why I ever married Pete Delevan. It happened two years ago. But I haven't lived with him for one day. He was a beast. My folks didn't believe in divorce, so what could I do? I told him to stay away from me, but he wouldn't. He hounded me wherever I went.

"My father used to run a trading post in the Labrador, and when he gave it up and came home he brought his servant, Chevik, with him. It was Chevik who helped me get away. He knew the Labrador well, and I asked him if he would bring me here and help me to hide. He did. He's faithful, Chevik is.

"He'd never seen Delevan, so when you asked him to guide you over this way he suspected you were the man. He told me about that meeting at Fort Chimo, how he had left you to starve and all that. Then when I told him that while he was at Chimo Delevan had tracked me with the aid of two villainous Frenchmen, he was very sorry. Delevan had whiskey, and with it he bribed most of the Eskimos; but Chevik and his brother, Tuktoluk, remained loyal, although they gave Delevan to believe otherwise.

"When you came in and told Delevan whom you were after, he threatened to kill you if I revealed my identity. I figured he would try to kill you anyhow, so I set Chevik to watch him. And Chevik saved you from drowning. I—I guess I've caused you an awful lot of trouble, Mr. Stryker."

"Mister? My front name's Ed."

"Well, Ed, then."

And she smiled up into his bruised face.

"No trouble at all, Jack," he lied nobly. "Just a little excitement."

CHAPTER VIII

OUT OF THE WHITE PERIL

ONE DAY, as the sun was making its brief appearance above the southern bulge of the earth, Monsieur De Loge, of Revillons, went over to pay a visit to his rival and friend, Donald Flemming, acting factor of the H.B.C. Post at Fort Chimo.

He said, "M'sieu, I wonder if dat dare-devil, M'sieu Stryker, has found himself a grave out dere near de Kuglictuk, or if he ees safe."

"It's hard to say, Mr. De Loge," returned Flemming. "He's an old-timer on the trail, you know, and maybe he's pulled through. Let's hope so anyway. But between you and me, I'd be damned if I'd take that trip for some mysterious person named Jack."

"It ees youth, I s'pose, *m'sieu*. Youth ees afraid of nodding."

The conversation was interrupted by a commotion just outside the door. There was a boisterous laugh, the snarl of a dog, and then the sound of a woman's voice.

The door swung open. De Loge stared, speechless. Flemming dropped his pipe. Ed Stryker, his face and *koolutik* sparkling with frost, rocked in with his arm around a very charming young lady.

"Hello, De Loge—Flemming," called Stryker. "How's everything?"

De Loge jumped to his feet and wrung Stryker's hand, and Flemming, his face beaming now, was close behind. Then they looked at the girl.

"This is Jack," laughed Stryker.

After that the factors argued at length as to who should act as host to Ed Stryker and the girl he had brought out of the wilds. They compromised. Stryker went with De Loge. Jack stayed with Flemming.

But first Stryker asked:

"Listen, Flemming. Pst! Is the missioner at the Post?"

Jack blushed. Stryker felt a little uneasy. Chevik shoved his head in the door and blinked. And the two factors looked at each other knowingly.

ESKIMO SORCERY ON BAFFIN ISLAND

SOME YEARS back—in early 1921, to be exact—Neakuteuk, an Eskimo headman belonging to the Kevetukmiut tribe, at Home Bay on the east coast of Baffin Island, got the idea into his head that he was Jesus.

Of course, he was a bit deranged. But the other Esquimaux of the village did not stop to consider this. They flocked to him, swore by him, and were warmed to the boiling point by his religious fanaticism.

This is a case in point to indicate the low mentality of the Eskimo; his mind under the influence of a stronger mentality is like clay in the hands of a sculptor.

Neakuteuk was omnipotent—all-powerful. He chose for his bodyguard Kowtuk and Kedluk. He took Munyeuk, a blind man, and tried through some occult medium to restore his sight. This didn't work at all, so the self-styled Jesus ordered poor Munyeuk killed.

Kowtuk and Kedluk promptly carried out this order. Another unfortunate soul was Semik, who was stripped, slightly wounded and left on the ice, where he froze to death.

It was rotten business. The natives' souls were in pawn. Neakuteuk swayed them like a strong wind bends weak trees. They all feared him. All except one, Kidlappik by name, who shot to death Neakuteuk when the latter was attempting to strike a woman with a hammer.

The Mounted got wind of it. They always do. Needless to say they cleaned the case up.

Take a look at Baffin Island on the map. Find Cumberland Sound, on the east coast just under the Arctic Circle. Bleak? No beauty spot, you can bet. Well, there is a Mounted Police post near there, at Pangnirtung Inlet.

In late February, 1924, a corporal and a constable left Pangnirtung with two dog teams for Home Bay, a couple of hundred miles due north across the wind-swept, ice-hummocked Baffin barrens. They reached their objective on March 8 and took a month to clean up the case.

Consider that the murders occurred in January, 1922, and that this patrol—McInnes and MacGregor—started out in February, 1924, two years later. This is one of the reasons why the Mounted is known the world over. The Mounted never forgets, never gives up, never loses out. No case is too old, no trek too arduous.

DEFIANCE VALLEY

**NORTHWOODS—
FLASHING REDCOATS
AND THE TERROR OF
THE UNKNOWN.**

LEE, CHUM, with weather like this we could make the old patrol in jig time. Then I could squat at the post, smoke the inspector's cigars and wait peacefully until my resignation papers arrive."

The speaker was Sergeant Pat Quinlin, of the Mounted, a young-old looking man, lean, blue-eyed, with a chiseled face seamed with the fine-weather lines that are the legacy of men who live in the open. The two were lounging on the sled and smoking their pipes while they "spelled" the nine dogs.

Constable Carlin, a young Englishman putting in his first term on the Force, kept twirling the thirty-foot dog whip meditatively around his mittened hand. He let off a little sigh and gave the whip a sudden snap, rising to his feet with a slight shudder.

Quinlin noticed it and asked—

"What's the matter?"

"Oh—" with a grimace.

"Come on, Lee, out with it now. What's ailing you?"

Carlin strode up and down for a short minute, then stopped in front of the sergeant and blurted out:

"I've—I've had a bad dream."

Quinlin stroked the stubble on his hard jaw and started to grin; then, throwing his hands aloft, he burst into a fit of laughter and almost toppled from the sled.

Carlin said:

"Yes, go ahead and laugh, but I tell you, Pat, it was the worst dream I've ever had. I'm not by nature a dreaming man. I—hell!—I feel pretty rummy over it. I dreamt we—the two of us— were set upon by a lot of cut-throats and that you were being tortured and all that sort of stuff. We were separated. Gad, it was all so vivid the whole affair still keeps dancing hazily in front of my eyes. I—"

"Lee," put in the sergeant, solemnly, "you'd better take some quinine tonight. Look out, chum, or you'll be shaking hands with the willows."

"Blast it, Pat, I'm all right otherwise; feel first rate. You may be right. The country may be getting on my nerves. My head doesn't ache; body's in fine shape. Only that bally old dream."

Quinlin sighed a sigh of the wise and got up, patting his companion on the shoulder.

"That's maybe it, Lee; the country. I've seen it get men fighting themselves and doing all sorts of lunatic things in my day. The thing to do, Lee, is don't think too much. Look at me. Glory be, I was never accused of over-taxing my think machinery. Never take things seriously—and least of all yourself. That is, if you're aiming to poke around this chunk of the world for some years. Dreams—*rats* for that stuff!"

Carlin tried to chuckle.

"Pat, you're a great man to have along. Always cheering me up and that sort of stuff. I'll hate to see you leave the Force at the end of the year, old sport."

Quinlin mused for a moment, started to say something, then changed his mind and knocked the ashes from his pipe. Stowing the pipe away, he rocked up beside Shag, the lead-dog, and cuffed him playfully on the ear. Then he looked back at Carlin.

"All right, Lee," he said in his brisk, though not harsh, voice. "Let's mush. We should make Ben Tobin's shack before dark and after that it'll be a long, tough trail to To-oot-aw-nek. Ready! Let's go!"

Carlin snapped the whip in the air. Quinlin struck out ahead

on broad snowshoes and spoke encouraging words over his shoulder to the big lead-dog. The outfit moved smoothly for a while through the shadowy aisles of tall spruce which, due to a recent high wind, were almost completely shorn of snow.

Carlin's young face still showed signs of worry. Quinlin, known far and wide wherever there was talk of trail and trace, as a hale and hearty, happy-go-lucky sergeant, plowed through the snow with a gay little song on his lips.

Many would regret his leaving the Force at the end of the year, when his third term would be up. But rounding thirty-eight, with money in the bank at Winnipeg and a desire to settle down, he had a site picked out in the Shamattawa country where he would build a trading post and live out his years in contentment and ease.

Thoughts of this nature were causing him to sing as he led the outfit from smooth going into a nasty stretch of muskeg, a trail full of bumpy hummocks and sharp-edged ridges that lacerated the dogs' feet. Carlin had his hands full keeping the sled righted while the sergeant pulled with Shag, the leader.

Two hours of this and they emerged upon a narrow waterway, where the going was good. Quinlin dropped back to the sled and trotted along at a leisurely pace beside the constable.

AT THREE in the afternoon they left level country behind and began to work up a tortuous trail towards the summit of a hogback. Heavy bush was here, overgrowing what little trail there was, and in places matted windfalls lay twisted in all manner of curious shapes.

It took them just two hours to make three miles and the summit, and dusk was beginning to fling out rapidly over the land.

At the top Quinlin brought the hard-breathing dogs to a stop and pointed into the valley below.

"Down there," he explained to Carlin, "is where old Ben Tobin lives. Ben's a funny old duck, Lee. Good as gold, but— well, odd. He's been trapping for about twenty years. And instead of trading hereabouts for grub and the like he drives his furs all the way to The Pas, gets good Dominion dollars and brings 'em back to this God-forsaken hole.

"He's been saving that money for twenty years; hides it some place, though only the Lord knows where. We've warned him about it. A lot of fellows know he hides it, and some day some one is going to get nosey—if you know what I mean."

"Yes, I understand," nodded Carlin, interested.

"He makes the statement sometimes that he's looking for some one dear to him," went on Quinlin. "Don't know whether it's a man, woman or dog, for he never says much. Just that he's looking for some one dear to him. And maybe that's why he's saving the money. Little daffy, poor old fellow, I suppose, so don't be astonished at anything he says."

Carlin nodded understandingly and twirled the whip in the air. But before he cracked it Quinlin laid a restraining hand on his arm and pointed to the valley floor. Black dots were moving on the snow; a dog team and a driver. Quinlin reached for his glasses, adjusted the focus and swept the distant outfit.

Still looking, he spoke to Carlin:

"Six dogs—toboggan—small man—"

A pause; then, suddenly:

"Hell, no, Lee, it's a woman. Her *capote* hood's thrown back and I can see a white face. Now what the—"

He stared at the constable with wide, popping eyes, astonishment written all over his face. He took another look through the glasses, then lowered them abruptly and whistled softly.

"Yes, she is white, Lee!" he clipped with a snap of his fingers. "A white woman way up this way. It's—by God, man, it's enough to make me believe I'm seeing things! Whip those dogs up. She came from the direction of Tobin's cabin. Ben ought to know something about her."

Carlin cracked the whip and the dogs went off with Quinlin half-a-dozen leaps ahead of the leader. By this time the mysterious woman was out of sight, swallowed up by the vast sweep of snow and tall timber and many lakes that sprawled all over this remote fringe of the world.

CHAPTER II

THE MYSTERY SHOT

QUINLAN LED the way down to the valley floor and proceeded at a lively gait in the direction of Tobin's trapping shack. Dusk was full upon them by this time and the stars were beginning to show faintly.

Rounding a sharp bluff, the sergeant espied a quarter of a mile ahead, a dark blot against the snow. He explained that was the cabin, as they drew nearer.

Carlin said:

"*This* would make any man daffy."

The sergeant chuckled as he drew up the dogs before the split-log shack and rubbed his hands together with pleasant anticipation.

"Lee, you might feed the dogs while I have a preliminary chat with Ben," he told the constable.

Then he pushed open the door softly, intending to surprise the old hermit as he had done many times before on his long patrol. The room was bathed in shadows. Only the rosy glow from the sheet-iron stove made objects faintly distinguishable.

The sergeant closed the door behind him softly and pulled off his mittens, bending his brows quizzically. No one greeted him. Nothing stirred.

He took a few steps forward, paused at the table and drummed thoughtfully on it for a moment with his fingers. As his eyes became accustomed to the gloom he could make out objects more clearly; the book-shelf, piled with ancient papers and magazines and worn old books; the roughly-constructed cupboard; in the rear, the bunk....

The bunk! *And something in the bunk!*

With quick steps he flung across the room and stopped before the bunk, and his body stiffened, held taut for a moment, and then relaxed. He leaned over the twisted body that lay there, ran his hand over the face, shuddered, then fumbled inside the rough woolen shirt. He brought his hand out slowly, reverently.

"Dear God!" he jerked under his breath. "Poor old Ben. Somebody got you at last—and you didn't find 'the dear one,' did you? Pretty tough, Ben."

The body of Ben Tobin was cold. With a prayer on his lips the sergeant turned away, went to the table and lit a candle. He stood by the stove and ran a studious eye about the little room. A stool, overturned, lay in a corner near the door. He picked up the candle and bent down to examine the floor. Blood spots.

"H-m-m," he mused, and stood erect.

He went over to the bunk, looked for a wound in the chest, found none, and turned the body over. The wound—an ugly knife gash—was in the back! Simultaneously with his discovery of this the sergeant's moccasined foot touched something on the floor that moved. Bending, he picked up a long, thin knife covered with blood—thinner than the hunting knife usually comes and constructed with a faun's hoof for a handle.

"Exhibit A," he said, grimly, as he placed the knife on the table.

Then he turned the dead man over again and folded the arms

across the chest. In doing so his fingers became entwined with some silky substance and, reaching down, he pulled from the lifeless hand a long strand of golden hair—*undeniably from a woman's head!* A little shocked, he held it aloft.

After a moment he said half aloud, "A woman's hair, and that knife looks suspiciously like one a woman would carry if she carried one at all. So help me, if she's guilty, whoever she is, she'll swing!"

He half-turned, to call Carlin. An explosion boomed in his ears, his brain seemed to snap, and he crumbled to the floor like a deflated balloon. Consciousness was not completely gone, but almost.

He was in a fog, unable to rise, unable to exert any muscle at all, not even those that controlled his eyelids. All the cords at the back of his neck seemed to have contracted and were now burning.

IT SEEMED an eternity before his eyes began to clear and he gained some control over his nervous system. The throbbing in his brain eased away and finally he fought to a sitting position.

He felt the back of his neck. Not much blood there. Merely a flesh wound. But the faintest flick of a bullet at that point is quite strong enough to numb the whole nervous system temporarily.

The sergeant got to his feet tentatively, found they served him fairly well, and discovered at the same moment that he still held the strand of golden hair in his hand. This gave birth to another thought and he gave a quick start toward the table, brought up sharply and clipped off an oath.

The knife was gone!

This in turn made him think of Carlin, and of a sudden he wondered why the constable had not come to his aid. Instantly he whipped out his service pistol and threw open the door—stepped out into the clear, frigid night which now seemed unreal and ghostly under the pale radiance of the Aurora.

No Carlin. No sled. No dogs.

He cupped his hands at his mouth and called—

"Lee! Oh, Lee!"

Only echoes mocked him. He went a little farther and studied the snow. To the south the trail was all mixed up—marked by the mysterious woman's outfit and by his own. It would be difficult, therefore, to pick out a new trail in that direction.

But to the north! There he found a new trail; the marks of a sled, of a dog team, and of a man on snowshoes. He bent down and studied these last marks—suddenly shot erect and sucked in his breath.

"By God," he muttered, "they're Carlin's tracks. He bought those snowshoes from a trapper who'd come over from the Labrador. Yes, sir, a snowshoe shaped like an egg—an Ungava Indian shoe—and I'll bet there's not another pair like 'em over this way. But—but, why?"

Perplexed, he strode back into the shack and replenished the dying fire. He had no equipment of his own, now, so he helped himself freely of the late Ben Tobin's larder. Ben wouldn't need it any more, anyhow.

"Yep, Ben, they got you," mused the sergeant with a mouthful of bannock. "But what's Carlin up to? His are the only tracks. No one with him. Looks like he fired that shot. But—hell!—he's always been on the level. H-m-m. And then he had a bad dream. 'S funny. Now, I wonder—I wonder if that young fool got love struck over that woman we saw.

"Perhaps he heard me say, if guilty she'd hang. But would he bump me off for that? Well, I'd say no, but then, on the other hand, maybe the North has got him. He hasn't seen a white woman for months and now that he's seen one it's gone to his head. Possible? Well, the knife is gone.

"Carlin, if he shot me, and his are the only tracks about, stole the knife to see the princess he's never met. There are possibilities there—damned if there aren't. Lee, old man, it seems you've got yourself in a devil of a fix. And I'm not going to like the business of taking you. But it's written in the Manual, and I've become so used to obeying it that...."

He sighed and shrugged his shoulders, as much as saying, "There's nothing else to do but keep on obeying it."

That night he slept at the cabin on robes spread in front of the stove, while on the bunk old Ben Tobin slept the eternal sleep. He was up before the dawn next morning. He tied the corpse in several wolf skins, carried it outside and hoisted it up into a tree by means of a rawhide line swung over a limb. He climbed the tree himself then and fastened the body to the trunk.

"No wolves 'll get you here, Ben," murmured the sergeant. "I'll get back in the spring and bury you."

After this he went into the house and ate a hearty breakfast. Some there were in the Force who criticized severely the sergeant's casual, unhurried manner of doing things connected with the law. But he could laugh up his sleeve at them all, for his record on the books was incomparable. His whole philosophy, as expressed by himself, was contained in very few words.

"Never take yourself seriously; you accomplish more in the end. Don't wait until you're positive before going ahead; take a chance. Three hits out of five is a good average—and look at the experience you get. Don't break your neck chasing a criminal. You'll get him in the end."

And that was why he was known far and wide as the happy-go-lucky, singing sergeant. And some said in whispers that he was hell-on-wheels when rubbed the wrong way. And it seemed, now, that Carlin had done a bit of rubbing.

CHAPTER III

WHEN BRAWN
MEETS BRAWN

"BUT I must follow the woman," he told himself, as he made a makeshift pack of a caribou-hide robe and stuffed it with the last of Tobin's provisions. "Carlin can wait for a while. Tobin has been killed. It's the murderer of Tobin I'm wanting—and the evidence hangs on a wisp of golden hair. Ah-r-r, it's a distasteful job all around, damn it!"

So he struck out southward, bending under the pack and the dead man's blankets, came to the spot where the woman's trail swerved to the eastward, and headed into a rugged, battered country unknown to himself, where in places the sullen ridges rose to the dignity of minor mountain ranges, and all about there was a tomb-like silence.

All that day he followed the trail made by her rackets and her dogs. At night he made a camp in the lee of a balsam grove and wrote at length in his journal. Finished, he braced himself against a stump and meditated over his pipe.

The sharp snap of a twig or branch in the gloom brought him out of his thoughts without a start but with a sudden concentration of the eyes on the brush directly opposite. He listened intently. Heard a crunching sound that was patently made by a falling foot.

Involuntarily, as was his habit in such situations, he began to hum a merry little ditty of the *voyageurs;* then arose, casually, and began gathering more wood for the fire. Little by little he worked towards the source of the noise. Presently he heard more crunching sounds, as if the feet were moving away.

Of a sudden he dropped the wood he had gathered and made a flying leap into the bush, landing flat on the snow. A gun cracked and lead whined just above him, but he was out of sight.

At the same time, however, he saw not six feet away a veritable giant of a man, a mighty cree Indian with smoking rifle.

"Don't make a move," lashed out the sergeant. "I've got you covered and by all that's holy I'll blow you up if you so much as move a finger. Drop that rifle!"

The Indian hesitated, guttural sounds issuing from his throat. Quinlin laid his revolver across his arm and shot at the stock of the Indian's rifle. The slug hit its mark and with a grunt of surprise the big fellow fell back and dropped the gun. Quinlin stood up and went forward.

"Get over to my camp," he said tersely. "And lively!"

With a black look delivered from under craggy brows the Indian moved out of the bush and stood by the fire.

"Sit down," Quinlin told him.

Hesitantly he obeyed.

Quinlin proceeded with: "Now what's the idea of poking around my camp, eh? And don't you know it's bad business to go shooting at a redcoat? Talk. Let me in on the why and wherefore, old boy."

Not a muscle in the carven face of the Indian moved. Even his lips seemed scarcely to move.

But he was saying, in a deep voice—

"Make no talk."

For a long minute Quinlin eyed him coldly; then—

"You won't, eh?"

The Indian moved his head in slow, determined negation. Then he leaned back, with one foot half outstretched towards the fire, and calmly began cramming tobacco into a greasy old pipe.

After a few moments the hard light in Quinlin's eyes became whimsical. He chuckled.

"Well, you're a determined devil, aren't you?" he said. "So be it. I'll have to arrest you for firing at an officer of the law. Consider yourself my prisoner. That plain?"

Without any expression whatever the Indian nodded his head. Then, with a sudden movement, his half-bent leg shot out and crashed into the fire. The hot coals flew into the air and drove the sergeant stumbling backward. With amazing agility for a man of his immense bulk the Indian vaulted over the fire and landed full upon the sergeant, and the next moment they were up on their feet and rocking back and forth in silent, grim combat.

NOW QUINLIN was no little man. He measured perhaps an inch over six feet, and his lean, tough body weighed something like a hundred and ninety. As men go, he was big, but alongside of the Indian he was small.

For this son of the woods towered up to nothing under six-feet-five, with a gorilla-like body that weighed at least two-hundred-and-fifty. In less time than you can tell it he wrenched the revolver from the sergeant's hand, threw it away, and locked him in his mighty arms.

Quinlin gritted his teeth and fought with the strength of a strong heart and a steel body. It was his courage, his spirit, that made up the difference in weight and size. Thus he found himself holding his own, but with nothing to spare, as they rocked, strained against each other under the cold stars. And only hard breathing and the muffled footsteps on the snow broke the stillness of the night which, though bitter cold, was without wind.

The breaks of the game don't always fall to the righteous. Quinlin knew he was licked, when carrying the fight away from the fire, he broke through an air-pocket in the crusted snow and one leg went down almost to the hip. The Indian gave a satisfied grunt and, as if in payment for the trouble he'd had, cracked the sergeant on the jaw.

"You'll pay for this," Quinlin chuckled grimly.

"Make no talk!"

"I'll talk as much as I damn well please. And, as I said, you'll pay for this."

The Indian was dragging him from the hole in the snow and towards the fire. He picked up the sergeant's pistol and pressed it against his back.

"Down," he ordered.

Quinlin sat down and stuffed his pipe.

"Well, you're top-dog right now, so what's your pleasure?" he sighed off philosophically.

After a moment the Indian asked:

"What do over this way?"

"I'm looking for—for my partner, Constable Carlin," Quinlin lied. "We got separated back there."

He jerked his head toward the west.

The Indian shot him a quick, searching look, then shook his head.

"Lie," he muttered.

"How do you know?" plied the sergeant with a sidelong glance.

"I know," was the only response.

"Then why ask me?"

For a long moment the Indian eyed him stolidly. Then—"Turn back."

"Who says so?"

"Me."

And he touched his chest.

The sergeant gave a short, harsh laugh.

"If that's what you want to talk about, old boy, save your breath. To that kind of talk I'm deaf, dumb and blind. When you talk that way I can't understand a word you're saying. So dry up and blow away. I'm in no great hurry. Keep me prisoner if you want. Do what you damn please. But—remember—in the end I'll get you. Take that in your pipe and smoke it, Sitting Bull."

A dark cloud swept over the Indian's face. Here indeed, he

might have thought, was a hard man to deal with. He arose solemnly.

"We go on," he said. "We talk with Master. Maybe he kill. Don't know."

"And who is the Master?"

"A mighty man. Him live 'Defiance Valley.'"

Quinlin scratched his chin.

"Never heard of the place."

"No," said the Indian. "No one outside know. No law ever reach Defiance Valley. The Master, law."

"Thanks for the information," put in the sergeant crisply. "And, mind, if the law has never reached Defiance Valley, be advised that it's on its way now in the person of Pat Quinlin, the same being myself, if you don't know. So let's get going.

"Oh, no, I haven't forgot I'm your prisoner, only, such little trifles don't worry me. Every dog has its day. But don't think I'm classing myself with dogs, though if I had the choice between their company and some men's, I'd choose the dogs."

The Indian scowled and mumbled deep in his throat. Then he said:

"Sleep here. Start dawn. Me watch."

"Suits me," Quinlin acquiesced nonchalantly. "I've got all the time in the world."

CHAPTER IV

SHADOW OF THE VALLEY

THE DAWN dusk was heavy upon the land when they struck out next morning. Quinlin led the way, while behind him the Indian strode with a ready rifle in the crook of his arm.

The perplexed expression on the Indian's face made it patent that he could not quite fathom out why the sergeant, though a prisoner, should keep whistling or humming a merry tune as he plodded on towards a rendezvous whose name smacked of evil and unknown things.

"Defiance Valley!" "The Master!" And the law had never been there!

At noon Quinlin, rounding a bend in a narrow waterway, saw up ahead a smoke, a sled and six lounging dogs. He slowed down and looked over his shoulder at the Indian. The Indian nodded understandingly and indicated with a gesture of his hand for the sergeant to keep moving. When they drew up by the campfire Quinlin looked around for signs of a human being.

After a moment there were sounds in the bush and a girl came out with an armful of sticks. She looked quizzically at the sergeant, then turned to the Indian as she threw the wood down beside the fire. Here there was acknowledgement in her gaze but no hint of greeting.

The Indian nodded, drew her aside and spoke in undertone. Quinlin watched her face out of the corners of his eyes. She kept looking obliquely into space as the Indian spoke, frowned now and then, then shook her head and shrugged her shoulders.

The Indian paused, spoke some more, and again she shook her head negatively. Finally she turned away from him with an impatient gesture and went about replenishing the fire.

IT WAS when she threw back her *capote* hood that Quinlin snapped his teeth together and sucked in his breath. Her hair was gold, all shimmering gold, tied in a simple knot at the back.

In the glow from the fire her face was radiant and more beautiful than he at first had perceived. He felt his breast, where was concealed his journal containing the single strand of golden hair that he had taken from Ben Tobin's lifeless hand!

They ate in silence. No one spoke. Quinlin realized that, although the girl seemed unfriendly to the Indian, she would join forces against himself if he tried to make a break for freedom. She did not cross gazes with Quinlin—gave him no attention at all. She ate, like the Indian and himself, in silence. The red coat he wore beneath his opened furs might just as well have been a rag for all she seemed to care.

At last, as he smoked his pipe, the sergeant broke the silence.

"As we may be able to converse more intelligently," he began, "than I have been able to with the Indian, I'd like to know what plans you two have in mind."

She stared into the fire as she answered in a quick, clear voice:

"Long Jim, here, says you refused to steer clear of the country. I don't see what you want over this way. Defiance Valley is not a healthful place for a redcoat to be heading for. Well, since you've refused to turn back, Long Jim is taking you to The Master. There's no telling *what* he will do with you! You're the first Mounty to leave the regular patrol and come over this way."

"Not because I'm out for a change of scenery," answered Quinlin, suggestively.

She gave him a sharp look.

He held her eyes and said—"Do you understand?"

Her big blue eyes widened and her pomegranate lips began to quiver. She flung a glance at the Indian—met a dark, portentous scowl there. The sergeant saw the exchanged glances and nodded to himself.

With a sudden toss of the head she rose and went over to her sled, rummaging aimlessly in the equipage. The sergeant thought he saw tremor after tremor pass over her small, well-knit body. The Indian leaned forward and bared his teeth.

"You make no talk," he hissed.

Flint was in the sergeant's eyes as he said:

"Put on a new record, Long Jim. That gets monotonous after a while. I have a habit of talking when, where, and how I please."

A sinister note came into Long Jim's tone.

"The Master will see you make no talk."

"Well, leave that to The Master, and you go shut your face for a while."

With an ugly rumble in his throat the Indian heaved over

and made a vicious pass with a clenched fist at the sergeant's face. Quinlin, quick as a flash, caught the flying hand by the wrist and with a deft jerk twisted the arm with such savageness that Long Jim was momentarily unbalanced.

Taking prompt advantage of this sudden whim of chance and most unexpected opening, Quinlin's free hand dived for the Indian's revolver, yanked it out, and as Long Jim tried to close the sergeant spun backwards and shot out his feet.

They caught the Indian in the middle in time to ward him off, and Quinlin then completed the backward somersault with the ease of an acrobat and landed square on his feet just as the Indian was lunging in a second attack.

"As—you—are!" commanded Quinlin, biting off each word sharply. "The breaks are against you just now."

At the same time he saw the woman flying toward a gun belt that lay near the fire.

"Madam!" he lashed out. "Not another step."

With which order he leaped back a pace and sent a fast shot at the revolver in the belt and smashed it. The woman stopped in her tracks with a sob of anguish. Long Jim had heaved forward with a vicious snarl, but in the twinkling of an eye the sergeant had him covered, his gun jammed against the big fellow's abdomen.

"Keep your hands up or I'll let daylight into you," he jerked out; then—"And back up! Lively! Show some speed. Madam, not another move out of you. As you are, there. Never mind backing toward that tree. I see the rifle leaning against it. The two of you, now, side by side."

He reached inside his fur coat and threw them a pair of manacles.

"Snap 'em on. One bracelet on your wrist, madam, and the other on Long Jim's."

His voice bore such a quality of command that the manacles were snapped on as soon as he had finished speaking. He relaxed a bit then and chuckled in his grim, harsh way. But in the woman's eyes was a defiant light.

Her chin was upflung, her usually full lips drawn in a thin line of determination. Her bosom heaved tumultuously and her hands clenched and unclenched continuously. Quinlin thought he had never seen a woman so ravishingly beautiful.

Presently he said:

"Now I have an idea that we all shall turn back—the three of us. We shall stop at a certain cabin, go over certain things, and then continue going back to The Pas, where a magistrate may ask you what you know about the death of one Benjamin Tobin. I am *positive* that *one* of you knows something about it."

Here his eyes were hard upon the woman; then they moved to the Indian.

"And I'm pretty sure the other has something up his sleeve. Now the both of you sit down."

WHEN THEY were seated he took out his journal, kneeled, placed it on his knee and with pencil in one hand and gun in the other he spoke:

"Long Jim, eh?" to the Indian, and he wrote down the name and general description of the Indian, inquiring his age, which was forty.

Then to the woman—"And your name, madam?"

"Rose."

"Rose what."

"Just Rose."

"You will have to give your full name eventually."

He tapped his pencil on the book, eying her frankly. He saw her own eyes were moist.

She was saying—"Just Rose."

"Age?" he asked at last.

"Twenty-three."

"Married?"

"No."

He wrote a few more notes, closed the book and stowed it away.

"Very well," he clipped in a matter-of-fact tone. "We'll start immediately. The two of you line up the dogs."

Reluctantly Rose called the dogs and she and the Indian, bound to each other by the handcuffs, lined them up. Meanwhile Quinlin gathered up the girl's and the Indian's guns, unloaded them and placed them on the sledge and stood by while the Indian and Rose threw their robes and blankets on. This done, they stood by for further orders.

The sergeant stood at some distance pondering over the situation. Finally:

"You'll ride on the sled, Miss Rose. You, Long Jim, will walk ahead of the dogs."

He threw the Indian the key. "Unlock the cuffs, take the one from Miss Rose's wrist and lock both your own wrists together."

"I don't have to ride. I'll walk," spoke up Rose.

"It happens, please, that I want you to ride," was the sergeant's peremptory reply. "Unlock those, Long Jim."

The Indian, muttering behind his teeth, unlocked the manacles and placed both bracelets on his own wrists. At an order from Quinlin he threw back the key.

"Very well, now," spoke up the sergeant. "Up in front of the team, and you, Miss Rose, on the sled."

Hesitantly she stood beside the sled, and tears were now rolling down her cheeks. Hard as the sergeant appeared to be in both manner and speech, his heart was as soft as those of most strong men. After a thoughtful pause he strode over beside her and patted her on the shoulder.

"Now don't go bawling, please, miss. Don't make my job harder than it is now. I—"

He stopped abruptly and flexed his lips. It wouldn't do to wallow too much in sentiment here. He must remember the

Oath, the Scarlet Manual, the Red Coat he wore. He steeled himself against any desire to comfort her with smooth words.

CHAPTER V

AN ENCHANTRESS?

HE SAID, coolly—
"Please, miss, the sled."

Instead of obeying she turned her face up toward him. It was moist with tears and her large, round eyes were eloquent of entreaty.

"Please—please don't take me out?" she faltered.

"I wonder if you do not know better than ask a man who wears the Scarlet such a question. Will you please get—"

"Oh, but you *mustn't* take me out! You mustn't! It—some one—I— Oh, you mustn't! Please! They'll—"

She broke off in a sob and grasped the sergeant's fur with shaking hands, pressed close to him and looked up at him with the most wonderful eyes he'd ever seen. Her whole soul—a soul crying out in anguish—was in those eyes.

"Not—not for my sake, but for some one else's," she pleaded.

"For the Indian's?"

"No. For—oh, for some one I love. Please, sergeant."

Held under a spell by her unfaltering eyes, possessed of a sudden, wild desire to break the Oath, he nevertheless said: "You ask this. You ask me for pity—you, who murdered Ben Tobin. Your hair—a piece of your golden hair was in his cold hand when I found him!"

She did not move. Only her soul seemed to shrink back in her liquid eyes, but they did not move from his. They held him—almost hypnotized him.

And then the thing happened. The Indian was upon him in a mad leap. While the woman had held him under her spell the Indian had edged around and taken one flying leap. He bore the outraged sergeant to the snow and at the same time drove his manacled fists against his jaw.

Quinlin went limp and lay huddled on the snow. Vaguely he could see the giant bend over him, remove his pistol. Heard his deep voice calling the dogs to action.

And then—again vaguely—the woman was bending over him. He tried to raise his hands but all power seemed to have deserted him. Everything seemed like a nightmare. She bent closer, touched his forehead with a soft hand, then suddenly kissed him on the lips.

And the next moment she was gone and he was trying vainly to struggle up.

Then he heard Rose and the Indian arguing. He didn't know if he were dreaming or if they actually were speaking. But he heard—

"We take him Master."

And from Rose:

"No, Jim. You were wrong in the first place—bringing him this far. He mentioned a partner—and the partner may be following this trail."

Then she knew nothing about Carlin! They had not crossed trails yet!

Consciousness faded a little more from Quinlin and he heard no more of the wrangle.

WHEN HE awoke it was getting twilight. A wind was rattling in the spruces. But otherwise there was no sound. The place was deserted. Near him lay his guns and his improvised pack. Doubtless the girl had seen to their being left. She would not want him to starve, possibly.

He sat up, rubbing his head; then arose shakily and went about building a fire.

"Pat Quinlin, you old fool," he said aloud. "H-m-m. Letting a girl put you in a trance with her eyes."

He paused and stroked his jaw meditatively.

"H-m-m. And then she kissed me. Rose. Nice name. Got nice eyes. H-m-m. I wonder if there's any chance of me being in love with—Rose."

Then, in a new tone:

"O, hang it all! What am I thinking about! I'm not an ex-sergeant yet. And there's no chance of her liking me. And, anyhow, there's the killing of Ben Tobin she must explain. It's written in the Manual. And I still have the golden evidence. Bah! This policing is a rotten game when you get to mixing with women."

Snow came with evening, driven down in blinding gusts and a rising wind. The sergeant raised a snow wall and fastened a blanket from the top of it to two sticks stuck in the ground. This in some measure warded off the snow and wind and permitted him to sleep, waking at intervals through the night to replenish the fire.

IN THE morning a white, virgin world lay about him. Trees snapped staccato-like with the cold.

"This makes another break against me," Quinlin mused over his breakfast. "It had to snow and cover up their trail. Now what—eh? Guess I've got to back-trail until I hit my patrol line, draft a new outfit from an Indian camp or some place and bring along an Indian boy.

"He might not know this country but those boys can generally hit it in the end—somehow or other. And Carlin. Like as not he's banging around the country half off his nut with that knife. I've been in much pleasanter situations—yes, indeed!"

But his spirit was still strong. When he swung the pack on his back and headed over the back trail he broke into a whistle and kept it up for an hour. There was no use in going ahead on scant rations, with an inadequate outfit, into a country he knew nothing about.

His ammunition was low. The only socks he had were on his feet, and in the cold regions a change of sweaty socks for dry ones every day is an old rule. Many a man has neglected this precaution with tragic results.

Once with a new outfit and an Indian to work the trail with him, he would return over this same trail to Defiance Valley, which, he presumed, lay somewhere to the eastward in a craggy, ragged country spurned by even the seasoned trappers.

"And then I must take Rose—Rose of the beautiful eyes and golden hair—I must take her in the name of the law. It's hard to believe she killed him. But the strand of hair—and she did not deny it. And who was the 'someone' she spoke about? Ah-r-r, damn this policing job!"

CHAPTER VI

STRANGE TRACKS

IT SNOWED again that night and was still snowing when he took up the trail in the morning. He had to work for the most part by his compass, until, in the afternoon, he began to recognize the country ahead and knew he was nearing the borders of his patrol.

He had hard going, for, due to a sudden rise in the temperature, the new snow lay soft and powdery, and he kept sinking through, even though he wore long, wide rackets.

At four he was on his patrol line. As night was near, he went off his proposed route in the direction of the late Ben Tobin's cabin. It would be his last warm shelter for many days, and perhaps he could find some clothing and food that he might have overlooked on his previous visit.

Dusk was gathering in rapidly, but even through the gloom he could see wisps of smoke rising from the chimney. He slowed down, a little perplexed; instinctively felt for his revolver. He pushed on after a minute, a bit cautiously, leaving the open trail and taking to the bush, with intentions of approaching the cabin from the other side, where there was no window.

"So far," he said to himself. "I'm a beaten man. Outwitted

first at this cabin, then on the trail by Long Jim, and then a third time by the woman. It won't read pretty in my report. So whoever is in the shack there, friend or enemy, it won't hurt for me to get the first peek. I must balance my report up."

He circled the cabin in the rear and began approaching it from the other side. He drew his service pistol as he reached the wall and began creeping around to the door. Here he listened. There was a light within but no sounds. He raised his hand to the door and began to ease it open on a crack. Then suddenly he whipped it open and swung up his pistol.

The place was empty. But there was a fire in the stove, and a bundle of blankets was on the floor, and the floor was wet from a recent visitor's dripping furs and moccasins. Quinlin took a step outside, scanned the murk, looked down at the virgin snow.

Yes, there were tracks! Tracks made by a long and narrow snowshoe about four feet long. Quinlin put a hand to his ear. Sounds were in the forest nearby. After a moment he nodded his head in comprehension.

"The stranger's gathering wood," he murmured and re-entered the cabin.

He took off his furs and hung them up. He stood over the nondescript pack on the floor, wondering whether the man would be white or Indian, good or bad. He pushed the pack over with his foot.

"May be just an honest trapper," he meditated.

He let the pack fall to its original position, and the slight jolt caused the blade of a knife to fall through an opening. It chinked against the floor.

Quinlin bent down, intending to thrust it back. But the shape of the blade caused him to hesitate. Then he abruptly yanked it out and shot to his feet as if propelled by a spring.

It was a knife that had killed Ben Tobin! The knife with the faun's hoof for a handle!

The sergeant, his jaw suddenly hard and his eyes glinting like chips of blue steel, flung to the center of the room and trained his revolver on the door.

"By God, this is a surprise!" he breathed.

After a moment he relaxed, put the knife in his pocket and sat down by the table, facing the door, with his gun leveled.

"I might just as well have remained here in the first place. But that's not Carlin's pack. And there's no dog team outside. Sure, this case is taxing my think machinery to excess."

His hand tightened on his revolver as he heard sounds just outside the door. Then the door rattled, swung open, and a furred figure rocked in with his arms full of wood. He kicked the door shut with his heel, looked up, gasped and dropped the wood where he stood.

The sergeant had half-risen, and now he shot erect, and the corners of his wide mouth drooped sardonically. He gave a short, harsh laugh and eyed the man coldly.

THE MAN was—Constable Lee Carlin.

"Pat! Lord, is it you?" Carlin's voice was choked with emotion.

He stumbled forward and grasped the sergeant by the shoulders, but felt the hard muzzle of his partner's revolver against his chest, and saw no hint of greeting in those steely eyes. He took his hands off and fell back a pace.

"Why, Pat! Why—"

Words failed him.

The sergeant said in a colorless voice:

"Until you can explain certain mysterious happenings to my satisfaction, constable, to you I am Sergeant Quinlin. Sit down."

Awed, speechless, Carlin felt his way upon a stool and stared with unseeing eyes at the table.

Quinlin, grim and unbending, sat down opposite him and with slow precision drew out the knife and laid it on the table.

"Can you explain how this came into your possession?" he asked.

"I stole it from the man who waylaid me."

Quinlin's eyes dilated.

"You what?"

"I—God, I see what's the trouble now. You think I played you false."

"With every good reason," was the sergeant's prompt rejoiner.

"But I didn't, Pat. How could you believe it?"

"I was knocked over with a bullet while examining the dead body of Ben Tobin in here. When I came to the knife I found beside him was gone. I saw no tracks except those made by your own rackets—and they led north."

"Now let me explain," put in Carlin eagerly. "While I was feeding the dogs I was put out—or nearly so—from behind. Dimly I heard the shot, and I thought later that you were killed. When I came to I was riding on our sled and my abductor was mushing behind *on my snowshoes,* and his own were on the sled.

"I started to brawl with him and he knocked me out for my pains. Then I asked him where he was taking me, and why. He said no place in particular—just to lead *you* on with suspicion against me. I mentioned the shot and he said he hadn't killed you—just put you out for a while. And why all these mysterious moves?

"'Why,' he said, 'to prevent a woman from being suspected.'

"And when I asked of what he just laughed. The next day

while crossing a lake the ice broke. We lost the sled and all the dogs. In the confusion he dropped the knife and I picked it up. He didn't know it. Then he said, 'Well, I guess we part now.'

'This is far enough.' And then he left me. I stumbled on a trapper's shack, but he had a touch of rheumatism and could only give me aid in the way of advice and a few blankets and provisions. I just got back here a little while ago."

Quinlin asked, "That all of it?"

"Yes, Pat. And so help me, God, it's true."

The sergeant extended his hand. "I believe you, Lee. I've been a blasted fool. Shake!"

And they shook, with their hearts in their palms.

Then Quinlin explained his own side of the story, and between them they tried to put two and two together. The upshot of it was, they became more entangled in the meshes of mystery than before. What connection had Carlin's abductor with the case, and with the woman, and where did the Indian fit in? And still further, who was The Master?—the super-power behind it all?

"Do you think he was killed for the money he was supposed to have concealed?" ventured Carlin, referring to Tobin.

Quinlin's idea was: "If a man committed it, yes; if the woman, no. Women very seldom kill for money. Remember that, Lee, in your dealings with criminals. We'll have to make tracks for Defiance Valley. The solution, if there is any, lies there. The fellow who got you mentioned no names, eh?—not even his own?"

"No, Pat. But he was concerned over the woman. An oldish fellow, not a bad sort taken by and large; regular sourdough. Medium sized, grizzled and rough."

"Well, I'm glad *we* two are straightened out, Lee. In the morning we'll start out for an independent trading post thirty miles west, draft an outfit and double back."

It took them just two days to make the thirty miles. After much haggling with the canny Scotch trader Quinlin succeeded in getting a nondescript team of seven dogs and a worn old Mackenzie toboggan. By a mere stroke of luck, Jerry Plate, a hard-bitten old crossbreed and old friend of Quinlin's, offered his aid as guide and general handy man.

"No, Pat, Defiance Valley ain't in my ken," he rolled off, "but just gimme a lay o' the land, an' I'll smeel m' way, I will. I'm just ripe f'r a tough trail, an' if I c'n help yer out, Pat, let's know."

He was a short, broad man, more white than Indian, with button eyes and a piratical mustache. He spoke out of the side of his mouth, spat often and copiously, and looked what he was; a hard boiled sourdough and a good man to have beside you in a pinch.

The three of them pulled out of the post with a mountainous load on the sled. Fine weather. Good going. And the dogs showed up better than Quinlin had thought they would.

ON THE morning of the second day they passed the death cabin and by nightfall they were twenty miles beyond. Quinlin had a general idea of the trail up to the waterway where Rose and the Indian had tricked him, and for two days he led the way.

After that he and Jerry exchanged ideas as they pressed on through a wild, raw country; up steep ridges, down through tortuous, yawning ravines where the snow lay in great windrows.

"Somebody's been through here," explained Jerry. "See that dead stump stickin' up outer the snow. See where it's been hacked wit' an axe? 'Course the campfire's buried under the snow someplace."

Another day passed, and still another. Jerry, scouting up ahead, brought down a moose with one shot.

"I never like t' waste bullets," he said dully, when Quinlin commended him.

On the tenth day after passing Tobin's cabin Carlin, taking his turn at breaking trail ahead of the dogs, caught sight of a moving shape in the forest ahead. He called out. The form stopped, looked around, and the constable called to Quinlin—

"A woman!"

Quinlin came up from the rear in long strides. As he did the woman dodged in the bush and began running away. Without a word to his companions, the sergeant set off after her.

He was a fast man on snowshoes, and in short time he caught up with the fugitive and grabbed her. But when he turned her about she was not, as he had supposed, Rose of the golden hair. She was dark and undeniably pretty—and frightened stiff, at the moment.

"Pardon me," he offered. "Thought you were some one else. You live here?" He swept his hand about vaguely.

"Yes," she replied in an awed whisper.

After a pause he said, "Defiance Valley?"

She gave a start—clasped her mittened hands to her breast. By this time Jerry and Carlin came trotting up with the dogs.

Quinlin was saying to the girl, "You will please show us the way to Defiance Valley."

Carlin, looking at her, could not suppress a smile. And the girl—she looked no more than twenty—smiled back wistfully with her dark, haunting eyes.

Jerry offered: "Pa'don, miss, but a little birdie tells me Defiance Valley ain't many miles from here. Be I right?"

Without a word the girl dropped her head in resignation, and with a gesture to Quinlin started off. The sergeant strode along beside her.

"What do you know about the Valley, miss?" he asked off-handedly.

She gave him a quick look but made no reply.

"You must know something," he plied.

After a pause she said: "I only know that if I am caught showing you the way, well—"

She shrugged her shoulders meaningly.

CHAPTER VIII

DEFIANCE VALLEY!

THE SERGEANT stopped her abruptly "You mean your life is in danger?"

"Anybody's life is in danger—who brings the law to Defiance Valley. Once you enter the Valley, you take your life in your own hands."

Carlin spoke up—"I say, Pat, it's kind of rummy to place the lady in a bad way."

Her eyes went soft on the young constable.

Quinlin was saying, "I was thinking the same."

But the girl said, "It's no use now. The thing is done. *There* is Defiance Valley!"

Through a rift in the trees she pointed to a column of smoke rising clear cut on the frigid air. As he looked intently, Quinlin could make out a cluster of buildings—possibly ten—deep in the center of the valley. And on all sides towered sheer walls of snow and timber.

"Surely," observed Carlin, "this is the end of the world."

The girl was saying—

"And now let me go."

With that she struck out, giving Carlin a last, blood-warming smile.

The constable shot at Quinlin:

"They'll do her harm, Pat. We'd better hold her."

"Lee, they haven't seen us yet. If we held her we'd bawl up the whole shooting match. Take it easy."

A moment later the girl was lost in the bush.

Jerry crammed a wad of tobacco into his mouth and said, "Now that we've found the Valley, let's eat. I'm so hungry m' stomach thinks m' throat's cut."

"But they'll see our smoke," put in Carlin.

"Naw. We'll just back-trail a mile. The timber'll hide us."

After supper they exchanged ideas on the method of entering the Valley. Carlin was a bit moody and Jerry began poking fun at him.

"Kinder stuck on the gal, hey, Lee," he chuckled. "Look out, boy. Women has made many a bloke sorry he took t' wearin' the Scarlet."

Carlin laughed away his discomfort. Quinlin looked into the fire. Of late Rose was always in his memory—her eyes, the kiss, and—yes!—the golden hair. He hated to think of her as a killer.

He hated to consider that she had enchanted him with her charms merely to give Long Jim a chance to strike him. He had never thought he was susceptible to such charms. He had considered himself case-hardened and callous to sentiment if that sentiment interfered with his duties as a policeman.

WHEN DARKNESS came he led Carlin away toward the valley, leaving Jerry with the dogs. At the brink he stopped.

"You'll stay here, Lee, unless I need you," he said. "I'm just going to scout around to get a lay of the land. If I don't return use your judgment. But I'll return. So long for a while."

There was no moon, and this in some measure aided him. It took him an hour to make the descent. Once on the valley floor he proceeded with the utmost caution, advancing by degrees through the dark forest. At last he was on the border of the little settlement.

Lights blinked here and there. Faintly he heard the mingled sounds of a fiddle and a feminine voice raised in song. In a clearing to one side half-a-dozen tents were pitched, and he could see dogs lounging about.

"Regular village," he mused. "Looks like the hangout for traders. Those are trail tents over there. And that big cabin in the center, there; that's where the music is coming from. H-m-m,

Got the earmarks of a trading post. Funny we never got wind of this place at headquarters."

Dodging from one tree to another, he worked nearer the large building. Presently the music stopped. Then the door opened and for a brief moment he saw Rose pause there, then close the door with a bang and walk off toward a cabin on the outskirts of the settlement.

The door opened again and a man, his face dark with anger, rocked out and strode after her in a business-like manner. He caught up to her as she opened the door of her apparent dwelling and forced his way in.

Quinlin drew his pistol and hastened toward that cabin, keeping in the shelter of the trees. When directly in front of it he went out into the open and crossed to the cabin. The one window was frozen and afforded no view of the interior. But he heard scuffling sounds. He hesitated for a moment, then gripped his revolver tightly and went over to the door.

He swung it in and with a quick movement stepped inside and kicked it shut behind him.

"Cut it!" he rasped out. The man had Rose by the wrists in a savage hold, and his eyes blazed as he whirled on the intruder. Rose's eyes went wide and a stifled cry came to her lips.

"You deaf?" the sergeant called to the man. "I said cut it—let go the lady's hand!"

The fellow was big, powerful and handsome in a reckless way. He released Rose's wrists and hooked his thumbs in his wide belt. His mouth sagged at one corner and his clefted jaw went hard.

"Who the hell are you?" he dragged out.

"Quinlin's my name, of the Mounted, and I'm telling you to lay off the rough stuff," was the crisp response.

The man shot to his full height as the sergeant threw back his furs and revealed his scarlet tunic.

"How did *you* get here?" he exploded.

"Walked. But never mind so many questions," Quinlin

advised. "I want the lady there—not you, though if you give me any lip I'll make you join us."

The man gasped.

"God, stranger, don't you know where you are? Ha! You're talking through your hat. You're lucky if you get out alive. With one yell I can bring a whole gang on you."

"If—I don't blow your head off before you yell," clipped Quinlin. "Are you the fellow they call The Master?"

"And what if I am—or not?"

"Nothing. But never mind the palaver. Miss, get your trail garb on as fast as you know how and take a pair of snowshoes. Lively, if you please!"

Again those wide, pleading eyes were upon him, and the lips began to quiver. Her hands started out in a gesture of anguished entreaty. But the sergeant, with an effort, remained cold and unbending.

And then—quite suddenly—her face froze and she went a little limp. The young fellow started forward. Quinlin felt a draft against his back and ducked sidewise against the wall.

The door closed and a tall, elderly man in the garb of a Jesuit missionary stood there with a restraining hand raised above his head. Rose disappeared behind a curtain. Her recent attacker stopped in his rush for Quinlin and fell back. Quinlin nodded to the missioner and lowered his gun.

CHAPTER IX

PÈRE LA BAU

T **HE MISSIONER** spoke: "Welcome, sergeant. It is indeed a surprise to see a stranger here—especially an officer of His Majesty's police. I am Père La Bau, and I minister to all creeds here in this sanctuary of the wilderness. But, I pray, Monsieur Bellamy"—here he turned to the other—"why all the disturbance?"

Bellamy without answering, clapped on his beaver cap and

strode out with averted eyes. Père La Bau followed his hasty exit with mildly amused eyes, then returned his gaze to Quinlin.

"You are after—that man?" he asked in his low, unhurried voice.

"No, Father," returned the sergeant. "The lady—in there. For certain reasons, because of certain evidence I have, she must come with me."

The missioner evinced no surprise. He drew an immaculate finger tip across his lower lip meditatively, then glanced up at the sergeant obliquely.

"It is too bad. We shall miss her. But—I say, sergeant, while she is getting ready let us sit down and have a smoke. I am eager for news of the outer world."

He waved the sergeant to a chair and sat down himself, drawing a pouch from his black robe and extending it. Quinlin stuffed his pipe with the proffered tobacco, lighted up and inhaled luxuriously. Then the missioner began loading his own, smiling and explaining his work in this remote section.

Gradually Quinlin began to sense a peculiar sensation, as if his head were floating up and away from his body. He felt sick at his stomach, and a mist seemed to be drifting in front of his eyes. He heaved up to his feet, and the room seemed to spin around.

He started for the door, but somehow or other he couldn't prevent his legs from taking him in circles. The last thing he remembered was the hazy, indistinct picture of the missioner still idly cramming tobacco into a little black pipe. He crumpled to the floor.

He had wild dreams, fantastic nightmares, in which he fought with dragons and fanged giants and all forms of weirdly contorted creatures. When he awoke from the unnatural sleep he was shaking in every limb and dripping with perspiration.

HE WAS in a small, ramshackle trapping shack, he guessed. It was pitch dark. There was no fire, and he shivered even under the mass of robes and blankets that covered him. He mopped the cold sweat from his face and fought to his feet, leaning against the cold wall.

"Some more nice stuff to write in my report," he mumbled grimly. "Either the breaks are against me or I'm a fool. Yes, I was a fool to go into that cabin. But I thought that roughneck meant harm to Rose. And then I wanted her. She must be guilty, else why should they all try to do away with me? And still—her eyes—her hair—all her loveliness... Hell, it's hard to believe she killed old Ben!"

He felt his way around the shack. His gun was gone. The mysterious knife was gone. The little hovel was bare of any furnishings whatever; not even a stool upon which to sit, not even a stove. The door was barred from the outside. There was no window.

After a while Quinlin sat down, suddenly shoved his hand into an inner pocket, then exhaled a sigh of relief. They had not taken his journal. He took it out, flicked back the pages and felt the strand of golden hair. Yes, it was still there—the lone piece of golden evidence.

He drew the robes closer about his body. He hoped Carlin had not, like himself, made any rash moves. He was glad he had brought along Jerry Plate. Jerry and Carlin ought to be able to help him. But would the girl who had led them to the Valley tell there were three? If she did, the game was well-nigh up.

The sergeant's ruminations were interrupted by the sudden opening of the door. A man came in, closed the door and lighted a candle that he held in his hand. He was not above medium height. His beard was scraggly; his eyes pale and whimsical. He grinned at the sergeant and set the candle on the mantelpiece.

"Greetin's, serge. Kind o' chilly in here, eh?"

"No chance of me sweating at all, stranger."

"'S right—perfectly right," nodded the man. "Don't think I'd keel over wit' the heat m'self."

Here, thought Quinlin, was a jovial rascal.

The fellow was saying, "I been sent here t' make you an offer."

"All right. Shoot!"

"You mayn't know it, serge, but you're about a mile away from the settlement, I been sent here to offer you—no t' ask you t' make believe you never saw Defiance Valley. In other words, t' clear out before somethin' happens t' you."

"Who sent you?"

"A lady—as fine a lady as ever wore a pair of moccasins."

"The lady called Rose?"

The man eyed him sharply. "Yeah—the same. She's took an oncommon int'rest in you, an' she's takin' an orful risk. Me, I'd guide you out, serge, because she asked me to. I'd do anything for Rose."

"Rather a gallant, eh?"

"No—hell, no. She nursed me through the scurvey once. I ain't f'rgot. She's all gold—like her hair—God bless her."

Quinlin thought over this for a minute. Then:

"Send Rose my heartfelt gratitude, but tell her I refuse aid. I am here for a purpose. And I shan't leave Defiance Valley until that purpose is realized. That's all."

The man shrugged his heavy shoulders. "Well you're fixin' f'r your own funeral, serge. But—lemme tell you somethin': You'll never take Rose out. If there was any chance o' you doin' it, me, I'd be the first one t' cook your goose. Get that, serge, an' don't think your red coat worries me any."

"H-m-m," mused Quinlin, "And who are you?"

"Well, there's some folks as call me 'Hell-bent' Jackson. I'll be givin' Rose your message. S'long." And with that he was gone.

Quinlin heard the lock snap outside. Then there was silence.

"Well," the sergeant told himself, "it sure seems the law is below par over this way. No respect for it at all. By hook or crook I've got to escape. Hell, I did better than this when I was a recruit. It's Rose that's getting me into all this trouble. But still I can't forget that kiss and the look in those eyes. And on the other hand, I can't forget the Oath, the Scarlet Manual!"

CHAPTER X

MEETING IN
THE MOONLIGHT

NOT UNTIL noon of the next day was food brought to the sergeant. He was pretty well fagged out when the door opened and the gigantic figure of Long Jim heaved in with a pot of steaming food.

"Well, we meet again," said Quinlin. "That was a rotten crack you gave me."

The Indian set down the food and backed to the door, where he stood with folded arms, his carven face cold and expressionless.

"The Master say eat. I wait till finish."

Quinlin was already chewing a wing of ptarmigan.

After a moment the Indian went on with, "I find and bring two men to Master. One man him wear red coat. Master lock up."

Quinlin swore under his breath. But he said, in an offhand manner, "That's too bad."

He finished the meal in silence and the Indian picked up the utensils.

"Any talk you want me give Master?"

Quinlin shook his head.

The Indian opened the door, passed out and again the lock snapped.

The afternoon passed slowly and with the coming of darkness a sharp wind began drumming against the cabin. As Quinlin was dozing off he was startled by the sudden opening of the door. White moonlight flooded in and outlined sharply in the doorframe was the shaggy figure of Hell-bent Jackson, with a gun in his hand.

"C'mere a minute, serge," he called in a low voice.

Perplexed, Quinlin got up and edged toward the opening.

Jackson went on—"That's far enough f'r a while. An' don't f'rget I got a gun on you. Now come out here where it's light."

Quinlin stepped outside. Standing some few yards away was Rose. He looked from her to Jackson quizzically.

"Well?" he asked tentatively.

Jackson jerked his head toward the woman. "Rose 's got somethin' t' say t' you. Go over to her. An'—remember—" He tapped his gun meaningly.

Quinlin moved over hesitantly. Rose avoided his gaze for a moment, then looked up suddenly and began in a quick anxious voice:

"I've come myself to beg you to leave. There is trouble on the way. Your two friends were captured shortly after you, but about an hour ago they attacked the guard and won free."

"Ah!" breathed the sergeant, "And?"

"Well, please accept the offer Jackson made. You're a marked man now for sure. I just heard The Master say he was going to wait until we got a blizzard—and he says there's one on the way now—then he's going to set you adrift in the country without food—without a rifle—without anything."

"The fiend!" Quinlin snarled out.

And Rose:

"So you will gain nothing by being so stubborn. It will mean your death—frozen stiff in all the white wilderness to the northward. Can't you see your fighting against a stone wall—you can't win? Jackson will guide you out. It's a crime to see courage like yours killed fighting against such odds. It's—"

"Perhaps you're planning all this to save yourself," Quinlin shot back. "You haven't explained certain things to me. You are still a wanted person—wanted in connection with the killing of Ben Tobin. I cannot give you my word that I'll leave Defiance Valley.

"I can't because I know I would come back. The law has been made a laughing stock of. Let them send me into the blizzard. Let them do what they want. If I don't win out others of the Force will. It may take months, years, but you can't beat us. In the end the law will be vindicated!"

She drew closer to him, a wild light in her eyes.

"But I shan't see you killed!" she cried. "I shan't. I'll take you away from here myself, in spite of what you believe about me." Then suddenly she seemed to crumple. "But—but Marie. Poor Marie!…"

"Eh—Marie?"

"Oh, will you please go?" she cried near his face. "For God's sake—for my sake! Go! Let Jackson take you out. But go! Go! *I* must stay here. Oh, you fool!—fool!—fool!"

She started to fling herself away from him in a fit of passion, but he caught her in his arms.

"Rose, dear Rose, in spite of what I'm given to believe, I—I love you, Rose."

He crushed her to his furs, kissed her pomegranate lips, and after a moment of resistance felt the kiss returned. Then, with a cry of pathos in her throat, she tore away from him and plunged into the timber, and choked sobbing reached his ears. With a shudder he stared down at the snow, and his eyes narrowed as he beheld lying at his feet the *knife that had killed Tobin!*

He stooped to pick it up, but the sharp voice of Jackson stayed him.

"I'll take that," were Jackson's words. "You better get back inside. You're a fool, serge, a bloomin' fool. Damme if you ain't. If a woman like that loved me I'd let the red coat go hang. Get inside, serge. You're a bonehead."

Quinlin watched him pick up the knife and stow it away.

"Jackson," he suddenly blurted out, "did she kill Tobin?"

Jackson's mouth drooped sardonically.

"That's a hell of a question f'r a man t' ask who's just told her he loves her. In the cabin, serge, an' sleep tight."

A MOMENT later Quinlin was alone in the little shack, his brain throbbing with a thousand conflicting thoughts. He had professed his love for Rose. He had kissed her and she had kissed him and he read all that was love in her eyes and her voice.

And in the embrace the knife must have worked loose from her person and dropped. He loved her. He did not deny it. But his love for the Scarlet he wore, for its traditions, its honor, was great, too. It is such crises as these that make or break a man.

"By God, I'll not leave," he suddenly ground out. "Who is Marie? Ah, perhaps the girl that showed us the way. And what is she to Rose? Hell, everything is so secretive. Nobody speaks coherently.

"They all talk in circles. Well, Jerry and Carlin broke loose—if they'll only stay loose. And The Master is going to send me off in a blizzard. That's certainly a bright idea—damn him!"

An hour later there was movement of some sort outside the door. Quinlin got to his feet and clenched his fists. It seemed to him now that the only way to win free was by a reckless move, trusting the rest to luck.

He made ready to spring, his muscles taut, as the door opened. He even sprang forward, but brought up suddenly when he saw his visitor, Father La Bau, accompanied by Long Jim.

"Ah, sergeant, 'tis only I," he murmured in his low, gentle voice. "Let us go in. The Indian, I presume, has orders to guard the cabin while we talk."

CHAPTER XI

PÈRE LA BAU SPEAKS

QUINLIN RETREATED into the cabin in perplexed indecision. The missioner was already lighting a candle.

After a moment he said, "First, sergeant, I'm sorry it was my fault that threw you into this predicament. I smoke unusually strong tobacco, and when one is fresh from the trail—and a hard trail—it is liable to make him groggy if he is not used to it. It was indeed thoughtless of me. And it is possible you thought I drugged it. Hence my amends, which you may or may not believe."

"It struck me as a drugged mixture," was the sergeant's frank but courteous reply. "However, supposing it wasn't, what is the object of your visit here."

The Jesuit Father drew a thoughtful finger along his lower lip. In the flickering candle light his eyes were opaque—seemingly transparent, now a pale blue, now gray, forever changing in color under light and shadow.

"My visit!" he echoed. "In the cause of humanity, I assure you, sergeant. This Valley contains some Godless men, and to them the law means nothing. The most of them have killed a man somewhere—sometime.

"Wherefore they are reckless, and some of them would be particularly pleased at the opportunity of shooting a redcoat. They would brag about it. And they have sworn allegiance to one man, and his word is law."

"The Master?"

"Some call him by that name," nodded the missioner. "He has but to say, 'Kill that man.' And *that* man, whoever he may be, will be killed. I am merely explaining this to show you how futile it is for one man—or two or three—to come here in the name of the law."

"And why do you remain here. Father?"

"Oh, I have my little flock," smiled the missioner. "And I live in hopes of some day converting the bad ones. And then I comfort those who die."

"My dear Father," put in the sergeant, "you have professed yourself a disciple of humanity. The law is a disciple of humanity, too. Why not unite? Why not divulge to me the methods, or what you know, of this clique?"

"I have given my word of honor to speak nothing of that sort, monsieur," replied Père La Bau. "I have revealed too much as it is, I fear. I have been allowed to speak with you and ask you to swear you will leave this Valley and forget you ever saw it—to swear by the Book."

The sergeant's face went grim.

"Father, I appreciate your kind indulgence, but my answer is—no! Within the year my services in the Force terminate, and, having not defiled the Oath and the uniform I wear in eight years, I shall not defile it now. The fools! Do they think they can do away with me and remain untouched.

"Are they blind to the Force's record? Do they forget that in the dead of winter two years back Corporal Tyson tracked a murderer from Fort Resolution to Coronation Gulf—a thousand miles of the worst country this side of hell—do they?"

The missioner recommended silence with a raised hand. "Very well, sergeant. I am sorry. I have only tried to help you to the best of my ability. Goodnight."

"Good-night, Father."

The missioner moved toward the door, opened it and started to go out. But he paused on the threshold and his hands started to rise slowly above his head. Quinlin, perplexed, moved over behind him.

Just outside the door stood Constable Carlin with his revolver trained on the black robed missioner. To one side lounged Jerry Plate, covering Long Jim.

"Pat, that you?" called Carlin in an anxious voice.

"The same, Lee, God bless you," sang out the sergeant. "Hello, there, Jerry." And to the missioner—"Please step outside, Father."

Jerry handed the sergeant the rifle he had taken from Long Jim.

Quinlin was saying:

"Father, you may return to the settlement. I am keeping the Indian as material witness."

The missioner nodded and then said, "I think it unwise of you, sergeant, to hold the Indian. You will bring all the dangerous element of Defiance Valley upon you. Merely my personal opinion, of course."

"Thanks, Father, but we must take him," answered Quinlin. "You may go."

Père La Bau bowed, turned and strode off into the darkness.

Carlin had manacled the Indian by this time.

Jerry said:

"Let's mosey along, Pat. We better hide up in the hills. Soon as they get wind o' this hell 'll pop. Lee an' me have been shot at more times 'n I c'n count. But we gave 'em the slip right along, eh, Lee?"

"Yes," spoke up the constable as they moved off with their sullen captive. "When you didn't come back, Pat, I started down into the Valley and soon found Jerry after me. We kept sneaking about until this Indian pounced upon us with half-a-dozen other rascals.

"We were locked in a cabin, where we learned that you, too, had been captured. In the night that girl—Marie—tapped on the window and when I opened it she passed me a revolver and I—I—"

"Go ahead, Lee, tell the truth," chided Jerry.

"I—I—"

Jerry cut in:

"He took the revolver, leaned out and kissed her, and the danged fools kept huggin' each other till I yanked him away. Haw! Haw!"

Carlin flushed.

"We—Jerry and I—attacked the guard when he brought us food. Jerry got his gun and we broke away, and ever since we've been looking for you. When we saw the Indian and the missioner heading this way we trailed 'em."

Long Jim's eyes darkened ominously as he heard Carlin's story and his breath hissed in his throat.

AT DAYBREAK they were two miles up in the spruce covered hills. It was snowing lightly, but enough to cover up their trail.

"The luck seems to be coming our way for once," observed Quinlin. "They'll have some time finding us."

They had no food. Their dogs and provisions had been gathered in by The Master henchmen. Food was a necessary item, so Jerry sacrificed one of his snowshoes by using the lacing for a rabbit snare.

"We can't afford to give our position by shootin'," was his comment.

They snared four rabbits and drank raw spruce tea. The site of their camp was on a sharp eminence that commanded a view of the country for miles about. As the day broadened they could see far away to the southward the cabins of Defiance Valley.

"With plenty of food and ammunition we could hold this hill till the cows came home," remarked Quinlin.

"But with on'y twenty slugs between us," supplemented Jerry, "it ain't so easy."

Carlin was trying to pierce the thin cloud of snow with his glasses.

"There's a lot of hustle and bustle down there," he said. "Groups starting out in several directions, and all armed. And it looks as though four are coming up this way. It's pretty far, but I think they're heading this way—four or five."

With the passing of another hour Carlin was positive that four men were heading toward their lofty retreat.

Quinlin said:

"We must trick them. Avoid any shooting. We'll waylay them,

tie 'em up and take their guns and ammunition. We need ammunition."

For the time being they bound the Indian hand and foot and secured him to a tree. Then the three of them started down the incline and waited in a thicket. Hours passed before the men came toiling up the rugged slope; four of them in single file and carrying rifles.

Quinlin was whispering:

"You fellows pounce on the first two. Leave the last two for me. Work fast, now. Club your revolvers and hit hard. Ready!"

The first of the four came rocking by the thicket. Jerry shot out and brought his gun butt down on the man's head even as Carlin bore the second fellow down with his clubbed revolver.

Quinlin caught the first of his two on the forehead and sent him reeling back against the other. In a flash he had the last man covered, while the other pitched unconscious to the snow.

"That gun!" he rasped out. "The revolver, too. Now open your coat!"

Black with rage the only conscious one of the quartette threw down his guns and pulled open his coat.

"That's the stuff," bit off Quinlin. "Take that knife from your belt. That's all. You may close your coat."

Carlin and Jerry were already hauling their men up the slope. Quinlin followed, while the man he had disarmed was forced to carry his unconscious companion. Once at the spot where they had left the Indian, Quinlin and his companions bound the prisoners securely with strips cut from the prisoner's own caribou-hide garments. Then Jerry built a roaring fire, so that their hands and feet, thus bound and preventing free circulation, would not freeze.

"Now," spoke up Quinlin. "There's a rifle for each of us and an extra revolver. Come here a moment, boys."

He drew Jerry and Carlin aside.

"Two of us are going down into the valley. Lee, I think you'd better come along. Jerry, you know you're not officially in the service. If you got banged up I'd have to explain a lot.

"So the best thing for you to do is remain here and guard these roughnecks. I'm going to clear this thing up now or be eternally damned. I've been made an ass of. I'll make 'em talk, the whole bloody lot of them!"

CHAPTER XII

HELL BREAKS LOOSE!

SIDE BY side Quinlin and Carlin swung down the slope. The sergeant's blood was up now. He had been rubbed the wrong way once too often, and his reckless gait and the hard, bitter set of his face made it patent that he was ripe for anything short of murder.

He was in no mood for words, as Carlin found out after a few unsuccessful attempts to start a conversation. The sergeant's replies were nothing more than clipped phrases and chopped off words.

As they reached lower country the snowfall increased, with a sharp wind at its back that whirled it in circles and corkscrew twists. The flakes doubled in size and evolved into pellets that slashed and cut like the tip of a rawhide whip.

"This will conceal our approach," ventured Carlin.

"Yup, Lee. 'S right," shot back the sergeant.

It took them just three hours to fight through storm and bush to the first cabin of the little outpost. They drew up on the lee side of a tree for a hurried consultation.

Quinlin said, "Farther on there's a sort of store. Suppose it's the general hang-out. Heard singing and dancing there when I first hit the Valley. It's likely that those who aren't searching for us are in there. Let's go!"

"Right-o, Pat," spoke up the constable.

They sank their heads in their furs and plodded on side by side. There was no need for a cautious approach now. The white cloud of the storm concealed them. A man passed within six feet of them and did not recognize them.

Quinlin led the way up to the trade store and they stood beside the window for a moment. It was so frozen that even by placing the heel of his hand against it Quinlin could not clear a space through which to look.

"Well, Lee, we'll have to walk right in," he explained. "For maybe a minute they won't recognize us, we're so covered with snow. We're the last people in the world they'll expect. Come on."

Quinlin pushed open the door and kept his head lowered as he went in. Carlin was at his heels. As he closed the door Quinlin, with a deft movement, threw down the heavy bar that locked it against intrusion from the outside. Out of the corner of his eye he saw six men gambling at a table near the great sheet-iron stove.

One leaned against the counter in the rear eying the card players in a detached superior manner. This man was Bellamy, the big, handsome fellow he had caught attacking Rose that night in the cabin where later he had smoked the fatal tobacco. None of the players looked up. Even Bellamy, who appeared deep in thought, did not stir.

Quinlin caught Carlin's eye and motioned to the men at the table. Then they strode forward. Both pulled their guns at the same time.

Carlin said:

"Every man keep his hands right where they are—on the table!"

Quinlin stood in front of Bellamy and eyed him coolly. The whole thing had been done in such a smooth, unhurried manner that Bellamy could not quite believe his eyes. His hand involuntarily slid toward the revolver at his hip.

"Cut it!" barked Quinlin. "Don't you recognize me, Bellamy?"

Bellamy suddenly exploded: "Crise-mighty! Where did you drop from?"

Quinlin laughed his short, harsh laugh.

"Kind of surprising, eh? From now on you and your bunch of roughnecks are going to get the surprises of your life. The law has come to Defiance Valley. I've met tough ones before like you. Now do what I tell you. Unbuckle your gun belt and let it drop. Now reach under your arm and pluck out that knife. I see the strap under your shirt. Come on. I've not got all night. Now keep your hands high and move over there with your playmates."

There was steel in the sergeant's voice and a bad light in his eyes. Bellamy, almost crying with baffled rage, rocked over by the others. His big chest rose and fell slowly, and the cords in his powerful neck bulged, and his face flamed red with uprising passion.

By this time Carlin had the others disarmed. Six guns and six knives lay on the table. Quinlin lined them all against the wall and then spoke to Carlin.

"There must be a storeroom here, Lee. Find it, will you?"

Carlin tried several doors in the rear and soon found the one that opened into the store-room. It was a cubby-hole of a place, dark, unlighted and without a single window.

"Just the place," chuckled Quinlin. "All right, boys, file into that room. Go ahead, Bellamy; you're the leader."

"By cripes, I'll—" started Bellamy.

But Quinlin cut him off with:

"You'll go right into that room; that's what you'll do. And no lip! Get along!"

Fuming with sullen rage, his eyes venomous, Bellamy moved reluctantly into the room and the others, four whites and two Indians, followed with black looks, curses and guttural snarls.

Quinlin saw the last man through the door, then shot home the bolt. He made the prison more secure by driving several spikes in the floor and bracing between these and the door a stout length of timber which he found leaning against the wall.

"That'll hold 'em for a while, Lee," he said.

Then there were sounds at the front door. Somebody was knocking. Quinlin went over quickly, threw up the bar and stood aside with drawn pistol. The door swung in and a fur-swathed man heaved in, rubbing the snow from his eyes and cursing the weather. When he looked up and beheld Quinlin he gulped and gave off a cracked chuckle.

"Oh, hello, serge. Where'n 'ell you blow from?"

"Hello, Jackson."

Hell-bent Jackson flung an eye around the room and frowned.

"Where's the crowd?" He caught his breath at sight of Carlin. "Oh, glad t' see you, cons'able. Too bad we lost that team."

"Team?" put in Quinlin.

Carlin leaped forward and caught Jackson by the shoulder.

"This, Pat—this is the fellow that waylaid me. This is the fellow that stole our outfit. *This is the fellow that shot at you and stole the knife!*"

"SO-O!" BREATHED out Quinlin. "So you're the sharpshooter that creased my neck back there in Ben Tobin's cabin!"

Jackson was unmoved.

"You must admit, Serge, I'm *some* shot. I could 'a' killed you dead, but I just wanted t' keel y' over f'r a while."

Quinlin eyed him searchingly.

"You're a cool devil, Jackson, aren't you? I'll bet you know more about this case than any other person."

"Think so, Serge? What if I was t' tell you I knew less'n you about it?"

"I'd say you were a liar."

"Yeah—I s'pose you would, so it's no use me sayin' it. I wish t' hell I did know somet'in' about it. Then I'd know where I stand. But this way— What the hell's all the noise about back there?" he asked abruptly, indicating the storeroom.

"A few citizens of Defiance Valley caged up," answered the sergeant. "I'll have to hog-tie you in another room."

"Who's all in there, Serge?" Jackson hastened on.

"I don't know 'em. Only one; Bellamy, they call him."

Jackson spat out of the side of his mouth with sudden gusto.

"He is, eh? That's the guy I'm lookin' f'r. He's gotta talk cold turkey t' me or, by cripes, I'll riddle him clean as a whistle."

With that Jackson clamped his jaw and started for the store-room. But Quinlin stayed him.

"Say, Jackson, hold on here. Give me that gun. Come on. Hand it over. You're under arrest, too."

Jackson whirled, his crooked mouth agape and his pale eyes wide.

"I tell you, Serge, I want that lousy pup of a Bellamy. He's *gotta* talk."

"Never mind. Personal grievances don't cut any ice with me. I'm in a hurry, so hand over your gun and we'll tie you up."

"You're in a hurry, eh? Well, God 'Lmighty, me, I'm in a hurry, too. What are you here for? You're lookin' f'r Rose, ain'tcha? Well, so'm I. But she ain't t' be found. There's some dirty work goin' on an' if this pup Bellamy don't know a thing 'r two about it I'll be a cock-eyed liar. You *can't* hog-tie me, Serge. I'm the on'y friend that gal has."

Carlin put in—

"Marie—how about her?"

"Gone, too. That room, Serge. Bellamy...."

For a while Quinlin was in a dilemma. Was Jackson lying? Or was he on the square? But time was precious, and he could not afford to consider it at length.

"Well, Jackson," he said, "we'll see Bellamy. But give me your gun."

Jackson handed over the revolver reluctantly.

"Just now you're top-dog, Serge."

Quinlin stood by the door with ready gun while Carlin threw open the bolt and kicked away the improvised jamb.

The sergeant called:

"Only you, Bellamy. And come out with your hands up. The rest stay in there."

Sullen, with hands raised, Bellamy came out. Carlin put home the bolt and then went over and dropped the bar across the front door, thus obviating a surprise-attack.

Jackson was saying, "Bellamy, what's goin' on? Where are the gals?"

Bellamy's lips curved into a sneer. "Go on, you traitor!" he snarled.

"I'm no traitor, you damn pup! I'm no friend o' these Mounties by a long shot, but they got the jump on me. I been huntin' high an' low f'r the gals an' can't find 'em. Now where the hell are they, hey?"

"I don't know."

"Liar! You'll never get that gal, Bellamy. She hates you. I'd rather see her dead than wit' you. You'll never get Marie. Rose won't let you an' I won't. I'd cut out your heart. Where are they, dammit? Where's Rose? Where's Marie? Speak, you big bum!"

"Don't call me a bum!" snapped Bellamy.

"Go t'ell. You're twenty-six kinds of a bum an' a couple o' pups besides."

Bellamy strained under this scathing tirade like a dog on a leash.

Quinlin put in:

"Easy, Jackson. That kind of talk's not getting you anywhere."

He turned to Bellamy.

"Are you going to speak? Tell what you know about the disappearance of the women?"

"I'll say one thing," bit off Bellamy. "I didn't know they had disappeared!"

Jackson lunged forward with—

"Liar!"

But Quinlin pushed him aside.

"Jackson, easy, I say."

"I'll—"

"You'll keep your mouth shut!" Quinlin cut in. "We'll have to take Bellamy's word for it. Haven't time to argue. All right, Bellamy. Back into the storeroom."

Carlin opened the door and said, as Bellamy backed in:

"If you've harmed that girl, Bellamy, God help you!"

And he slammed the door against the big fellow's smirking face.

Quinlin stood pondering over the situation. Finally:

"Jackson, as man to man who killed Ben Tobin?"

"I don't know, Serge."

"Rose?"

"If she did, d'you think I'd tell *you?*"

"No; I suppose not."

"But she *didn't*," Jackson flung at him.

"Then who did?"

"Don't know."

"Trying to shield her, eh? I admire you for that. Then if you believe she *didn't*, Jackson, can I place you on your honor until we find her? You seem to think she and the girl called Marie are in jeopardy. If you know she's not guilty—"

"Maybe she can't prove it, Serge."

"Can you?"

"No, but I believe her. Stake m' life on her. She knows a lot but she don't talk. But I say she's innocent. An' until we find her, Serge, I'll play square. After that I'm for her an' against you, even t' the point o' killin'."

"Jackson, you're a strange man. No wonder they've named you 'Hell-bent.' But I'll take a chance on you."

They muffled themselves against the storm, buckled on their rackets and stepped out into the swirling clouds of snow. Great windrows were piling up against the cabins. The wind, pounding down from Hudson's Bay, was at the height of all its mad, chaotic fury; whistling, screaming, booming in the big timber with maniacal abandon.

It caught Carlin and bowled him over, and Quinlin, reaching to help him up, felt it cut his face like a cat-o'-nine-tails. Jackson, tough old sourdough, fought for his balance while he drew his parka hood closer about his face and cursed in his throat.

It was a blizzard such as neither he nor Quinlin had seen in all their years of trail pounding. The wind looped and dived downward, drove horizontally, crosswise, up and down, so that no matter how the men tried to hide their faces it found them out and tried to crush them. Holding on to each other, they struggled up against one of the cabins and leaned there.

"'S tough!" gasped Jackson.

"Damned tough!" supplemented Quinlin.

Carlin was struggling for his breath.

"God! If—if she's out in this hell…" He choked.

And at the same time Quinlin was thinking of Rose. She could never exist in a storm like this. It would crush a man—a strong man—before very long. He prayed for her—hoped she was safe until they could reach her, if ever they would.

It would be difficult to suppose what was going on inside the rough, tough, hard-bitten old soul who called himself Hell-bent Jackson.

Quinlin was yelling in his ear—

"You've been through all the cabins?"

"Yep. Both gals are gone."

Quinlin hugged the wall, wondering how on God's earth he could find them, when he hadn't even the remotest idea of their whereabouts. Here was a blizzard so furious, so destructive, that it cut and battered him even while he stood by the cabin; so dense that he could see scarce six feet into the white cloud. In desperation he called out to Jackson:

"Any cabin in the hills where they might find shelter?"

Jackson's voice came in snatches, tossed about by the wind:

"One t' the north… three miles… east… two miles."

And Quinlin yelled back:

"We've got to take a chance. They couldn't travel far in this. They didn't go north, because we had a camp up there and I didn't pass anybody on the way in. We'll take a chance on the one to the east."

CHAPTER XIII

THE TEETH
OF THE BLIZZARD

THUS THEY went off into the eye of the gale, one plodding behind the other, with Jackson in the lead because he knew the way. There was no mercy in that storm. Straight down from the Baffin ice fields it roared in its blind, passionless fury, knocking over trees, snuffing out the lives of countless small animals and trying the mettle of men.

It was molten. It gave no quarter. It struck and struck again, and the men went to their knees in bitter resistance to its brute strength. They did not speak. They could not have spoken had they tried.

They only grasped each other's arm and, thus locked, fought up to their feet, doubled their bodies against the wind and forced their way ahead with the grim doggedness of men who are used to fighting raw nature not only with their brawn but with their sand and grit as well.

They went a mile, fighting every inch of the way, and then drew together behind a matted windfall that offered some little protection from the wind. Quinlin grasped Jackson's head in his hands and yelled next to his ear:

"Know where you are, all right?"

And Jackson clamped his own mouth to the sergeant's ear and bawled:

"Half-way, Serge. Everything O.K."

Then Quinlin shouted into Carlin's ear that all was well and asked the young constable how he felt. Carlin shouted back he was in fine shape, but the sergeant could see black frost patches growing on his mate's face and his eyes were red and raw, with the salt rheum freezing on the lids.

"Good man," Quinlin said to himself and pressed the constable's mittened hand in his own.

A MINUTE later they were pressing on, fighting up through a country thick with bush and jackpine, so steep in places that they had to haul themselves up by grasping the bushes.

It seemed hours before they won to the summit, and by this time night was full upon them and the storm still in mid-career. They struggled desperately along the backbone of the ridge until suddenly there loomed up before them the squat form of a cabin. They stopped, the three of them, and huddled together.

They could see near the cabin two sleds almost buried, and here and there were groups of dogs burrowing in the snow.

Jackson said, "Me, Serge, I'll rap on the door. When they see it's me all alone they'll let me in. I'll take a long time gettin' in, an' you an' your pardner, who are gonna hide at the corner, 'll rush around an' break in behind me."

"You're double-crossing 'em, Jackson," Quinlin barked.

"Serge, I'd double-cross any one of them if I thought it'd save those gals. Let's go."

Jackson zigzagged ahead and Quinlin and the constable hid around the corner of the cabin. Jackson worked up to the door and let his hand thump against it. He waited a moment and struck it again, after the manner of a man who is too feeble to knock vigorously. When the door opened he swayed on his feet, tried to remove his rackets and purposely slumped down. Rough hands reached down and hauled him inside.

At that moment Quinlin and Carlin, having removed their snowshoes, bounded for the door and burst in. In a flash Jackson was on his feet. The man who had let him in snarled out a string of curses in French and English and hacked at him with a knife. Jackson ducked the thrust and cracked the fellow on the jaw with his revolver.

Carlin and the sergeant, covered with snow and ice, charged three men who had risen from comfortable seats by the stove and were now yanking at their weapons.

"In the name of the law—" began Quinlin.

But one fellow had his gun out and was swinging it in a line for the sergeant's chest when Carlin lunged over and cracked the man's wrist with the barrel of his own revolver.

Quinlin ducked a wide shot and from an awkward position put a neat shot through the fellow's forearm, while Carlin rushed the other and bore him crashing against the wall with such force that the man sank down senseless from the impact.

At that instant the door that led into the rear room opened and Père La Bau, clothed in his sombre black robes, stood framed in the doorway with a shocked expression on his face.

"Children!" he exclaimed. "Shooting! Knives! What's the meaning of all this?"

Quinlin was in no mood for gentle words, though he tried his best to be civil.

"Who's in that room, Father?" he asked, crisply.

"Why, no one, sergeant. I pray, be seated there."

"Father, the law will respect you so long as you respect the law," snapped Quinlin. "Personally, I think you have not aided justice. You have thwarted it several times. It is my wish that you remain quiet and do not take too much advantage of your station. This is time for action—not idle talk. What do you know about the women called Rose and Marie?"

"I know nothing sergeant."

"What are you doing up here away from the village with two sleds and two sets of dogs?"

"I pray, Sergeant, am I answerable to such questions?"

"If your interest is with humanity and justice, yes. I am treating you with as much partiality as I am able. You are wearing my patience severely, Father."

Jackson, with an oath, started for the next room.

"There's only one way, Serge, an' that's t' go right in."

Père La Bau drew himself up to his full height and looked down at Jackson with a cold, agate stare. Jackson made to shove him out of the way, but Quinlin stayed him.

"Jackson," he rasped out. "Lay off. I'm handling this. Lay off, I tell you."

Jackson retreated slowly, his hands clenched.

Quinlin said:

"Father, I shall have to look through that room. Please step aside."

The missioner raised a hand.

"Sergeant—"

"Pardon, Father," Quinlin cut in. "I must see that room."

With that he strode forward and Father La Bau, his lips taut and his eyes narrowed, stepped aside.

Quinlin struck a match as he went in with ready revolver. In one corner, clasped in each other's arms, Rose and Marie crouched.

"Thank God!" breathed Quinlin.

Then his mouth went hard and he whirled about and confronted the missioner.

"Again you have tried to thwart the law, Father," he ground out. "Why are these women here?"

Père La Bau smiled and drew a finger tip across his lower lip.

"I brought them here because there was a disturbance in the Valley," he answered easily.

They locked eyes for a long moment.

Then Quinlin said:

"It would be proper for me to say I believe you," and turned on his heel.

"Lee," he addressed the constable, "go outside and see what you can do with the dogs. Line up one team. That's all we'll take."

Then to the missioner:

"We are taking one outfit, Father, and we are taking the two women—in the name of the law. Some of these fellows are banged up, so you'd better look after them."

Père La Bau bowed stiffly, his face an expressionless mask.

Carlin was pulling on his mittens as he moved towards the door, but before he reached it, it whipped open and half-a-dozen men surged in with roaring guns. Carlin hurled himself backward.

Jackson made a leap for the rear room, and Quinlin grabbed the constable by the collar and swung him in behind Jackson. Then he sent three fast shots at the attackers, knocked one over and retreated into the back room, slamming shut the door against an Indian's face and shooting home the bolt.

"Jackson… Carlin!" he called.

"Here, Serge," jerked Jackson.

And Carlin was at his side in an instant.

The sergeant said:

"No door in here, eh? But there's one parchment window. Cut it away. Take the women. Clear out. Hurry! They're break-ing the door. I'll hold 'em back… give you a chance to get a start."

"But—" began Carlin.

And Quinlin rasped:

"No talk. Quick! The window—break it open while there's a chance."

He found a table and put it against the door, adding to this his own braced weight. Jackson was opening the window. Carlin was bundling up the women. The sergeant had both guns out and his shoulder jammed against the table.

Of a sudden he felt warm, dry fur against his face, then two soft, white hands. He looked around and found Rose looking up at him.

"My dear, go—go with Jackson and the constable," he jerked out. "I'll hold them off—"

"But you come, too. They—they'll—"

"Rose, dear, please go. The door is breaking. Get a head start."

"But you—you, Pat," she cried, in a choked voice. Then she clutched him tightly and kissed him many times on the lips.

"Rose, for God's sake, go!" broke forth Quinlin. "Jackson—I say, Jackson, will you take Rose here. Hurry, Jackson."

Jackson came over and by sheer force tore her from the sergeant. She screamed. She cried. And as Jackson put her through the window she called:

"Pat, come to me. I love you, Pat. Oh, how I love you!"

CHAPTER XIV

SAND AND GRIT!

A **ND THEN** she was gone, swallowed up by the storm. But the words still rang in the sergeant's ear and kept echoing through his brain. They thrilled him to that point where he felt he could lick any man under the sun.

He realized that he was fighting a losing game at the door. He knew that eventually the door would break down and it would be a case of one man against many. But the women had to have a start, and by keeping the split-log table braced against the door he would hold the attackers back long enough to make that head start possible.

When the door finally broke in he leaped back in the shadows with his shoulders hunched and his guns clapped to his hips. Daggers of flame slashed through the gloom, the explosions indistinguishable from the mad noises of the storm. One of the attackers pitched head-first across the upturned table and another recoiled from the room into the arms of those behind him, his face frozen in a twisted grimace.

The sergeant stood with his back to the wall, a motionless, grim figure with death in each hand. The doorway was cleared of any human target for the time being. The broken door and the heavy table, heaped across it, prevented a combined attack. A few shots cracked, fired at an angle through the doorway and missing Quinlin by a couple of feet. He answered sparingly, just to show them he was on the job.

Presently he heard a voice yelling:

"We want those women, sergeant, an' we want 'em now. If you don't give 'em up they're gonna get hurt."

For answer Quinlin sent a shot through the doorway. Then he moved toward the window, firing at intervals to keep the doorway clear. He won to the opening, put a leg over the sill and swung out into the storm-tossed night. For a moment he stood by the window and emptied his one gun at the doorway.

At last he turned, crept to the corner of the house and found his snowshoes as he had left them. He strapped them on with difficulty, reloaded his empty revolver and rocked off into the blizzard.

"Well, I hope Jackson and Carlin are out of reach," he muttered. "Those fellows back there'll throw a fit when they find out the trick. Well, I've been getting the bum breaks long enough. About time luck came my way."

He bit his way northward into the storm, and before very long a mask of ice covered his face and beard and his furs became matted and frozen. He fell many times, caught in a baffling vortex of cross winds that twisted him to his knees. But he was up in a minute, fighting on, while all about him great trees gave up the fight and crashed down, carrying smaller trees with them. Men were to remember that storm; men who ordinarily were not startled by the wrath of the North.

Quinlin fought with all the spirit and courage of his great heart. For a while he forgot he wore the Scarlet. He was fighting on toward Rose. Somewhere in the white maelstrom ahead Rose was waiting for him. He did not think of her as a suspect in the murder case of Ben Tobin. He thought of her only as an adorable woman who had kissed him, clung to him, fought to stay with him and cried out her love as Jackson carried her away to temporary safety.

He was fighting towards her—towards Rose o' the golden hair and rich red lips. And the storm tried to drive him back, knocked him all over the trail, pounded him mercilessly and sent him reeling and staggering from one tree into another.

"Kind of… tough… going," he gasped.

Finally he lost all sense of direction. His hands were too numb to feel for his compass. He dared not remove his mittens. Without quite realizing the fact he began going down grade, slipping, sliding, but somehow or other maintaining his equilibrium in spite of it all.

Down—down, until he found himself on a level trail, with the wind scooping down into the valley and twisting and snarling about his body like a mad ghost of some prehistoric monster.

He kept going—just going, without knowing where. The gray light of another day showed feebly through the blizzard as he tottered out of the scrub spruce, passed two cabins without seeing them and by accident walked against the door of a third with such headlong force that the impact sent him to his hands.

Then the door opened and he rolled across the threshold, and lay on his back, blinking up at the weazened face of an ancient squaw who was hauling him in out of the doorway. He was already working up to his feet when she closed the door. He fought erect, spun across the room and brought up with a jolt in a big, rough-hewn chair.

"Where am I?" he jerked out with an effort.

Already the squaw had a pot of strong, black tea before him.

" 'Fiance Valley," she muttered.

"Eh? Defiance Valley!" exclaimed the sergeant.

The woman nodded.

Quinlin sipped the steaming tea and felt new life running in his blood before the pot was half finished. He did not speak with the old Indian woman until the pot was drained. He let his whole battered body relax and puffed on his pipe. The squaw sat on a mat near the stove and worked dyed porcupine quills in a new pair of moccasins.

"Where husband?" Quinlin asked.

"Gone *Kisse-Manito,*" she answered, without looking up.

"Dead, eh? H-m-m. Where all the men?"

Here she made no answer.

Quinlin ventured:

"Looking for me, I'll bet—eh?"

Her bony fingers moved faster, but she lowered her head and made no answer.

Quinlin laid one of his guns on the table where it would be handy and finished his pipe in silence. The squaw, he guessed, would not speak. She had upheld the tradition of the trail by sheltering him from the storm. That done, she was under no obligation. It is possible that if the opportunity presented itself she might be inclined to drive a knife between his shoulder blades. Quinlin knew Indians.

He helped himself to more tea, inspected his feet for signs of gangrene, found none, and prepared to leave. He thanked the squaw for her service, pulled on his mittens and pushed out once again into the storm. The wind was blowing itself out. The snow was less dense now and fell at a steady pace.

Quinlin plowed along until he found himself standing in front of the big trade store. He listened at the door—heard no sounds. He lifted the latch cautiously, then swung open the door and leaped in. The place was deserted. The store-room door had been battered down and lay in pieces on the floor. He looked in the living quarters in the rear. Deserted, too. No fires in the stoves.

"The whole bunch are on our trail," Quinlin mused. "Which means trouble ahead."

From the stock he took a new pack-sack, loaded it with provisions, crammed his pockets full of cartridges and added to his armament a new .303 British rifle.

"There may be some long range work," he reasoned.

CHAPTER XV

SIEGE

ON THE way out he skirted the settlement, keeping to the woods, and headed for the shaggy hills that lifted themselves to the sky in the north. The snow continued to thin out, and when he left the settlement behind not a flake fell from the clouds.

But he foresaw a still, bitter cold that would gnaw the bone right to the marrow. Somewhere in the white wastes were two women in jeopardy, and with them two men who would fight to the death.

And somewhere else was the redoubtable Jerry Plate whom the sergeant had left alone on the mountain top in charge of five prisoners. There was no telling what had happened or was happening to any of them.

Quinlin kept to the timber, avoiding the open trail. The day was becoming crystal clear and he might be seen by the enemy. Too many lives were in danger for him to take a chance. He passed the little shack where first he had been held prisoner, and some inner instinct prompted him to turn off and look it over. He found it locked from the outside.

But a voice called:

"Dam' yer t''ell, if yer don't open the door an' unhook me I'll do murder when I *do* get free! An' I will, mind!"

Quinlin's heart beat faster. It was the familiar voice of Jerry Plate.

"Jerry! God bless you, Jerry, it's Pat here!" the sergeant yelled.

"Pat! You, Pat! Well, blow that lousey lock off an' onhook me."

It took four shots to shatter the lock, and the sergeant rushed in and found Jerry tied hand and foot and almost freezing to death.

Jerry was saying:

"I feel ashamed, Pat. The beggars tricked me. That big Injun, Long Jim—a sly fox. I'm squattin' b' the fire an' he's squattin' on t' other side an' all of a once he shoots out his foot an' it rains hot coals on me."

"An old trick of his, Jerry," said Quinlin as he helped the old sourdough up. "Played it on me also. And they brought you here and skint out, eh? H-m-m. And then they went to the tradehouse and freed Bellamy and his bunch. Yep. It works out that way."

"What?" asked Jerry.

"No time to explain. Here, chew on this chunk of bannock and limber up your muscles at the same time. No time to lose."

TEN MINUTES later Jerry was strapping on a pair of dilapidated snow-shoes he found in the shack. Side by side he and the sergeant struck out, with Jerry packing the latter's extra revolver. Steadily they worked up into higher country, and towards evening they heard shots somewhere in the wilderness before them.

"The parties have met," remarked Quinlin. "As I figure, Jerry, there are about twenty-five or thirty cut-throats against two men and two women." With this he gave a brief explanation of the case of Hell-bent Jackson. Then— "The outlook is pretty rotten. Stretch your legs, old boy!"

Reaching the summit, they found the timber stunted but thick, with all about matted windfalls that hindered their progress. They heard more shots— nearer this time. They began going down hill, and then in the growing dusk Quinlin spotted a cabin way down in the bottom of the ravine. Jets of flame were spurting from the window. Men were moving about in the bush down there and shooting at the window.

"The whole gang is there," observed Quinlin.

Jerry spat out tobacco juice and flipped his revolver in the air.

"The show is on, Pat. I'm ripe for anyt'ing. Let's horn in."

Creeping from tree to tree, crawling through bushes, they crept down towards the ravine. The moon came up early and shone with a pale, silvery radiance upon the virgin snow. Countless stars were in a cold blue sky; not many clouds were afield.

From their vantage point Quinlin and Jerry could see the dark shapes of the attackers edging closer to the little cabin. Shots barked loud and clear and echoed far off in the ravine.

While the sergeant was intently watching the maneuvers, Jerry lay down on the snow, laid the barrel of his long revolver across his left arm and fired the first shot. One of the dark figures seemed to sit down peacefully enough, but the next moment he rolled over side-wise. There was a stir in the ranks of the outlaws.

At that instant a burst of flame came from the cabin and another figure pitched to the snow. Jerry spat, took careful aim and let go another slug. It hit its mark and put another fellow out of business.

"Hate t' go wastin' shots," the old sourdough drawled.

A volley was returned but all the shots went wild.

"Now," suggested Quinlin, "let's change our position."

They crawled thirty yards to one side, advanced a little farther into the ravine and stopped behind a twisted heap of fallen trees. A fresh volley broke out from the cabin and drove the outlaws back some few yards. A group left the main party and began worming up the slope in search of their new adversaries.

Quinlin said, "Let's keep moving around and down until we flank the main body. We must keep them guessing."

Cautiously, on hands and knees, they continued working in an arc until they reached a point on the outlaws' flank. This main party was again creeping up on the cabin and for a few minutes there was a warm exchange of shots between it and the defenders of the cabin.

Quinlin and Jerry joined in and the attack from this new quarter was so unexpected that three of the outlaws went down before the others realized the situation and flung themselves back in mad haste.

The group that had started out in search of Jerry and the sergeant found them out by the gun flashes and swooped down in that direction. Quinlin heard them coming, crouched lower in the bush and picked the leader off as he leaped over a fallen tree. Jerry followed up with two fast shots that caught the next fellow in the same act and dropped him like a log.

Some in the main party were now directing shots in the sergeant's direction, and this volley drove him and Jerry farther down into the ravine while they still kept picking off the fellows in the other group, until but two remained out of six. These two gave up the cause and dashed back to the main attack.

"Hit?" Quinlin flung at Jerry as he reloaded his rifle.

"One bounced off m' head an' I feel a stingin' in m' left calf. On'y flesh cuts though. You hit?"

"Scratched on the right thigh; that's all."

The next move showed that neither of them was lacking in nerve. Side by side they began forcing the fight, advancing on the outlaws and keeping up a steady fire as they crawled ahead under the bushes, with lead whining past their ears and kicking up the snow in their faces. Those in the cabin increased their fire, too, and the night was wild with gunfire and yells.

The outlaws began to break and scatter, and in their mad confusion they afforded easy targets. Through a rift in the foliage Quinlin caught sight of a tall man in a long fur coat. He paused with his finger on the trigger, for under the white moonlight he recognized Père La Bau, and the missioner had a smoking rifle in his hands. The next instant he was lost to sight.

Then the cabin door opened and Carlin and Hell-bent Jackson burst out in pursuit. Quinlin and Jerry straightened up and went along with great leaps. The four joined, shouted greetings and proceeded after the fleeing outlaws.

Jerry was the first to catch up with the rear guard and Hell-bent Jackson was a few steps behind him. Quinlin and Carlin came up on either side and for a moment there was some fast and furious gun talk. Jackson went down, cursed at the top of his voice and heaved up to his feet again.

Carlin and Bellamy were at each other with clubbed rifles, and Jerry and the Indian Long Jim had thrown aside their guns and were doing some clever knife work. Quinlin had caught sight of Père La Bau again and was running him down. The missioner suddenly stopped, whirled and fired point-blank. The slug whanged by the sergeant's face and clipped off part of his beard. The next moment he was upon the missioner and knocked aside his gun as it boomed a second time.

CHAPTER XVI

SHOWDOWN

"**D**ROP THAT gun!" snarled the sergeant.

They closed, and as they did Quinlin realized he had a powerful man to deal with. If he was in doubt when they began he was positive when the man broke and sent him reeling against a tree with a terrific crack on the jaw; then quickly removed his cumbersome fur coat and charged again. There were no black robes now. He was in rough woolens, and a cruel, twisted leer was on his face.

Quinlin ducked a hard-driven right and drove two fast jolts to the man's abdomen. He received a glancing blow on the cheek that almost snapped his head off, caught a follow-up square on the other cheek and ground his teeth in pain. For a moment he lashed out wildly until his head cleared, then lurched back, stopped abruptly and met the next rush without moving an inch.

He broke under the man's guard and beat a tattoo on his ribs until the latter clinched and then hurled himself away. Quinlin went after him and knocked his head back and forth with two lefts and two rights that hit square on all tries. Then they closed, crashed to the snow and rolled down the incline to where Carlin was telling Bellamy to get up so that he could knock him down again. By some trick of his trade as an all-around brawler, Jerry had disarmed the Indian and was backing him against a tree. Jackson sat on a stump, doubled up and groaning.

Quinlin and La Bau brought up with a thud against a tree and as they struggled to their feet the sergeant freed his right and whipped it to La Bau's jaw with such steam behind it that the latter's head snapped back, cracked against the tree and the man dropped without a sound.

Bellamy was out. Carlin was snapping handcuffs on Long Jim's wrists.

"Pat, I just *knew* you'd come," he cried. "We were in a rummy situation down there. The rest of the gang cleared out, but we'd better get down to the cabin. Jerry's cut up a bit and Jackson says he's passing out. God, that man is a fighter and a reckless devil."

"How are the women?" Quinlin asked.

"Shaken up, Pat. Rose has been calling us all kinds of cowards for letting you stay to give us a start. And Marie—"

"I can guess the rest, Lee," cut in Quinlin jocularly. "But let's trot these birds down there."

Carlin walked Long Jim down at the point of his gun and Jerry unceremoniously grabbed La Bau and Bellamy by the feet and hauled them along sled-fashion. Quinlin picked up the broken, shattered man who called himself Hellbent Jackson.

"Pretty bad, Jackson?" he asked as he carried him down.

"Yeah, s-serge. Bound out, I reek-reckon. Can't get... m'dam' breath. Figure I'm carryin' eight slugs now, not—not countin' 'em as went clean t'rough. Purty—purty tough f'r a man t' carry eight slugs, serge... not countin' 'em as went clean t'rough, y'understand."

"You'll be all right," Quinlin said, and he knew in his own heart he was lying.

"No, serge. M' innards is gittin' all mixed up wit' each other. C'n feel it. An', Serge, Rose loves you, she does. You... must believe her... Serge."

WHEN THEY reached the cabin Quinlin laid Jackson tenderly on a bed of wolf skins. Rose was at his elbow, her eyes big and moist.

"Pat, you—you won through," she half whispered.

"Yes, Rose, dear, because I saw you loved me." And he lifted her chin and kissed her.

"Hur—Hurray f'r... the Serge!" jerked out Jackson, smiling even while he was dying.

Bellamy and La Bau had come back to consciousness. Carlin stood over them with his gun while Jerry made life miserable for the Indian Long Jim. Quinlin left Rose and confronted the two white men.

"One of you two is the ringleader—the Master," he said crisply. "Which one?"

Bellamy moistened his lips and looked at La Bau. The latter drew a finger tip across his lower lip meditatively and regarded the sergeant obliquely:

"Well," he began, "I am called The Master."

"You—a missioner—a Jesuit!" exclaimed Quinlin.

La Bau chuckled cynically.

"Merely for effect—the robes and that stuff. I never dealt

directly with my men. Bellamy, here, was my lieutenant. He gave out orders and said they were from The Master. None of the men really knew who The Master was, except Bellamy, Long Jim and the women. And the role of missioner? Merely a whim—and then it brought in contributions from transient trappers for a proposed mission house—which never was to be built."

"You cur!" rasped out the sergeant; then leaned closer and asked, "And what do you know about the killing of Ben Tobin?"

La Bau gave a hollow chuckle and shook his head negatively.

"He lies!" cut in Rose.

"Eh?" jerked Quinlin.

"He lies!" she repeated. "He engineered the whole thing. One night a man came in from the outside to escape the law. He was a professional killer and he told a story about a man named Mr. Tobin who kept a lot of money in his cabin. Said he was going to get Mr. Tobin after a while. Bellamy pumped him, found out where the old man lived and then a few nights later one of the Indians put the informer out of the way.

"La Bau wanted me to go and find out just where Mr. Tobin hid the money. I refused, even though he called himself my foster father. Then he said he'd give Marie to Bellamy if I didn't do as he told me.

"Marie is the daughter of a Doctor Wallace who came through here twelve years back with his wife in an effort to teach the Indians sanitary conditions. They died themselves during that same winter and Marie was left with an Indian woman who later became La Bau's servant.

"I love Marie with all my heart, so to save her from Bellamy, whom she despised, I set out with Long Jim. La Bau never let me go far alone, for fear I'd run away, and he always kept Marie under watch, for he must have known I wouldn't leave her. Hence Long Jim's company.

"I had no plans. But I was bound to save Marie at all costs.

I found the old man home, and when he saw me I thought he'd gone mad. He got a picture from a wallet and studied it and me. He asked me who I was. I said just Rose. Then he threw his arms around me and cried, 'Oh, God, I've found my dear one!' *I had found my father!* He said La Bau had run off with my mother when she was eighteen and I was two. I never knew. Mother died young. La Bau never told me.

"I wanted to stay with my father. He wanted me to stay. But there was Marie to think of. I said I had to go back. I told him why they had sent me and he told me where the money was hidden, and I swore I'd never tell.

"Then Long Jim, who had been waiting outside, came in and I told him to get out. He laughed and came forward toward father and I drew my knife—the only weapon I had at the moment—and threatened him with it. He wrested it from me, and as father ran to the wall for his rifle, Long Jim flung the knife and it caught father in the back."

The sergeant raised his hand and turned to the Indian.

"Do you hear that, Long Jim?"

An animal snarl grated in the Indian's throat and his eyes stared hard at the floor.

"And Rose is Tobin's daughter?" Quinlin swung on La Bau.

"Has she not said so, monsieur?"

"Ah-r-r, you beast!"

And Rose went on—

"I can't understand how I ever pulled the knife out, but I did and dragged father to the bunk. He died feeling my hair, which he said is like my mother's. Long Jim was hunting high and low for the money. He couldn't find it and he attacked me. I hit him with a stool and ran out.

"I ran back with a gun, but he had barred the door. Then I drove off and left him probably hunting for the money. I wanted to kill him, but after thinking a while I knew it would put La Bau in a rage and he would give Marie to Bellamy. I resolved not to let on that I had found my father."

Hell-bent Jackson was struggling for words.

"Serge, she didn't even—even tell me... best friend. I'd tagged behind Rose an'—an' Jim. Didn't trust that Injun. But I busted... snowshoe... stopped t' fix it... they got way ahead. Met Rose comin' back alone all skeered... asked her... wouldn't tell. So I goes an' looks f'r un'self. An' I finds a Mounty feedin' his dogs an' hears noise in the cabin.

"I scrapes a bit o' snow off the winder an' sees another Mounty an' he's holdin' up a knife I knew belonged to—to Rose... there. So I sneaks around, leans over an' cracks Carlin on the bean wit' m' rifle, takes a careful shot at the serge an' puts him t' sleep.... Knife on the table.... Oh, Serge, I can't talk no more. S'long, Serge. S'long, Rose... like yer hair... all gold...."

CHAPTER XVII

VICTORY!

"LEE," **SAID** Quinlin to the constable, "it fits in with your story. Hard man, Jackson, and he's just died hard. Twelve wounds."

He turned back to Rose.

"But, my dear girl, why didn't you reveal all this at first?"

"I couldn't. I didn't dare. Long Jim warned me on the trail when he brought you into my camp. He said I was to say nothing—said I should remember Marie was a pawn in The Master's hand and her fate rested on my silence.

"It was hard to give in to the killer of my father. But there was Marie. I tried to be patient, resolving that some day he and La Bau would pay. And I knew that some day La Bau would want me. He was just holding off, playing with me like a cat. You—you can't imagine....!"

"I can," murmured Quinlin in a hushed voice; and then he turned on La Bau. "You heard all of that, La Bau. God help you at the hands of a jury! And Long Jim didn't find the money—eh?—after killing old Tobin."

"Evidently, no," purred La Bau. "There is, Sergeant, no blood on my hands. I did not order Long Jim to kill Tobin. I—"

A horrible snarl rattled from the Indian's throat. He whirled on The Master, and, though manacled, clamped his grotesque hands around La Bau's throat and bore him back against the floor.

"Lie!" he roared. "You tell me kill Tobin if him show fight."

Quinlin and Carlin flung themselves upon the Indian and tried to tear him loose. But Long Jim was raving mad, and the blows they struck seemed only to increase his fury. Finally his effort slowed down and at last he sank down on The Master with a chilling rattle in his throat.

Quinlin rolled him off and found a knife sticking in his chest. The hilt was still grasped in La Bau's dead hand. He had pressed it up into the Indian even while the latter was choking him to death.

"Well," mused Quinlin, "so Long Jim killed Tobin. It took us an awful long time to find it out."

"It was kinder roundabout," put in Jerry. "But then it led t' the findin' o' Defiance Valley. Pat, they ought t' make you 'n inspector f'r this haul. Bellamy, here, is still alive, an' we'll see he stays that way. It'll make a better case in court if you got at least one o' the ringleaders."

WHEN THEY drove back into Defiance Valley a day later the place was deserted. The cabin doors swung open in the wind and the cabins themselves were empty and bare. The big trade house had been cleaned of everything but the stove and the rough furniture.

Trails led away in all directions, made by those who had fled the country and taken with them as much as they could carry. Not even a dog remained.

Defiance Valley was dead. The Master was dead. Long Jim and many others were dead. And so was Hell-bent Jackson, who died fighting for a woman who once had nursed him through the scurvy.

Quinlin and Rose were standing in front of the trade house.

Quinlin was saying, "And not even Jackson knew that La Bau was not a missioner but in reality The Master?"

"No, Pat. Jackson often told me he hailed from the States, where he had done a bit of killing. And he had been in the Klondike. He served under Bellamy and the unknown Master like the rest of them, but he always took it upon himself to watch over me. Bellamy used to plead with me to get Marie to live with him, and that night you came he actually attacked me because I refused, as usual."

"Yes, Rose, under the rough Jackson was a knight. He believed you in spite of all the evidence against you. And I—I didn't, Rose."

"It's the way of the Scarlet, Pat. You would have broken all its grand traditions by doing otherwise. And I love you for it—and for your courage—and for you, Pat."

"I loved you, my Rose, from the first. Was always thinking about you—your eyes—your kiss—your golden hair."

Here he paused and took out his journal, flipped back the pages and drew out the single strand of hair upon which he had believed a woman's destiny hung. He raised it and let it be snatched away by the wind.

"We'll leave it here, Rose, in Defiance Valley," he said. "For why should I hang on to one when I have a whole head of them now?"

"Oh, Pat—!"

"And, Rose darling, when my term is up this year we'll go down into the Shamattawa country and establish a trading post. 'Tis a great country, Rose; strong woods, much trade, and not so far from God's Lake, where each year there is the greatest Christmas celebration on the frontier. And, Rose, you'll be loving me always?"

"Always, Pat," she whispered, and nestled in his arms.

Had they looked around the corner they would have seen Carlin and Marie in each other's arms.

While inside the trade house the redoubtable Jerry Plate chewed tobacco and spat copiously into the wood-box, explaining to the morose Bellamy the danger of playing with dynamite, fire and men who wear scarlet coats.

" 'S bad business, mister. Them fellers is harder t' kill 'an anyt'ing I know. O' course, if you *do* kill one, why, your goose is cooked f'r sure. Might just as well walk t' the nearest post an' give up. Me, I'd a sight ruther fool around wit' dynamite 'an a Mounty."

"Oh, go t' hell!" exploded Bellamy.

"Not yet. I'm goin' right wit' Sergeant Pat. I'm goin' t' start buildin' his tradin' post in the Shamattawa country, so's him an' the wife—which she'll be 'fore long—c'n move right in when Patrick leaves the Force."

ON THE way out the sergeant stopped at the cabin in which old Ben Tobin had died. He lowered the frozen body from the tree and placed it on the sled. Rose wanted to be near her father's grave. And while Quinlin did this, Rose pried out one of the great stones that formed the fireplace and from the hole pulled a moosehide pouch packed with her father's hoarded wealth. It was his dying wish that she should takes it.

Today, if you will go to the end of steel on the Hudson's Bay Road, and from there work southeastward by river, lake and portage, you will come to a river that the Indians call Shamattawa. It is a country of majestic pine and spruce, where in the summer the flowers bloom in great profusion and the star-gemmed nights are cool and haunting.

Near the river you may come upon a large trading station and on the main building see a sign bearing the legend:

SHAMATTAWA TRADING COMPANY, LTD.,
QUINLIN, CARLIN & PLATE.

TRAIL TALES OF THE NORTH:

THE FREIGHT OF HONOR

I REMEMBER that night well. Cold, it was, with a sharp wind beating a rat-a-tat in the spruce scrub as it pounded in across the freezing lake. We sat bundled in our blankets around the fire; three of us, "Free-trade" Jim, Ramblin' Dad, and myself.

Jim was what his name implied: a free-trader with a line of traps running up in the Churchill River Country. Ramblin' Dad had another name, but Jim dubbed him Ramblin' Dad, and I thought the sobriquet quite appropriate.

Old he was, gnarled and twisted, but tough as hickory. He had poked around every place in Canada worth the poking. Long years of lonely campfire nights had made of him a gifted story teller.

No, he was not a success, just a drifter, a ramblin' old man, and, strange to say, a champion of the red man, though he had fought against Louis Riel in the Rebellion and was wounded at Cut Knife in the old, bold days.

Somehow or other we got into an argument. I believe I started it. Apropos of nothing, I passed a remark about having part of my outfit swiped by an Indian who had packed some of my stuff through big timber.

When I disengaged the Indian, I left my stuff near the river, intending to camp there, and paid a visit to the trading store. When I returned I found a frying pan missing, also a new four-point blanket and a pair of mittens. Of course, the Indian had flown too.

"Wal," drawled Ramblin' Dad, and paused a whole minute to get control of his chew, "Injuns have a habit o' doin' that ef you don't impress it on 'em t' leave the stuff alone. Had the same thing done on me, but you got t' understand the Injun afore you c'n go for t' criticise him. They's on'y one Injun in Canady wuth talkin' about, an' that is the Cree. Dog-Ribs ain't wo'th their salt, so far as that goes. But the Cree is mighty good, lemme tell you.

"The white man has learned the Cree to steal. It's kinder borned in a Cree t' pinch somepin' nor other on a white man fust chance he gits. It's kinder handed down, you might say, from his forefathers, 'cause in the old days they was a heap o' white scum up in the Territories, thievin' an' cheatin' an' robbin' the Cree right under his nose.

"Wal, a'ter a while Mr. Cree got on t' this monkey business, an' a'ter that, wal, it's jest tit for tat, kinder speakin'. The sons up an' learned it from their fathers, an' their son's sons up an' learned it from 'em. So, Mr. Writer Feller, you got t' take sech things inter consideration afore you go shootin' off about damn thievin' red men. I ain't no story writer, but, jus' the same, mebbe I understand a heap more about the Injun 'an you fellers think you do—no hard feelin's, now, mind you.

"Jest you go an' put an' Injun on his honor an' on his honor he'll stick come hell an' high water. I got a good example t' prove thet what I say ain't all cheap talk."

I told him I'd like to hear it. He shifted his chew to the other side of his mouth, spat copiously into the fire, and leaned farther back into his robes. Jim got up, swore at the rising wind, and piled more wood on the fire. Then he sat down and stuffed his pipe with my H.B.C. cut-plug.

Ramblin' Dad went on:

"This thing happened way up t' the north'ard, in the Etawney lake country, where they's some o' the finest Crees in the country.

Mebbe it was ten year ago—can't remember prezactly—but nemmine that. I was kinder down on m' luck an' workin' a twelve mile trap line wit' hopes of mebbe cleanin' up enough t' hold me through the summer.

"They was a big famine up that way that year an' more snow an' cold 'an I ever seen or ever hope to. I was livin' in an' old shack that was so full o' holes I had t' wet the walls an' ceilin' so's they'd freeze shut. Heap o' wolves in the country, too, lean shanked fellers jest achin' t' gobble me up.

"Wal, they didn' get me, but somehow nor other the damn beggars busted into m' shack when I was out on the line an' cleaned me plumb outer grub. Yes, sir, when I got home the skin winder was torn out an' the place was a danged mess, wit' not a single crumb o' grub left. You c'n imagine, o' course, how I felt, me a hun'red miles from the nearest post; an' mebbe I didn' call them there wolves some purty names.

"I tried huntin', but as I says, a famine was in the land, they was a storm ev'ry other day, wit' the spirit thermometer way down lower 'an what I calls cheerful, an' me wit' a touch o' liver t' boot. At last, seein' no hope, I closed up the shack an' started t' mush f'r the post, bein' wit' out food two days when I started.

"Sure 'nough, fust day out a blizzard hauls off an' slams down from the Bay, an' when it blows over I'm plumb tuckered out. Come a'ternoon an' I'm lookin' f'r a nice place t' drop down an' cash in m' checks, when I see a sled outfit plowin' across the lake wit' a man staggerin' along in the lead.

"**WHEN I** meet him I find he's an Injun, an Etawney Lake Cree. Fust thing I asks f'r is a hunk o' bannock, but the Cree shakes his head an' says he ain't had nothin' t' eat hisself in four days. Wal, I says we're both in the same boat kinder. Then he says he's bound f'r a good camp that's nearer 'an the post an' I should tag along an' ride on the sled if I want.

"I didn't pile on the sled then, but I joined up wit' him, because, as some wise feller once said, misery likes com'ny. We run into bad weather next day ag'in, an' both of us made a man trace an' pulled wit' the dogs. Boys, you ain't got no idea a-tall how that there blizzard whooped down from the Baffin ice fields an' belted us, me an' the Cree an' the dogs, all over the place.

"It was plumb hell, I tell you. Our parkas was nothin' but two overcoats o' ice stiffer 'an pine board, an' the ice formed around m' eyes an' nose so thick that I couldn't hardly see or breathe. Purty soon I flopped down, got up an' tried to haul some more, but these here legs o' mine seemed plumb daid, an' down I went ag'in.

"Wal, the Cree, not any too good hisself, heaved me on the sled an' hauled wit' the dogs hisself. But a'ter a while I found I couldn't lay on the sled atall account o' freezin'. So I tumbled off, got t' m' feet an' stumbled along, though unable t' take a hand on the trace. Most times I had t' hang on t' the gee-bar f'r support.

"An' that night, damme, I got the su'prise o' my life. I found that all along there was a sled-load o' grub. Yes, sir, the sled was packed wit' flour an' beans an' bacon a-plenty. The wind was screamin', an' I tried to ask the Cree why the hell he'd kept this mum. Reckon he couldn' hear me, an' I took it into m' head to rip off the caribou-hide wrapper an' help m'self.

"But when I started this the Cree chucked me aside an' through the cloud o' snow an' wind I could see he had a gun on me. It was no use argyin'. Wit' all the noise o' the storm I couldn't hear m'self think. But he kept the gun on me, an' sat on the sled all that night keepin' the gun on me.

'An' him, mind, half starved hisself.' I got right ornery over it, but he held the drop on me, an' next day, wit' the storm still hell-bent, he made me mush ahead o' him, takin' m' gun at the same time. Purty soon, though, I couldn't walk or even crawl, an' kept topplin' over every couple yards. The Cree, mind, instead o' chuckin' me aside or puttin' me on the sled, heaved me over his shoulder an' hung on t' the gee-bar, half caved-in like he was.

"Wal, come late a'ternoon an' he's on his knees more 'an he's on his feet, but he still hung t' me like I was wuth somepin', an' I could see he was gettin' weaker an' weaker. I got often his back, then, an' both of us took t' crawlin' an' pullin' wit' the dogs, makin' about a mile in two hours. M' innards must 'a' all gone wrong, though, 'cause purty soon I jest rolled up in a ball an' went t' sleep.

"The Cree must 'a' trucked me into camp, 'cause I just opened m' eyes as the factor of a sub-station was takin' me off the Injun's shoulders. An' then the Injun caved in.

"Now, lemme tell you sompin', young writer feller, about the honor of a Cree. That there Cree was sent wit' that sled o' provisions from the main post to this here li'l sub-station I been speakin' about. The factor at the main post told him point-blank that them provisions was for a station hard-hit, an' that under no circumstances which somever should he touch 'em. The Cree swore he wouldn't touch 'em.

"An' he didn't! Holed up by a gale, his own supply ran out. The station grub was there, but the Cree had swored he wouldn't touch. *He went wit'out grub eight days an' I had t' go wit'out it, an' all the time it was there on the sled jest f'r the takin'.*

"Now, young feller, c'n you tell me o' one instance where a white man has stood a test o' honor to his word like that?"

Well, I might have brought a few instances to mind, but I didn't. From that night I haven't judged the Indian so harshly. And I have a good friend in Ramblin' Dad, wherever he may be today.

THE BLACK FOX SKIN

BAFFIN LAND—
ESKIMO WIT AND
THE SUNNY TRAIL OF
ARCTIC ROMANCE.

FEBRUARY IS a windy, messy month in Baffin Land. The northeasters pound in from Baffin Bay almost continuously. They gouge out the sand bars in the fjords and inlets and in places the ice pans look like vast stretches of sand paper.

These winds are so strong that they can spin an Eskimo *komatik* (sledge) around like a top; they can knock over a good sized dog and make a man swear a cobalt-blue streak, what with the dogs falling over each other and tangling the traces.

Young Peneloo had come up the Pangnirtung valley from Pangnirtung against strong headwinds on a rugged, ice-hummocked trail. He blew into the little settlement at Merchant Bay at the tail-end of a blizzard, with his dogs fagged out and himself half-frozen and half-gone.

He had done a bit of bartering in the lonely post at Cumberland Sound, and his *komatik* was heavily laden with trade goods for the men of the settlement, whose business he had transacted there.

He stumbled into the igloo of his brother, Mikah, who attended to him and in short time Peneloo, strongest of all the young men of Merchant Bay, sat back in his caribou robes and smoked his pipe with an air of supreme satisfaction.

"And how is Tilcoon?" he inquired at length, in Eskimo.

Mikah rubbed his fat nose and regarded the bowl of his pipe for a long-minute.

"Tilcoon is well, Peneloo," he returned vaguely.

Peneloo gave his brother a sidelong-glance.

Finally—"I do not like your tone, Mikah," he said. "Is there something the matter with my beloved?" He threw off his robes. "I shall see," he stated simply.

Mikah raised a restraining hand.

"Sit down, Peneloo," he recommended. "There is rumor—"

He hesitated, screwing his finger in the bowl of his pipe.

"Yes, Mikah?"

"There is rumor, my brother, that Ivahluk, the son of Ahlaveetah, is seeking the hand of Tilcoon."

Peneloo's immobile face showed no hint of emotion. But inwardly there was a faint stir, an insidious gnawing at his heart-strings. He was poor—this young Peneloo. The previous spring and summer he had lain ill in his *tupik* and young Tilcoon had nursed him.

He had not been able to contribute his amount of sealskins to the mighty Ahlaveetah, headman of the settlement and father of Ivahluk, who Mikah said was seeking the hand of Peneloo's beloved, the beautiful Tilcoon.

At length he said in a colorless voice:

"And Tilcoon?"

"The ways of women are strange, my brother," philosophized Mikah. "She has done some walking with Ivahluk and watched him hunting the seals on the ice pans. But I do not know how she feels about it."

"I shall speak to Tilcoon," Peneloo said after a moment.

He remained in his igloo all that afternoon, smoking his pipe in silence. In the evening, under the cold sheen of a new moon, he drew his sealskin *netsik* about his strong young body and headed for the igloo of Tilcoon, who lived with her brother and mother.

He paused just outside the entrance, knelt and looked into the interior. He saw Tilcoon and Ivahluk sitting side by side, conversing in low tones and apparently wrapped up in each other. Peneloo looked away, blinked his eyes and twitched his lips. After a moment he rose and quietly stole back to his own igloo.

"Mikah, my brother, I leave at dawn for the ice fields," he said in a quick, unnatural voice.

"And why?" Mikah asked with an oblique glance.

"To hunt the seal and the *oo-jouk*."

"But it is not yet time, my brother," remonstrated Mikah.

Peneloo said:

"But I go, Mikah."

Mikah regarded his brother for a long, silent minute, then nodded his head slowly after the manner of the wise. No doubt he divined that some turmoil in Peneloo's heart was driving him away from the settlement to the bitter, wind-ridden reaches of the ice fields. This—and *not* the call of the seals.

BREAK OF dawn found Peneloo busy over his small *komatik*, lining up his seven dogs, each of which was attached to the sledge by an individual trace—Eskimo fashion. Mikah stood aside and puffed his pipe in a stolid silence.

"I am ready, Mikah," Peneloo announced at last, and they shook.

His long walrus hide whip snaked out and ended with a sharp report.

"Hoo-eet!" he called, and the dogs strained in the traces and started off.

"Ouk! Ouk!" he yelled a moment later, and the team swung to the right and headed for the open bay.

He circled the settlement and soon left it behind. He ran at a steady, tireless pace beside his *komatik* round a promontory and began to hug the eastern coastline of Baffin Island, heading due north.

To the east stretched the illimitable vastness of ice and dead sky, with here and there on the frozen surface dark lines that were leads. To the west, inland, grim and craggy headlands soared heavenward in cold, silent majesty.

At the same even pace he traveled five miles, six, seven. The temperature rose, and by and by he was running with his *netsik* open, perspiring freely. At noon he stopped in the lee of an ice-hummock for his meagre meal.

Gazing backward across the great sweep of bare ice he saw a dark, moving speck. It grew larger and, curious, Peneloo waited an hour and then another, until he made out the figure as that of Tilcoon. With a sudden beating of his heart he left his outfit and loped toward her, unable to think clearly for some minutes.

They drew up before each other and Tilcoon, bowing her head, remained motionless and silent.

After an interlude of silence Peneloo ventured—

"Why do you come, Tilcoon?"

"Because I love you, Peneloo," was the quick, breathless rejoiner.

Peneloo thought over this for a minute. "You do not love Ivahluk?" he asked tentatively.

"I love only you, Peneloo."

"But you walked with Ivahluk. Last night Ivahluk sat with you in your mother's igloo and you seemed pleased."

"Ivahluk is the son of Ahlaveetah," replied Tilcoon. "Ahlaveetah is all-powerful. It is not good to offend the son of the all-powerful one. I do not care for Ivahluk. I love—only you—my Peneloo."

"Then I may speak to the great Ahlaveetah about our marriage?"

Tilcoon nodded.

"I love you, Peneloo."

Peneloo lost no time in back-trailing. His heart sang. Tilcoon ran beside him, tireless as he, a fit mate for so noteworthy a hunter as young Peneloo. The cold stars were beginning to gem the gloom when they drove into the settlement.

They went straight to the big igloo of Ahlaveetah and found audience after an hour's waiting. Ahlaveetah was an ancient man, with a cavernous face, tiny, inscrutable eyes and a slash of a mouth that clamped between the thin lips a greasy pipe. Peneloo bowed.

"I would wed Tilcoon before the spring hunt on the ice fields," he began. "I love Tilcoon and Tilcoon loves me."

Not a muscle twitched in the blanched old face. Ahlaveetah puffed his pipe slowly and studiously, then removed it from his mouth and ran a hand across his lips.

"Before the spring hunt?" he asked in a toneless hollow voice.

"Before the spring hunt," reiterated Peneloo.

Ahlaveetah took three more puffs and knocked the ashes from his pipe. His eyes settled on Tilcoon.

"Do you not know, Tilcoon, that Ivahluk loves you and has asked me to grant his marriage to you?" he asked.

Tilcoon was taken aback, but she batted not an eye. She only shook her head in slow negation.

" 'Tis true," said Ahlaveetah. And then to Peneloo: "Peneloo, my son, you are greatly in debt. Last spring you caught no seals. You caught nothing. It is doubtful whether this spring you will catch enough to clear you of debt. You should not consider marriage in your present state."

"But I love Tilcoon," persisted Peneloo. "I *will* catch enough this spring to pay you all and more."

"That is but idle talk, Peneloo," chuckled Ahlaveetah. "Ivahluk caught many seals last spring. He is as good a hunter as you, Peneloo. This spring he will catch more. He too loves Tilcoon and is more worthy of her."

Tilcoon, not wanting to offend the headman because she feared his wrath for both Peneloo's and her own sake, remained silent, although bitterness was in her heart. Peneloo boiled with silent, suppressed rage.

"I swear, Ahlaveetah," he said, "that I will pay my debt. I swear it!"

Ahlaveetah started to wave him away, but paused in mid-career and stroked his bony jaw. A crafty, steely light grew in his eyes. He settled back in his robes, stuffed his pipe and lighted it.

Presently he said:

"Peneloo, some there are who call you a great hunter. I believe Ivahluk is greater. I have a test. To-day Keechoo came in from a hard trail to the westward. He says there is a precious black fox some one hundred miles to the west and south, in the Penny Hills. He says he has never seen one like it.

"It eluded his rifle, and had he not been low in food Keechoo would have stayed many days and weeks to obtain it. But he had little food, and in the Penny Hills food is scarce.

"You and Ivahluk will go into the Penny Hills and bring back to me this marvelous black fox. The one that finds it and brings it to me, him will I consider the best, and to him will I grant Tilcoon.

"But, remember. *No rifle shall be used! No knife shall be used!* Trap the fox, then break its neck if it still lives when you find it. But no wound or bullet must mar the pelt!"

LATER THAT night Ivahluk and Peneloo sat before the headman in the igloo and Ahlaveetah again went over his proposition.

Outside, later, Ivahluk said to Peneloo:

"I shall win. Tilcoon will be mine."

"No; *I* shall win, Ivahluk," returned Peneloo. "Tilcoon *is* mine."

And still later Peneloo met Tilcoon in the shadow of her igloo.

"I love only you," she told him. "I will kill myself if I have to marry Ivahluk."

"Never fear, Tilcoon," Peneloo soothed. "Be the first to greet me when I bring back the black fox skin."

But as he plodded home to his igloo, Peneloo was not so sure that he would be the victor. He had but a few traps, and they were poor things at best, while Ivahluk had the pick of his father's collection. It was unfair to begin with, but Peneloo was not disheartened to the point of despair. He *must* win—for the sake of Tilcoon.

IVAHLUK LEFT an hour before Peneloo on the following morning, choosing his own route to the remote Penny Hills. Peneloo left with Tilcoon's warm words ringing in his ears and began the hundred mile trek over one of the bleakest, loneliest lands in the world.

With the wind at his back, he made good time all that day, and his dogs were in fine fettle when he began to enter rough, ragged country on the second day, entering into the first stages of the Penny Hills—gnarled, twisted mountains covered with ice and snow, where in the warm months waterfalls roared and boomed and streams rushed white and frothing to the polar seas.

But in winter it was a dead, white-and-gray land, all silent and gloom, with once in a while the far-away roar of a mighty glacier pitching into some rocky abyss.

Peneloo found bad going in the afternoon. The land was becoming a mass of jagged hummocks, and more than once the sledge turned over and the dogs, frightened, started brawl-ing amongst themselves. A sharp wind drove down and the loose, sugary snow spiraled about and cut Peneloo's face sharply.

Leaving his dogs at the foot of an ice bluff, he chopped footholds in the ice and ascended in this manner to the top, from which point of vantage he scanned the surrounding ter-ritory, looking for the landmarks that Keechoo had given Ivahluk and himself in order that they might locate the region where he had seen the fox.

He did not find these landmarks, but at nightfall he ran into Ivahluk and they both camped on the same spot. After the meal Ivahluk showed Peneloo the two five-foot fox traps that Ahlavee-tah had given him. Beauties, they were.

"It is unfair," said Peneloo.

"Are not my father's traps also mine?" chuckled Ivahluk.

"It is unfair," repeated Peneloo; then added, "But I shall catch this black fox if he is here in the Penny Hills."

Ivahluk laughed aloud—a taunting laugh—and chewed on his pipe stem in pleasant anticipation of his victory.

They parted before the dawn dusk.

Before starting, Peneloo melted snow and with this re-iced his *komatik* runners for the day's hard going. At ten rain began to fall; a thin, icy mist that before very long covered Peneloo's sealskin garments with a layer of ice.

In the afternoon the rain stopped, the temperature plum-meted and a bitter, slashing wind drove in from the east and knocked the outfit all over the trail. Peneloo could barely keep his footing. The dogs slipped on the icy ridges, fell, got mixed up in the traces and fought together on general principles.

Later on Peneloo sighted a short, blunt eminence, and at the foot of this was a long, narrow lake, with two islands in the center. Peneloo knew, then, that he was in the locality where Keechoo had seen the fox. He made his camp at the base of the bluff, and farther down the lake, on the opposite shore, he saw signs of Ivahluk's camp.

THE GRIM contest started in the morning. Peneloo baited and placed his own ancient traps, and besides this constructed a few snares and a deadfall. He spent the morning on his trapline, and on the way back to his camp passed Ivahluk and exchanged greetings.

"Very soon I shall possess the black fox—and then Tilcoon," called Ivahluk.

"The black fox will be mine," returned Peneloo and continued toward his camp.

Next day his heart thrilled. He caught sight of the black fox slinking between the ice-hummocks—a rare, precious animal. His hands gripped tighter the rifle he carried. He could have shot the fox, but Ahlaveetah would not have it so.

Later he saw the animal approaching one of Ivahluk's double-spring traps. He crouched down, tense, his heart throbbing, as the fox edged closer to the baited trap. He thought of jumping up and chasing the fox away, but honor was one of the things that made up his code.

The fox circled the trap warily. It approached the thing of steel, backed away, sniffed the snow, started to go away but returned again. It extended a tentative paw, drew back, and then looked about coyly. Chunks of ice lay near the trap, loosened possibly by Ivahluk's recent visit.

With a deft movement of the paw the fox flipped one of these chunks at the trap. The piece of ice hit the bait pan and the steel jaws snapped shut. The fox leaped in the air and spun around, disappearing in a flash. Five minutes later it slunk back, circled the sprung trap and finally robbed the bait.

Relieved of the awful tension, Peneloo returned joyfully to his camp. And on the tour of his own line he found every trap sprung and robbed of the bait. Ivahluk met him the next day. "Peneloo, that is a devil fox," he said. "It has robbed all my traps."

"And mine, too," rejoined Peneloo. "Twice I could have shot the fox, but we vowed before Ahlaveetah not to use gun or knife."

Indeed, the black fox seemed possessed of an uncanny knowledge. The deadfalls that Peneloo and Ivahluk built were soon destroyed. Day after day the traps were sprung and robbed.

The men were at their wit's end. Food was running low. One day Peneloo found wolf tracks, followed them and brought back to camp three dead wolves. These he divided with Ivahluk.

Ivahluk said, "The fox is possessed of some evil spirit, Peneloo. Let us return without it."

"And Tilcoon?"

"I will give up my claim for her, if it is you she loves."

Peneloo did not reply for several minutes. Finally— "Spoken like a true brother, Ivahluk. But I will not return until one of us has taken the fox. We know it is here. One of us *must* catch it."

"But food is low, Peneloo," persisted Ivahluk, "And what are traps to a devil-animal like that?"

"One of us must bring back the fox," Peneloo said with philosophic finality.

Next day Ivahluk took his rifle and, scouring the country, returned with two wolves, one of which he gave to Peneloo for dog-food. With nightfall a blizzard came; an unleashed, ranting maelstrom that howled and screamed along the crags and boomed through the chasms.

It blew holes in Peneloo's igloo and he was kept busy patching them up. The dogs could not find shelter and he piled them inside the igloo with himself. All that night the storm raged in high fury, and in the morning a white, echoing silence hung over the Penny Hills.

Peneloo had to dig himself out through the top of his igloo, so deeply was it buried under the new snow. When he made the rounds of his traps next day it was to find them sprung and robbed, as usual.

For a while afterwards he was half-inclined to accept Ivahluk's offer and return to Merchant Bay empty-handed. He sat in his igloo, smoking his pipe and trying to figure out some way of catching the fox without the use of gun, knife or trap.

He tried to remember chance meetings with clever white trappers farther south, where there was always talk of traps and furs; tried to remember if somewhere, sometime, he had heard of other methods of catching the precious black fox. But all without avail.

Where else had he met white men? There was the policeman in the red coat who two winters back had stopped at Merchant Bay on the way north to Kevetuk. Then there were two-other redcoats way up at Ponds Inlet, near Eclipse Sound. And some years back a sealing schooner had dropped anchor in Merchant Bay. Had the white men talked of traps then? No; they hadn't talked of traps at all. But....

Of a sudden Peneloo sat bolt upright. He had never moved so suddenly in all his life before. His eyes widened and stared eagerly at the snow as he recounted the visit of the white sealers. Then he got to his feet quickly.

"It may work," he whispered. "But I must wait until it is very cold out."

THE THREE days that followed were of normal temperature. Both Peneloo and Ivahluk hunted wolves and realized four between them. On the fourth day the temperature began to drop, and on the fifth it went very low, a still, bitter gnawing cold.

Peneloo met Ivahluk starting out for his morning tour.

"Ivahluk, I think I am going to catch the fox," he said.

"It is not possible," snapped Ivahluk, now grown sullen from lack of food.

"Perhaps by nightfall the fox will be mine," Peneloo observed as they parted.

He reached one of his traps, removed it from the peg and placed his hand-ax flat on the snow, fastening the handle to the peg. Over the flat steel side of the blade he spread a thin coating of grease, barely covering the surface. This done, he slung the trap over his shoulder and hid behind an ice hummock twenty yards back.

He waited there for three hours, almost numb with the cold. Presently there was a stir behind him and, looking around, he beheld Ivahluk.

"Traps robbed again," Ivahluk grunted, disconsolately.

Peneloo said, "Crouch here with me, Ivahluk, and perhaps you may see me trap the fox."

Ivahluk dropped down beside him and lighted his pipe. Silently they waited behind the hummock. And a little later both saw the fox slinking toward the spot where Peneloo had placed the ax.

Peneloo was crouched on his knees, ready at an instant to spring up. Ivahluk, perplexed, kept looking from the fox to his companion, wondering what it was all about.

"Remember, Peneloo; no bullet," he cautioned.

"No bullet," breathed Peneloo, his eyes riveted on the fox.

They saw the animal again kick pieces of ice at the mysterious object. But nothing snapped. After a while the fox edged closer and flicked it with its paw. Again no snap—no sound at all. The fox backed away, circled the thing and then worked closer to it again. Again the paw flashed out and nothing happened.

For a long minute the fox stood stock-still regarding the thing that would not jump as the other things had jumped. Then the paw went out again—slowly this time. It touched the thing, stayed there and still nothing happened.

Then the head went forward bit by bit, and the tongue came out.

Peneloo was tense. He watched the head go forward, saw the tongue go out, and tightened his leg muscles for a sudden leap. Then in a flash he was up and dashing across the snow. Ivahluk, still unable to understand it all, flung after him.

With mighty bounds Peneloo reached the spot where the fox was struggling frantically with the greased ax. He swung his clubbed rifle over his head, missed the fox and swung again.

This time the heavy stock came down just behind the animal's ear and broke its neck. In a moment it gasped to death.

"How?—" began Ivahluk, astounded.

Peneloo's heart was singing.

"Ivahluk, you must wish me luck," he said. "Tilcoon will be my wife."

He extended his hand, and Ivahluk grasped it.

"Yes, Peneloo. She loves only you," he answered. "But the fox...."

Peneloo said:

"Do you remember when the white man's ship came to our settlement?"

"Yes, Peneloo."

"There was one white man amongst them when we all feasted on the shore and they had a little box that made music. I remember it was very cold then. This one man dropped his knife on the snow when we sat down to eat. When the food was passed around he took a chunk of meat in his hand and looked for his knife to cut it.

"One of our brothers picked the knife up from the snow and handed it to the white man. Right away the white man cut off a piece of meat and when he put it in his mouth the ice-cold tip of the blade stuck to his tongue. It was very painful, and took some time to get loose. Do you remember that, Ivahluk?"

"Yes, Peneloo."

Peneloo bent down and turned the fox on its back.

"You see, Ivahluk," he explained, "I thought the same thing might work with the fox. I put just a little fat on the ax, and the ax was so cold the fox's tongue stuck to it long enough for me to kill him—without a knife—without a bullet."

"Peneloo," said Ivahluk, "you are a good hunter, and Tilcoon will find in you a good husband. Henceforth we shall not be rivals—but friends, Peneloo, my brother!"

And on that they shook.

TRAIL TALES OF THE NORTH:
LAW OF THE TRAPLINE

"POACHERS?" ECHOED Ramblin' Dad, holding a flaming splinter to his pipe.

The two of us were enjoying our after-supper pipes in a split-log trapping shack near Old Wife's Lake. Ramblin' Dad had hung his several pairs of socks over the red-hot "jerry" and was warming his bare feet in the ruddy, cheerful glow from the grate.

I was trying to mend a snowshoe I had broken that afternoon in a rotten bit of muskeg where our trapline ran. Not much of a trapper myself; just trying to make enough money, at the time, to get a few miles nearer home.

I'd asked Ramblin' Dad if he'd ever had any dealings with fur poachers during his more or less itinerant career in the land of the long cold.

"Poachers?" he repeated again, inhaling the fumes of the rankest tobacco I've ever seen a man smoke. "Yeah, some; not much, though. Y'see, it's a kinder law up this away f'r one man t' leave another man's traps be. I mind one case, howsomever, when I was hangin' around the Athabasca country, many's the year gone.

" 'Course, I've heard tell of others, at some place nor other, but this one here was the on'y one which in I was an int'rested party kinder."

He paused to get a better grip on his pipe and to scratch thoughtfully the heel of his left foot.

After a moment I prompted:

"You say you were an interested party?"

He stopped scratching his foot and nodding, spat into the wood-box.

"Yeah—kinder." His old eyes twinkled.

"Well?" I urged, laying aside my unfinished snowshoe to relight my pipe, and Ramblin' Dad went on.

" 'Twas over in the Athabasca country, in the good 'ld days, m' frien', when Athabasca Landin' was the gateway t' the Slave country, when Resolution was doin' the biggest trade of any post in all Canady, and when me, I was young, no more 'an thutty, and runnin' m' trapline 'tween La Biche an' Big White Fish. Naw, La Biche ain't what it useter be, m' frien', nor I ain't like I useter be, me wit' m' liver botherin' me now an' kinks comin' in m' knees.

"But, as I says, I was runnin' m' trapline outer La Biche, an' a purty wild young chum I was in them there days, allus ready to shake wit' a man an' allus ready t' knock him flatter an' a flapjack if he got t' sayin' things unpleasant kinder t' m' ears. Yeah, an' many's the time me, I was knocked flatter 'an the flattest flapjack goin'. But that ain't either there nor here, as you say now an' then.

"I'd put three years in that there neck o' the country an' made out purty good. Sandy McAllister was doin' fine at White Fish, me at Big White Fish, an' Rube Trask makin' a fortune at Hart's. Injuns was all around an' doin' fair t' middlin' too.

"When I come back the fourth winter they was a stranger in a shack a mile up the lake from me. I dropped in t' say howdy t' him an' glad t' see a new man an' hopes he makes out good 'an all. I tell him m' name an' he says his is Burt Hackett an' glad t' know me. Older 'an I was a bit, an' looked purty good t' me, and we got along purty good.

"Somehow nor other I wasn't gettin' as much outer the traps like I did the other years. This kinder got me sore, 'cause I'd bragged a good deal t' Hackett 'bout the pelts I'd bagged las' year, an' tol' him how many I was goin' t' catch that there year an' all. Yes, sir, most o' m' traps might just as well ha' been a stick a wood in the snow f'r all the good they did.

"Twice in a week m' five-foot fox trap was robbed o' the bait an' sprung, an' m' deadfalls wasn't get-tin' much neither. I tol' Hackett 'bout it an' he complains the same way. His trapline was 'bout so big like mine an' his luck was even poorer, him havin' less pelts on his loft 'an even me.

"Wall we began right then, an' there t' wonder if some poacher wasn't gettin' familiar wit' our traps. Hackett didn't think so hisself much, claimin' mebbe it was a bad season, that's all. But me, snoopin' 'round the Injuns' camps, an' findin' as how their traps an' deadfalls was workin' good, got t' thinkin' that mebbe some sneakin' Dogrib was gettin' careless wit' his life kinder by liftin' pelts.

"Me, I'll bank all I got on the honesty of a Cree, but when it comes t' Dogribs, wal, the deader they be the better I like 'em an' they was a Dogrib camp near White Fish.

"Wal, anyhow, me an' Hackett makes it up between us t' keep a lookout on each other's traps, an' we worked in shifts day in an' day out, as well as durin' the night. I didn't see nothin' on m' own watches, but once nor twice Hackett said he heard someone snoopin' in the bush but didn't see nothin'.

"Then come a day when Hackett stomps over t' m' shack an' says he's piped strange tracks around some of our traps. Me an' him went over our traplines an' sure enough I saw strange tracks made by a snowshoe longer 'an the kind me an' Hackett wore.

"T' keep in closer touch, I tol' Hackett t' move his stuff down t' my place, an' he did that right off an' we bunked t'gether. We kept a closer watch 'an ever, an' one day, damme, I found bits a black fur stuck t' one o' m' fox traps, which tol' me plainer 'an day that the trap had been robbed of a blackie.

"I c'n tell you, mister, I was mad as blazes an' ripe f'r anything, murder included. I was young an' strong as an ox an' skeered o' no man under the sun. A man gets a blackie once in a blue moon, an' t' be robbed o' one is enough t' drive you crazy.

"I raved up an' down the cabin an' come nigh t' rippin' the bunks offen the wall, I was that riled an' all. Hackett kep' follerin' me an' tryin' to get me t' sit down an' eat an' not go ravin' like a madman. Nex' day I seed them there strange tracks ag'in an' tried t' foller 'em, but somehow nor other they just natcherally disappeared in the spruce scrub.

"That was the year we had the big blizzard over that way, an' she shore was some humstitchere, runnin' a close second t' the one I got mixed up wit' in the Etawney Lake country when that there Cree Injun I tol' you about made that famous musk' on no rations. Wal, this here blizzard played the merry ol' hell wit' the country an' goin' out t' look over the traps was plum' outen the question.

"Me an' Burt Hackett just stayed bottled up in our shack an' played two-handed poker f'r terbaccy, me losin' all m' terbaccy an' Hackett give me the ha-ha an' then lent me some. 'Gimme it back when you're through,' he says.

"An' when I was through I give him it back all that was left, which was the ashes. Burt thought that was a good joke an' had a big laugh, an' so did I.

"A'ter the blizzard kicked over, me an' Burt had to hack our way out inter the open wit' axes. It got t' be all mighty cold an' that there spirit thermometer went bobbin' way the de'il below what I calls balmy an' cheerful kinder. I headed f'r m' own trapline an' Burt Hackett headed f'r his'n.

"'Long 'bout noon I'm shot from ambush. Bullet smacks m' pipe outen m' mouth an' plum' ruins it. I mind I flopped down, yellin', 'Why the hell don'tcha shoot one o' m' ears off 'stead o' m' pipe! On'y got one pipe, an' they're two ears.'

"Wal, they was lot o' thrashin' about in the bush an' me, I tried t' trail the son-of-a-gun, but lost him. Anyways, I found his tracks f'r a while an' then lost 'em in the spruce scrub. But them tracks was just like the ones me an' Burt Hackett had saw 'round about our traps.

"**WHEN I** reached the cabin I found the door swingin' in the wind, an' when I went inside, holy dam', the place was a wreck. Flour spilt over the floor, shelves tored down, most all o' the provisions gone—Burt Hackett's an' mine—an' ev'ry pelt that we owned was gone too. Oh, me, I was a wild younker, an' I come dam' night t' tearin' the shack apart I was so all-fired ravin' mad.

"Burt Hackett came in wit' a few pelts an', seein' what happened, stood in the door an' swore f'r five minutes straight. Somepin' hadder be done. They was on'y a week's grub left. Burt said if I'd look a'ter his traps as well as m' own, he'd make a flyin' dash t' La Biche an' get enough grub t' last us f'r the rest o' the season. I was gettin' t' like Burt, an' when he up an' offered t' make that there trip I got t' likein' him more, an' I said I'd keep an eye on his traps.

"Wal, we whacked up what provisions we had an' Burt left f'r La Biche. That was the last I ever seed o' Burt Hackett."

"How come?" I cut in, a little surprised.

"Yeah, I never seed Burt Hackett since the time he shuck m' hand in the cabin door, his blue eyes lookin' honest as any I ever seed."

Ramblin' Dad scratched the heel of his left foot with the big toe of his right.

"Yeah, Burt Hackett did me dirt. When I reached La Biche I thought mebbe Burt had got lost or killed or somepin', but the factor said a gent answerin' the description I gave had stopped there all right wit' a fortune in furs, sold 'em an' moved on. He also sold a pair a long snow-shoes—extra that he didn't need kinder."

There was a moment of silence, during which Ramblin' Dad screwed a finger absently into the bowl of his pipe. Then he sighed.

"Yup, mister," he drawled on. "Burt was double-crossin' me all along. He had a cache in the spruce scrub where he hid the stolen pelts an' the long snowshoes, which same he wore when robbin' the traps, t' make it look like someone else. Smooth as oil, Burt was. He did away wit' the grub so's someone 'd have t' pull out f'r more. Yeah, I'll ne'er f'rget that there Burt Hackett long as I live."

"And you never saw him again?" I asked.

Ramblin' Dad bent his ancient head far back and stared with squinted eyes at the low roof. He let a cloud of that rank tobacco smoke envelope his head until his features were indistinct. Presently his voice floated to me as though it came from a great distance.

"Wal, y' see, a lil' while a'terwards Burt was shot an' killed in a cabin on the Doobawnt. They found Burt on the floor, his gun in his hand an' one bullet discharged. Burt was deader 'an a doornail."

Pause. More smoke, the rankest stuff I've ever smelt. Then:

"O' course, they was a feller as tried t' say he saw me headin' f'r Burt's cabin the night he was killed, but he wasn't sure, 'cause they found another feller on the Doobawnt as looked somepin' like me...."

His voice trailed off and he puffed in silence.

After a moment I found myself saying, "The law of the trapline—the unwritten law—"

"Unwritten, y' say?" droned Ramblin' Dad, scratching his left heel with the toe of his right foot.

"If you ask me, mister, I'd say this here law o' the trapline is written wit' the blood o' such men as has gone ag'in it—she's writ deep an' red, f'r all t' see, an' them as ain't color blind oughter see it."

I nodded, picked up my unfinished snowshoe and went on fixing it. Ramblin' Dad knocked the ashes from his pipe and reloaded it again, with the rankest tobacco I've ever seen, or ever hope to.

TRAIL TALES OF THE NORTH:
PATROL OF COURAGE

THERE WAS a crowd of us lounging around the big glowing stove in "Free-trade" Jim's store deep in the strong woods of the Etawney Lake country. Ten, all told, if I remember rightly; Jim himself and Ramblin' Dad, an ex-Mounty, giving the good old frontier the once-over before leaving for his home in England. Then there was a Frenchman on his way to the seal hunting trade, three 'breeds, a Dutchman, a stolid Cree and myself. We all had eaten overmuch at supper and were drowsy and listless in the warmth of the room, until the ex-Mounty, apropos of nothing, scratched his tousled head and remarked:

"Heard Doak was killed by an Eskimo up North."

"Corporal Doak?" asked Free-trade Jim.

"Uhuh. Funny. Eskimo thought he might be hung for the charge they had against him. Drew a gun on Doak, hoping Doak would beat him to the draw and kill him. Seems this Eskimo would rather be shot than hanged. Killed Doak. Too bad.

"Me—the biggest job I ever had was arresting a Doak for running rum to an Indian reservation. Three years on the Force and never shot at or called on to shoot at any one."

"'S tough," droned Ramblin' Dad, spitting at the woodbox and missing it by a foot.

Free-trade Jim, who was a very neat man, gave Dad a dark look and booted the woodbox nearer him. Dad looked at him whimsically, and Jim found it hard to suppress a wry smile. But he looked away quickly and spoke to the ex-Mounty.

"Doak was a good man, all right," he said. "Years ago I knew a corporal who was the toughest, most hard-boiled hunk of humanity I've ever run across, and at the same time the bravest. Courage is a hard thing to define. A woman who runs into a burning house to save her baby is not necessarily courageous; she's just a mother acting on instinct.

"A man in mortal combat, with blood in his eyes and ears and throat, who fights until he drops, is not really prompted by valor or courage; he's just temporarily insane. A man fighting on and on through a blizzard with the bottom of the thermometer, is merely obeying the primal law of self-preservation. But this Corporal—he had courage, so cool it made you shiver.

"Educated, he was, when he wanted to be, but most times he talked in the vernacular, and he sure was case-hardened four ways from the jack, what I mean. At that time I was banging around the country north of Resolution, hunting blackies, but the Corporal, plowing south on patrol, said I was hunting me a nice white grave.

"Well, when he found me, it sure looked as though I was hunting a grave of some kind. A gang of mongrel Indians from the Yellow-Knife cleaned me out of grub, and my feet were getting sore as the devil and I had a rotten cough in my chest that wasn't doing me any good either.

"Well, the Corporal found me in my little shack pitching and tossing on my robes, with the single room so cold icicles were hanging from the roof and walls.

"'Huh. This looks messy,' I remember hearing him say, and he took off his mitts and leaned over me. Then he got some brandy from his kit and gave me a stiff shot that tingled my whole body. And I heard him say, 'Huh. With damn near four million square miles of Canadian terra firma to pick from, it gets me, it does, why some blasted fools pick out the worst they can find.'

"'Here this bloke hasn't a crumb of grub, and me blowing in from the Coppermine on short rations myself. Something tells me this thing isn't going to be exactly a strawberry festival. Blast the blooming bad luck!'

"Myself, I was too all-fired played out to argue with him, and after he had fed me on steaming porcupine broth and bathed and bandaged my swollen feet, he went out to tend to his dogs.

"Then he came in with more wood, got the fire going, and paraded up and down that cabin for an hour cursing the country, the Indians that had stolen my grub, himself, me, and the bad condition of the wheel-dog's feet. I'll say frankly, now, that he did get on my nerves, what with his parading up and down and eternal swearing.

"But when, on the next day, he went out in the teeth of blizzard, fought it for five hours until he got a ptarmigan so's he could make me some broth, why, I began to feel differently toward him.

"When he came in then he looked pretty much fagged out, and when I remarked about it, he gave me a harsh laugh and said, 'Who's fagged out. Just out for a little stroll; that's all. Picked up a ptarmigan on the way.' But I knew that he had actually gone out to get that bird with intentions of staying out till he got it.

"He stinted himself on food and fed me well. And he seemed to take wonderful care of his big lead-dog, a scarred and malevolent brute that he called Duke. This dog looked like a cross between a wolf and a Mackensie River hound, and he sure was a leader if ever there was one.

"**NEXT DAY** the Corporal said to me, 'Well Jim, we've got to shake a leg. Looks like we've got to live off the land too. You'll ride on the sled and no arguments.' Of course, I had to ride. I couldn't have walked had I wanted to. My feet were in terrible shape, and my chest burned with that awful cold I had.

"Well, we struck out for Clinton Colden Lake, where the

Corporal said there was an itinerant missioner and doctor who might be able to help me. I rode, of course.

"The Corporal rocked up ahead of the team, breaking trail, and telling his leader, Duke, how many biffs alongside the ear he'd get if he didn't follow right behind. Man and lead-dog were harsh, yet I once saw the man divide the last pound of fish between himself and the dog.

"Cold, gray days. You know the kind I mean—when the air is so still it seems frozen and you imagine sometimes you can reach out and grab a hunk of it. The horizon disappears in a misty veil of pulseless mist. When objects on the wide white plains of snow seem farther away than they really are, reversing the optical illusion on the desert where objects seem closer.

"So for day on day this hard-bitten Corporal plugged ahead of his hardbitten lead-dog. Then we lost the wheeler. Poor brute just keeled over. Duke, enraged at this, whirled and pounced on him, and the Corporal, letting out a string of sizzling oaths, rapped Duke on the head with the butt-end of his whip.

"But the wheeler died and we fed him to the other dogs. Next day the dog that had taken his place by the sled, got his two hind legs smashed when we all pitched over a cut-bank. Bad luck. Gad, you should have heard the Corporal stamp and rave about.

"After that, more bad luck. A blizzard. And some blizzard, let me tell you. It—"

"I mind the time," cut in Ramblin' Dad, "when I was up here some year agone—"

"You told us about that six times already, *m'sieu*," put in the Frenchman; then to Jim, "You were about to say?"

Ramblin' Dad spat next to the wood box. Jim went on:

"It struck us, this blizzard, about fifty miles out from Clinton Colden Lake. Wind? In all my experience I've never seen it blow like it blew then. The world seemed gone mad. It tore through the scrub timber moaning and screaming like a million lunatics. It whipped the snow in all directions, and each particle of that snow was like an individual knife-thrust. In the midst of it the third dog, without food for three days, cashed in his checks.

"Then we were alone, the Corporal and his brute of a lead-dog and me. Once, getting rash and desperate, I tried to get off the sled. But the Corporal, now pulling with the dog, let go the trace, cursed me to Hades and bundled me back again.

"'We don't need you. Duke and I are just having a little fun. Now stay the hell under the robes and don't let me see you getting off again.' And he went on pulling with the grizzled Duke. Oh, he was a hard man, I tell you, and seemingly without any sentiment whatever.

"Yet he had courage. God, but he had courage! And the irony of it, when his legs went back on him the second day of the blizzard. *Mal de roque,* I think it's called, when the knees become kind of paralyzed and keep buckling all the time.

"Time and time again he fell, crawled on hands and knees with the trace still over his shoulder, struggled up, fell again. That, you will say, was the instinct of self-preservation. All right, but here—here is courage.

"Finally he could no longer get along. My cough was coming back, my feet were just as bad, and I was weak generally from lack of food. I was sinking, and the Corporal knew it. His own legs were useless.

"At last he stopped in the lee of a tamarack clump and took a few blankets, his gun and ax and kit from the sled. And the storm was still in mid-career, the wind gone mad, the drifts piling high and the whole world a vast white tomb. He threw what he'd taken from the sled on the ground and said to me:

"'All right. Duke, there, knows the trail to the settlement at Clinton Colden as well as I do. He'll get you through quicker than if I flopped along on hands and knees. When he gets you through, old man, I'd appreciate it very much if you'd have them send someone out for me. Here's the whip. I'll be here. Get going. You ought to make it in a day or two.'

"Well, sir, that just about drove me wild. Of course, I refused flat to leave him there. You know how it is. You, any one of you, would have done the same. He sat there on the snow, not a smile on his face, and ordered me to proceed to Clinton Colden Lake or he'd knock the living hell out of me. I refused, tried to heave off the sled. He heaved himself over toward me, let rip with a blow that caught me on the chin and knocked me half-unconscious.

"When I came to I knew the sled was moving. Duke, that great old brute, was pulling his heart out through the white cloud of that devilish blizzard. Somewhere back along the trail I knew a very tough, very hard-bitten Corporal, was helpless with *mal de roque*. I almost cried out in rage, but the dog plugged on.

"God, how that dog worked and toiled through that chaos. His feet were ripped wide open, frozen with blood. His breath froze on his grizzled face like a white mask. Panting, he dragged me into the settlement at Clinton Colden Lake, his hind legs useless, only his forelegs dragging me along and his ice-covered body squirming snake-fashion.

"They had to carry me from the sled, and I told them about the Corporal, where he was, what he had done. They had to carry Duke, too, or what was left of him, for the poor, dear brute had breathed his last as he drew me into the settlement. This tooth I wear here on my watch chain? One of Duke's teeth. Great dog....

"And the Corporal? They found him all right. I understand they found him huddled in his blankets, trying to write in his diary the incidents of his patrol, the condition of the country, the scarcity of game; all this so that the next man to take over his patrol would be well informed.

"For, you see, the Corporal had an idea that he was making his last report, that the blizzard would get him and kill him before help arrived. But they saved him. And the first thing he said, when they put his weary body on the sled was, 'Well, how did that blasted trapper and my dog make out?'

"And when they said the dog had died after the awful trek, the Corporal said, 'Huh. He died like a gentleman, didn't he, boys?'

"One of the men said he shed a tear, but another said he swore fearfully for some reason or other. I understand he left the Force a term later and went overseas with the first Canadians. Killed in action, I think, at Vimy."

Courage?

I thought so. We all did, in fact.

THE BIG MOON LAKE PATROL

FAR NORTH—TYSON OF THE MOUNTED HITS THE CAIN TRAIL.

THE HEAVY door of the split-log cabin banged open and wind, snow and Corporal Chet Tyson came in all together.

Constable Ike McClusky, his feet perched atop the table and a ragged magazine in his hands, twisted his head around, took his pipe from his mouth in order to spit, and remarked:

"Whativer the divil's the idee of lettin' so much cold in ever-r-r-y time ye open the door, Chet? Blast me, but ye're an inconsiderate sort o' man."

Tyson was heaving out of his furs vigorously. He beat his ice-caked bearskin gloves against the closed doors. And all the while ignored Constable McClusky—completely. Finally, when he was stripped down to his tunic, he began unbuttoning this in a thoughtful manner with one hand and scratching his head with the other. Then, reverting to his usual brisk manner, he chafed his hands and grinned down at the Irishman.

"Well, Ike, old chum, why the devil haven't you got the table set and the grub out? I'd like to see myself blow in once and find your nose elsewhere besides in a blooming book. Man alive, is that old lady ever going to stop sending you books! Since you caught that killer on the Baker Lake Patrol and got your name in the papers, Lord, you've got more letters, photographs and books than I can count. It's—well, it's worse than being an actor."

"Is it jealous ye are?" sneered the rocky constable.

"You bet I am," chided Tyson, and made a pass at McClusky's jaw.

McClusky slammed down the magazine, heaved to his feet, squared off, and for several minutes the two men sparred back and forth across the cabin. Tyson was the more agile of the two—a lean, black-haired, black-eyed, capable young man—and he kept shooting tantalizing jabs to the rough-hewn constable's wind.

"You haven't touched me yet, Ike," chuckled Tyson, rapping his partner's nose.

"Blast me, Chet, I'll smear ye ag'in' the wall." And the constable rushed, swung hard, missed the quick corporal and drove his fist so hard against the door he howled aloud.

Tyson laughed, ran to the table and sat down, grinning across at the red-faced McClusky.

"All right, Ike," he said. "Setting-up exercises are over. If you don't get the grub started darned soon I'll tear up your magazine."

"Ye will, will ye?"

"Just as sure as I'm sitting here."

"Well, thin, ye black-eyed divil, I'd better be doin' as ye shay. Sich a glutton ye be, Chet, Always eatin'. Humph!"

With which observation the abashed constable, nursing his fist, began rattling the pots and pans with a lot of unnecessary noise.

Tyson washed up, and while the meal was making sat down at the table and wrote in his journal. These two, handling the Big Moon Lake Patrol in the country east of Artillery Lake, got along together admirably. Tyson had come over from the Great Bear region recently, after making a splendid record there, and McClusky had been sent over from Baker Lake. They had been partners some years before when Tyson was still a constable and he and McClusky had worked the Saskatchewan plains on intermittent patrol. Tyson was known for a rather hard man in more ways than one, but he and McClusky, forever poking fun at each other, paired first rate.

Even now, while Tyson was trying to write, McClusky banged the cooking utensils and explained in a booming voice all about the story he had been reading when the corporal blew in. But Tyson had the ability to concentrate, and the constable's words rolled off him like water off a duck.

But presently the corporal lifted an ear. "*Sh!* Shut up, Ike. Listen!"

Tyson, getting up, strode over to the door, put his ear to it. A faint, dull knock sounded on the boards, Tyson stepped to one side and flung open the door. A form, swathed in furs and snow, pitched in, groaned. Tyson slammed home the door.

McClusky set down the tea kettle slowly and arched his red eyebrows.

"Well!" he breathed out.

Barked the corporal, "Snap into it, Ike! That brandy!"

Tyson rolled the stranger over, tugged at his furs, pulled back the *capote* hood that was rimmed with ice and snow. The man's lips, frost-blackened, fluttered.

"Know him?" called McClusky, lumbering over with a bottle of brandy.

"Yup. Chap named Trudeau. Got a young wife and a shack just north of that hogback I told you about. But I wonder what the—. Here, give us the brandy, Ike. Yank off his footgear. Feet may be bitten. Hands all right."

Rapidly, deftly, the two partners worked to restore the man Trudeau to consciousness. His feet were in good shape, McClusky discovered.

"Good," bit off Tyson. "I'll handle him, Ike. Dammit, don't you smell the grub burning? What this bird needs is a load of hot grub and a smoke."

McClusky had a sweetly sarcastic remark all ready to get off, but he suddenly changed his mind and dived for the stove.

Trudeau was beginning to whisper now and move his fingers. His eyes blinked, but refused to stay open. Tyson, all eagerness, leaned closer to catch the murmured words.

"Amy... ma beloved... cabin... gone... *Dieu!*"

Unconsciousness seemed to overtake Trudeau again. Words failed him and his body went limp. Tyson shook him, tried to rouse him. Then he carried him over to one of the bunks and laid him down. There he paused to scratch his head. After a moment he went over to the rack, took down his trail togs and heaved into them while he spoke to McClusky.

"Ike. I'm going to blow over the hogback to this bird's shack. Got an idea there's some dirty work knocking about the country. Work on him and try to get him talking. Meantime I'll snoop around and see what's up. No, I'm not eating now. Just pour me a cup of that tea and a hunk of bannock. Dammit, I could go a good meal, too."

McClusky's eyebrows bent together. "Well, say, Chet, old timer, ye stay here an' lemme go. C'mon, Chet. Ye been bangin' around all day an' I been warmin' the chair here. Just sit yersel' down an' lemme—"

"Ike, will you clamp your mouth and pour me that tea and attend to Trudeau there?"

Tyson was pulling his hood close about his face. He began chewing on a piece of bannock while McClusky poured the tea. He took the beverage steaming hot, smacked his lips, pulled on his mittens and picked up his rackets.

"S'long, Ike, old chum," he called as he went out.

"S'long, ye black-eyed divil of a man," boomed Ike.

His rackets once on, Tyson bent his head against the driving snow and followed the shore of the lake northward. Darkness was full upon the land, and windrows were piling high in all kinds of curious shapes. Tall spruces came down to the lake from all directions, making a wall that was blacker than the night. The wind rose and fell, rose and fell, touching odd, wild notes as it bore down through the forest. The trees groaned, their pointed tops reeling in the white gloom. The ice on the lake cracked with a muffled boom.

Leaving the lake, Tyson paused to verify his bearings, then swung a little to the west and plowed on through the swirling clouds of snow. For a while he left the tall woods and cut across an open stretch of hummocky muskeg, where the wind and snow skimmed along and tore at him with persistence, like an invisible hand. Once it actually turned him around. This made him a trifle angry.

"Oh, *will* you!" he clipped, addressing the gods of the wild, and immediately set a stiffer pace.

It was five miles from the cabin on Big Moon Lake to the little shack in the sheltered valley just north of the hogback. It took Tyson almost three hours to make the trek. At first he had trouble in locating the cabin. In the white cloud of the blizzard he missed his trail for a while, floundered about in a savage mood, and at last picked it up again.

"That's twice in a week I've missed a trail," he told himself; then added, "Seems, Chet Tyson, you're falling down on the job of patroling."

Quite suddenly he came upon the cabin. It was a low structure, built solidly enough, and hemmed in all around by snowdrifts, except where the passageway ran to the door. He opened the door without a moment's hesitation, found the interior pitch dark and quite as cold as it was outside. With numb fingers he searched his pockets for a match, found one after a moment and lit a candle on the table. The yellow glare grew and flung patches of light and shadow around the room in fantastic shapes.

"Oh-ho!"

The corporal stopped dead in his tracks as his foot touched the stiff hand of a man lying on the floor. He took the candle from the table, put it near the man's face, felt for signs of life. There were no signs. The man was dead. But who was he? Tyson looked the face over closely.

"H'm. Stranger in this part of the country."

It was a black-bearded face, not so good to look at; a rough cut, badly constructed face, with beetling brows and a heavy jaw.

"We'll, mister, guess I can't do anything for you," said Tyson, putting the candle back on the table. "But, now, Trudeau's wife…. Where the devil can she be?"

He lugged the dead man across the room and laid him on a bunk. The wound, he discovered, was directly over the heart. The bullet was lodged, possibly, in the spine. Had Trudeau killed the stranger? Or had his wife done the deed?

"Blamed if I can tell offhand," mused Tyson. "But I'll find out soon enough."

He made a thorough search of the floor and found, in a dark corner, a revolver with three cartridges exploded. Then he took the candle and examined closely the walls and ceiling.

"Well, I guess the shooting didn't happen in here," he reasoned. "No bullet marks. Unless—h'm—unless the door was open and they flew outside."

He stowed the revolver in one of his pockets, drew his hood about his face, pulled on his mittens and bent down at the door to put on his snowshoes. Closing the door, he plunged down the path and struck the back-trail. The wind still whistled and wrapped blinding sheets of snow about him; the trees swayed mightily, their tops mingling.

Muttered the corporal: "Seems most folks generally pick out bum weather to do their killing. Never consider the Law at all. Now, last night was clear and not much wind. But, no, it's got to happen on a night when it's not fit for a wolf to be out. Blast the breaks of this game!"

It was well past midnight when he reached his post on Big Moon Lake. He pushed open the door, then stopped on the threshold, perplexed. The place was empty. The stove was losing its red glow. He closed the door with a jerk of his shoulder and crossed to the table. There was a note:

Dear Chet: Trudeau came to when I wasn't looking. Grabbed his clothes and busted out. There's some grub left on the stove. I'm going after Trudeau. It's funny. Can't understand.
IKE.

Tyson swore under his breath. What the devil was going on, anyhow? Did it mean that Trudeau had killed that stranger and was trying to get away? The corporal, turning the thing over, poured out some tea and ate some bacon straight from the pan.

"Best thing to do, I guess, is wait here till Ike gets back. No use in me meandering around on a skylark. H'm. Bacon's good."

He finished eating and went to pacing the room with his hands clasped behind his back. In his mind there was no doubt that Ike would bring back Trudeau. The big Irishman was not exceptionally bright, hence he made a good partner for Tyson, who was really the brains of the patrol; but good old Ike hung to a trail like a bloodhound, and in a tight corner he was worth a dozen "bright" men.

But as the hours dragged on toward morning there came no Ike. The snow stopped, puffed itself out in fits and starts. The temperature plummeted. The cabin snapped, and hoar frost formed on the walls and ceiling.

Tyson's lean, muscled face became hard with genuine gravity. He cracked fist into palm with a sudden impatient oath, bundled on his furs and, grabbing up his rifle and rackets, banged savagely out of the cabin. Daylight comes late in those high latitudes, and as yet only the faintest hint of a gray dawn was in the east. Tyson cursed the state of things as he plunged into the spruces.

"There's something wrong else Ike would have been back before this," he told the world at large.

There are some men who go through a state of adverse circumstances calmly and methodically. Tyson was not that kind of man. He was by nature a brusque, somewhat aggressive man, capable of making quick decisions in a pinch, sometimes a little harsh, as the law is apt to make a man, but always on the square. When things went wrong too steadily, being the type of man he was, he worked himself into a healthy state of anger.

Thus he plowed on over the virgin snow giving vent now and then to his feelings in heated words, but always pushing on steadily and tirelessly.

He set a course for Trudeau's cabin, working on a hunch, hoping he might unveil some new evidence there. Trudeau's cabin was, after all, the hub of the mystery, and it was possible that, like a magnet, it would draw back those connected with the crime. Further, it was the most logical objective. He held no very great fear for Ike, for he knew Ike was capable of handling himself. But the downright strangeness of it all got on his nerves badly.

The dawn was broad upon the wilderness when he caught sight of Trudeau's shack nestling snug and peaceful down in the valley. What gave him pause was the spectacle of a thin column of smoke rising steadily on the clear, frosty air.

"Oh-ho!" he clipped, and swung down the trail with a new eagerness.

He approached the cabin in a roundabout way. Pausing outside the door, he removed his mitten from his gun hand, drew his service pistol and, with a clamped jaw and a tense body, whipped open the door and leaped in.

He found himself confronting a woman—a woman with eyes red and swollen from too much crying. She was pretty, and, standing erect, she faced the corporal unafraid.

"How do you do, Madame Trudeau," nodded Tyson crisply.

He kicked shut the door with his heel, put away his pistol

and flung open his furs—or, rather, he paused in the act. His eyes, roaming to the bunk, stopped there, narrowing and taking on a cold, glinting film. His lips drew hard against his teeth.

The corpse he had left on the bunk was gone.

His eyes moved, fixed their flinty, boring stare on Amy Trudeau. She had not uttered a word thus far. She just looked—that was all—looked with eyes that were brimming with a sort of wild pathos. Her hands kept fumbling frantically with a locket she wore about her neck on a long chain.

"Well, Madame Trudeau...."

"*Oui, m'sieu?*" pathetically.

The corporal stroked his chin. "What—h'm—what did you do with the body?"

Her eyes grew suddenly wide, shot with terror.

"*Body?*"

"Yes, madame. The body that was on the bunk last night."

Her hands fluttered to her face, pressed her cheeks in a frantic gesture.

"*Dead?*" she breathed.

"Quite dead, madame," nodded the corporal.

She let out a wild scream and fell across the table, her hands gripping its rough edge until they turned pure white at the knuckles. She broke into a low, agonized moan that shook her whole body.

The corporal stroked his jaw and then scratched his tousled head in perplexed indecision. Here was a delicate situation, and the corporal was not what you might call a delicate man.

He thought, "Now I wish Ike was here. Ike is a big gentle rogue, with a lot of blarney on his tongue. But me...."

He ground his hands together and took a turn about the room. Imagine trying to talk to a woman in such a state. Tyson was not a man who could work up an oily, wheedling tongue. The fibre of him was too tough, like the harsh, strong land that had nurtured him from childhood.

He took a great breath, preparatory to handling the woman in his most brusque, official manner, just as the door slammed open. He was sent reeling across the room by the sudden impact from some powerful body.

Immediately, even as he was tumbling, he yanked at his service pistol and tried to twist around before he fell. But a stool was in his path and this toppled him in a heap so that he landed hard on the side of his face. This caused him to bite off a muffled oath and become distinctly peeved.

He struggled madly to his feet, swung around and slashed his pistol through the air. Even so the door slammed shut and he was alone in the cabin. *But he had seen Trudeau!*

"By the Lord Harry!..."

He bounded for the door and pulled at it. It gave way not more than an inch. The chain-bolt on the outside had been thrown to.

He tried again, using all his strength and a string of choice epithets, neither of which proved effective.

"By God, this patrol's going to the dogs! I deserve to lose my stripes for this!"

He flung furious eyes about the room, strode over to the stove and came back with a steel poker. This he wedged in the space between the door and the frame, which the chain allowed, and tried to pry it open. But the chain was stout.

Finally, pressing against the bar with one hand and gripping his pistol with the other, he fired through the opening and smashed the chain apart.

"Now!" he clipped, with a bad glint in his eye.

He buckled on his rackets and flung away from the cabin in a wholly righteous wrath. Trudeau and his young wife were lost to sight. One cannot travel over virgin snow, however, without leaving tracks.

"We'll see who's going to make a bum out of the Law," Tyson told the silent, white-mantled forest. "We'll see, and if we don't, then, so help me, I'll shed the scarlet and go selling ribbon in Eaton's."

He sped on through the clear, crisp air. Not a breeze was moving. The pointed spruce tops pointed to a sky of such pale blue color it was almost white. The trees snapped sharply. A big snowshoe rabbit skimmed through the thickets. A porcupine coiled up into a bristling protective ball.

The corporal was a fast man on snowshoes, and before very long he heard sounds up ahead that evidenced the closeness of the pursued. Soon after he caught sight of them running along the backbone of a ridge. He fired a shot in the air, but this did not stop them.

He quickened his pace. At the same time he wondered what had happened to McClusky. Had Trudeau killed him? Well, there was Trudeau up ahead, and if he had, well, in a short time his wife would be a widow.

Tyson gained steadily, topped the ridge and swept down toward a frozen waterway. He saw the woman trip and Trudeau stop to help her up.

He shouted, "Stop there, Trudeau, or I'll shoot!"

Trudeau was speaking to his wife with a lot of gestures, urging her to go on and leave him behind to stop the corporal. She refused, and by this time Tyson was closing down on them. He had his gun leveled, while neither Trudeau nor his wife were armed. As Tyson reached them, the woman, all fury, flung herself upon him. He could have shot her easily, but instead he tried to brush her aside.

Then Trudeau also was upon him, a wild, reckless, passionate man. Together they went down, while the woman fell aside.

Trudeau fought like a lynx for possession of the gun. Tyson was in the throes of a silent rage. He showed the Frenchman what strength was in that lean body of his. The snow flew about in clouds as they rolled about, trying to break each other's grip.

They struggled up, still locked, with Trudeau trying to twist the gun from the corporal's hand and the corporal determined to have it otherwise.

"Trudeau, you damned fool, this won't get you anywhere!" Tyson ground out as he rushed the Frenchman against a tree.

For a brief moment he relaxed completely, then exerted a sudden strength and heaved Trudeau over his shoulder.

The woman screamed as her husband hit the hard crust on the back of his neck. Tyson swung clear and had both Trudeau and his wife covered when the man staggered to his feet.

"That one fooled you, didn't it, Trudeau?" he clipped.

The man and wife flung themselves into each other's arms, sobbing.

"Come, now," said Tyson. "Up ahead of me, and make tracks for Big Moon Lake. Get going, please."

Trudeau put his arm around his wife's waist, and together they started off, the man silent and the woman crying. Tyson kept behind them, his hand on his gun.

"Well, I guess I don't go selling ribbon," he told himself.

IT TOOK them just two hours to reach Big Moon Lake, and another fifteen minutes to reach the detachment post. Tyson, standing to one side, ordered Trudeau to open the door. The Frenchman, his arm still around his wife's waist, pushed open the door, and Tyson went in directly behind him.

The room was cheery and warm. Ike McClusky was rising solemnly from beside the bunk. He closed a Bible and placed it on the table. A form lay on the bunk, covered completely with a blanket.

Ike said, "So ye got Trudeau, Chet?"

"Yup. But who just died?"

"Well, I don't know. Didn't give his name. Ye see, Chet, when Trudeau ran off I follered the divil, or tried t' foller him, I should say. But thin I got mixed up in the storm an' stumbled over the feller that just is after breathin' his last. No, he wasn't shot or even wounded, Chet. Just plain broken down wi' both lungs gone. Well, it was me dooty t' foller Trudeau, an' it was likewise me dooty t' try t' save a dyin' man. I choosed the last-named dooty, Chet, an' stayed here wit' him ever-r-r-y minute. He just died.

"He tol' a queer story in between his ravin's. Sid he killed a man just before I found him. Sid he'd follered this man two hundred miles because this man brought shame unto his fam'ly... his sister, I think. Sid he killed this man, but I didn't see any dead ones around, Chet."

"I did," said Tyson, and turned to Trudeau and his wife.

Trudeau spoke up—"M'sieu, I took dat body from ma cabeen. I come home ver' late from ma traps. Ma Amy no dere, but Ah find de body. Ah t'ink Amy she shoot an' keel dis man an' run off. Ah go look, fall down hill, which mak me ver sick. Ah come here 'most dead, hear you, M'sieu Tyson, say you go look ma cabeen. Ah wait you gone, den rush out, tak short cut you don' know, but you get dere first, an' den leave. I tak de body away anyhow, hide eet. Ah want to do dat before you reach dere, but ah was late."

Tyson silenced him gently with an upraised hand and turned to his wife. "And you, madame?"

"Ah lost maself in de storm, m'sieu. Ah nevaire saw body you talk of. When you ask me about body I t'ink you mean ma husband dead, you see. He was not home, an' I worry. Ma mind she all was mix up, an' when you say to me, body...."

"I see," nodded Tyson. "General confusion all around. All right, Trudeau, you get the body you hid, and then both of you can go home. By the way, Trudeau, if I were you I wouldn't go trying to beat up a Mountie again."

"But, m'sieu—"

"I understand," said Tyson, "but I know several mean chaps on the Force who'd pull you in just for that. All right, get that body."

Their eyes shining radiantly, Trudeau and his young wife went out in each other's arms.

Tyson said, "I thought for a while I had a rotten job to do—take a man from his wife, and them not married a year yet. Sometimes, Ike, a fellow wishes he'd never taken to wearing the scarlet and gold. Now—"

He stopped, for Constable McClusky had dug up another magazine and was settling down comfortably behind it.

Tyson groaned, made a wry face and lit his pipe. Then he sat down with his journal and began writing down the incidents of the first crime on the Big Moon Lake Patrol.

TRAIL TALES OF THE NORTH:
ALONE

THE BUNCH of us were sprawled in split-log chairs around the long cylindrical stove in Free-trade Jim's post up in the Etawney Lake country. We all had eaten over-much and I guess everyone—there were five of us—felt drowsy, for the room was warm and the snow drumming against the window made a fellow relish the comfort of the big, solid trade-room.

Jim was staring lazy-eyed at the red glare in the grate and absently poking tobacco into his pipe. Ramblin' Dad was lounging on the small of his back with one leg outstretched and the other dangling over the arm of the chair, and, as usual, he was exploring what few teeth he had left with a shaved-down match. The other two men were an Indian agent and a trade-hunter for Revillons.

I remember that Ramblin' Dad was beginning to snore in an off-tone key, and I guess my own head was beginning to nod, when the door whipped open and a cloud of snow surged in. Then the door slammed and we saw a young chap sagging against it, his knees shaky, his young face worn and dark with frost-bite.

The Revillons man leaped from his chair and caught the stranger as his knees buckled. We all bent over him. He was saying:

"You men are real—eh? Think— think, I've been alone for more than half a year! Alone—alone! What agony! Oh!"

He gripped our hands to make sure we were real, laughing

and crying at the same time. We undressed him and put him to bed, and Jim's Indian boy made some steaming porcupine broth and attended him.

Soon we found ourselves back, in our chairs by the stove, but no one was drowsy now. Ramblin' Dad worked his mouth silently for a moment and took a tobacco shot at the wood-box. As usual he missed it, and, as usual, Jim, who was a very neat man, gave him a dark look.

"Seen the time I was alone f'r nigh onto a year," Dad said through his chew. "Didn't mind it much."

"You!" Jim drawled, and paused to light his pipe. "You were born to the wilderness. Your old man fought off Indians while your mother nursed you. You, of course, can't understand what it means for a new cub in the country to be alone—like the man that just blew in. I can understand just how he feels. I went through it myself when I came into the wilderness thirty years ago. I was twenty then. I learnt a lesson, too.

"I came up as a factor's apprentice, and they shipped me north to the Lac la Rouge country. I was young, as I say, and pretty cocky, too, and the country held no fears for me at all. I stayed for a year at that post and then I was drafted by a post on Lake Waterhen, something like a hundred and fifty miles to the westward. I started out with an old sourdough called Henry Binns. Henry was bound for Lac des Isles to join his partner, and Lake Waterhen post was on his route.

"Henry was all right, take him by and large. He had what you might call a sense of humor. He was always poking fun at somebody. If there was nobody around but his dog he'd poke fun at it, and even get the dog sore. Henry was that kind of man. He never took anything or anybody seriously.

"I think humor is one of God's greatest gifts to man, but, let me tell you, there are some men who become exasperatingly funny. Henry got more men sore in his time than I can count by what he called a fine sense of humor. Either Henry was wrong or those men could not appreciate humor. But this outlandish funny streak of his was worth a fortune to him, for it helped him keep a happy state of mind when prospects looked blue, and through the worst storms he plowed chuckling at some joke he'd played on somebody or some joke he was going to play.

"I was young at the time and Henry everlastingly made fun of me; the way I swung my snowshoes, the way I ate my food. You see, Henry would take a chunk of pork in one hand and a knife in the other and lop it off and guzzle it down that way. He drank his tea without milk or sugar. When I sneaked a pinch of sugar in mine he'd give me the merry old haw-haw. When he ate fish he'd cram it in his mouth and keep spitting the bones out as he chewed. Yes, sir, Henry was a regular died-in-the-wool sourdough.

"I began to get sore as the devil on the second day out. I had to take a hand at breaking trail ahead of the three-dog team, and Henry would whip them until they were at my heels. Then I'd take a spill, for it took me an awful long time to get used to snowshoes, and while I was trying to get up Henry would haw-haw his head off and pitch handfuls of snow in my face. I'd get up cursing a blue-streak, and he'd laugh so much he couldn't stand up.

"We got mixed up with a blizzard after we passed Smooth-stone Lake. It was my first taste of real dirty weather on the trail, and of course Henry had to be there to laugh himself sick at the tenderfoot way I blundered along. For a spell I tried to look at the funny side of it, too, but, man alive, it was beyond me to take a headlong spill down a cut-bank as a joke. Henry did and had to hold his stomach he laughed so much.

"My face was ripped by the ice in that fall, and I didn't feel funny, and I was unable to hold my temper, and I took hold of Henry and pitched him headfirst in a snow-bank. Do you know, gentlemen, that Henry came out of that snow-bank spluttering and laughing to beat all Hades? All that day while the blizzard lasted he joshed me and told me he knew a little girl six years old at Pelican Narrows who could teach me how to pound a trail.

"Consider that I was twenty at the time and kind of touchy. I tried my best to hold my own on the trail, but the continuous haw-hawing of Henry made me do some of the most blundering things.

"I stood it for another day. The storm had stopped and it got bitter cold, but neither cold nor storm could break up Henry's funny streak. That night I decided to sneak away and reach Lake Waterhen on my own hook.

"I didn't take anything but what belonged to me, and I left Henry most of the grub. I had a compass and I used it. I traveled all that night, for the Northern Lights were on duty and when they passed out the moon was bright and the trail was good. No, I simply couldn't stand Henry around any longer. I was afraid if I did I'd maybe hurt him, for I was a big husky in them days and I packed a wallop.

"I kept on the go all the next day, for I wanted to get 'way ahead of Henry. No, the trek didn't wear me out. I could stand it and a lot more in those days.

"I made my fire that night and sat by it, smoking. Then I began to feel the awful lonesomeness of the land. Strange to say, I missed Henry's voice. I missed the playful growls of the dogs.

"It was one of those still, cold nights, with a lot of white moonlight on the snow and a lot of strange sounds now and then in the timber. A place may be lonely enough, but when an owl lets off a solitary hoot, why the place seems a hundred times more desolate.

"Maybe you don't understand me. Maybe you've never been alone in the wilds. No, it wouldn't stir me now. But I was only twenty then and actually alone for the first time.

"I figured that if I had a tent it wouldn't be so lonely. Did you ever stop to think that a trapper hibernating in the woods for a season might go nuts if he didn't have a tent or a cabin to sleep in? It's the sitting underneath the stars and being able to look for miles and miles that makes you feel so lonely and so small in the wilderness. I know many a good man would never think of spending a winter inside without a dog for a companion. I know a man who trapped a bear cub just so's he'd have company.

"This being alone sure did wear on me—more than Henry's funny streak even. It's bad to have too much imagination in this country. It will get you to shaking hands with the willows if you don't look out.

"Even the next day I couldn't shake off the feeling. I actually prayed for a storm, for this at least would kill the silence and give me a lot to do plowing through it. But no storm came. There was nothing but a pale sky and a wilderness of snow-drenched spruce with not enough wind to rustle the branches. Once or twice I saw a snowshoe rabbit or a porcupine, but nothing else.

"The swish of my own rackets began to get on my nerves. I tried singing to keep myself company, but the air was too cold and stung my throat. The snow-glare pained my eyes. I began to wonder if maybe I was on the wrong trail.

"Over the fire that night I couldn't get any comfort out of my pipe. The moon came up late and stared coldly at me through the trees. I began to miss Henry's chatter more than ever. I actually missed his making fun of me. Think of it! I couldn't sleep.

"No, I wasn't afraid. I don't think I've ever been really afraid of anything. But, dammit, I couldn't stand the awful silence and solitude, the staring into space, the feeling that I was so small in that great white wilderness!

"I started off before daylight. I couldn't bear the inactivity. I traveled hard, setting a stiff pace over the windswept hills and down through the still, brooding valleys. Finally I saw a level hand of whiteness that was a frozen river. I knew it must be the Beaver, and that there must be an Indian camp nearby. And, yes, sure enough, there was.

"I ran toward it, glad as a baby, my heart so happy it hurt. Go ahead and laugh, Ramblin' Dad! Maybe you're laughing and trying to cover up a similar memory, or maybe you've never been alone. Yes, I was so happy I near bawled.

"As I ran forward who should step out of one of the teepees but Henry, twirling a whip around his hand!

"I stuck out my hand to shake. I had almost reached him when my snow-shoes crossed and I took a header.

"Henry spread his legs and threw back his head and haw-hawed till he had to hold his stomach. I got up and haw-hawed back at him! The *two* of us kept up the haw-hawing business until Henry could hardly stand! Then we went on to Lake Waterhen. We kept haw-hawing each other all the way.

"Whenever we met after that I always managed to beat Henry to the haw-haw....

"This being alone doesn't get me any more, but to this day I'll go twenty miles out of my way if it takes me in the company of another man. You can bet that any man who lone-wolfs it isn't worth his salt. He isn't human if he doesn't like human companionship. That being alone when I was a youngster sure taught me a thing or two—something you missed, Ramblin' Dad."

"Yeah," muttered Dad, and spat next to the wood-box.

"Missed that too!" said the Revillons man.

Jim, who was a very neat man, gave Dad a hopeless look.

TRAIL TALES OF THE NORTH:
CACHE LAW

W**E HAD** been having fine weather right along; crisp and clear with a good crust on the snow and plenty of game in the land. Clouds in the sky by day were few, and as for the nights—why, I've never seen better. Stars without number, plenty of moonlight, just enough wind to stir the fire and make it cheerful while "Free-trade" Jim and I lounged on our blankets and smoked our pipes.

Jim, by the way, had left his post in the hands of Ramblin' Dad and was making a trade-hunting trip along the Churchill near North Indian Lake, and I was tagging along with him. So far business had been pretty good, and Jim was in extremely good spirits and full of yarns. I remember, toward evening of one day I spotted a cache carefully concealed in a matted windfall. I pointed it out to Jim, who was up ahead of the dogs, and he came back and stared at it for a long minute.

"Reminds me," he started, and then said, "but wait till we make camp tonight."

That, I knew, meant a good yarn, and I was always ready to squat down and listen to Jim's reminiscences of trail and trace.

Night came, finally, and the crackling of wood in the fire, and the sizzle and smell of frying bacon mixed with the tang of wood-smoke. And after that a pipe of peace, a comfortable position, with the dogs digging holes in the snow nearby and overhead the clear, clean night-wind brushing along the spruces.

"Well, Jim, I think you've got something to tell me," I prompted.

"Have I?" He looked across the fire quizzically; then, "Oh, yes. About the cache." And he threw a few more sticks of wood into the fire.

"The grub cache," he went on, regarding his pipe, "is probably the most sacred thing in the North. No, maybe a woman is more sacred, but, anyhow, it comes next—even above the so-called law of the trapline. I mind a case many years ago over in the Burntwood Country. I came over that way when I left the Old Company and joined up with an old-timer named—let's see—h'm—Joe Corson, I think, he called himself. Yep, Joe Corson; that was his name, all right. We stocked up at Nelson House, but we didn't have any dogs, and so we didn't take much grub along. Joe said it would be enough for a while and he'd make a trip back for more provisions later in the winter. He had a dumpy little trapping shack up that way. It was so full of cracks when we got there that we had to throw water over it and let it freeze to keep out the wind.

"We had plenty of traps, though, and as I was new in the game and that particular neck of the country I let Joe map out the trapline. Joe was a good old sort, honest as the day is long, and the traditions of the North country were rooted deep in his rough old soul. I think he'd been to the outside only about three times. His stay there was short because he said the cities were too lonesome for him. Imagine! Well, that was Joe—born and bred beyond the frontier and unable to get along without it.

"For a time the furs ran pretty good—nothing extra, mind, but enough to get along on. And Joe was good company, too. He was a little man, terribly bow-legged, and never shaved, and he never hurried himself. Even his speech was slow. He'd take a half-hour to tell a tale that you'd tell in, say, ten minutes or so. And very often, if he forgot himself, he'd tell the same tale over; but I'd always listen, for I figured he might get grumpy if I interrupted him.

"One day I happened to be meandering around the country near our trap-line, and I saw a couple of men making a cache down in the valley below the hill where I was standing. I started down there to say hello to them, but by the time I reached the spot the men had gone on. It was a cache something like the one you saw back there, fixed in a windfall, and that's what made me think of it.

"Well, I wandered on. When I got back to our shack I found Joe lying in the bunk with a bad cough that rattled his chest in a way I didn't just like. I didn't mention anything about the cache business to Joe because his bad condition made me forget all about it. We had some quinine along and a jug of brandy, and I made a hot punch and made Joe take it right away. But I guess the cough had got a good start on Joe, and next morning he was in a pretty bad shape and couldn't get up. Oh, he tried to all right, for Joe was that kind, but his old legs buckled and I had to help him back into his bunk.

"I bagged a porcupine that morning and fixed Joe up a good steaming broth. Between attending to Joe and keeping the fire up and running the trapline, I guess I didn't have much time for anything else.

"Our grub box was pretty empty. It was around that time that Joe had figured on making a trip to Nelson House for another supply. But he was down with the grippe bad, and of course making the trip was out of the question. I couldn't go either because I had to stay with Joe. In fact, I was up most of every night with him, getting him a drink, and holding him up while he coughed. His head he said was hot as a furnace and nigh to busting, and every little while he wanted a cold cloth to lay on his forehead.

"Well, the days and nights dragged on, and Joe instead of getting better either stayed at the same level or got worse. The grub box was empty, and I was using the tea leaves twice. Joe had reached that stage where he wanted something all the time, like sick people get, you know. I tried to tell him that we were cleaned out. Being sick like he was, and almost out of his head with those headaches, he got unreasonable and accused me of holding grub back on him. This made me sore at the time, but I kind of realized he couldn't help it and tried to look at it that way.

"But things got worse. We got a rip-snorting blizzard that lasted two days and drove all animals to cover. I had to dig my way out to the open. I was getting desperate, and the thought of the grub cache hidden by those two men began to work through my brain and kind of made me shudder. When Joe took a spell at sleeping, which wasn't very often, I sneaked out and plowed over the hills to the cache. I walked around it, I'll swear, a dozen times, wondering what to do. At last I turned and ran away from the cache as fast as I could, I'd come so near to breaking it.

"When I reached the shack I found Joe raving to beat the band, and the best thing I could give him was spruce tea. We'd used all the brandy and quinine besides the grub. Joe accused me of all kinds of things, of trying to persecute him, of trying to steal his pelts, of leaving him there to croak. I took it all without saying a word. After awhile I didn't hear much what he said. I was so busy thinking about that cache.

"I didn't know what to do. If I broke into the cache I would be violating the iron-bound code of the woods and liable to be shot down or swung from a limb. If I didn't get good grub and tea and some medicine for Joe he might pass out. I tell you, my friend, for a twenty-five-year-old youngster I was in an awful predicament. I didn't sleep a wink that night. I sat by the fire and smoked my pipe until it got so hot I had to lay it down. I got cold cloths for Joe's head and tried to soothe him. When he'd doze off for a little while I'd squat by the stove again and think till my head hurt too.

"In the morning Joe's headache seemed to leave him a bit, and I could talk sensible to him. But his chest still hurt, and his joints hurt, and he couldn't raise an arm. Yes, he began to talk sensible, but he was in a critical condition and without food he might pass out any day.

"At last I came to the decision that I'd have to break the code of the woods to help Joe. There was plenty of bannock there, and for my own part I could live on that, stale as it was. But Joe needed something strengthening. So I left the shack and followed our trap-line to that valley. Running was poor, and had been there, lately, and not a trap was sprung. I didn't even see a rabbit track.

"I reached the cache and hung around for fully a half-hour before I could get up the courage to break into it. But at last I did. I found some tea, some flour, a side of bacon, some sugar, a box of quinine and a package of matches. The two men who had planted it would probably rely on its being there when they returned from the North. You can't imagine how rotten guilty I felt when I stole back to the shack with that outfit! When I came in Joe was half-awake, and when he saw my arms loaded that way he blinked and watched me while I pulled the, stuff out. I didn't dare look at him, but went right about preparing a meal.

"At last Joe asked, 'where'd ye git thet there?'

"I just mumbled something and put on water for the tea. But Joe was determined. He called to me again and wanted to know where the stinking hell I'd got the grub. Even then I didn't say anything, but went over to him with a dose of quinine. Joe shoved it away and glared at me in a way that made me feel my guilt more than ever.

"'I don't take thet there ontil ye tell me where ye got it!' he declared. I told him never mind, he was sick and needed it. He replied that he'd croak before he'd take it without first knowing where it came from.

"Well, I spilled the story at last, and Joe got into such a rage that I thought sure he'd pass out right there. He told me to take the stuff right back where I'd got it from, every crumb of it. I put up a stiff argument, but he would have none of it. He said he wouldn't take a bit of it if he died that night, and I wouldn't dare to take it either, else he'd shoot me.

"You see the kind of old-timer Joe was? Yes, I had to take the grub back. Joe wouldn't let me keep it. In a way I was glad. His headaches left him. I scoured the country from morning till night for a stray bit of meat, and once in a while I snared a rabbit.

"It took Joe a long while to get better, but he did, finally, and when the break-up came we were ready to go out. Joe managed to walk a little, at least enough to reach Nelson House.

"Strange to say, after I'd replaced the cache Joe never brought up the thing again. Even so I knew then how sacred the grub cache was, and I was proud to have for a partner a man who even in the face of death upheld that inviolable law of the woods. Such men as Joe, my friend, are the kind that have made the North what it is today—a land of unwritten laws and traditions, with the law of the grub cache one of the sternest of all.... Pass me the tobacco."

I threw him my pouch and knocked the ashes from my pipe.

I guess he's right about this cache law.

EAST OF BIG MOON

SUB-ARCTIC—CHET TYSON OF THE MOUNTED PLAYS JUDGE AND JURY IN A BAFFLING, PRIMAL DRAMA OF THE OUTTRAILS.

OUTSIDE THE night was cold and clear. Stars winked. A moon shone. The lake-ice cracked with a subdued boom. Within the cabin it was warm and quiet and cheerful. The sheet-iron stove glowed red. Streamers of lavender tobacco smoke rose from two pipes and rolled lazily beneath the low ceiling. The two men were silent, steeped in thought. They were playing checkers, and the board was almost clear. They were in their shirt-sleeves, but on the back of each chair hung a scarlet tunic. One of the players was a tall, lean, hardbitten man in his thirties, black-haired and black-eyed, with the hall-mark of command stamped on his dark, weather-seared face. The right arm of the tunic that hung on his chair bore just above the elbow the downward-pointed V's that showed his rank of corporal. The other player was some years older, with a broad red face and hair to match—a whale of a man, thick in the neck and chest and wide as men come in the shoulders.

"It's your move, Chet," said the red-haired constable.

"S' I see," droned the corporal studiously, and then moved.

The constable smacked his big hands together and grinned from ear to ear.

"Ho-ho, Chet, ye divil, I've got ye again! See here. One, two, thr-r-ree. An' now, me man, ye owe me smokes f'r a month t' come. It's so-o simple, Chet."

"S' I imagine, Ike," said the corporal, with a yawn. "Didn't think I owed you that much smokes, though."

"Oh-ho, ye didn't! Just wait." And the constable drew from his pocket a little book and turned back a number of pages. "See. Ye've lost exactly a hundred an' twenty-eight games, an' this one makes a hundred an' twenty-nine. If ye lose four games in a day, I smoke yer tobacco. If I lose four, then ye smoke mine."

"But wait a minute, Ike. How many games have I won?" Ike's eyes popped wide.

"Won! That's just it, ye dommed idiot. Ye ain't won a single game!"

"O-oh!" exclaimed the corporal softly, and stared at the table. "I haven't, eh?" Then he straightened up and glanced at his watch, saying, in a brisk voice: "Anyhow, Ike, it's your turn to cook. Stir your carcass and get things going. And, by the way. The bacon you made last night was stiff as wood, and I never tasted such rotten tea before. The bannocks also were rather—"

Ike glared.

"S-a-y, just a minute, ye big stiff! If me cookin' don't suit ye, thin go do it yerself. The front that ye put on sometimes sure makes me want t' knock the livin' hell out o' ye, ye black-eyed divil of a man."

The corporal, with his tongue in his cheek, gave his mate a sidelong whimsical look.

"I give up, Ike. You are an excellent cook. In fact, I've never seen a better."

"Ah-r-r, go way wit' ye, Chet!" roared the constable, and then getting up, wiped his mouth to hide a smile and began slamming the cooking utensils around with a lot of unnecessary noise

The corporal scooped up the checkers, piled them into the box and put it up on a shelf built over the bunk in the rear. He then went to the hand-made cupboard and brought what few dishes they used over to the table, where he began banging them down with much gusto.

Ike would not be outdone, and so he started banging the stove-door open and shut and shuffling the fry-pan around and whistling to beat the band. He did all this with a grave face, yet

just behind the lips there lurked a world of mirth. He looked over his shoulder, and the corporal looked at the same time, and their eyes met and they both grinned rather sheepishly and eased up on the hullabaloo.

They got on admirably, these two, Corporal Chet Tyson and Constable Ike McClusky, of the Big Moon Lake Patrol. In line of duty the corporal had a name for being exceptionally hard-boiled, but he was not entirely without humor, and he and Ike whiled away the long days and nights of the sub-Arctic by forever poking fun at each other. As may be supposed, Tyson was a lamentable failure when it came to checkers, and at times he cursed heartily the well-meaning lady in Calgary that had sent them the outfit.

Ike had several correspondents in various cities, and he received batches of magazines with every courier that passed on the way north. While Ike was an accomplished talker, he was backward with the pen, and Tyson wrote most of the letters that his partner dictated.

Between them they set out the steaming meal and faced each other genially across the rough-board table. Both were hungry, and talk lagged until they leaned back expansively with their tea before them, when Ike began to relate very dramatically a story he had read that day in one of his magazines. He was working up to a slashing climax, his face florid and his hands gesturing wildly, when the sharp bark of a rifle, muffled to a degree by distance, cut him short. The shot was mingled with the faint, hoarse scream of a man.

Tyson put his cup down and looked at McClusky. Ike drew the back of a hand across his mouth and looked at the corporal. As one, they rose.

"Sounds dirty, Chet."

"Sounds dirty, Ike."

They kicked back their chairs and pulled their tunics on quickly and silently. From pegs on the wall they took down their black fur coats and caps. From one corner McClusky brought the rifles, while from another Tyson brought snowshoes.

Drawing on their bearskin gloves they stepped out into the Arctic cold and bent to buckle on their rackets. The crust of the snow was hard as ice. An east wind drummed in the dark spruces. The lake shone like a giant pearl under the pale radiance of moon and stars. Tyson touched his partner's arm.

"Sounded like it came down wind Ike."

"Sounded that way, Chet."

"Let's go."

They moved eastward, away from the lake, passing into a dense forest where the moonlight played in vagrant streaks like white rapiers. Their rackets grated on the hard crust. Their breaths spumed out like silver clouds. In rhythmic haste they swung ahead, Tyson six feet in the lead. After a while they stopped, looked at each other, lifted ears to the wind.

"Hear anything, Ike?"

"Not a thing, Chet."

"Neither do I. Let's split. If you find anything fire a shot. I'll do the same. Go down through that valley. I'll work the ridge and the draw beyond. All right?"

"All right."

"See you again, Ike."

"S' long, Chet."

They parted. In a few minutes McClusky was lost in the

gloom of the valley trail. Tyson swung upward along the ridge, stopping at intervals to listen intently. Only the sound of the wind in the spruce-tops reached his alert ears. Once an owl hooted three times, and the wind carried the echoes from valley to valley. Once, too, a timber wolf's call came wailing from an immeasurable distance, and died like a forlorn soul. But otherwise the mottled wilderness slept in its robe of cold starshine.

Tyson reached the backbone of the ridge and shot dark, questioning glances into the bush about him. Below stretched the other valley, black and mysterious. The corporal moved slowly, attentively, along the rim of the ridge, his rifle resting in the crook of his arm. He was calm, collected, alert to every little sound. He had a name where men are measured by their sand. Some, of course, remembered him with bitterness. For he was the law.

He stopped suddenly. His hands tightened on his rifle.

"Something down there," he thought, peering into the valley. He had heard a rustling noise in the thickets.

He started down the slope, moving from tree to tree swiftly, cautiously. A big, web-footed snowshoe rabbit shot across in front of him. His rifle came down with a snap.

"Dammit!" he bit off under his breath, and eased his rifle back. "Guess that's what I heard."

The bush became dense, the trees crowded, the going hard. He progressed with some difficulty, his ears strained to catch every sound. Soon he came upon a narrow, winding footpath. He remembered it was the route used by trappers without sled or dogs. It led from the lake over the ridge to Hank Langdon's trading station. Here the going was easier. He descended more rapidly for a time.

Suddenly he stopped; so suddenly, in fact, that he almost lost his balance. Another step and he would have stumbled over the huddled figure of a man that lay in his path. He looked all around, listened, then bent over the body, rolled it over on its back.

"Nasty!" he muttered, with a slight grimace, as he saw the dark hole in the temple.

The man was old and grizzled. His clothes were nondescript, a cheap mackinaw lashed around the waist with a piece of *babiche*, worn moosehide moccasins, strips of blanket wound around his legs to serve as leggings. In his right hand was gripped a forty-four revolver. Tyson went through his pockets, but found nothing by which he could identify the man.

He stood up, pondering. Then, thinking of McClusky, he fired his rifle. After a moment he knelt down again, took the gun from the dead hand. One shell had been fired. Powder dust was still fresh around the muzzle.

"Devil of a place to commit suicide," thought the corporal.

He shoved the revolver into his pocket. A sudden idea struck him, and he snapped his fingers. He looked at the man's wound again, straightened with a snap and bit off:

"By cripes!" For a long moment he was silent. "Now, why didn't I think of that before? The bullet entered the left temple. This chap's gun was in his right hand. I've never heard of a right-handed man shooting himself in the left temple. Rotten business!" he ended with a snap.

Impatiently he waited for his partner. A half hour passed, but there was no sign of Ike. Tyson cupped his hands to his mouth and shouted. No answer. He fired his rifle again. Only its lonely echo came back. The corporal swore and smacked fist to palm savagely. He jammed his hands into his pockets and waited fifteen minutes longer. Then, finally, he heaved the dead man over his shoulder and began toiling up the slope. Once at the top, he again called Ike's name. Again his echo mocked him—nothing more.

"Now, what?" he asked himself. "What the devil's happened to Ike? I wonder if he's gone right on to Langdon's place and maybe got into a conversation with some old sourdough. But Langdon's got no use for the red. Well, anyhow, I'd better park this old fellow at the cabin before I do anything else."

With which he struck the back-trail, bending under his cold, stiff burden. Half an hour later he pushed open the door, kicked it shut with his heel, and laid the corpse in one corner. He went over to the stove, replenished the fire and began stuffing his pipe.

"It's funny," he mused. "There was only one shot. I can swear to that. Yet here this fellow had his gun in his right hand and a hole in the left temple. It doesn't look logical. And what the devil's happened to Ike? And who is this fellow? Questions! Sure, if I keep on I'll be asking myself questions all night!"

He threw a blanket over the dead man, took up his rackets and his rifle and went outside. Ike was in his thoughts now. He must find Ike. He struck the east trail into the big timber, the trail he and Ike had taken but two hours before. The wind had shifted from east to northeast, and was a little sharper, whipping up stinging snow particles from the crust. But the sky was faultlessly clear, the stars brilliant, the moon now soaring majestically overhead. Under other circumstances the hard young corporal would have enjoyed the jaunt in the crisp, bracing air.

But not so now. He had to be alert, sensitive to every slight noise in the wilderness, on his toes for immediate action. He felt that somewhere in those woods all was not well. He reached the spot where he and Ike had parted company, and took the direction that he remembered Ike had taken. This led him down into a valley so dark that not even the moonlight filtered through. Once he stumbled and swore briefly but violently. Things like this irritated the corporal. He had, at times, a temper.

He reached the bottom of the valley, calling loud and long for Ike. He looked obliquely upward and listened. No answer came. Presently he moved along, and then he saw a shadow that was darker even than the shadows cast by the tall spruces. And this shadow was moving away with what the corporal thought was rather panicky haste.

"Say, there!" he shouted.

The shadow kept moving. The corporal, clamping his jaw, moved after it with a grim glint in his eyes.

"Say, you, hold on! If you don't I'll pot you!" he ripped out.

The shadow slowed down, hesitated, finally stopped and crouching, turned about reluctantly. Tyson was no fool. He dropped down behind a bush.

"None of that," he called out. "Stand straight up, drop your gun and see how high you can reach. Now stay that way." He started on, adding, "Any tricks and see what happens."

His rifle resting along his hip, he strode out of the bushes and up to the waiting figure. Approaching closer, he slowed and chuckled in his grim, hard way.

"A woman, eh?" he droned, and stopped, eyeing her narrowly.

The woman made no answer. She was wearing a white-fox *capote,* with the hood thrown back, but even in the gloom you could see that she had black hair, oceans of it, and a face that, though tense and a bit strained, was singularly beautiful. Some years back a romantic Frenchman down Lac la Ronge way, having imbibed too freely of rank rum, had told the corporal to his face that he was no man because a pretty face failed to turn his head. The corporal at that time had just mushed in on hard trail from He a la Crosse, and his temper had been very near the surface. He had promptly taken the Frenchman by the seat of his pants and pitched him through the door into a snow-bank.

He was symbolic of the Force, the corporal, and it takes a man of steel indeed to deal the same justice to a woman that he would deal to a man. He was saying, now:

"Madame Duval, I believe?"

"Oui, *m'sieu.*"

"What are you doing over this way, at this time of night, please?" Madame Duval seemed bewildered.

"I—I— Ma dog, he run away."

"No men at the post?"

"Oui, but I—I come."

"So I see," nodded the corporal sagely. "Frankly, madame, I don't believe you."

"Oh, *m'sieu,* it ees true. I swear it!"

"By le bon Dieu?"

She shrank back, her midnight eyes wide. The corporal nodded to himself and changed his tone.

"By the way, have you seen my partner? You know, M'sieu McClusky, he of the flaming hair. Have you?"

She shook her head vigorously.

"Non, non! I have no' see."

Tyson thought for a moment, then bent down and picked up her rifle.

"Very well," he said in a matter-of-fact way. "I will see you back to the post."

"Oh, but I can ver' well go alone, *m'sieu,*" she cried.

"Nevertheless, madame, I insist on escorting you back to the post," persisted Tyson, his eyes shrewd and penetrating.

"Non, non," she began.

But the corporal took her arm gently but firmly and guided her through the bush. He thought he heard a sob of anguish catch in her throat, but he was not sure. At any rate, he remained unmoved and kept propelling her onward with that same gentle firmness he had at first exerted.

"I am looking," he said, "for my partner, who has disappeared in these woods. I'll see what they know at the post about that and—h'm—another thing."

Young Madame Duval buried her head in her *capote* hood. A tremor ran over her body. The corporal sensed it through her furs and smiled grimly to himself. He had mentioned nothing regarding the dead man he had found. For the time being, he was not of a mind to.

So they went on, side by side, and soon they rose up to a ridge from the crest of which they could look down toward a frozen waterway. On the banks of this river clustered a settlement of log-cabins. Lights blinked there.

"Funny," said Tyson. "Lights at this time o' night. Most folks are asleep at midnight, usually."

Madame Duval made no answer, and after a moment the corporal led her riverward. They crossed the ice, and Tyson made for the cabin in which lights shone. This was Langdon's trade-store, a rendezvous for the good, bad and indifferent that drifted over the white frontier. He pushed open the door and motioned for the woman to go in. Then he followed her, slipping off one glove and gripping his rifle near the trigger.

A conversation that had been under way immediately stopped. Two men sitting at a table looked up. The one was low-built, bull-necked, shaggy. Hank Langdon. The other was big, young and burly, with an unkempt stubble of beard, insolent eyes and a loose mouth. Paul Duval.

"Hello," jerked out Tyson, booting shut the door.

The two men nodded hostilely. Duval got up and rolled over to his wife.

"Where you been?" he snapped.

The woman tried to silence him with her eyes. He gripped her by the wrist, jerked it savagely.

"Enough of this," cut in Tyson, pushing him away casually. "Sit down."

Duval glared at him, his fists clenching. Obviously the man was drunk. Tyson cut him with a razor stare.

"Sit down!" he rasped, the muscles at his mouth corners tightening. Duval, muttering in his throat, backed up and sat down. Tyson turned to the woman.

"You, too, madame," he said.

He threw open his furs. His scarlet tunic was worn and faded from much usage. His eyes were regarding Langdon impersonally. His thrust was direct.

"What do you know about Constable McClusky?"

Langdon's thick brows bent together in a puzzled frown.

"McClusky? Me? What you mean, Corporal? I don't get your drift." He looked from the corporal to Duval perplexedly, and then back to the corporal again. "McClusky? I ain't seen the cons'able in a month."

Tyson thought over this momentarily. Then he turned to Duval.

"Did Madame Duval's dog find its way home?" he asked.

Duval snarled.

"Nevaire knew dat dam' wife o' mine had a dog."

The woman hid her face in her hands. The corporal's lips drew down in a bitter grimace. Langdon threw a black look at his companion which might have meant, "you fool!"

"Madame," spoke up Tyson, "again I ask you to tell me why you were over near Big Moon Lake at such a late hour?"

The woman moaned. Her body shook. She sprang to her feet, her face pitiful in its anguish.

"I weel not say! I weel not say!" she cried, and slumped back to the chair again. Duval took a crack at the table and heaved to his feet, taking in a reef on his belt.

"By dam', she have no' tol' *me* yet where she had been. An' she weel tell me or by le diable...." He strode over to his wife and grabbed her roughly by the shoulder.

"You cut that stuff!" ripped out Tyson, without budging.

"By dam', ees she not ma wife, eh?"

"Cut it, I said! I'm dealing with madame right now."

"She ees ma wife."

"You blasted idjit, come away!" boomed Langdon, rising, purple with rage. "Come away an' sit down."

"I'm handling this, Langdon. Back to the table, Duval, and not another chirp out of you till I say so. I can see there's something dirty here. You, Langdon, are scared stiff over something. And you're afraid your chum Duval, who is drunk to the ears, will spill the beans."

"There ain't nothin' wrong," rumbled Langdon, eying the corporal evenly.

"Oh, no? Well, sir, let me tell you there is. My partner, Constable McClusky, has mysteriously disappeared in the valley south of the lake trail. We were out for—well, just for a walk, to brace us up. We parted for a short time, and my partner disappeared. Some short time later I came upon Madame Duval in that valley. She seemed very nervous. I come here past midnight and find you two deep in conversation. What's it all about, eh? Constable McClusky is missing. One of you knows about it."

"That's a lie," growled Langdon.

Duval leaned back and leered.

"Mebbeso eet was ma wife have wan leetle affair d'amour wit' M'sieu McClusky."

Tyson's breath hissed through clenched teeth. Madame Duval sat erect abruptly, her eyes two great round orbs.

"Paul, you *lie!* You lie! Oh, mon dieu!" Duval's cruel insinuation had cut her to the core. He said to Tyson:

"Well, *m'sieu,* eef M'sieu McClusky is missing, an' ma wife was in de same valley, den sure she must know somet'ing. If she weel not talk, give her to me. Ha! *I* weel make her talk."

Tyson thought, "You skunk!" But he said:

"The law doesn't operate that way."

For some minutes now an object lying on the mantelpiece under the gun-rack had attracted his attention. Now he strolled over that way, and saw out of the corner of his eye that the two men were watching him closely. Once by the mantelpiece he swung about abruptly. Langdon and Duval looked away and stared at the table.

"Which one of you owns the silencer here behind me?"

Langdon and Duval looked at each other for a long minute. Then Langdon looked away and said:

"Me."

Tyson nodded, reached back, took hold of the silencer, and examined it casually.

"Been used recently, hasn't it, Langdon?" he asked in an offhand manner.

"Naw. Not f'r a long time. Bought it from a feller needed grub," said Langdon.

"Funny," Tyson went on. "This smoke grime doesn't seem very old."

Langdon and Duval looked at each other strangely. Then Langdon looked at his hands and shrugged his shoulders.

"Naw, haven't used it in ages, corp."

Tyson looked up to find Madame Duval's eyes riveted on him. But she looked away with a slight gasp and fidgeted. The corporal laid the silencer back on the mantel. Silence hung like a dread pall in the room. Then the corporal said, quite simply, "Found a dead man on the trail that leads from your place to the lake, Langdon."

Three persons started. Duval. Langdon. The woman. The corporal followed up this neatly dropped bomb shell with:

"Come on, now! Spill it! What do you know? One of you knows. Maybe all of you." With a quick step he was beside the table, his eyes shooting sparks. "Duval? Langdon? Out with it!"

The two men stood up. They eyed the corporal narrowly.

"You're takin' a lot f'r granted, corp," dragged out Langdon, hooking a thumb in his vest-pocket.

"And I'll bet you I'm not far off, either. That silencer has been used only a short time ago. That stranger, perhaps, was on his way over to see me about something. One of you birds clamped the silencer on your rifle, trailed him and potted him in the temple. Then you crept up and pulled off his own revolver and stuck it in his hand. But one of you pulled a bonehead trick. *You shot him in the left temple and shoved the gun in his right hand!* Now, by God, which one of you?"

Langdon took a deep breath and still stared at the corporal.

"It's your silencer," Tyson told him.

"Ain't used the silencer in a month, corp," Landon growled.

"Mebbeso ma wife use eet," purred Duval.

Langdon's jaw went hard. Tyson's eyes contracted. The woman cried:

"Paul, Paul, what you say? What you say? Mon Dieu! I? Me? Non. Non! You do not mean eet, Paul! You—you— Oh!" She shrank back across the room, pressing her hands across her eyes as though to shut out some horrible nightmare.

Duval turned to Tyson.

"Eef mebbeso ees possible. Oui?"

Tyson stared him down. After a moment the corporal said:

"What evidence there is, yes, points toward Madame Duval. It is likely that I shall have to take her south as the killer of that stranger and perhaps, too, of Constable McClusky, not yet accounted for."

Duval shrugged his big shoulders, spread his hands palmwise.

"Well, most surely, me, I weel not ah—interfere wit' de law."

Inwardly Tyson boiled, but he said nothing, for a long minute. It was Langdon who spoke next, and his voice was thick.

"The madame don't go south, corp," he said, and then jerked a thumb toward Duval. "There's your man."

Duval sucked in a breath through clenched teeth and swung back, his eyes suddenly shot with black passion. With a quick movement he whipped out his knife and lunged for Langdon. Tyson, ready for just such a move, sprang over and jammed his rifle into Duval's ribs.

"Drop it!" he clipped.

Duval brought up sharply, his loose lower lip quivering with passion.

"You—you—" he jerked out, his eyes glued fiercely to Langdon.

"Go ahead an' call me what you like. Yeah, I squealed. But if you hadn't tried to blame it on the madame, I'd ha' kept me mouth shut. You're low, Duval. There ain't nothin' lower 'an you. Try t' blame it on your wife!

"Yeah, corp, he's your man. His wife won't miss him. He's treated her worse 'an I used t' treat my old woman, an' I wasn't gentle either. He killed the stranger. Feller named Hastings, old-timer. Seems Duval swiped money from him over on the Doobawnt. Knew lot o' other things 'bout him. Came here f'r the money. Duval kicked him out. Hastings said he'd go over an' spill all he knew 'bout Duval t' the Mounties—meanin' you. An' he started, an' Duval took my silencer. I guess I got a lot o' explainin' t' do, but the madame goes free. She didn't know anything 'bout it."

"I did," spoke up the woman tremulously. "I heard de talk between Paul an' de stranger, an' when Paul go I leave later, t'inking mebbe I stop him. But I get lost, me, an' den I hear shot way far an' I make for dat way. But eet is ver' dark an' I go slow, an' den I see Mountie, an' I t'ink he hunt Paul an' I mak a sneak in bush. An' when Mountie pass I heet him on de head wit' ma gun an' drag him though bush to li'l trappin' shack, where I tie his hands an' feet, an' when he come to I tie cloth over mouth."

"You can find the shack?" Tyson shot at her.

"Oui. I find now."

She had swept Duval entirely out of heart. Only in name was he her husband and not for long, either. The wheels of justice would move swiftly. And for the woman, mercifully. A great sense of duty, as between wife and husband, had in the beginning driven her to save her husband, although there had been no great love between them. But Duval's vindictive cowardice had killed even that.

Tyson was clamping hand-cuffs on his prisoner.

"I'll take you along now," he said grimly.

Duval remained silent, sullen.

Langdon said:

"Maybe I'd better tag along, corp, an' see the madame gets back safe t' her cabin. Maybe you'll need help gettin' the cons'able t' the lake."

Madame Duval led the way out and across the frozen river, and her step was not reluctant. Behind trudged Langdon, whose general code perhaps was not righteous. Yet, like most men of his stamp, he held a good woman's honor sacred. Duval's head was bowed; he was a broken man. The hard young corporal brought up the rear, his rifle hovering near the small of Duval's back. He was calm, collected, showing no signs of elation. To him it was just another incident of the white frontier, a raw bit of life, a drama played by a noble woman and a man utterly without honor.

WEEKS LATER the corporal and Ike McClusky sat in their cabin on Big Moon Lake, immersed in thought. They were playing checkers, and the board was almost empty.

"It's your move, Chet," said the red-haired constable.

"S' I see," droned the corporal studiously, and then moved.

The constable smacked his big hands together and grinned from ear to ear.

"Ho-ho, Chet, divil, I've got ye again!" And Ike jumped the corporal's last two men. "It's so-o simple, Chet."

"S' I imagine," said the corporal. "Duval said it was simple to beat the law, too. He swung yesterday."

"An' his poor little wife, she that whanged me on the head, God bless her, has gone back t' her folks on the River du Rocher. Pst! An' she siz anytime I'm down that way I should drop in t' see her. Bet she didn't tell ye that, Chet."

Tyson put his tongue in his cheek and said:

"It's your red hair that attracts women, Ike." Ike growled:

"Ah-r-r, go way wit' ye! An' mind, me dear corporal, ye owe me tobacco f'r two months t' come."

"Two months!"

"Yes, two months. Ye have lost altogether two hundred and sixty games." Tyson stroked the rough stubble on his jaw.

"But, Ike, how many have I won?"

"Won? That's just it, ye dommed idiot! Ye ain't won a single game!" With which Ike leaned back and threw out his chest proudly. The hard young corporal grinned.

TELL IT TO THE MOUNTED

**IN SUNSHINE OR
BLIZZARD, HELL-
HOLE OR HEAVEN,
FRIGID TUNDRA OR
MELLOW ARCADY—
FROM QUEBEC TO
CALGARY AND FROM
THE YANKEE BORDER
TO THE POLE—YOU'LL
GET ACTION IF YOU
TELL IT TO THE
MOUNTED!**

WHEN CORPORAL KIRK plugged into Nelson's Camp that raw December night he felt just a little weary and grouchy and out of sorts. He had been on the prod for ten days through a rotten strip of country; scraggly muskeg and stunted spruce, or no spruce at all—raw stretches of open country where the wind drove sharp as a knife. To make matters worse, his Indian dog-driver had never seemed sure of the trail.

Yes, Kirk was a little on edge. He had been promised a month's leave that would have included Christmas with his folks in Calgary. He had prepared to take a respite from the wilderness. In fact, he had been ready to leave the detachment post when Corporal Pendleton arrived from the north on a sledge driven by two Indians. Porr Pendleton—a physical wreck, half out of his mind with the chills and fever.

Staff-sergeant McQuade had said, "Sorry, Kirk; you'll have to go north. Pendleton says he left Constable Flint in charge. I'll let you have Pendleton's journal so that you may get a slant on things as they are round about Nelson's Camp. Flint will probably tell you something, too."

Kirk had not tried to hide his disappointment.

McQuade repeated, "Sorry, Kirk," and then added, "You know, Nelson's Camp is no beauty place, and I want a man there I can rely on. You'll find it interesting. Those two Indians who brought Pendleton in refuse to go back so we'll have to round up another."

Billy Jack was the other, and now he was driving the six-dog team into Nelson's Camp. He was a dirty little runt, but a willing worker despite the fact that he made some lamentable blunders.

The Camp, comprising about a dozen cabins of varying size and quality of structure, nestled in a bowl-like valley through which coursed a narrow, frozen waterway. The hills that almost completely surrounded the Camp were not high, and the forest growth was stunted. Thickets, however, were plentiful, and in the southern part of the valley there was plenty of muskeg. An unlovely country, with its scrawny hills and wind-blown willows, but otter, mink and beaver were to be trapped along its brooks and its fields of muskeg.

This particular pocket of the Northland was new to Kirk, and he didn't like it. He didn't like its frozen swamps and its stunted spruce. But, then, it wasn't up to him to choose his posts. He wore the red coat with its corporal's stripes, and he took order from McQuade, who in turn took orders from the Division Superintendent in Prince Albert, a thousand miles or more to the south and west as the crow flies.

The early twilight of the North, that so quickly turns to darkness, was settling over the land when Kirk, tramping at the head of the dogs, looked about for signs of the police cabin. A man swung out of one of the cabins, and Kirk called to him, asking for directions.

"Keep right ahead. It's the last cabin. You can't miss it," the man explained.

Kirk moved on. A crisp, sharp wind blew in his face. A dog barked, and then growled in its throat. Kirk had never met Constable Flint. A new man, he had been told, nearing the end of his first term. He hoped Flint would be a decent sort.

He reached the last cabin, saw a light in the window, heard voices. He raised a mittened hand and Billy Jack brought the dogs to a halt. There was boisterous laughter in the cabin, loud guffaws. Kirk frowned and looked about, thinking perhaps he had stopped at the wrong cabin. He went closer, after a moment, and saw the R.C.M.P. sign over the door. Then he turned and took a few steps toward Billy Jack.

"Feed the dogs, Billy, and put up your camp here for the night," he said.

Billy Jack nodded, and Kirk again turned to the cabin. This time he heard a harmonica, stamping feet, and a woman's laugh. His lips hardened and his tall, clean-clipped frame straightened with a military snap. He strode forward, laid his hand on the door, and pushed it open.

A girl, evidently half-breed, was dancing atop the table, and half a dozen men were keeping time with their feet. One played furiously on a harmonica. Another sat on a tipped chair with his feet perched on the edge of the table. It was on this man that Kirk's cold, gray eyes settled, as he leaned back against the door and drew off his mittens. There was a bottle on the table and several cups. All the men, including the one on the tipped chair, appeared to be slightly intoxicated. The half-breed woman seemed none too sober, either, for she kept on dancing and laughing and paid no attention to the newcomer.

The man on the tipped chair took his feet down from the table and stared. He was a young man, rather good-looking despite the fact that his tousled hair hung partly over his eyes, and his face was badly in need of a shave. His scarlet tunic was unbuttoned, rumpled, and stained. In a half-hearted way he began to button it. He muttered something under his breath and the harmonica player stopped. The others stopped stamping, and the girl on the table sat down, dangling her legs.

Kirk said, briefly: "Please be good enough to clear out. I've come to replace Corporal Pendleton. Kirk's the name."

The girl slid from the table. The men got up and edged toward the door.

"Glad to meet you, corporal," ventured one tentatively.

The girl rolled her big dark eyes as she sauntered by Kirk with her hands on her hips.

"Me too, *m'sieu?*" she purred.

"You too, mademoiselle," clipped the corporal.

He opened the door, and she passed out, not without another warm look cast over her shoulder at the corporal. The men followed her, and Kirk closed the door. Then he drew off his furs, hung them up and stood facing the one man who still remained.

"Flint, I suppose?"

The man nodded. Kirk sat down and began stuffing his pipe.

"You know," he said after a moment, "this is bad business. You're drunk now, Flint, and it's the last time I want to see you this way. It's all right to have a bottle—I've got one—but it's bad business throwing a party this way and having the town in. Who's the woman?"

"We call her Nellie," Flint muttered.

"Better stay away from her, too. She's no good, Flint, and," he slowed down, pointing his pipe at the constable, "if you keep mixing with her you won't be either."

Flint swung on his chair and brought a big hand down on the table. "Just what are you driving at, corporal?"

"Don't get theatrical. You know what I'm driving at. When you wear the red coat, mister, you've got to wear its traditions and wear 'em well. I'll admit it's a blamed heavy burden, but you knew that when you took the oath. And—Indian—women—are—taboo. Get me, Flint?"

Flint's bleary eyes narrowed, then widened.

"I get you, corporal," said he.

"Then don't forget. I had to plug up to this God-forsaken hole instead of winging south for a month's furlough, which I'd been promised. I don't know how long I'll be kept here, but while I'm here this camp gets run as it should, and there'll be no more parties spread in this little shack. By the Lord Harry, I never saw such a dirty dump, Flint. I'll have to get it cleaned up a bit."

"I've heard," put in Flint, leaning on one elbow, "that you're a stickler for the law as it's written."

"That's possible. Maybe I am."

"And I've heard you're a pretty-well-tough bird."

Kirk leaned forward and tapped the table with a forefinger.

"Flint, you'll find out just how tough I am if you try to act nasty. Talk to me when you're sober."

"I'm sober now."

"You're drunk."

"I tell you—"

"*Shut up!*" Kirk's voice had the crack of a rawhide whip. "I said you are drunk!"

Flint stood up, swaying on his feet, his mouth sagging at one corner.

"Damn you, Kirk, I don't like you " he snarled and swept the bottle up in his hand. "What's more, I'll drink when I please, where I please, and with whom I please."

"Put that bottle down!"

Flint chuckled and raised the bottle to his lips. Kirk leaned over and yanked it from his hands, smashed it to smithereens against the wall. Flint swayed, a murderous look in his hazy eyes. His right hand twitched, then dived for his revolver. With a snarl Kirk knocked over the table, lunged after it and caught Flint's hand as it was pulling the service pistol from its holster. With a deft twist he tore it away and sent Flint crashing to the floor.

Flint hit hard, for he was shaky in the knees and he was a hard-bodied young man. He rolled over and lay with his face pillowed on one arm. In that position he fell into a sodden slumber. Kirk sat down, looking at him, scratching the black stubble on his cleft chin.

"A pretty mess," he mused to himself. "Flint, something tells me we're not going to get on so well. I'm sorry. Hate to be at odds with a mate. But this—this is a devil of a beginning. Drunk—a 'breed woman prancing on the table—attempt to shoot me— And I was to spend Christmas in Calgary. Blast the luck!"

The door opened and Billy Jack came in with Kirk's trail equipage. The Indian looked at the red-coated figure on the floor, blinked, but said nothing. Kirk rose.

"Put those things in the corner, Billy, and help me get Constable Flint to his bunk," he directed; and added, as an afterthought, "The constable isn't feeling so well. Just fainted."

Billy Jack blinked again, dropped his bundle in the corner, and shuffled over to help Kirk. Between them they carried Flint to his bunk. Then Kirk dismissed the Indian and sat down again. Almost immediately there was a sound at the door. A moment later it swung open, and a girl started in.

She stopped with one foot across the threshold. Her eyes grew wide with surprise. Her mouth opened, but uttered no sound. Wisps of golden hair, escaping from her toque, blew across her flushed, startled face. Only a moment she stared, then backed out, slammed the door and was gone.

Kirk leaped to his feet, and rushed outside, but she had disappeared. The sharp night wind cut him to the marrow and he stepped back, lingering in the doorway, searching the darkness with keen eyes. Finally he went inside and closed the door.

"Who was that?" he asked himself. "It seemed she didn't expect to find me here. She is no 'breed. Probably after Flint. H'm. I wonder how many more women this Flint knows."

He piled more wood into the sheet-iron stove, while Flint snored.

CHAPTER II

KIRK MEETS MacMAHON

THE MORNING came around with a light snow puffing out of the east. Kirk had the fire going and breakfast on when Flint climbed out of bed.

"Morning, Flint," greeted the corporal briefly, placing some slices of bacon in the fry-pan.

"Morning," Flint muttered.

He washed his hands and face in a basin of water and ran a comb through his hair. Kirk went on with the breakfast, whistling to himself. No more conversation passed between them until they faced each other across the table. Then Flint said:

"I suppose I acted rotten last night."

Kirk chuckled. "I'll say you did. Have a piece of bannock."

"I was drunk," Flint averred and repeated, "I was drunk."

"Worse than that. You were crazy."

"I suppose so. I want to apologize."

"Good enough. Have more bannock."

They ate for a while in silence. Flint seemed nervous. He kept running a hand through his hair and casting furtive glances at the indifferent corporal. He gulped his food and left half of it unfinished. He was almost choked drinking his tea, it was so hot. While Kirk was still in the middle of his meal Flint rose and paced back and forth. Kirk was not disturbed, though. He ate lustily, and when the last crumb and the last drop of tea were gone pushed back his chair, crossed one leg over the other, and lit his pipe.

"Now," he began, flipping the burnt match into the wood-box, "we can do business. I've been reading Pendleton's notes. He says you made a circular patrol last month covering three hundred miles in three weeks, and found the Indians in good shape and fairly prosperous. From his notes I gather that Pendleton considered you a valuable man.

"About this Nelson's Camp. Nelson, I understand, died a long while ago, but the place still retains his name. Pendleton seemed to think there was some underhand work going on—but he's very vague about it. He remarks a certain hostility shown by most residents to the law. How do you feel about that, Flint?"

Flint moistened his lips and hesitated for a long minute.

"I haven't noticed any hostility," he dragged out. "I—I did a lot of patroling, you see, while Pendleton paid more attention to the settlement."

"I see. The people here, I suppose, trap for a living."

"That's all," Flint jerked out.

Kirk regarded him keenly for a minute.

"Say, Flint, don't you feel so well? You're nervous as the devil and seem afraid to talk. What's ailing you"

"Oh, I'm all right. I'm all right."

"Then let's get together. I'm up here for God knows how long, and we ought to be friends. I'm damned easy to get along with, Flint. Last night—well, I was pretty sore. I had cause to be, but let's drop it. I've got a fresh razor in my pack—a spare one—and you'd better use it. It'll brace you up, a good shave. I'll look the settlement over and drop back for a chat later." He got up, his lean, weather-roughened face crinkling in a smile, and laid a hand on Flint's shoulder. "Buck up. I may be a stickler for the law as it's written, old timer, and I do get tough at times, but I've been policing ten years and I've mixed with some pretty tough people. If you treat me white, Flint, I'll treat you white. Treat me dirty and I'll treat you dirty. But meet me half-way and you'll find how nice we'll get along."

He struggled into his furs and went outside. When he had closed the door Flint buried his face in his arms and muttered to himself. Then the constable got to his feet, clenching his fists and his jaw, and groaned deep in his throat:

"My—God!"

Kirk, having fastened on his snow-shoes, plowed through the fine, driving snow. He felt pretty well this morning. He had blown in last night in a bad mood and Flint's disgraceful behavior hadn't made it any sweeter. But he was willing to let that blow over if Flint would play the man. He had to live with Flint, and if you are forced by circumstances to live with a man on the remote rim of the world, it's not politic to hold a grudge, for in raw places men's nerves get raw, and anything is liable to happen. Kirk knew, for Kirk had bunked with many men by many a lonely trail.

He passed a few shacks, and after a while stopped before a square, well-built cabin with the word "Store" painted over the door. He entered this, and was met by a large, heavy man with a bushy red beard and beady black eyes.

"So you're the new corporal" the man boomed.

"Yes. And whom have I the pleasure of addressing?"

"MacMahon—Alex MacMahon. We're mostly kin in the valley, from fur back. There's Don MacMahon, an' Andy Mac-Mahon, an' Bob, an' the MacDonalds. Have a seat, won't ye?"

Kirk sat down and gave his name. A fire roared in the big stove. He noticed there was not much stock in the trade-room. The single counter in the rear was bare, and there was the faint smell of old dust. Alex MacMahon himself seemed dusty.

"Do much business here?" Kirk ventured.

"Not much—no. We're just like a big family, corporal, though I do a little tradin' with such as might pass our way. Our traps run pretty fair, an' in the summer we raise what vegetables we can."

The door opened, and a man bearing an armful of wood entered. He looked neither to left nor right, but walked with a measured tread and dropped the wood beside the stove. Then he turned slowly and looked at MacMahon with a blank, unwavering stare. MacMahon snapped his fingers, and the stranger bowed stiffly, turned on his heel and strode into the rear. Kirk looked after him, mildly perplexed. MacMahon saw he was interested and remarked, tapping his temple:

"He does the chores 'round the place. Ye mustn't mind him, corporal. Little queer in the head, but a harmless, good-natured soul. We call him Johnny. He just drifted in some time ago, an' he seems to like the place, so we keep him on."

Kirk nodded and dismissed the subject.

"About how many persons live in the valley?" he asked.

"Well, say twenty, an' we're all kin. There's about six families, of course, there's an Injun camp two miles up the valley near the muskeg, but I don't know just how many's there. My wife died seven years back. There's a squaw takes care o' my kitchen."

Kirk spent about an hour with him, gathering bits of information about the valley and the surrounding country. When he left MacMahon shook his hand with apparent warmth, but in those small, beady eyes Kirk thought he saw a fleeting glimpse of mockery. His own good-bye was formal and perfunctory. He said he hoped he would have the pleasure of seeing MacMahon often.

Leaving the store, he so relished the brisk clean snow that he decided to explore a little farther through the valley. He nodded to several mackinawed men who passed him evidently headed for the store, and the nods he received in return bore a note of reserve and vague mistrust. He noticed two more cabins and placed their location in his memory; a gradually he was getting the lie of the land.

After about half an hour of brisk snowshoeing, he sensed that someone was dogging his steps. He stopped casually and looked about, and saw another figure come to a halt. He stood regarding it for several minutes. When it did not move, he approached it. It was Johnny. The man seemed to be well in his twenties, and there was something pathetically inquisitive in his round eyes.

"Do you want something, Johnny?" Kirk gently asked.

The man stared at him.

"Who are you" he asked in a flat voice, pointing a finger.

"Why I'm Corporal Kirk, of the Mounted."

"Corporal Kirk, of the Mounted," Johnny repeated, without shifting his gaze. After a pause he asked: "Who am I?"

Kirk put a hand on his shoulder. "Why, you're Johnny. Come on. You'd better go back to the store. I'm going that way."

He took Johnny's arm and walked with him in the direction of the store. When he left him there, Johnny touched his arm and asked: "You're...?"

"Kirk—Corporal Kirk."

"Kirk... Kirk... Kirk," Johnny kept mumbling as he shuffled into the store.

CHAPTER III

THE BEGINNING
OF DISASTER

KIRK HEADED back for his cabin. The feathery snow whisked and spiraled around him, clinging to his furs, and as he was now heading into the wind it nipped his face sharply. But his blood was healthy, and it tingled in his veins under the brisk exertion.

Presently he noted an indistinct figure coming toward him, stumbling a trifle from what he guessed was too much haste. Before they passed he saw that it was the golden-haired girl who had looked in at his cabin last night. She was hurrying, and he thought he heard her sobbing. As they drew nearer she reeled and almost collided with him. He caught her arm and steadied her.

"Oh… excuse me!" she gasped.

"That's all right," he assured her. "Pardon me, but you seem to be in trouble. I am the new corporal—"

"No—no—everything is all right," she hurried, smiling through moist blue eyes.

"I just thought—"

"No; thanks—very—very much."

Her white teeth flashed against red young lips in another brave smile.

"Well, if there's anything wrong," he told her, "anything at all, of any nature, you know you just have to tell it to the Mounted, and we'll do our best."

"Nothing—nothing wrong," she hastened to declare.

Then she pushed on, and the corporal watched her until the driving snow put an impenetrable curtain between them. He snapped a heap of snow from one of his rackets and continued toward his cabin, mildly perplexed. The wind was whistling shrilly about the little cabin when he arrived, and it didn't take him very long to unbuckle his rackets and shove open the door.

Flint, who had been pacing the floor, stopped and regarded Kirk obliquely. The corporal was heaving vigorously out of his furs. He remarked: "If this wind changes, Flint, you'll see the mercury drop out of the bottom. Boy, I'll bet the wind raises the devil around this bald spot. No big woods to shunt it off. Think of the soft jobs the boys in K-Division have. That's the Division I used to belong to; I was at Medicine Hat for a while and then they ticketed me to Stand Off. But there's no park lands and no tourists to take care of on good old F-Division, eh, Flint?"

"I don't know much about K," Flint replied, sitting down on the bunk.

Kirk had his furs off and was cramming tobacco into his inevitable pipe.

"Did a lady drop in a little while ago, Flint?"

Flint started, then settled back again.

"A—lady?"

"Blonde lady—very beautiful, Flint. Fact of the matter is, I've never seen a more beautiful lady in my life."

Flint shook his head and said: "No lady was here—Kirk."

Kirk's eyes narrowed. He was on the point of saying something, but he pursed his lips, crossed the room and looked at the fire, which he replenished. Then he sat down at the table with Pendleton's journal.

"Well, I made a little tour, Flint," he remarked after a while. "I had a long talk with Alex MacMahon, and he's told me a lot about the valley and its inhabitants. Passed several other men on the way, but they weren't very friendly. Say, that Johnny's a queer one, isn't he? MacMahon says he's harmless, though. Ever have any trouble with him, Flint?"

"Who? With Johnny? No. No trouble with Johnny."

"H'm," Kirk droned and became interested in Pendleton's journal.

During the next few days the corporal busied himself exploring the valley. He was out from dawn till dark, making notes in his own journal, estimating the amount of timber, remarking on the living conditions of the white families and the vague quality of unfriendliness that was displayed by most of the men. He spent a day in the vicinity of the Indian encampment, rendering medical attention to a sick squaw, and ordered a group of young boys to clean up the camp and burn the refuse. When he reached his cabin that night he said to Flint:

"Sanitary conditions in that Indian camp were rank. You should have had them clean up, Flint. We've got to look after the poor beggars and try to stop the blasted plagues that sweep them every so often. Now in about a week I'm going to send you on a little patrol to that Cree camp fifty miles or so north. Pendleton's last report says there was quite a bit of sickness there."

Flint and Kirk, it seemed, did not click. Kirk had tried his best to be amiable, but Flint talked very little and always seemed to be brooding. Sometimes he had nervous spells, when he paced the room incessantly. At night he rolled and tossed in his sleep.

"Buck up," Kirk told him, clapping him on the back. "Is it the country that's getting on your nerves? Forget it. Throw yourself into your work, take an interest in it, write down your impression of the land and the people. Buck up, Flint, or you'll be shaking hands with the willows."

Kirk was beginning to consider himself Flint's keeper. He had seen the cruel, lonely North break the spirit of more than one good man, and he feared that it was breaking Flint. He was not a sentimental man, still he felt sorry for the constable. He was a toughened campaigner who had lived through a dozen arctic winters and seen the North at its worst. He knew how men crumbled at this fag end of the earth.

IT WAS dusk, and he was heading for their cabin after a day spent in increasing his knowledge of the valley. It was bitter cold, with the air clear as crystal, and his breath drifted from his mouth like silver clouds, forming gleaming ice particles as it settled on his two days' stubble of beard. He was in good spirits, though. Flint would have the fire going cheerily and a steaming meal awaiting him.

He reached the cabin, jabbed his rackets in the snow just outside the door, and rocked in. There was an immediate stir, the scraping of a stool, and Kirk found himself staring at Flint and the half-breed girl called Nellie. She crouched behind Flint, holding one of his arms, her lips puckered, her dark eyes wide and startled.

Something inside Kirk rebelled. A hot rush of anger swept through his veins. He called himself a fool for having softened against Flint. The man was no good. He had disgraced the uniform he wore in more ways than one. The corporal's face was lined with bitterness, and his lip curled in a snarl.

"Flint," he ripped out, "send her away! You've broken your trust. You're no good. The only time a woman is allowed in here is when she's on a mission pertaining to the law. Your friend is not here for any such purpose. And, Flint, you've been drinking again."

"That's my business," Flint snapped.

"And mine. *Care*-ful, Flint. You know what I'm going to do. I'm going to send you on the longest patrol I can think of."

"Like hell you are!"

"Never mind. Chase your little friend."

Flint's jaw went hard. He put his arm about the girl's waist, defying the corporal. Kirk strolled over and placed his hand on her arm.

"Come on, miss," he said softly.

"Damn you, leave her alone!" Flint cried, and smashed Kirk flush on the jaw.

The corporal reeled away, tangled with a stool and toppled to the floor in a heap. Flint released the girl, an ugly look in his eyes as Kirk clambered back to his feet and rushed for him. There was no gentleness in Kirk's eyes, either. He rushed the constable to the wall. They closed, reeled furiously about the room and spun to the floor.

Kirk was on top, and he intended to stay on top. He had the better of the situation, when Nellie, her dark eyes blazing, picked up the heavy stool, crept up behind him and brought it savagely down on his head. The corporal slumped without a groan. Nellie shoved him aside, and Flint got to his feet, stumbling to the pegs where his trail togs hung.

"Come—come, Nellie," he gasped. "I think—you've killed him."

"Where—where?" she cried.

"I don't know. Here—put your coat on. Hurry!"

Flint struggled frantically into his furs, helped Nellie with hers. She clung to him for a tense moment.

"*Cheri*—you love me?" she asked.

"Yes, of course! God, yes! But come, we must hurry! No—he's not dead—just moved. But when he comes to...."

He yanked open the door, almost shoved Nellie out, and rushed after her. It was dark. The wind was raw. A white wisp of a moon hung among the frigid stars. The spruce scrub rustled and the wind scooped up flurries of stinging snow from the crust. The man and the woman ran into the night, close beside each other.

The corporal lay on his back, arms outstretched, eyes closed, his face pale with a ghostly pallor. His fur coat was open, and the yellow light from the lamp shone on his scarlet tunic. The wind beat a tattoo on the single window. Wood crackled in the stove. Kirk groaned—faintly.

CHAPTER IV

THE MYSTERY OF NANCY

SOMETIME LATER—PERHAPS an hour or so—there was a knock at the door. Kirk by this time was on his knees, with his hands braced against the floor, trying to get up. His head was clouded, his vision blurred. He did not hear the knock.

After a while the door opened a crack, remained that way for a moment, then swung a little farther. A white face looked in—a white face framed in the hood of a white-fox *capote*. It was the golden-haired girl. Her eyes were big and round as she watched the man kneeling on the floor. She saw he was struggling slowly, gropingly.

She entered, closing the door softly, looking quizzically about the cabin. She approached Kirk, drawing off her mittens, and stood over him for a moment in perplexed indecision. Then she bent down and grasped his arm.

Kirk felt that someone was trying to help him up. He struggled with concentrated effort to do his share, and made his feet, swaying unsteadily, with everything about him vague and misty. But someone was steadying him. He dragged his feet across the floor, felt with one outstretched hand the bunk post and, turning a trifle, let himself down.

The girl found a bottle of brandy in the home-made cupboard, and poured a little between his lips. It shot through his system like fire. He glimpsed, indistinctly, a white face swimming before his eyes, and oceans of golden hair. Then the picture disappeared. His vision began to clear, though his head throbbed with pain. Presently he turned, saw the girl sitting on a stool nearby, watching him with wide eyes and parted lips. She smiled.

"I—you feel better?" came her low, soft voice.

"Thanks… yes… a little."

"Is there anything I can do?"

"No… nothing. It was lucky… I had my furs on. The collar was up… deadened the blow."

"Somebody attacked you?"

"Yes… some unknown assailant… from behind."

"Unknown?"

"Yes… And, by the way, I'd like to… thank you sometime… if you'll tell me where I may find you."

"I'll probably see you again," was her reply.

"I won't keep you any longer. I'll be all right soon. Your… name?"

"Oh… Nancy."

She drew her *capote* hood over her head, piled more wood into the stove and, with a last smile at Kirk, departed. Kirk lay back for a while with his eyes closed. After a while he pulled himself to a sitting posture, removed his furs, and opened his tunic. He was getting up, to try out his legs, when a man entered cautiously, closed the door, and stood looking at him.

"Oh, hello, Johnny," greeted the corporal. "What can I do for you?"

Johnny stamped the snow from his moccasins.

"A lady just passed me and said you were ill, and maybe I should come and see if you needed any help."

"No, Johnny, I guess not. Little shaky yet, but I'll be all right. By the way, did you see anything of Constable Flint?"

Johnny started, frowned at the floor as if puzzled.

"Constable Flint?" he asked slowly.

"Yes, Johnny. You know, my partner."

Johnny seemed perplexed, and he shook his head.

"No-o... no-o."

Kirk sat down wearily, holding his head. Johnny stood motionless, hands at his side, his body erect. He puzzled Kirk. He always spoke in a hushed, restrained voice, and his eyes stared blankly, with now and then a fleeting spark of eagerness in them, as though he were struggling to grasp something in his mind. He puzzled Kirk, and Kirk didn't feel in any mood to solve puzzles. He told Johnny he'd better run along. Johnny bowed stiffly, turned on heel and tramped toward the door. He put his hand on the latch, paused, and glanced around.

"Constable Flint?" he asked slowly.

"Eh? Flint? Oh, yes. But that's all right, Johnny. Better hurry."

Johnny pulled the door open, and a huge muffled man, who apparently had been just about to knock, bulked in the doorway.

"Oh!" grunted the man. "This where you are. I been lookin' all over for you."

"Come in," invited Kirk.

"No, thanks, corporal. I just come for Johnny. Didn't know where he was. Alex sent me. Alex is my brother. I'm Don MacMahon."

"You didn't see Constable Flint, did you?" asked Kirk.

Again Johnny started. Don MacMahon shot a rapid, dark glance at him and fairly hauled him out of the cabin. Then he looked at the corporal.

"No, I didn't," he rumbled, and pulled the door shut.

Kirk frowned. He hadn't failed to notice that quick glance of MacMahon's at Johnny. Something in that. One thing was apparent. MacMahon didn't want Johnny in Kirk's company.

He had almost jerked him from his feet. Something—yes, something was in the wind, mused the corporal, and returned to his bunk.

In the morning he made an early breakfast. The dull ache was still in the back of his head, and he had nothing but bitterness in his thoughts for Flint. He cursed himself for ever having felt sorry for the man. Well, Flint would pay for it now. He'd put Flint's nose to the grindstone. Kirk was the seasoned campaigner, now, the man who had a name for being a stickler on points of the law—and a name, too, for being a tough bird. Flint had pushed him one step too far, and there would be no retracing those steps. He'd strip the constable's red coat from his very back.

He banged out of his cabin following breakfast, strapped on his rackets, and rocked toward Alex MacMahon's store. He found Alex puttering around the stove. There were two other men in split-log chairs, smoking pipes.

"Good-morning," clipped Kirk, kicking the door shut with his heel. "I am looking for Constable Flint. The constable has been rather ill lately, and I fear he's wandered away from our cabin."

"That's too bad," Alex sympathized, pulling at his red beard. "No, I didn't see him, corporal. Brothers o' mine, Andy and Don. You seen the constable, boys?"

They shook their heads.

Kirk pursed his lips in a gesture of impatience. He was on edge again, and his head pained him fearfully. Another man would have stayed in bed, but Kirk's was a restless nature.

"You're sure of that?" he shot at them. He pointed a finger at Andy. "You were one of the gang in the cabin the day I arrived. That 'breed woman—who brought her there that night?"

"Nobody," said Andy, "unless it was Flint."

"Where does she come from?"

The three brothers looked at one another. Then Alex said, "We don't know, corporal. She just drifted in."

"She had to live some place. Where did she live?"

"Well, you see, corporal, we don't know much about her at all," replied Alex.

Kirk snorted. "That's surprising. Maybe Johnny might know. Get Johnny in here."

Again the three brothers looked at one another. Don and Andy stirred uneasily on their chairs. Alex shifted his weight from one foot to the other, gingerly fingering the end of his beard. "He's gone out to cut some poplar poles," Alex explained.

The words were scarcely out of his mouth when the door leading into the rear room opened. Johnny came in and marched up to the stove, to inspect the fire. Kirk eyed Alex darkly and breathed a silent oath.

Don rose. "Listen, corporal, you can't depend on what Johnny says. Ye know how it is with Johnny."

"I can't, can't I?" was Kirk's shot. "I guess I can depend on him as much as I can depend on anyone else around here. It strikes me that all of you are trying to put obstacles in my way. Johnny," he continued in a different key, "I wonder if you know where that half-breed girl called Nellie lives."

Johnny regarded the MacMahons one after another, then stared at Kirk. "Nellie hasn't been around today. Nellie takes care of the kitchen."

Kirk chuckled drily. Alex fell back a step, his hands clenching, a suppressed snarl in his throat. His two brothers looked at each other and sat erect on their chairs. Kirk bit the three of them with an icy stare.

"So that's how we stand," he observed, drawing on his mittens. "I guess Pendleton was right, saying the folks in this valley were rather hostile to the law. Pendleton's an easy-going, gentlemanly chap. You may find me not so easy-going and not so gentlemanly. I'll probably have more to say to you later."

With that he left them. When he reached his cabin his head was spinning, and he took a dose of quinine and lay down. About an hour later the door opened and Billy Jack shuffled in. Billy had been visiting some friends in an Indian camp to the eastward. He pulled over a stool and sat down by Kirk.

"Big news," he grunted. "Come here before. See white squaw go in here. Me hide in bush. See white squaw come out. Me go in, see you gone. Me follow white squaw."

"What did she look like? How long was she in here?"

"Dam' fine white squaw—pale hair. In here mebbe ten minutes. Me follow."

"Where'd she go?"

Billy Jack pointed north. "Got shack by lake."

Kirk got up, walked around the cabin.

"Wonder what she wanted."

He stopped by Flint's bunk. He noticed that it had been disturbed. He noticed, too, that the balsam-stuffed pillow had been torn open at one corner.

"She's taken something," he told himself. "I wonder what." He turned to Billy Jack. "Let's go take a look at the shack, Billy."

"Um," Billy grunted.

Kirk pulled on his trail togs, musing, "I wonder what's going on. I wonder what Nancy took from Flint's pillow. Nancy and Nellie: are they both in love with Flint? Funny. Are they against me as well as the MacMahons? Blame it, I wish Pendleton hadn't gone under. I'd be almost in Calgary now. Blast the luck—and blast this policing game!" He buckled on his revolver. "All right, Billy; let's go."

CHAPTER V

BILLY JACK BLUNDERS

BILLY JACK waddled ahead of the corporal on broad snowshoes. Thus far the going was smooth. On either side of them were groves of slim poplars, and brush sprouted everywhere. They were still on the valley floor. Presently they reached and crossed the narrow waterway. The ascent became gradual.

"I wonder you didn't approach the lady when you saw her coming out of my cabin, Billy," Kirk remarked.

Billy Jack shrugged. "How me know you not in cabin? Um. Me go in when white squaw leave. Cabin empty. Me follow."

They marched on in silence. The going became more arduous. Kirk plugged along grimly, his head a little clearer than it had been that morning. Nellie had dealt him an awful blow with that stool, and might have split open his head but for the heavy fur collar that padded the blow. But Flint would pay for it—Flint would pay for it all.

Billy Jack stopped, casting a dubious eye about him.

"What's the matter, Billy, lost your way again?" Kirk asked.

Billy made no reply, but continued looking about. Finally he turned to the left, grunting with satisfaction, and Kirk followed. They plodded along for about half an hour. Again Billy stopped, scratched his chin, and peered intently through the forest. Kirk leaned against a tree and waited for Billy to make up his mind. This had been a regular occurrence all the way up from detachment headquarters—this getting lost.

"Uhuh," Billy grunted, which meant that he hadn't lost his way after all.

They went on, crossing the ridge. Billy seemed to have the trail pretty well in hand now. His stride was deliberate. After a while he muttered over his shoulder to Kirk and pointed to a small lake that gleamed through the scrub timber. He kept on until he neared the lake, swung sharply and followed its shore line for about five minutes, then stopped and pointed ahead.

Kirk saw the cabin and nodded. They moved on. He found it to be a nondescript affair, with a warped roof. No smoke issued from the chimney, there were no signs of life, but on the snow were the faint impressions of snowshoes. He rapped on the door. Only hollow silence answered him. He looked around at Billy, who was scratching his chin, with a frown on his face. Kirk knocked again. Billy cleared his throat.

"Make mistake. Wrong cabin—wrong lake." He pointed northeast. "Think cabin that way—mebbe."

Kirk groaned. "Billy, you've lived all your life in the woods, and you're the rottenest trail hound I know or ever hope to know." The door creaked open under his hand. "Guess this shack's deserted," he murmured, stepping into the dark interior.

A voice barked, *"Stick 'em up, Mounty!"*

Kirk's teeth clicked. He was standing in the doorway, furnishing an excellent target, and had not a chance in the world to draw his gun. He heard the movement of feet, and several hoarse whispers, and knew that more than one man confronted him in that gloomy cabin. A huge figure bulked at his side and relieved him of his service pistol.

The voice from the farther darkness said, "Get that Injun. I'll 'tend to the Mounty."

The man who had taken Kirk's gun lunged outside, while the other advanced with leveled revolver. He was huge, too, with a broad, flat face.

"Wasn't expectin' to run into you, Mounty," he said. "Saw you when you didn't see us, an' popped in this shack."

"What's the big idea?"

"You'd be surprised. But you been surprised enough, so I won't tell you. What you doin' over this way, anyhow?"

"Chasing butterflies," replied Kirk, sitting down.

His eyes were accustomed to the gloom now, and he could distinguish objects more clearly. It was a bare shack, and apparently hadn't been occupied for some time. His huge captor stood spread-legged before him. Well, a fine mess he was in now. He might have known Billy Jack would blunder. But then, he mused, he was somewhat at fault himself; he should not have walked into this trap so easily.

The man who had gone after Billy Jack returned empty-handed.

"Can't find him. He faded out, an' I'm not goin' meanderin' around an' have him pot me from ambush."

Kirk could see that this man was pretty young, though he bore a sharp resemblance to the other. Possibly father and son. Good for Billy Jack! He had eluded them!

The two men drew away from Kirk, though each watched the corporal and kept his gun handy while they conversed in low whispers. From their gestures Kirk divined there was a difference of opinion over something, but after a little apparent haggling they seemed to agree with each other. The elder of the two moved over and said to Kirk:

"You'll stay here a while, Mounty. I'm going to stay with you. M' friend's got to leave us on important business."

"I don't know what you birds have got against me," retorted Kirk, "I never saw you before."

"Nothin' personal, Mounty. It's the red coat."

The younger man, nodding briefly to the other, put his rifle under his arm and went out.

"You c'n smoke, Mounty," announced Kirk's jailer.

Kirk stuffed his pipe and lit it. "You must be a fool, stranger, to think you're going to get away with this."

"We're just goin' to keep you here a certain time. Then you c'n walk out."

"What will be happening elsewhere while I'm kept here?"

The man shook his head. "That ain't for you to know."

It was cold in the cabin. Both Kirk and his captor sat wrapped tightly in their furs. The day dragged by. Dusk rushed across the wilderness, and the cabin became darker. The men could scarcely see each other. Kirk saw his captor's face indistinctly; it seemed to float bodyless in the gloom. His own hands and feet were numb, and he felt chilled through to the marrow.

"How much longer do we hang around here?" he asked.

"Don't know. Maybe all night, an' all tomorrow."

"That doesn't sound cheerful. Mind if I stand up and move my arms and legs a bit?"

"I'm close by. Mind how you move 'em, though."

Kirk got up, flexed his arms and legs briskly. Then he sat down again, loaded his pipe, and struck a match. The glow glinted on the big man's revolver. The man watched him shrewdly across the littered table.

It grew so dark within the next hour that neither could see the other. Once or twice the man with the gun heard Kirk shift on his stool.

"Not a move, Mounty," was the sharp command.

It began to snow. They could hear the pellets driving against the roof. The wind was rising, too. It must have been near to midnight when the door opened and a man bulked there, saying:

"It's only me, pa."

He slammed the door against the wind and snow, and the man at the table struck a match.

"Got back at last, eh?"

"Yeah. We got him."

"Good. Got a piece o' *babiche* on you? We'll tie the Mounty up."

One held a revolver against Kirk's back while the other bound his feet together. The old man said, "We figure you'll get them knots open in an hour or two. It'll keep you warm tryin'. Take his knife, lad."

"I'm glad you're doing this," Kirk flung at them. "I'm glad because it'll make your score bigger to even."

"S' long, Mounty," was their retort, as they departed.

Kirk bit off a warm oath. He sat for a while motionless where they had left him on a heap of rubbish in one corner. His legs were bound at the ankles and just above the knees with tough lengths of *babiche*, intricately knotted. He began working on the knots with numb fingers, wondering meanwhile what the younger of the two meant when he had said, "We got him." Whom had they "got"? Did it mean they had killed someone— the young fellow and his gang? He had said "we," so there must have been others besides himself.

It took Kirk just about an hour to free himself. He jumped to his feet, stamping the floor to restore circulation, swinging his arms vigorously back and forth. Then he stepped outside to look at the weather. The snow was driving hard. He felt around the dark room for his snowshoes, found them, and buckled them on. He struck a match and looked at his compass for bearings. Could he depend on Billy Jack's statement that the golden-haired woman's cabin was northeast? He took into consideration the fact that he was unarmed, and knew only too well how miserably Billy Jack could bungle things. He decided finally to head back for his cabin until the storm was over. Billy Jack no doubt would turn up sooner or later. Also, a gun was a necessary item in this lawless pocket of the wilderness.

CHAPTER VI

LEAD FLIES

KIRK REACHED his cabin at dawn, with the storm still in mid-career. He was pretty well fagged out, and the tip of his nose was frost-bitten. He attended to this before he started a fire in the stove, cooked a hot meal, and sat down to it with an appetite such as he had rarely felt before. He cleaned up completely, pulled his chair closer to the stove, and got his pipe going.

He hoped Billy Jack would show up soon, else he would have to scout around for that cabin himself. He believed that the cabin Billy spoke of was the key to the mystery—the cabin and the girl with golden hair. That girl had taken something from Flint's bunk—something, perhaps, that might incriminate Flint if he, Kirk, were to find it. He remembered the day he had passed the girl on the trail, during that light snowfall, when he thought he had heard her sobbing. Ten to one, she had been in this very cabin, and Flint had said something, or done something, to upset her.

As for the half-breed girl Nellie, Kirk considered her as

nothing more than a passing light o' love in Flint's career. Still, in a way, she had been the cause of Flint's disgraceful behavior. And she had fled with Flint, God knew where. Nancy, the golden-haired girl, might be in love with Flint—cleanly in love with him. Her recent actions seemed to justify that point of view.

"Flint was living under a mental strain of some kind," Kirk mused.

"Something was weighing heavily on his mind. I'd speak to him at times and he wouldn't hear me. He'd get those nervous spells. Once I thought he was about to make a confession of some sort. I'm sure when I get Flint I'll have to send him south. I couldn't live with him again. Rum makes him lose his reason. It was Nellie who brought that rum in, for it wasn't mine—or his. I—"

His ruminations were cut short by a sudden sound at the door. He took his pipe from his mouth and got up as Billy Jack struggled in. Billy was supporting another person muffled in a white-fox *capote*. At a glance Kirk recognized Nancy. He put down his pipe and jumped to close the door.

Billy was grunting and breathing hard, but he helped the girl to the big split-log chair and eased her down.

"What happened?" Kirk shot at him.

Billy made a few aimless gestures with his hands and said, "Get lost big storm. Try get back cabin we find by lake. Get lost. Ugh. Find her in storm pretty dam' sick. Bring here."

"That's once your bungling did some good," remarked Kirk. "Shove that tea on the front of the stove."

The corporal opened the girl's *capote*. She was not entirely unconscious. She seemed weary, very tired, and her eyes refused to stay open. He pulled back her hood, then pulled off her knitted toque, and a sea of shimmering gold hair rippled down over her shoulders. Kirk found himself wondering why such a beautiful creature should be living in this remote region. Women—pretty women—white women— were rare on the trails that he knew. They had always been rare, for it had been Kirk's lot to be handed raw, lonely stations and tough, bitter patrols. He had earned his reputation early for being a capable man, and he had been living up to it ever since.

He rubbed the girl's hands briskly in his own. When the tea was hot he held a cupful to her lips and she sipped it slowly. After that he managed to draw off her *capote,* placed a rude, home-made pillow behind her head in the big chair, propped her feet on a stool, and piled more wood into the stove. She fell asleep there, utterly exhausted, while Kirk sat with his elbows on the table, studying her, and Billy Jack snoozed in a corner.

For four hours she slept. Then one of her feet slipped from the stool and her eyes flickered open. She stared for a full minute without turning her head. Presently her eyes shifted and fell on Kirk.

"Oh!" It was a whispered gasp, scarcely audible.

"Billy Jack brought you in," Kirk explained. "You were tuckered out. Feeling all right now?"

"Sleepy," she said, pushing back her hair. "It was good of you to look after me."

"Nothing at all."

"I feel rested. It's nice and warm in here." She smiled at the corporal, but Kirk's face was serious.

"Your coming here," he said, "has saved me a little trip. You see, I was going to pay a visit to your cabin."

"My cabin?"

"The one beyond the valley. I was going there to ask you a few questions."

She sat erect, a wary look creeping into her eyes.

"I—I don't quite understand, corporal."

"You will presently, Miss Nancy. My main question is: What did you take from that pillow?"

She caught her breath and dared not meet his gaze.

"I still don't understand you, corporal."

"I think I've been pretty plain. You were in this cabin yesterday while I was out, and you removed something from the pillow on that bunk—Constable Flint's bunk."

"I was not in here," she said.

Kirk replied, "My Indian saw you, and he followed you to your cabin."

This shot hit the bull's-eye. She sprang to her feet, trembling, her hands clenched.

"You are lying—lying!" she cried. "You have no right to say such a thing. Please give me my *capote*."

"Will you please sit down?"

She stamped a foot. "I'm going out!"

"On the contrary," the corporal told her, "you are going to remain a little while and tell me a few things."

"I am not!"

"In the name of the law, you are."

She made a rush for her *capote*. The corporal caught her arm with gentle firmness. In a like manner he steered her back to the chair. She was furious— beautifully furious. Her cheeks were flushed and there were dark fires in her eyes. She shook off his hand, sat down abruptly, and showed him the back of her head. He moved around so that he might face her, and she promptly turned her face in the opposite direction. Kirk stroked his jaw for a thoughtful moment.

"There are certain things I must know," he said, "and I'm sure you can help me out. Constable Flint has disappeared. I am inclined to believe you know the constable very well. When you looked in at the door that night you expected to find him here. When you saw me instead you were surprised, and ran off. If anyone knows where he is, you do, because you came here to get something of his from that pillow."

She whirled on him. "You've tricked me—you and your Indian! You sent him to bring me here. And I thought—he— was—helping me."

"I didn't send him—not a bit of it. Billy got lost himself. He knew nothing of my suspicions."

"You lie!" she cried, springing to her feet. "You were afraid to look for me yourself—"

"I—afraid?"

"Yes. You—afraid! Do you know that I was coming here, to ask your aid—to ask you to help me? No, you don't. Well, I know something, but you'll never learn it. I'll never tell you. I know a lot. I hate you—despise you! You think of nothing but your red coat—nothing but the law. You're inhuman! You would arrest your own brother!"

"If I had one, which I haven't," came the corporal's steady voice, "and he wilfully challenged the law, I might."

"Oh, you—you beast!"

She sprang across the room and picked up her *capote*.

"Now I'm going. Try to stop me!" she dared.

Kirk took a step forward. A small revolver appeared in the girl's hand, and Billy Jack, who was in the corner behind the corporal, moved uneasily.

"Put that gun down!" Kirk snapped.

She was moving toward the door. Now her back was against it, and her hand shook as she leveled the gun at Kirk. The corporal, steel in his eyes, took another step.

"One more and I'll shoot!" she screamed.

"You shoot and I'll—"

Her revolver cracked and spat hot lead. Kirk stopped in his tracks, clasping a hand to his side and grimacing. He swayed a trifle, and Billy Jack rushed to steady him. For a brief instant the girl stared, horrified, then cried out, "Oh, God!" and disappeared.

"I'm all right, Billy," Kirk muttered through clenched teeth. "Help me to—that—chair. Put on some water to heat. That's a good boy."

He sat down slowly and opened his clothing while Billy

heated water. The bullet, he found, had passed right through, probably nicking a rib; not a deep wound, for it had struck the edge of his body at the waist, shocking his system more than anything else. He told Billy to get his medicine kit, and set about cleansing the wound.

"Billy," he said, "I'm beginning to think I'm a worse blunderer than you."

CHAPTER VII

THE COMING OF BRISTOL

THE STORM lasted three days. Kirk remained in the cabin, looking after his wound, while Billy Jack made the meals, brought in wood, and kept the fire going.

The corporal had no visitors during that time, and there was no word of Flint. He would have to place a charge of desertion against the constable now. It was a distasteful duty to perform, and there was no doubt in his mind that he would apprehend his man. He disliked figuring in a departmental scandal, but he had no choice. It was in line of duty.

On the fourth day, when the storm was blowing itself out, and the little cabin was almost buried in high white drifts, a stranger sagged in. He was weak on his feet, and Billy Jack had to help him to a chair. When the man shoved back his *capote* hood Kirk saw a blood-stained bandage about his head.

"Well, I thought I'd never make it," were his first words. "Great Godfrey, this neck of the country is rotten! Got a shot of rum—anything hot?"

Kirk motioned to Billy Jack and the Indian brought out the brandy. The man poured himself a generous portion and threw it down, smacking his lips. He looked at Kirk steadily for a minute.

"My name's Bristol. What's yours?" Kirk told him. "Seems I've heard of you before. Humph! That brandy is the thing to put life in a man." He took another drink. "Well, corporal, there's going to be hell to pay. Just take it from me. I'll hate to do it, but I've got to. Yes, sir, I've got to. I suppose you'll get blamed for it—part of it, anyhow. It will put a blot—a rather smudgy blot, I might say—on the otherwise, well, immaculate escutcheon of F-Division. I'm not blaming you outright, but the responsibility was in your hands."

"What are you driving at, Mr. Bristol?" Kirk asked, perplexed.

"Well, the particulars were explained in the message," said Bristol.

"In what message?"

"There was only one."

"I don't understand."

"That's too bad," said Bristol. "Anyhow, they got the money—every blasted cent of it. Ten thousand Dominion dollars."

Kirk smacked the table.

"Explain yourself! I never received a message. I don't know what you're talking about."

Bristol breathed out, "Oh!" and took another drink. "You didn't get a message? You say you didn't get a message asking if it were possible to supply a police guard from Blowing Lake to Post Cheer Up?"

"I did not."

"Why, we sent a messenger here with that request and received a reply saying you could, and that a Mounty would meet us at Blowing Lake. There's a bad crowd between here and Cheer Up, and we wanted to play safe."

"When did you receive the reply, and who signed it?"

"Three weeks ago, signed by Constable Flint. He explained he was alone at that time, but was expecting a corporal any day, and to expect a guard at Blowing Lake."

Bitter turmoil was beginning to seethe within Kirk.

"And what happened?" he asked.

"What happened?" Bristol chuckled drily. "We were robbed. My mate's dead on our sled outside, and my call was close. Flint met us, all right, and when we were attacked by half a dozen men he stood aside, scared stiff. Didn't raise a hand. He disappeared with the rest. I'll swear he walked us into that trap. He looked guilty as hell, corporal. Ten thousand good Dominion dollars! What a scandal!"

"You're sure of this?"

"Am I sure? Sure I'm sure. Go out and take a look at poor Jennings. Shot clean through the head, clean as a whistle. Poor old Jennings!"

Kirk did not go outside to look at Jennings. He sat down by the table, his face gray with a terrible grimness, his soul shocked to the very core. He felt that if Flint were to walk in he would choke the life out of him. He could not speak for some minutes, he was so awed, so choked with rage, so unutterably shocked at this tragedy.

Tragedy it was, to him—nothing less. Jennings shot through the head, and killed. Bristol with a bloody bandage around his head. Flint a traitor to the traditions of the Scarlet Manual—running with outlaws. It seemed incredible, despite the poor opinion Kirk already held of him. Flint had gone the limit. He could do nothing more to add to the fierce, bitter hatred Kirk was nursing against him. Kirk had never believed he could hate, despise, loathe a man the way he hated, despised and loathed Flint.

He had his back to the wall now, this corporal who had a name for being a tough bird and a stickler on points of the law. He would have to fight alone. Well, he was used to it; he had fought alone before.

He said to Bristol: "This ten thousand dollars... whose property was it?"

"Northeast Fur Company, and we were taking it to their post at Cheer Up. It was for a trade campaign. They were going to pay cash for pelts right in the woods instead of the usual methods of barter."

"Would you recognize the men who held you up?"

"It was pretty dark. I might, but wouldn't say for sure. Had their faces pretty well covered up. They were all big men—six of them, I counted. When that bullet bounced off my head I didn't see or hear a thing for quite a while."

"I'll get on the job," Kirk assured him. "And by the way, you'd better let me look at your head."

"No hurry. Might look at it, though, when you get time."

Kirk found the wound to be superficial, washed it, and applied a fresh bandage. Bristol was dead tired. Kirk told him he could use one of the bunks if he wished. Bristol didn't hesitate, and went right to sleep.

Leaving Billy Jack to take care of the fire, the corporal put on his trail togs and took a revolver that he had been thoughtful enough to bring from detachment headquarters, along with his regular service pistol. He left the cabin, his first day out since Nancy had shot him, and strode along at a moderate pace. The day was bright and clear, with the fresh snow from the recent storm lying about in great windrows. There was not much wind, but the mercury was low.

One hour later he reached Alex MacMahon's store. Alex was sitting by the stove with his brother Andy. Both looked sharply at the corporal as he entered.

"I don't suppose," Kirk began, "the woman Nellie is back."

"No, corporal," said Alex.

Kirk resumed, "Two Northeast men were robbed last night near Blowing Lake, and one was killed. I guess they thought they killed the other too, but he was only knocked out. They got ten thousand dollars."

"Goshamighty, that's too bad," rumbled Alex, fingering his red beard.

"It certainly is," nodded Kirk; then, "I want to have a few words with Johnny. Will you get him?"

Alex looked at his brother and shifted uneasily.

"He—he ain't around just now, corporal."

"I'll wait," said Kirk briefly, and took a seat, stuffing his pipe.

There were a few minutes of silence. Then Alex offered, "Well, now, corporal, ye see, Johnny was in all night. Fact is, we don't 'low him out, for fear he might wander away an' get lost. Ye know how it is with Johnny."

"I know. I'll speak to him, at any rate," was Kirk's terse reply.

Johnny came in ten minutes later, stamping the snow from his moccasins. Kirk told him to sit down.

"Johnny, were you out of the house last night?" he asked.

"No, I wasn't out of the house all night," answered Johnny.

"Was Alex home all night?"

Kirk's hand rested meaningly on his gun. Johnny did not answer immediately. He looked at Alex and encountered a black stare. He moistened his lips and glanced at the corporal.

"Don't be afraid to speak, Johnny," Kirk encouraged. "You shall have the protection of the law."

"No, Alex wasn't home all night," Johnny ventured. "Alex came in at daybreak—Alex and Andy."

Alex's fist clenched and his red beard shuddered. Kirk turned to him.

"Where were you all night?"

Andy put in, "You've got a nerve, corporal, asking so many damn questions. Alex an' me were out, an' where we were is none of your business, as far as I can see. But if it'll make you feel easier, we were playin' cards at Ted MacDonald's place, an' you can ask Ted."

"Being kin of yours, he'd say yes," Kirk clipped, and stood up. "I'm not through with you yet, though I'm leaving you just now. And, by the way, I'm taking Johnny with me."

Alex raised a hand. "Now, listen, corporal, you can't go by what Johnny says. What's more, we need Johnny t' do the chores around here an' help in the kitchen."

"You'll have to do without him. Come on, Johnny," ordered the corporal, taking the man's arm.

Andy, a gaunt man, climbed to his feet.

"Say, you leave poor Johnny alone, mister. Don't ye go per-secutin' Johnny."

"Don't worry. I'm merely going to ask him some more questions about Nelson's camp." Kirk opened the door, nodded for Johnny to precede him.

"You'll regret this," Andy snarled.

"No. But I think you will," the corporal retorted.

The two brothers shook with silent rage as Kirk closed the door. Andy drew his gun and started for the window, but Alex grabbed his arm and held him in check.

"Easy, Andy. We'll shoot only when there's nothin' else we can do."

CHAPTER VIII

THE CABIN BY THE LAKE

WHEN KIRK reached his cabin with Johnny, he found the door swinging wide. He was keyed for danger. The moment he saw this he pulled his revolver and told Johnny to step to one side. Then he advanced obliquely and peered in. He saw only the dead body of Jennings lying in one corner with a blanket flung over it. Kirk swore under his breath. Bristol's team was gone. Bristol was gone. Billy Jack was gone.

"Now what the devil happened?" the corporal bit off savagely. "I can't leave this place for a short time but something pops. This kind of business would drive a man to drink! Come inside a minute, Johnny, till I think."

They went in and Kirk disgustedly examined the room. Had Bristol been handing him a lot of fairly tales? Had he driven off Billy Jack at the point of a gun? This didn't seem in the least plausible. Bristol had told a straightforward story, and he had been pretty fagged out when he told it. There had been nothing secretive, nothing evasive, in his manner of relating what had happened. And there was the body of Jennings, his partner, silent testimony of a clash with guns.

What about Billy Jack? Whatever Billy's shortcomings, Kirk had come to trust him as he trusted few Indians. Billy was a lamentable blunderer. He made the most absurd mistakes, from losing a trail to burning a whole batch of bannocks. But he had always tried to please, and in more ways than one he had revealed deep regard for the corporal. Of the two, he would condemn Bristol before even thinking of condemning Billy Jack.

"Johnny," he declared at length, "you'd better stay with me. I don't think you'll be safe with the MacMahons after what you said today. That is really why I brought you along."

"I am glad to stay with you," agreed Johnny, bowing stiffly.

"Then you'll have to hit the trail, for I've got to find Constable Flint."

Johnny started, and Kirk thought he saw some kind of struggle going on in the man's eyes. It baffled him.

He asked, "Why do you look that way, Johnny, every time I mention Flint's name?"

"I—I don't—know," the man answered vaguely. "I don't know."

"Do you remember Corporal Pendleton?"

Again that look. "Corporal... Pendleton." He regarded Kirk with those disquieting eyes. "Are you Corporal Pendleton?"

"No. No, Johnny. My name is Kirk."

"Oh... Kirk."

Johnny's mind seemed to be forever wandering in a cloud. Kirk gave it up. He realized that Johnny was incapable of any continuity of thought.

"We're going to hit the trail," he said, and got together his light equipage. He was resolved to stay out until he caught Flint, or Nellie, or the golden-haired Nancy. He loaded the grub-box with only the essential staples. With Johnny's aid he carried the body of Jennings out to the shed in the rear, and barred the door. Then he lined up his dogs; they had been taking life easy in the small kennel, and were eager for the traces.

"You take care of the gee-bar, Johnny," Kirk directed. "I'll mush ahead of the dogs."

There was a fresh trail leading north from the cabin, and he judged this to be Bristol's and Billy Jack's, for there were the marks of a dog team and two sets of snowshoes. Johnny seemed pleased to have charge of the sledge. With a brief word to the lead dog Kirk started off.

When they reached the waterway the corporal lost the trail. The high wind that had accompanied the recent storm had swept the frozen river furiously, and there were long stretches of bare ice, with big drifts banked along the shores. The river's course was northeast. For a time Kirk swung along in that direction on its slippery surface, thinking he might pick up the trail again, but it is not easy for dogs and men to travel on bare ice. After a while he veered into the northern shore.

Beyond the ridge, according to Billy Jack's statement, was the cabin of the golden girl. Just where that cabin was situated, Billy had failed to show him, but Billy had said the girl's cabin was by a lake, and Kirk reasoned that by scouring the country beyond he ought to come upon it eventually.

He did not try for speed. Speed would have been impossible, anyway, with the huge drifts and the tangle of timber knocked down by the last storm. That night he chose a camp on the northern slope of the ridge, and Johnny built the fire. The night was clear, with a moon and a multitude of stars, and later the aurora began to pulse on the Arctic rim and fling its ghostly banners across the wilderness.

At daylight they were on the move again, beating slowly back and forth, searching everywhere for some signs of habitation. It was toward noon that Kirk, coming upon a narrow creek, decided to follow its course. An hour later he led the way through a scraggly field of muskeg that soon developed into a small lake. On the northern shore he saw a faint blue column of smoke.

"I'll take a look at that, Johnny," said he. "We'll drive into the willows with the team. You'll stay behind while I go ahead alone."

Leaving Johnny and the team in a well-concealed spot, he

pushed on. It did not take him long to come within sight of a small, squat cabin nestling in a grove of spruces, almost hidden from view. He did not know for sure whether this was Nancy's cabin, but some inner sense whispered to him that it was; he felt in his bones that within that wilderness cabin was concealed something or somebody who would go far toward clearing up Flint's disappearance and the reported robbery.

He made a cautious approach, bending over as he crept toward the rear of the structure, where there was neither door nor window. Reaching this, he paused to listen for sounds, and hearing none removed his rackets and proceeded around the side of the cabin. There was a window here. He crept by on hands and knees just under it. He passed the front window also. Then he was standing before the door, his revolver drawn, his left hand raised to rap.

He got very close to the door indeed, and when he knocked he held his hand tight against it, so that the moment it was opened he could force it in.

At his summons there was a stir inside. He heard the latch being lifted, and his hand closed tighter over his gun. The door opened on a crack. An eye regarded Kirk questioningly. He heard a gasp.

Immediately he flung his weight against the door and forced his way inside, a sharp command on his lips:

"Not a move!"

He had expected to find more than one person, and for a brief moment he was a little disappointed. At any rate, the one person he found there was a big factor in his scheme of things. Nancy shrank back under his flinty eyes.

"Well," he said, "your shot didn't do much damage. I suppose you're surprised to see me dropping in like this."

"I—I'm glad it wasn't serious," she offered in a choked voice. "I didn't mean to shoot."

"Just so. Well, I am still looking for Constable Flint. Are you going to tell me what you know about him?"

"Oh, I don't know anything!" she cried.

Kirk pondered a moment.

"That something or other you took from the pillow in my cabin; was it a letter from the Northeast Trading Company about—"

"What do you mean?" she flung at him her hands clenching.

He advanced a step. "You know what I mean, and I wish you would give up pretense. You are making it very difficult for me to treat you with respect. You've blocked any attempts I've made to vindicate the law; you've lied repeatedly. You even went so far as to put a bullet through me. Now you know a lot I am trying to learn. You know all about Flint. You know where he is. You know there was a robbery the other night—"

She muffled a gasp with her hand, and a hunted light appeared in her eyes.

"You know these things," Kirk went on. "I am ready to grill you night and day until you tell me what you know. A man has been killed, Flint has disappeared, and now my Indian has disappeared."

The hunted light in Nancy's eyes changed to a flame of defiance.

"Suppose I refuse?"

"You won't."

"I will. I do refuse. Your red coat?" She laughed lightly. "It means nothing! Now what are you going to do?"

She taunted him. She stood with her hands on her hips, her chin tilted, a gentle hint of mockery in her eyes. Kirk was perplexed. He was not used to dealing with women. Men he could handle, but women were different; they caused all kinds of complications. At last he said, "I can place you under arrest."

"For what?"

"You forget," he explained, "that you shot me. I still carry the wound."

The sound of voices precluded any answer she might have made. Kirk snapped alert.

"Get in that corner, please," he ordered. "I'll open the door."

He stepped to the door, still keeping his eyes on the girl, and waited for the newcomers to approach.

"Not a move," he warned her.

There was a loud rap.

CHAPTER IX

KIRK GAINS A POINT

KIRK LIFTED the latch, and stepped behind the door as he pulled it open. Two men swung in—two big men, with rifles under their arms. Kirk kicked the door shut behind them.

"Drop your rifles!" he barked.

The men stopped, stiffened, and looked from Nancy to Kirk in frank bewilderment. Their eyes clouded. They were the two men who had kept Kirk captive in that deserted shack not so many days before.

"Put 'em down!" Kirk repeated.

Reluctantly they dropped their rifles. Kirk told one of them to back up beside Nancy. He ransacked the other's pockets, relieving him of a revolver, then searched the one beside Nancy and unearthed another six-gun.

"Now all of you may sit down," he told them. The two men removed their coats. He asked the older man, "What is this lady to you?"

"Nancy's my daughter," was the grumbling reply. "Joe, here, is my son."

"What's your name?"

It came reluctantly—"Barrett."

"Any kin to the MacMahons?"

Old Barrett scowled. "God f'bid!"

"I want to know," Kirk went on, "why you kept me in that cabin. I want to know what your son meant when he said, 'We got him.'"

Father and son exchanged glances, and Nancy bit her lip, turning from one to the other. Kirk said: "A man was killed that same night. Is that whom you got?"

Old Barrett snorted, "No! Joe didn't do anything like that at all. It was somethin' else, Mounty."

"Well, what was it?"

Nancy put in, "You—*you* wouldn't understand. You never—never would understand."

"Quiet, Nancy," advised Barrett solemnly.

"A man was killed," stated Kirk, "and ten thousand dollars were stolen at Blowing Lake. If you men had no connection with the robbery and killing, why was I held in that cabin? Answer that!"

"Mounty," ground out Barrett slowly, "we refuse to talk."

"You do, eh? It looks to me, Barrett, as though you held me there while the robbery was going on."

Joe snapped, "The robbery wasn't done that night! It was—"

"So!" Kirk exclaimed. "I know it wasn't done that night. I just wanted to see what you would say. Your tongue slipped, didn't it?"

Barrett cast a dark look at his son. Joe made a wry face, realizing he had blundered. Kirk went on:

"Your daughter knows a lot about it, too, I'll wager, and I have been urging her to tell me something of Constable Flint. All of you are acting very stubborn. If you persist you cannot expect too much courtesy from me. I'm up here to see that the law is maintained, and I'll not have it disregarded. I'll clean up this blasted case if I have to arrest every person within a hundred miles. And I'll begin, Barrett, by arresting your daughter."

Barrett started up.

"Sit down!" rapped out the corporal.

Barrett grated, "You'd better begin, Mounty, by arrestin' Alex MacMahon an' his kin."

"Why so?"

"You might get back that money."

"*Father!*" Nancy shrieked.

"Quiet, gal," droned Barrett. "I'll not have the Mounty on you f'r what is somebody else's doin's. You've done enough, sacrificed enough as it is. I'll not stand f'r it."

"Nor me, pa," added Joe, seriously.

"I wish you would explain," Kirk persisted.

Nancy grasped her father's arm.

"Don't, father, don't. Please—please—don't!"

Barrett stared at the table. He patted Nancy's hand.

"Mounty," said he, "there's things we can't explain. But if you want to get that money back, Alex MacMahon's your man. Don't ask me how I know."

"To prove your faith, one of you will have to guide me by the quickest route to Nelson's Camp," said Kirk.

"If one of us Barretts showed his face in Nelson's camp there would be shootin'," said the old man. "We got no use for each other."

Nancy said, "I'll guide him to the entrance of the valley. I know the way by heart."

"No, sis, you leave it to me," argued Joe.

"I'll go," Nancy persisted, and took her *capote* from the rack. "But you shouldn't have talked so much. Only God knows what will come of this!"

In a few minutes he was dressed for the trail. She gave the corporal a curt, frigid gesture indicating her readiness to start.

"I have a dog-team down the lake a ways," he said. "Barrett, you'll see me again if I don't get all the information I want."

He started off, with Nancy behind him, and in a little while reached his team. Johnny was sitting on the sledge. He rose as the corporal arrived. At sight of him Nancy frowned quizzically, but said nothing.

"All right," Kirk snapped. "You'll lead the way now."

"Follow me Mounty," she shot back with a note of derision.

No words passed between them. Kirk had to marvel at the way she could plow along ahead of the team, never faltering. He felt a little sorry that circumstances were forcing them to hostility. He wondered vaguely if it were worth a man's while to wear the scarlet tunic, to carry its laws into the far places, to serve under its stern code. Ten long years of it had hardened him, and sometimes he was harder than he imagined himself to be. He had money in the bank. Quite a few times during the past year he had entertained thoughts of resigning when his present term should expire, but something held him on. He had been faithful to the Force. He had tacked up no mean record as a man-trailer, and for handling Indian troubles. Leaving the Force would be like saying good-bye to an old friend. Something else would have to come into his life—something with a stronger pull than the brave old Force.

Nancy plugged on resolutely, and when Kirk offered to break trail for a while she refused with a curt, "Never mind!"

"What time do you think we'll reach the valley?" he asked.

"Maybe eight tonight."

More silent plodding; more beating through heavy thickets. Four hours to go, then, by Nancy's reckoning. Day was already beginning to wane. They stopped to spell the dogs, and Kirk took time to stuff his pipe and enjoy a smoke. Nancy remained silent, and Johnny leaned against a tree, a forlorn figure.

They were making ready to start afresh when a flurry of snow winged out of the sky. The wind grew as they pushed on, whipping the snow furiously about. Nancy bent her head low and drove on. Kirk pounded along at her side, while Johnny strode at the gee-bar.

The dogs strained in the traces, pulling faithfully, while daylight faded. Nancy stumbled once, falling headlong, and Kirk lifted her up. She shook herself free and continued without a word. An hour or so later the snow thinned out and finally stopped, but the heavens still looked sullen. Kirk judged they would get more later on.

They began to get into a hilly country, and Kirk thought he recognized a creek they passed. They toiled up a sharp slope. When they were at the top Nancy pointed to a few pin-points of light that gleamed in the darkness beyond.

"You ought to know where you are," she said. "There's Nelson's Camp. I'll turn back now."

"I think you ought to camp here till morning," Kirk suggested.

"I'm used to traveling at night. If the storm holds off I'll be all right. Good-bye."

She turned and without another word strode off. He watched her until she disappeared, wondering if he were doing a wise thing in letting her go. He looked down into the valley, where the cabin lights flickered.

"Let's go, Johnny," he called, and started down.

CHAPTER X

THE DOWNFALL OF ALEX

THE SIGHT that greeted him in Alex MacMahon's store was surprising, to say the least. He had left Johnny outside with the team. Now he closed the door behind him, hand resting on his service pistol.

There was much merrymaking. Alex was there. He had his arm around the half-breed girl Nellie, and a glass of liquor in his hand. Her eyes sparkled. She snuggled comfortably in Alex's generous arm, smiling at him coquettishly. Half a dozen other men lounged about, and one was playing a harmonica.

"Shut up!" Kirk roared.

The harmonica player almost choked. Alex set down his glass, patted Nellie's shoulder, and disengaged her arm from around his ample waist. Andy MacMahon was there, and he spat disgustedly. Nellie sat on the table, dangling her legs, and smiled invitingly at the corporal. Alex saw this and gave her a black sidelong look. The corporal's glance was not exactly black, but it cut Nellie like a knife, and she very impudently projected her tongue in his direction.

Kirk saw that he was with a hard-boiled crowd, and rather relished the atmosphere. He could let himself loose, and he had a particular appetite for hard-boiled eggs just now. He leveled an arm at Alex. His words snapped out with a rasp.

"Where is the money you robbed from those men bound for Cheer Up?"

The shot was direct, altogether unexpected. Every man in the crowd stirred, and some growled. Alex planted himself squarely and pulled at his beard.

"You talkin' t' me, corporal?"

"Now don't pull any comedy. I'm talking to you, and you're going to answer me or I'll turn this place upside down."

"You're doin' some mighty tall talkin'," chimed in Andy.

"*You* clamp your jaw!" bit off Kirk; then to Alex, "and you find that money you've got, and find it blamed quick."

"I tell you corp—"

"No alibis!" Kirk pointed to a small door in the left rear corner. "What's behind that door?"

"Just a storeroom, that's all."

"That's enough." Kirk turned to the others. "All of you march into that storeroom—all of you except Alex."

Andy raised a hand. "Now, lookit here—"

"*You* lead the way!" Kirk hurled at him.

Andy scowled and moved reluctantly toward the storeroom. The corporal's temper was at high-tide now, and he demanded more haste. Alex stood beside Nellie, muttering in his beard, scowling darkly. Kirk drove the men into the storeroom, shot home the bolt, and regarded with keen, piercing eyes the half-breed woman and the man beside her. He remembered that this same woman had dealt him a vicious blow once, and he was minded not to have it happen again. He took out his manacles. "Come here," he called to her.

Alex protested, but the corporal said, "Mind your own business," and clamped one of the bracelets on Nellie's wrist. The other bracelet he fastened to a ringbolt in the wall, from which hung a number of traps. She flashed her teeth in a brazen, insolent smile, but Kirk paid no attention to her.

"Now, Alex," said he, "shell out, and don't try my patience."

"I tell ye, corporal, I don't—"

Kirk took three fast steps and jabbed the muzzle of his revolver against Alex's stomach. Alex almost fell backward from sheer surprise. Kirk jabbed him again and backed him across the store into the rear room.

"You don't have to tell me anything," he said. "Just think hard and turn over the cash."

Alex shoved out his jaw. "I don't know anything. You can't shoot me down. Now what are you goin' t' do?"

"You're a clever bird, Alex. No, it would be against the principles of the Force. I'll try something else, though. Walk into the store."

Back in the store, Kirk edged toward the front door, opened it, and called to Johnny. When Alex saw Johnny enter his face flamed with rage, and his breath hissed through clenched teeth.

"So that's who told you, eh?" he snarled.

"Not a bit of it," Kirk replied. "But perhaps he can tell me where your strong-box is. Can you, Johnny?"

Alex's hands writhed at his sides. He mouthed incoherent oaths, and almost wept for pure rage. Johnny marched into the rear room with comic dignity, and Kirk prodded Alex in after him. Johnny went straight to a closet and dragged out a heavy chest. He opened this and took out a small metal box, secured by a heavy lock. This he held in his hands and looked at Kirk. Alex sank to a chair, muttering bitterly.

"Where's your key for this?" Kirk asked him.

"Ye found that; now find the key!"

Kirk took the box from Johnny, set it on the table, and blew off the lock with two shots. The box was loaded with crisp bills and gold and silver coin.

"Here y'are, Alex," the constable said. "Just as I thought. You can't beat the Mounted. Now, of course I am going to hold you for the killing of a man named Jennings. That will be two counts; robbery and murder. When I find Flint, I guess I'll have things pretty well cleaned up."

They went into the store again, and Kirk stared long and steadily at Nellie.

"Where'd you leave the constable?" he asked her.

"In de woods, *m'sieu.* Heem go 'way from poor Nellie. Nellie stay wit' Alex—heem buy her nice clothes an' mooch ring."

At this instant there was the sound of voices outside. Kirk strode quickly to the door, listening, his eyes still on Alex. He jerked the door open. Two figures stood by his sled. A voice called:

"Hello, there, mister! Say, by Godfrey, could you tell us where we are? I've an Indian here who is about the rottenest guide in the whole Dominion. Now he's trying to tell me he knows this team, but I've given up taking any stock in anything he—"

"Come in, the both of you," Kirk directed. "He knows the team all right."

Billy Jack came shuffling in, and a grin, rare visitor on Billy's face, crinkled his dark skin. Bristol took one look at the corporal and sighed with vast relief. Then he spotted the handcuffed woman and the glowering Alex.

"What's up?"

Kirk said, "I've got your money."

"No!" Bristol exclaimed.

"Give him the box, Johnny," Kirk said.

Bristol grabbed the box and stared at the money. Immediately he sat down and began counting it.

"It's all here," he agreed, finally. "These other bills and loose change, though, aren't mine."

Kirk asked, "But what happened to you and Billy? When I returned to that cabin you were gone."

"It was this way," Bristol exclaimed. "I lay down, you remember. Well, after a while I woke up and remembered my dogs hadn't had a bite to eat for a long while. So I got up and told Billy about it, and we went outside to feed them. While we were doing this two men passed. It wasn't till after I'd fed the dogs that their faces struck me as being familiar. They looked something like the crowd that held us up. I asked Billy if he knew the country nearby, and he said yes. So I got him to come with me and trail those two men. Well, I don't know. Billy kept going and going, and we didn't catch sight of the men, and finally I came to the conclusion that Billy didn't know any more than I did about the country. We've been lost ever since. Come to think of it, that man there looks mighty like one of those roughnecks that held us up. What's more, around the eyes he looks a damned lot like one of the men that robbed us—and particularly like the man that shot Jennings. I remember the eyes, corporal."

"I'm holding him," said Kirk, "and there are others bottled up in that storeroom. Now I'd like to appoint you and Billy Jack as guards here, while I go on and finish up this case. We'll put Alex in with the rest, and the woman can take them food. This place is in police hands now. I'll post a notice to that effect."

"Glad to," nodded Bristol. "I want to see the man that shot poor old Jennings get his. I'll watch 'em, corporal."

Billy Jack grunted his willingness to help, and Alex was shoved in the storeroom with the rest. With Bristol on guard, Kirk and Johnny lay down for a few hours. They would be off at daybreak.

CHAPTER XI

THE BLIZZARD

KIRK LEFT after an unsuccessful interview with Nellie. He had tried to get her to tell him more about the constable, but she only laughed and rolled her eyes at the corporal and patted his arm caressingly. He pushed her away gently but firmly. She tossed her head at him and flashed white teeth, her dark eyes sparkling. He had cursed under his breath and finally left her, reflecting that she was bad company for any man who wore the scarlet.

"No doubt she twisted Flint around her finger," was his thought. "An insolent, shameless woman, and dangerous as fire."

He trudged ahead of the team in the cold gray twilight of early morning. Johnny was at the gee-bar. The sky was sullen, and it seemed that a storm would break before very long. But storm or no storm, Kirk was bound to see this thing through in the shortest time possible.

It seemed logical now that Flint, not being in the company of Nellie, would be near or in communication with Nancy. With Flint in his hands, everything would be cleared up. It would go hard with the constable—disgrace to the uniform, a prison term, and the contempt of men. Nancy would protect him, and here the corporal would have a time of it. In a way Kirk admired that golden girl—admired her for her loyalty to the hunted man. But his personal sentiments must not interfere with his duty as an officer. The damage that Flint had done was irreparable. He must pay for it.

Musing along these lines, he swung his broad snowshoes with practiced feet. A raw, ragged country swept away on all sides, with here and there humpbacked ridges bulging from wind-lashed stretches of frozen marshes. Under the dull, leaden gray sky it presented a picture of consummate loneliness. Its stunted trees, sprawling in irregular clusters, added to it a note of ravaged wildness, and an occasional lake seemed only to accentuate the desolation.

They stopped once to spell the dogs, and Kirk said to Johnny, "How long ago did you drift in here?"

"I don't know."

"You haven't been here always, though?"

Johnny shook his head.

"Where did you come from?"

"I can't remember. I don't know."

Kirk regarded him critically, while he puffed a fresh pipe. A strange case, this Johnny. He had joined the corporal's cause without a moment's hesitation. He worked faithfully, and outside of his inability to think rationally, Kirk could see nothing very wrong with him He was best described as "simple."

"You are sure you don't remember Corporal Pendleton?" Kirk put to him. Again there was that apparent struggle in his eyes, and then a sudden flash of intelligence that Kirk had never seen before. Johnny started, and cried:

"I…" but his voice trailed off, and the old blank stare came back to his eyes. "I—I don't remember," he ended quietly.

They moved on in silence.

Just before noon Kirk, who was still in the lead, came upon a huddled figure lying on the snow. He knew it was Nancy before he bent down. When he turned her over he saw a still, white face, with wisps of golden hair across the forehead.

He shook her, but her body was limp in his arms. He carried her to the sled and laid her on the blankets, felt her pulse, and detected a faint beat. He yelled for Johnny to build a fire, wrapped her in the sledge-robes, and poured some brandy between her lips. He chafed her hands vigorously in his own. Her face was pale and serene and beautiful.

Johnny got the fire going, and Kirk drew her near its warmth, watching eagerly for the girl's eyes to open. When they did open they fell on him, scrutinized him gently, and the young lips smiled. He smiled back, and fixed the robes more securely about her. Her eyes closed. She sighed peacefully, and the smile slowly faded from her lips. Kirk stayed by her side, and Johnny made some grub.

Then the sky, which had brooded all morning, was blotted out by a sudden deluge of snow. The wind rose, the snow became thicker, and the storm rushed to mid-career with wild fury. Nancy wakened again, with the wind roaring about her. Kirk was very near her, sheltering her from the brunt of snow with his own body.

"Feel better—a little?" he asked.

"All right—but my ankle is sprained. I took a header on the way back from Nelson's Camp, and had to crawl on hands and knees. I must have become exhausted."

"Yes. We found you lying in the snow."

"I was afraid the storm would break," she said. "It was threatening."

"Well, we'd better push on to your cabin. We'll get snowed under here. Your ankle needs tending to, and you need a good rest."

"You were heading for the cabin?" she asked, tremulously.

"Yes. I recovered the money. Alex MacMahon and some others are under arrest. The only missing link now is Constable Flint. But let's not talk about it. We'd better be on our way."

She started to reply, but Kirk had risen abruptly and was looking after the dogs. They set off in the face of the blizzard. Before long men and dogs were covered with snow. Kirk stopped at intervals to clean the robes that covered Nancy.

At the gee-bar plodded Johnny, steady as a machine, the snow clinging to the dark stubble on his face. Progress was not swift. They were traveling right into the wind, and the snow kept piling on their rackets and on the sledge.

They passed into a grove of poplars, where the wind whistled and boomed violently, and all was chaos and bedlam. That mad wind tore from all directions, it seemed; it leaped with diabolical suddenness from a new quarter and almost knocked them down, as if with malicious intent.

Kirk shielded his face with an arm, and the dogs, their bellies touching the snow, hauled in a kind of panicky haste. Johnny gripped the gee-bar grimly, his face shining with snow and ice particles, and Nancy huddled deep in her robes, scarcely visible.

Kirk battled his way onward, turning now and then to yell encouragement to the struggling lead-dog, whose breath spouted out like clouds of pale smoke. The wind buffeted him, clubbed him, made him stagger, but he plugged on with dogged persistence, remembering that beyond the edge of the poplars was a field of muskeg, and beyond the muskeg the lake and the cabin. He could make it; Johnny would make it; the dogs would make it. He had been at close grips with the North before; he knew the mad, savage fury of the North—knew its brute strength, its ruthless, devastating force.

A rending crash sounded so near at hand that he stopped, tensing. He half-turned and through the white cloud of the blizzard saw a tree hurtling down to earth. He cried out and lunged for the sledge, where he thought it would strike, but Johnny had seen what was coming also. With a mighty effort the half-wit hurled his strength against the sledge and pushed it forward. The tree missed, but Johnny went down under its impact without a cry.

Kirk blinked his eyes, shuddering a trifle, his hands clenching in his mittens. Nancy had uncovered her head at the sound and was looking about with round, excited eyes. She shouted something, but the wind gobbled her words. Kirk sagged toward the fallen tree, and fell on his knees beside the motionless body of Johnny.

"Poor... Johnny!" he muttered, spitting the ice from his lips.

He pulled off his mitten and felt for signs of life. Yes, there was a pulse. With his hand-ax he chopped away the snow and thus was able to drag Johnny out. Nancy watched him toiling in the wind and the driving snow. Now he stood over the unconscious body, looking about thoughtfully, seemingly unaware of the snow that pelted his face. He bent close to Nancy and raised his voice.

"Keep under the robes. I'll have to carry Johnny."

The sledge wasn't big enough to hold two. Kirk got Johnny on his shoulder and trudged up ahead of the team, yelling to the dogs. Bending under his burden, which by no means was a light one, he staggered on. Staggered describes it exactly. Once he toppled to his knees, breathing hard, got a better grip on his burden, rose slowly and lunged ahead.

He reached the muskeg. Here the wind, slashing across the bare country, struck him like something molten. The flying snow seemed as hard and as dense as ice. It drove the breath from his lungs, so that he paused, swaying, to gasp. The lead-dog, almost blinded, plowed into his heels and almost upset him. He reeled back to the sledge, half-bent.

"You—all right?" he yelled. "We'll —be—there—soon."

"I'm all right," cried Nancy. "But you...."

He did not wait to hear the rest, but lowered his head and plowed on. The shaggy team snaked out and toiled behind him. Kirk fought his way inch by inch across that muskeg and finally reached the lake. He could feel the ice forming around his eyes and on his lids; he could feel ice on his lips and nostrils. The weight of Johnny was breaking his back, and his head spun with the vast exertion. He followed the shore of the lake, reeling drunkenly, wondering just when his legs would buckle.

Eventually he reached the cabin, and fell against the door with his burden. He leaned there, fumbling for the latch-string, found it, and jerked. The door opened abruptly and he pitched to the floor. He lay there for a moment, then squirmed from under Johnny and hauled himself to his feet. He went outside, to find Nancy crawling from the sled toward the doorway. Despite her protestations he lifted her in his arms and carried her inside. He placed her in a rough-hewn arm chair.

As he backed away his knees buckled and he spun to the

floor. He was not completely out, however. He managed to raise himself to one elbow, and found Nancy kneeling beside him.

"What can I do?" she cried.

"I'm—all right," he jerked out. "You might—if you can—look after Johnny—till I get my breath. Nobody else here?"

"I don't see anyone. They are probably out looking for me."

She scrambled over to Johnny and unloosened his trail clothes. There was a welt across his head. He was still unconscious, and Nancy poured water between his lips. Kirk, seeing this, pulled a flask of brandy from his pocket and told her to give him a taste of that. Meanwhile he dragged himself to his feet and, removing his furs, dropped into a chair. He was up in a few minutes, however, to place Johnny on a cot, and noticed that Nancy was having a hard time of it getting about with one sprained foot.

"Better sit down," he urged. "I'll fix the stove. Johnny will come around. I'll watch him."

"God knows what would have happened if you hadn't found me!" she exclaimed. "I would have perished under the snow."

Kirk said, "You mustn't forget that Johnny saved you from that tree. He shoved you out of the way, and took a nasty crack himself."

"I'll not forget," she promised; then, suddenly, "Oh, I wish—I wish you were not a Mounty!" Her voice trembled.

"Sometimes I wish the same thing," he replied, and went to look at the stove.

Stuffing it with wood, he sat down beside Johnny, saw that he was breathing normally, and gently patted his arm. Nancy had gone into the other room to look after her ankle, and Kirk sat alone with his pipe, puffing moodily. The storm was still in mid-career, whistling across the wastes, booming against the cabin.

Kirk faced the door. Presently he became aware that the latch was moving up and down. He was comfortable, and didn't feel at all like getting up, but it began to dawn on him, after a moment, that a hand, and not the wind, might be pulling at that latch-string.

He walked across the floor and raised the latch. As soon as he released the door he felt a weight against it. A fur-swathed figure pitched headlong inside. Kirk pulled it all the way in, then slammed the door against the storm. He leaned down and turned the figure over.

His eyes narrowed, and a bitter smile pulled at his lips.

CHAPTER XII

THE TOLL OF THE STORM

NANCY, COMING from the other room, called, "What's the matter?"

Kirk twisted around and said, "Flint—at last."

Nancy put a hand to her breast. Her eyes dilated, and a cry escaped her lips. She stood there, a pathetic little figure, a braid of golden hair trickling over each shoulder.

Kirk removed his eyes from her to study the bearded, frost-bitten face of the man on the floor. He began unbuttoning the fur coat, then tried to remove the mittens, but they were frozen to the hands and would have to be thawed. He ran his hand under the man's shirt, felt about, put his ear down. He could detect no heart-heat, no sign of life.

He straightened, saw a little mirror on the wall, and removed it. This he polished to a clear surface and held over the man's mouth and nostrils. He found no film of breath on the glass. The man was dead.

Kirk looked at Nancy. His face told the story.

"Dead?" she asked weakly.

He nodded and crossed the room to replace the mirror. When he turned Nancy was kneeling by the body, her head drooping, her hands clasped together. She did not touch the body. She kneeled there like one in a trance, and Kirk heard her sobbing brokenly.

He went over slowly, after a few moments, gently raised her, and placed her in the arm-chair. Then he pulled the lifeless body to one side of the room and threw a blanket over it.

"Death," he said, "often saves a man a lot of disgrace. Flint—"

She lifted tear-stained eyes, and for some reason he stopped.

There was a sound from the cot where Johnny lay. He had turned and mumbled something. Kirk strode over to him. As he stood beside the cot Johnny's eyes opened and stared up quizzically. Kirk was instantly aware that he had never seen that clear, intelligent look in the man's eyes before. Even as he looked Johnny sat up, felt his head, and winced.

"What the devil happened?" he asked, his voice quick, with a new note to it. He looked up at Kirk. "Where have I seen you before? Did Pendleton get there all right? Must have been a dirty crack I got. It seems as if I've just come out of a crazy dream. There was a crash, and then somebody was carrying me, and it was snowing like blazes. Say, there's a storm going on now." He looked at his clothing, frowned perplexedly. "Where's my uniform?"

Kirk shot, "Who are you?"

"Me? Didn't Pendleton tell you the name—Flint?"

"Flint?" Kirk exclaimed. He whirled and looked at Nancy. She was holding a hand to her throat, and seemed very frightened. "Did you hear that?"

"Ye-es," she choked.

"And that man on the floor is?…"

"My brother…. Tom Barrett."

The corporal groaned, "Good God!" and then was silent for a full moment, regaining control of himself.

The real Flint asked, tentatively, "What's the matter?"

"The matter is a lot," Kirk told him. "Why, man alive, do you know you've been wandering around for a month or more, out of your mind? You didn't know your own name, you had never heard of Pendleton, and you were doing chores for Alex Mac-Mahon!"

"Doing chores for Alex MacMahon!"

"Exactly. Until I took you under my wing."

Flint leaned back. "Faintly I remember some things, but it seems like a dream. MacMahon was no friend of mine. I went there one night to remonstrate with him for giving a half-breed woman named Nellie too much liquor. Why, it seems like only last night. There were some other men there, and—yes—Tom Barrett. Nellie—brazen little brat—went to take a drink of rum while I was speaking—to defy me, of course. I knocked the cup from her hand, and Barrett—Barrett, I remember—came at me with a heavy stool. He must have hit me, for after that there was—a dream. It is all very uncanny, corporal. Pendleton had been gone two days when it happened."

"And you've been out of your mind from that time till a while back, a tree fell and hit you—shocked your nervous system and cleared your clogged brain. See that heap in the corner? It's Tom Barrett, whom I believed right along was you. He has your uniform on now. He impersonated you."

Flint said, "He was wild over Nellie."

Nancy pleaded. "Don't speak too harshly of him, please. Tom was—well, weak. He couldn't let whisky alone, and father almost disowned him. As it was, he did chase Tom from here. Tom drifted down to Nelson's Camp, where he met Nellie. He lost his head over her—lost his head and his reason. Whisky always made him dangerous, and he couldn't let it alone. When he hit you that night, constable, he was very drunk—he told me everything a few days ago. While you were unconscious they searched your pockets and found that message from the Northeast Company. They dared Tom to pose as you, and then somebody—Alex probably—sent a letter to the Northeast, signing your name, to the effect that you would meet their men at Blowing Lake.

"It was really Nellie who made Tom keep up the pretense and wear the uniform. For one thing, she liked the uniform, and she told Tom she wouldn't love him any more if he took it off. Then she wanted some gold bangles and dresses. It was planned that Tom would get a thousand dollars if he met the Northeast men at Blowing Lake and walked them into a trap where Alex and his henchmen were lying. Try to understand that to begin with poor Tom was weak, that he couldn't let whisky alone, and that Alex supplied him generously with drink. Then consider the powerful hold this half-breed woman held on him; she drugged his reason as much as the whisky. But the bitter part is, she was not sincere.

"You see, she left Tom. Tom played his unlovely part; he met the Northeast men at Blowing Lake, led them into the trap, and one of them was killed. He told me Alex fired the shot. It was just before that I had pleaded with my father and brother Joe to help me get him from that crowd. They would have nothing of it, but at last I won their consent, and they promised to get him. That was the night you were held captive in that cabin. Father held you there while Joe and I got Tom, who was hiding in a cave nearby with Nellie. I stayed with him while Joe went back to get father, but Nellie pleaded with him, and he ran off leaving me.

"After the robbery Nellie left him, and this broke him up altogether. He didn't go for his share of his money. Nellie said she was going to live with Alex. It was Alex, you see, who had set her on Tom, and he must have promised her some reward. Tom was tricked all around. He was a fool, and he was weak. I tried my best to shield him. He had left some papers of his in that pillow, and I went to your cabin one day when you were out and took them.

"Now he's dead. He had a bad lung, and this storm must have killed him. He was in hiding about five miles north of here. Tomorrow I was to have taken him supplies and civilian clothes. He was going to escape into the Northwest—or try to. I don't suppose it would have done much good. Father and Joe were hard. Some people would say they were right. Maybe they were. But Tom had been good to me, and I thought I could help him. Poor... Tom."

Kirk glanced at Flint, then they both stared at the floor for a long minute.

"I'm sorry," Kirk breathed at last. "I've misunderstood things from the beginning. I've always called my Indian Billy Jack a blunderer, but I think I am a bigger one."

"Oh, I can't blame you," Nancy told him. "I have a lot to apologize for. I was very rude, and I might have kil—"

"There is nothing to apologize for," he cut in.

Flint said, "About that Northeast money, corporal?"

"Safe and sound," Kirk replied. "That reminds me. We'd better get back to Nelson's camp. My Indian and a Northeast man named Bristol are guarding Alex and his cutthroats. Don't you remember we left them there?"

"Not clearly. That all seems like a dream. I remember clearly only up to the time Tom hit me. The dream begins there and ends when there is a crash—the tree falling, you said—and I am being carried through a storm. The rest is all muddled up—just like a dream."

"Well," Kirk stated, "we'd better mush. This will make a pretty story, and I'll have some report to write up. There's frozen fish on the sled. Will you go out and feed the dogs?"

Flint left and Kirk got slowly into his furs.

"You will probably take your prisoners south?" Nancy ventured.

"Yes, as soon as I can get away."

"Are—are you coming up this way again, do you suppose?"

He shot her a furtive glance. She seemed very wistful.

"I might," said he. "Oh, yes, I might—that is, unless Pendleton is sent up again."

After a pause she went on, "You know, I *have* been awfully mean to you. I shouldn't have been. But you understand now, don't you? I hope you do. I said I hated you, but I didn't. I've found you are not really so hard as you seem at times. You were only doing your duty. I hope you'll forgive me for everything—

for the shot, too. I was nervous. The gun went off. I was horrified!"

"I understand," he said, smiling.

"Will you shake my hand?"

He reached out, took her hand, and held it in his own. They
looked into each other's eyes and seemed to be drawn into a
world of their own.

The spell was only broken when Flint banged open the door
and stamped in. Then Kirk dropped her hand and rubbed his
jaw.

"Well, let's go," he remarked to Flint.

On the way out he looked at Nancy again, and thought he
saw her lean toward him, thought he saw a beckoning warmth
in her moist eyes. But he wasn't sure.

Flint called him, and he closed the door, carrying with him
a picture that haunted his memory all the way to Nelson's Camp.

CHAPTER XIII

THE LAST BLUNDER

KIRK AND the constable mushed into Nelson's
Camp just in time for trouble. Swinging through the
valley, they heard hoarse shouts and yells, and Kirk broke into
a trot ahead of the dogs. When they drew up before Alex's store
the place was in an uproar. Stools and other objects were being
hurled about, while fists were flying freely.

Kirk broke through the door, Flint at his heels. The corporal
dodged a bottle that hit the wall behind him with a crash and
fell in a hundred pieces. He saw Bristol shooting rights and
lefts to Andy's face. Billy Jack was having a knife duel with one
of the MacDonalds. He saw, too, young Joe Barrett and old
Barrett, the latter tussling with Alex MacMahon.

Kirk started to yell for order, but was promptly tackled by
Don MacMahon. He received a terrific blow on the side of the

head, then Don gripped his gun hand and rushed him to the wall.

Kirk rebounded and they both spun to the floor, rolling over and over, still locked together. Kirk managed to tear loose his left hand, and drove it smashing between Don's eyes. Then he wrestled himself out of Don's grasp and scrambled to his feet.

He fired his gun three times.

"Lay off!" he roared. "Cut this out, or I'll start some real shooting!"

The men broke, panting and winded, and glared at the corporal. Flint had them covered too, from the other side of the room.

"No more, now!" Kirk warned. "Billy, come here. You, too, Bristol."

Billy shuffled over, looking a trifle sheepish, and Bristol came along dabbling at a cut over his left eye.

"What happened?" Kirk asked.

Billy Jack looked at Bristol. Bristol took in a reef on his belt and cleared his throat.

"Well, that half-breed woman started it," he explained. "It was this way. She asked me if I had taken the ten thousand from Alex. I said no—said Alex had taken it from me, and I was just recovering it. Well, what she wanted to know was if Alex had any more money. I said I didn't know, but explained that if she meant the ten thousand, no. She looked at the few dollars and loose change in the box, and spat on them. Then she walked over, stood in front of the storeroom door, and began calling Alex some of the rottenest names I ever heard a woman use—'breed or otherwise. She said he was a fool—an old fool, at that—said she knew a trader over near the bay who would buy her clothes and gold rings. She said that's where she was going, and Alex could go to hell. She spat at the door, stamped her feet, cursed like the devil. Suddenly there was a string of shots and I saw her tumble to the floor.

"At the moment I was sore as anything. I pulled open that door. Alex was standing there with a smoking revolver.

"The prisoners all rushed me. As they did so the front door smashed open, and in came those two men. Before I knew it they were fighting beside me and Billy." He pointed to old Barrett and Joe.

"I see," Kirk nodded. "Well, everything's cleared up. Alex will swing for the murder of Jennings—and Nellie. Where is she?"

"Behind the storeroom door—dead as a doorknob."

Kirk walked over and pushed back the door, grimacing. Yes, Nellie was dead—the inevitable end of a bad woman. He turned away and strode over to confront Barrett.

"I left your daughter at your cabin," he said. "Found her with a sprained ankle in that storm."

"Me an' Joe were lookin' for her," Barrett replied. "We thought she'd got stuck in the valley. We heard shootin' here an' looked in."

"I'll not bother you any more," Kirk told him gravely. "Your son Tom is dead. The storm got him."

Barrett looked at Joe. Both lowered their heads and murmured a prayer. They turned, then, and without another word to anyone, filed out.

Kirk looked at Alex. "Well, the game's up, isn't it? A fine mess you're in. You haven't a chance in the world. You'll swing, all right. You've noticed, of course, that 'Johnny' has changed. He's Constable Flint now, and Tom Barrett is dead. Nellie is dead, too. Aren't you the fine fixer? You got Nellie to turn on Tom Barrett, and then when she saw you hadn't any money she turned on you. You might have known that."

Alex tugged at his beard, shooting a sidelong glance at Flint.

"Rather a rotten trick you played on me, Alex," remarked the constable. "I hear I was doing chores for you. Yes, I remember it, as one remembers a dream. It's beginning to fade already."

Alex growled in his beard.

Kirk said to Bristol, "This, you say, is the man who shot and killed Jennings?"

"At first I wasn't so sure," Bristol replied. "I'm sure now, though. His actions and his eyes—there's not another pair of eyes like 'em." He paused, pointing to Don and Rob MacMahon. "These are the two Billy and I followed that day. They look mighty like two of the bunch that held us up, too. But Alex fired the shot. I'm going to swear to that. Guess he suspected I knew all right, because when you left Billy and me here as guards he kept talking through the door, wanting to do business with me. Nothing doing. Old Jennings was a partner of mine. I warned Alex he couldn't tell me anything—that he'd better tell it to the Mounted."

Kirk nodded. "You see, Alex, we've got a number of counts against you, any one of which is enough to finish you. There will be Andy, Don, Bob, and the MacDonalds to keep you company. I'll bet every one of you gets a sentence. You can make a fool of law just so long, but there's a limit."

The prisoners were placed under heavy guard. Bristol and Billy Jack were pressed into service again. Billy was on Kirk's shift, while Bristol stood guard with Flint. Kirk was kept busy. His journal was far behind. He spent much time to bring it up to date. This was no small job, for there was a great deal to make note of. Many times he put questions to the prisoners and jotted down the answers.

Then he made a trip to the Indian encampment at the other end of the valley. The trip south with his six prisoners would require a large quantity of food and blankets. He would need at least three sleds and six extra men to handle the dogs, and make and break camp. Flint and he would be kept busy guarding the prisoners. Billy Jack would go with them, but Bristol was taking his own outfit, with the body of Jennings and his recovered money, on to Post Cheer Up.

After a great deal of talking, Kirk managed to enlist five young Indians. At Nelson's Camp he rounded up eight dogs and two decrepit sledges.

On the day before he planned to depart, he wrote a letter and called in Billy Jack.

"Billy," said he, "take this to the cabin by the lake, to the lady with the pale hair. Come right back, though, because I may need you around here."

Billy Jack blinked, grunted, took the letter, and shuffled out. Kirk, cleanshaven now, mused over his pipe. This catch would be another star in his eventful career. McQuade would shake his hand and his eyes would shine. The Division Superintendent would compliment him. Then the incident would pale, and he would be sent off on another long, dreary patrol, farther north than ever before—Baffin Land, perhaps.

Late that afternoon he was making further notes in his journal when the door opened and Nancy stepped in. Her cheeks glowed red from the clean Northern air. Her eyes sparkled.

"Hello!" he exclaimed, rising. "Didn't you see Billy? I sent a note to you."

"No-o," she replied, throwing back her hood. "That is, no note. But Billy—Billy is outside. I came here with him."

"Why, I gave Billy a letter for you. A few farewell words."

"I'm sorry," she offered.

"Oh, that's all right. But this trip wasn't necessary. I'll bet you are tired—"

"You—you didn't say I should come?" she asked wistfully.

"I didn't, but—that is—I'm glad you're here...."

He took her hand. He thought she leaned toward him, thought he saw a beckoning warmth in her dark moist eyes. He wasn't sure until his arm had slipped around her, and she had raised her lips, clinging to him. Then he was quite sure.

"You'll come back?" she whispered.

"I will come back," he told her gently.

There was a sound at the door. Kirk released her, stepping to one side. It was Billy Jack who shuffled in, blinking guiltily under the corporal's stare.

"Billy," said Kirk, "I sent you off with a letter this morning. What happened to it?"

Billy shifted uneasily. "Um—me lose letter. Reach cabin—no letter. Me say you want lady come quick."

Kirk advanced stiffly, and Billy shrank back, blinking rapidly. Then Kirk broke into a grin and clapped the Indian on the shoulder.

"Billy," he said, "you are the *best* blunderer I've ever met!"

THE Nebel LIBRARY

THE COMPLETE
CASEBOOK OF SGT.
BRINKHAUS (IN 2015)

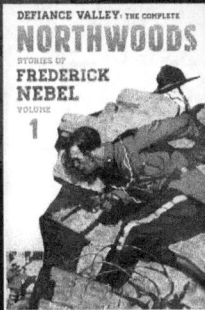

DEFIANCE VALLEY:
THE COMPLETE
NORTHWOODS
STORIES VOLUME 1

STREET WOLF: THE
BLACK MASK STORIES
OF FREDERICK NEBEL

LOOK FOR THE COMPLETE ADVENTURES OF
GALES & McGILL, VOLUME 1, IN 2015!

THE Nebel LIBRARY

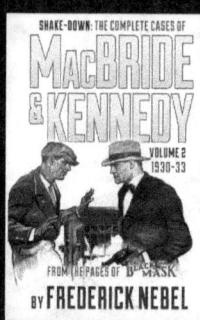

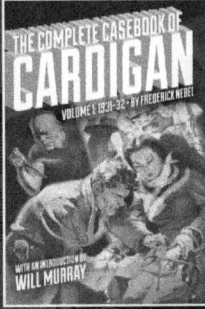

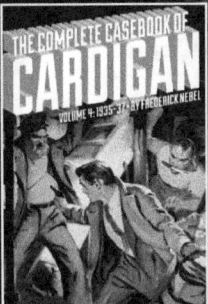